David lea...
hers with...
the charge...
them at th...
Christie re...   ...powerful
attraction she felt for him was reflected in
his own eyes, and her pulse raced.

Slowly Christie eased her hand away
from his, a half-smile on her lips. She had
met too many correspondents who left a
trail of broken hearts behind them.
Exciting though it might be, a love affair
with David Cameron was courting danger.
As if he could read her mind, David smiled
ruefully and twisted the gold signet ring on
his right hand.

'David! There you are. Keeping busy
with the staff, I see.'

Christie looked up as Caryn Kelly swept
up to the table and slammed her black
Chanel bag on to the table. Caryn coolly
returned her gaze. 'I came to find David,'
she stated possessively, marking out her
territory without delay.

Christie extended her hand in greeting,
but Caryn had already turned away. She
slipped her arm through David's as he
stood up to meet her. 'I'm sure you've been
soaking up the hero's tales of war. David
has a very wide fan club, you know. I'm
just lucky he spares so much of his precious
time for me. He's so loyal.'

Was Caryn warning her away? Christie
glanced at David again. The expression she
read in his eyes was not one of love. Just of
sadness.

Hard News

Tess Stimson

Mandarin

A Mandarin Paperback
HARD NEWS

First published in Great Britain
by Mandarin Paperbacks
an imprint of Reed Consumer Books Limited
Michelin House, 81 Fulham Road, London SW3 6RB
and Auckland, Melbourne, Singapore and Toronto

Reprinted 1993 (four times)

Copyright © Tess Stimson 1993
The author has asserted her moral rights

A CIP catalogue record for this title
is available from the British Library
ISBN 0 7493 1447 8

Printed and bound in Great Britain
by Cox & Wyman Ltd, Reading, Berks

For my darling Brent
Amoud Fiki

Acknowledgements

There are so many people who contributed to the writing of this book that it is impossible to thank them all.

But it is with particular gratitude I thank Louise Moore, my Editor, whose friendship, support and humour made *Hard News* so enjoyable to write.

And my thanks too to all those at ITN and CNN who helped in the writing of this book. Whilst none of them are characterised directly on these pages, all opened the door to a world I would otherwise never have known.

I owe a deep debt of gratitude to my friends and family; to my parents, Michael and Jane, whose wisdom, humour and love have never failed me; to Chantal and Francois Guillot, who were there at the beginning and made me believe almost anything is possible; to Sunnie Mann, who gave me that first chance to write and who is so much missed.

A special mention must go to my computer genius Ian Penberthy. Without him this book would still be a microchip.

My thanks, too, to all those whose opposition made me so determined to write this book.

But most of all, to Brent, my hero.

Cyprus, February 1993

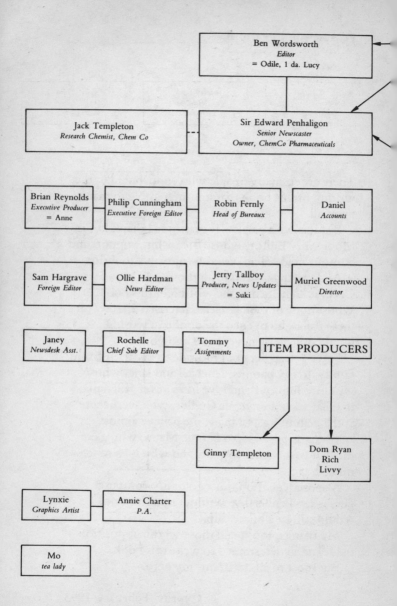

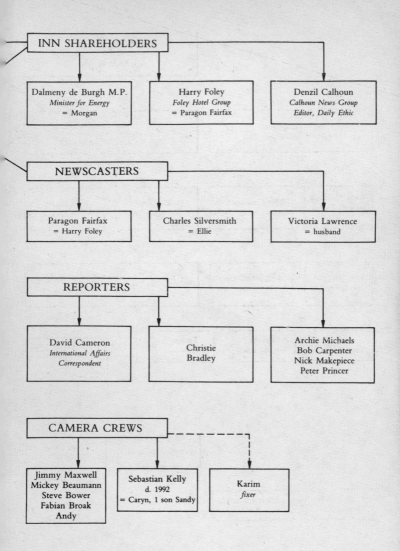

INN SHAREHOLDERS

Dalmeny de Burgh M.P.
Minister for Energy
= Morgan

Harry Foley
Foley Hotel Group
= Paragon Fairfax

Denzil Calhoun
Calhoun News Group
Editor, Daily Ethic

NEWSCASTERS

Paragon Fairfax
= Harry Foley

Charles Silversmith
= Ellie

Victoria Lawrence
= husband

REPORTERS

David Cameron
International Affairs
Correspondent

Christie
Bradley

Archie Michaels
Bob Carpenter
Nick Makepiece
Peter Princer

CAMERA CREWS

Jimmy Maxwell
Mickey Beaumann
Steve Bower
Fabian Broak
Andy

Sebastian Kelly
d. 1992
= Caryn, 1 son Sandy

Karim
fixer

Prologue

For a moment, all he could see was her breast. Her pink nipple was taut with desire, the soft, creamy skin around it smooth and translucent. She ran her hands over the satin swell of her chest and cupped her firm breasts in her fingers, their tips teasing the buds of her nipples with gentle, erotic strokes. Slowly his eyes travelled the length of her body as she moved her hands lower, his breathing accelerating as he appreciated the voluptuous curve of her hips, the milky whiteness of her thighs. Languidly her legs opened to him, inviting him towards her.

As police officer on duty, he almost failed to hear the telephone ring.

With a sigh of reluctance, he tore himself away and reached for the receiver, turning down the television volume as he picked it up. His eyes remained transfixed by her body on the screen as she conveyed her siren message in silence.

His arousal faded instantly as he listened to the words, scrabbling for a pen to write them down.

The moment they had finished he slammed his fist down on the cradle of the telephone to sever the connection, and began redialling the emergency number. The woman was forgotten. He glanced at his watch, sweat beading his brow.

1

'Chief? We've had a warning. Code words verified.' He ran his hand through his hair and stared at the paper in front of him. 'We've got twenty minutes.'

Chapter One

Ollie Hardman was not having a good day.

He had known it was going to be a bad one when he woke up half an hour late that morning, his hangover beating a military tattoo inside his head. His pessimistic prediction had been further confirmed when he reached inside his wallet and found the five hundred pounds he had withdrawn the previous day was gone.

Ollie's rising had been slow, despite the lateness of the hour. He had spent five minutes face down on the bed contemplating the grimy floor of his bedroom hoping the world would stop spinning. It hadn't. Bright, wintry sunshine streamed through the uncurtained window. An acrimonious divorce had put paid to such luxuries as curtains – not to mention the sofa, wardrobe, dining-table and chairs, and as many fixtures and fittings as his ex-wife had been able to remove from their home when he was away at a News Editors' conference. He had returned to find his flat completely empty, bar the bed and television. Taped to the blank screen had been a note, succinct and to the point. 'You can keep this. I'm citing it as co-respondent. See you in court. Jeannie.'

Ollie had not been too distressed by the loss of his wife, although he missed the curtains. She had been right, of course; like most journalists, he was married to his job. In Ollie's case, however, his relationship with INN was more in the way of a passionate love affair: filled with sleepless nights, thankless tasks and the occasional stab in the back.

Ollie Hardman had been a talented regional television reporter in Manchester when he had met his wife, who had been dazzled by his local fame and potential fortune. Six months later, she had been forced to flee with him when a string of gambling debts he could never pay had driven him to move to London, as far away as possible from those colleagues who would happily take an arm and a leg in lieu of the cash.

Fortunately Ollie's change of address had coincided with the formation of an ambitious international news station, whose stated aim was to rule the globe in terms of television news. In less than a year, INN had bureaux in more countries than almost any other news channel, and almost as many viewers. INN's Editor, Ben Wordsworth, followed a policy of poaching the best reporters, news-men, editors and camera crews from the other networks, so that INN quickly built up a reputation as the fastest and most accurate service of them all. Its news output was divided into two services: a domestic news channel which covered UK news twenty-four hours a day; and an international channel which took domestic news updates but was largely concerned with worldwide news stories. Ollie was just one of many news hacks happy to jump ship and join the burgeoning station as its Home News Editor. To him fell the responsibility of ensuring that the domestic news maintained INN's high and exacting stan-dards.

Ollie shook his head and glanced at his watch. 7.49. He had been on shift since 8.00 that morning . . . well, 8.35 by the time he reached the INN building . . . and still had more than another four hours to go. Midnight beckoned him like a beacon of hope and respite. Still time to make up that missing five hundred pounds.

He kicked back his chair away from the Home News Desk, a piece of furniture shaped like a square 'U' which had him at its centre. For once the telephones had stopped ringing. Ollie glanced around to tell his newsdesk assistant to mind the shop whilst he stretched his legs, but could not see her. Sod it, Assignments was AWOL as well. Probably chatting up his mistress on the telephone in one of the empty edit booths where no one could overhear him. For someone whose job was to organise and allocate which camera crews should cover which story, and how they should get there, his personal life was a bloody mess.

Ollie stood up. If the world fell apart, someone else would have to pick up the pieces for the next five minutes.

He moved towards the atrium, glancing sourly up at the immense glass and chrome structure that was INN's headquarters. Sodding monstrosity. Twelve storeys high in the heart of London, the building towered above its neighbours, just a short walk from Euston Station. The vast atrium bit out the heart of the building, making it resemble nothing so much as a giant square polo. Into the basement two floors below street level a pond had been built, surmounted by a rockery from which flowed a gentle waterfall. The News Mall around it contained half-a-dozen souvenir shops, selling mugs, T-shirts, pens and stationery imprinted with the green and silver INN logo, or the face of its illustrious editor, Ben Wordsworth. Visitors could stand with lifesize cardboard cut-outs of the station's star reporters and newscasters to have their photograph taken. Occasionally the genuine article was detailed to go down to the ground floor and meet the tourists first hand. A small theatre played a half-hour documentary describing the founding of INN on a repeating loop to an eager audience, who then hurried to join the tour of the building which optimistically promised to show them real journalists at work. A fast food hamburger joint was at one end of the mall, an expensive Italian restaurant – always fully booked – at the other. In between was a Taco Bell and a boarded shop-front which had once been a health food shop. It had gone bankrupt within six months of opening. Next door was a hairdressers and the photography studio of a new fashion magazine.

Birds who had found their way into the building flew around the atrium, perching on the elaborate modern art sculpture which was suspended down the entire twelve floors of the building. Ollie knew that those swaying coloured pipes had cost more than twice his annual salary, and to him they remained an ugly eyesore. They had nearly killed one of the secretaries crossing the atrium floor one Sunday evening, when the wires holding them had snapped and the whole structure came crashing down. Fortunately the INN building had already closed to visitors for the evening, otherwise the result – not to mention the publicity – could have been disastrous. The secretary had been given a pay rise, the coloured pipes rehung and the whole matter discreetly forgotten.

Ollie made his way through the double doors to the coffee pantry, punching the requisite buttons to obtain a cup of the brackish liquid that masqueraded as coffee. He mooched back to the Newsdesk, nodding at Sam Hargrave, the Foreign Editor, as he sat down. Sam's desk was a mirror image of his own, positioned so that the two together formed an 'H'. Thousands of pounds and God alone knew how many time and motion studies had gone into proving that this was more efficient than any other combination could possibly be. Ollie's personal opinion was that it put him far too near his boss, that miserable runt Brian Reynolds, whose task it was to oversee both Home and Foreign Desks and make sure that no decisions were ever made.

Ollie looked up as Janey, his newsdesk assistant, returned from her gossip by the printer, bearing a large cup of coffee and brandishing a Danish pastry.

'Sorry I was so long, Ollie,' she panted, throwing her plump figure into the chair on his left. 'I nipped out to the sandwich bar for a decent cup of coffee. Thought you'd prefer it to that dishwater from the machine.'

Ollie grinned. 'What would I do without you?' he said, biting deeply into the pastry and taking a swig of scalding coffee at the same time.

'Ask me that in five minutes.'

Ollie looked up suspiciously. 'Why?'

'Just saw the roster for tomorrow. We've only got two crews to cover the whole day – and that includes the early crew,' Janey said, sipping her drink from the polystyrene beaker in her hand and leaving a bright pink impression of lipstick on the side.

Ollie slammed his own cup down on the desk. 'How the hell am I supposed to cover the entire day's breaking stories with two bloody crews? It was bad enough today, with only three. Christie's got Andy for her undercover special on the teenage drug ring, and the early crew knocked off at four. That only leaves us one, and they're down at Westminster.' He frowned as he scanned the list Janey offered him. 'This is hopeless. Where the hell is Assignments?'

'Don't give Tommy a hard time,' Janey said, sliding her chair back to her side of the desk. 'For once it's not his fault.'

'Yeah? How do you figure that one?' Ollie said, already reaching for his diary and dialling one of the off-duty cameramen's numbers, intent on getting some cover into the building for tomorrow.

'If you're looking for someone to blame, try Ben. Our revered Editor has assigned two two-man crews to shoot round the building, to present a documentary on INN to HRH when she opens it next week.'

Ollie groaned in disbelief. He knew it was pointless to even debate the Editor's decisions. Once Ben Wordsworth had made up his mind, the decision was final and no correspondence would be entered into.

'Meanwhile, we can forget the nurses' strike, the leukaemia kid and the PM's meeting with the farmers. Christ, I hope the bloody Queen appreciates it, if the world goes bang and we miss it.'

'I blame the ozone layer, myself,' Janey said, tapping into her computer and scanning the news wire services to make sure there was nothing they were missing. 'Never mind, Ollie, at least we got through today OK.'

'So far,' Ollie said, crossing his fingers. One of these days, a late breaking story would make a nonsense of their pared-down rosters, and they would be creamed by the opposition. 'When's Christie due back?'

'She'll be at that party filming until midnight at least,' Janey said, checking Tommy's Assignments roster. 'She'll edit tomorrow if she gets some good stuff; should be able to get a nice piece together for the Early Evening News slot.'

Ollie nodded his thanks as one of the many telephones on his desk began to ring. 'Cheers. Don't worry, I'll take that.' He picked up the telephone. Thank God it was a quiet night. He couldn't wait to get home.

The driver of the 18.45 express train from Gatwick Airport to Victoria Station had no idea he had only seventeen minutes left to live.

There was no indication that this journey was different from any other. The computer proclaimed that everything was in order as the train hurtled along the track. There were no malfunctions. The weather was clear.

Judy Coleridge entered the driver's cab and smiled.

'Last run for you tonight, Tobe?'

The driver glanced at his watch and grinned back. 'Always takes the longest, doesn't it? Never mind, should be back in time for The Bill . . . that's if I don't end up having to bathe the kids.'

Judy shook her blonde head. 'You fraud. You know you like it more than they do.'

'Yeah. Well.' He stretched and yawned. 'Busy tonight?'

'You're not kidding. It's like the bloody rush hour out there. Train's full of people coming back from their holidays; if I fall over another straw donkey I'll scream.'

'Alright for some.'

Judy gazed through the window as if for inspiration. She saw only darkness rushing by. 'Yeah. OK, I'd better get back. See you.'

Toby acknowledged her with a wave over his shoulder as she left the driver's cab, turning back immediately to re-check his computer. Judy made her way along the swaying train, steadying herself as she paused between carriages. The automatic doors hissed open as a lurch of the train put her in range of its sensors, and she adjusted the ticket machine against her stomach, pulling the straining tunic around her ample frame. She knew she could do

9

with losing a few pounds, but she was too happy at the moment to think about that.

She smiled softly as she contemplated the tiny diamond solitaire on her left hand. It had only been there for three weeks, and still felt new and a little alien. She kept stealing glances at it as she punched the tickets of the passengers in the crowded carriages.

A group of pensioners waved at her as she moved towards them, and Judy waggled her fingers back in greeting. Probably going on to see a show in London. She caught the misty look an old couple exchanged as they handed her their tickets. If she and Geoff were still that mushy about each other when they were that age, she'd be more than happy.

Judy tapped the legs of a young girl who was resting her crepe-soled shoes on the seat opposite her, and the girl whipped her feet down with a guilty start. Her boyfriend nuzzled her ear, and the girl blushed. God, they make me feel old, Judy thought, smiling wryly. Can't be more than fifteen.

She pushed her ash-blonde hair back from her face and sighed as she moved into the next carriage, her feet aching with weariness. Perhaps when she and Geoff settled down, she'd be able to take a job a bit nearer home. This shuttle meant that she was on her feet most of the day, trekking backwards and forwards along the carriages. Mind you, could be worse. At least she had someone special to go home to. Judy glanced at the young couple sitting stiffly beside each other on the seat at the end of the compartment. They'd obviously had one hell of a row; from the way the woman was looking at him, he must have been up to no good. Judy's heart clenched as she thought of Geoff. She would be devastated if she ever found out he had cheated on her. She smiled and forced herself to relax. As if he ever would.

'Well, give her the tickets,' the woman hissed, digging an elbow sharply in her husband's ribs. 'She doesn't want to stand about all day.'

Judy gave her a sympathetic look as she moved away, shaking her head as their argument resumed, *sotto voce*. Most of the other passengers stared out through the windows, skilfully ignoring the disruption.

Judy glanced at her watch as she edged around the battered suitcases that straddled the aisle, trying not to disturb two sleeping children cradled in their parents' arms. 7.11. A charter flight must have just landed at Gatwick. God knows how these people afforded it: holidays somewhere warm enough to give them a tan like that didn't come cheap, not in March. Credit cards and overdrafts, probably.

She passed into the next carriage and stiffened as she sensed the tension. A flicker of fear ran through her as she saw the five young men who were standing in the aisle, beercans clutched in their hands, the empty tins rolling around the floor a testimony to the amount they had already consumed. Warily Judy eyed the stuffing that spilled from the seats they had sliced open, wondering if she should go back to Toby and arrange for the police to be waiting at Victoria to meet the train. She could see several passengers crammed in the corridor at the end of the carriage, driven away by the threat of an ugly incident with which they had no desire to become involved.

She hesitated, uncertain whether to retreat, and suddenly one of the boys laughed and flung a half-empty can of lager at her. Judy opened her mouth to cry out in alarm.

The cry never came.

The one-hundred-and-eighty-seven passengers on board the train felt the crash before they heard it. The carriages swung crazily from the rails and lurched to the right. The lights inside them flickered and died. In the

11

darkness, the carriages hung skewed at a forty-five-degree angle, and seemed to hover, frozen in time, as if deciding which way to fall. A child plunged screaming through the window, breaking glass slashing his body as he fell. Screams echoed up and down the corridor, and the piercing wails of terrified children filled the air. For a timeless moment everything had stopped.

Then the frozen tableau came to life and the train teetered and plunged down the embankment. The eight carriages twisted away from each other, their couplings snapping apart like cotton. People spilled from the train and were crushed beneath its weight as it fell. As if in slow motion the carriages tumbled down the steep slope, rolling over and over, the metal of their sides bending and ripping like tissue paper. Trees skewered them through the windows, impaling passengers thrown against the glass. Like marbles scattered by a careless child, the carriages fell in different directions, heedless of what lay in their paths. With a thunderous roar, three of them slammed into a row of small houses hugging the bottom of the slope. The walls collapsed and disintegrated under the impact, the carriages embedded in what were once bedrooms, living rooms, homes. Dust flew upwards, and the sound of breaking glass, collapsing buildings, and, above it all, the screeching of metal, filled the night.

As abruptly as it had started, the noise stopped. The debris of train and houses finally came to rest. For a moment, the scene was still.

And then the screaming began.

Christie Bradley ran a hand through her golden hair and leaned back, one slim leg bent beneath her so that her foot rested against the wall. She glanced at her watch surreptitiously as she sipped an unmentionable wine from a plastic cup, considering how to execute a strategic withdrawal from the earnest young man talking to her without seeming unforgiveably rude. She wondered if she cared if she seemed unforgiveably rude. She had long since ceased to understand the topic of conversation, her boredom threshold a milestone passed many minutes ago. Desperate measures were called for.

Slowly she reached down to the message master clipped to the waist of her black silk dress, and switched the delayed action button. Ten seconds later the shrill bleep pierced the pounding thud of the music, and Christie unhooked it thankfully, reading the blank LCD screen with an expression of profound concern.

'Terribly sorry . . . must dash,' she said apologetically, easing her way around the startled young man. 'It's always happening.'

Christie darted across the crowded underground cellar before he had time to object, weaving her way around sweaty bodies. The music reverberated off the grey concrete walls, a heavy, pulsing rhythm that lacked either tune or lyrics. She fought her way past couples festooning the hallway and leaned against the wall with a sigh of relief. The things she did for a story.

She pulled up the thigh-high black suede boots she was wearing, smoothing her silk dress down. She hoped the teenage drug baron she was shadowing would make an appearence sometime soon. She wasn't sure how many more student parties she could stand.

With a sigh, she pushed her dishevelled hair away from her face and made her way into the kitchen, hoping there was something left to drink. It would almost certainly be unpalatable – why was it people always brought wine they would never choose to drink to these parties? – but the way she was feeling, methylated spirits would have been acceptable provided the proof was high enough.

A tall, unappealing youth dressed in a hooded sweat-shirt and wide jeans blocked the doorway as Christie turned to leave. His unnaturally bright eyes raked her body, his interest obvious as he registered her firm breasts and the long legs that emerged from the black sheath she was wearing.

'Can I help you, gorgeous?'

Christie eyed the shoulder-length curls, the silver rings on his fingers, the designer trainers with the regulation lack of laces. This boy might not be selling the drugs she was chasing, but he probably knew a man who did. Christie smiled, arching one eyebrow with exactly the right amount of mingled anticipation and disdain.

'I'm open to suggestions,' she said, smoothing her dress with a gesture that invited his eye to follow her hand as it ran over her breast and came to rest on her thigh. 'Anything to offer?'

The youth grinned, plucking at his grimy sweatshirt. 'Could be. Don't go away, sweetheart.'

Christie nodded. The microphone she had just activated should be able to pick up his every word when he returned.

She reached for a half-empty wine bottle on the sticky table in front of her, pouring a generous slug into a plastic cup, then replaced the bottle amongst its dozen empty fellows that were scattered across the table, and turned to search the room for her cameraman. Damn. Knowing

Andy, he was probably already upstairs with the juvenile sex siren he had started chatting up the moment he walked through the door.

'How's it going?'

Christie started as her producer, Dom Ryan, appeared at her elbow. 'At last, a friendly face. Don't drink the wine, it's lethal.'

Dom grinned. 'Too late. You're talking to a lost cause.'

Christie smiled as Dom searched for a bottle that had not already been emptied. 'How the hell do you find these parties, Dom? You must really know the right people.'

'Yeah, well they're more my generation,' Dom teased. 'But don't worry, I love an older woman.'

Christie shook her head, laughing despite herself. Dom Ryan was only twenty-one, and had been assigned to the production team at INN for less than four months, but she was impressed by both his talent and his enthusiasm. He had been shadowing her reporting for the last three weeks, and had already proved himself to be intelligent and persistant. Christie had no doubt that he would make an excellent television correspondent, given the right chance.

Suddenly she noticed an attractive man of around her own age moving through the crush of people, the long-haired teenager at his elbow. 'Dom, go and get Andy for me,' she said, her voice low. 'I'm miked up, but I need some pictures if I'm going to get enough to stand this story up.'

Dom nodded, his hazel eyes sparkling with a mixture of excitement and admiration. He knew Christie Bradley was one of International News Network's top correspondents, and not without good reason. In the three years she had been with INN, she had already gained a number of major exclusives, had tasted war in the most dangerous corners of the world, covered famine, corruption and

15

human tragedy. She had risked her life more than once to get a story, her reporting style renowned for its cool, daring, and above all fair approach.

Dom's appreciation of her was far more than just professional. Christie was also one of the most arresting women he had ever met. Her lips were a little too full, her cheekbones a touch too high, for her to be considered classically beautiful, but she possessed an inborn character and style impossible to emulate. Her rich-gold hair tumbled to her shoulders, framing a face whose skin was smooth and translucent. Her body was slender and supple, her movements graceful. But it was her eyes which really drew attention. They glittered like liquid emeralds from beneath dark lashes, changing from sea-green to the deepest malachite depending on her mood.

She could wield a rifle with expertise, function for days without sleep or food, gain the trust of terrorists and government officials alike. She possessed ruthlessness and allure, humour and compassion. They were a lethal combination.

'So you're looking for a little fun, darling?'

Christie glanced up at the man in front of her, replacing her cup on the table and allowing her gaze to travel over him with an expression of mild interest. 'And that's what you're offering?'

'Could be, sweetheart.'

'So why don't we talk about it?'

Suddenly, over the throbbing music, Christie heard the shrill, impatient tone of her bleep, and with a sigh of resignation, she reached for it. The young man backed off abruptly, staring at her.

'You're Christie Bradley,' he said accusingly, suddenly recognising her. 'The TV reporter.'

Christie sighed. Great. End of story. 'You got it,' she

said coolly. 'And this is my Newsdesk. Excuse me.'

She spun the LCD display towards her, and pressed the illuminating button with practised swiftness. It had to be important for the Desk to be bleeping her on this sort of investigative report, since she was not the duty night reporter. Working for a twenty-four-hours-a-day news channel was not all fun and games. In the dim light she could just make out the message, and she turned towards the staircase, wondering where the telephone was located. She noticed Dom working his way down the crowded staircase from the main entrance on the ground floor, and waved her hand high in the air to attract his attention, miming the use of a telephone as she fought her way to the foot of the stairs.

Dom nodded at her to follow him, and turned around, not even attempting to speak over the din, as they struggled past people up to the landing, and shut the door to the pulsating cellar down below with relief.

'Newsdesk,' Christie said succinctly.

Dom was already dialling the direct line. As soon as he heard the number ringing, he handed the receiver to Christie.

'Hi, Ollie, Christie here,' she said swiftly as soon as the telephone answered. Dom saw her nod twice as she listened, scribbling a maze of hieroglyphics into her notebook as she did so.

'OK, Ollie, I'm on my way. You might find Steve and Jimmy at the Gatwick Hilton – I know they were staying somewhere around there, because they were due to fly out to Corfu to do that holiday villa story tomorrow morning. I'll call you when I get to Heathley.'

She pushed the notebook back into the pocket of her jacket, and started heading towards the door. 'Andy,' she said, as the slim cameraman appeared at the top of the stairs, tucking his shirt into his jeans. 'Get the crew car and follow me. I'll take my own; we may need the extra wheels when we get there.'

'What's the gen.?' Andy asked, falling in beside her as she ran down the steps towards her car.

'Train crash out near a village called Heathley, halfway between London and Gatwick Airport,' Christie said, unlocking the door of her red MG BGT. 'No idea what caused it.' She glanced at her watch. 'It's almost eight now. We'll newsflash as soon as we can, but Ollie wants us to throw a piece together for the Late News show at ten.'

'That's going some,' Andy shouted across the road as he unlocked the large Volvo estate that INN used as a crew car. 'I'll see you there: I have to go via my flat to pick up some more tapes.'

He drove off. Christie turned to Dom. 'OK, this could be very messy, but you'll certainly see how live television works.' She opened the boot of her car, sitting on the rim and tugging off her suede boots as she spoke. 'Want to come? I could use a hand; we won't have anyone else there for quite a while.'

Dom nodded, trying not to blush as Christie reached into the back of her sports car, and pulled out a pair of black jeans. He glanced in the side-mirror as she slid them on beneath her dress, which she pulled over her head without ceremony. He prayed his excitement did not show as she revealed a breathtaking glimpse of creamy white breasts and hard, pink tipped nipples, before tugging on an outsize sloppy-joe jumper over her jeans.

'Never travel without this lot,' she grinned at him, slipping on a pair of worn trainers. 'Always happens when I'm wearing the most impractical outfit I possess. I can hardly go on camera in that lot when I've got mangled bodies in the background.'

Christie slithered into the MG and reached across to

18

open the passenger door. As Dom climbed in, she handed him a bundle of crumpled and much-folded maps.

'Can you find Heathley on that for me?' she asked, turning the ignition and sliding the low-slung car into the road. 'Forget the A23 . . . the roadworks are a nightmare.'

Dom studied the map, twisting it this way and that to see by the light of passing streetlamps as they whipped down the street. 'Do you know what happened?'

'Impossible to say yet,' Christie answered. 'Someone living near where the crash happened telephoned the Newsdesk. It sounds bad. Apparently a train just came off the rails and plunged down the siding. Hit a row of houses.'

Dom thought of the carnage that must be awaiting them. He had never even seen a dead body. Until he had joined INN, most of his time had been spent covering Arts Festivals and local celebrities. Suddenly he would be facing the kind of sight that made experienced rescue teams sick.

Christie caught a glimpse of his face in her side-mirror. Poor kid. She shivered as she drove. She knew how bad it would be, the sleepless nights she would have because of this. Every shattered body meant a shattered life, and that was something she would never come to terms with, however many times she saw it. In the end, for journalists, and for most of their viewers, it was just another story: tragic, terrifying, but part of someone else's life. But for those crushed beneath the wreckage, and the people who loved them, Christie knew it was a story that would have no happy ending.

After half-an-hour's driving, Christie saw the police tape fluttering in the wind as Dom directed her down the road which led to the centre of Heathley. Her car screeched to a halt beside it, and she glanced at her watch

19

as she leaped from the MG, an expression of polite authority on her face as she pulled her Press card from the pocket of her jeans. 8.31. Christie approached the policeman guarding the tape as Dom reversed the MG out of the way.

'Christie Bradley, INN,' she said, proffering her card. 'Is there someone I can talk to about the accident?'

The policeman sighed and took the card from her hand, perusing the photograph carefully for a full thirty seconds. Sexy piece. He glanced up at Christie, and his expression of mild lust was replaced by one of wary respect. He removed his walkie-talkie from its holster and turned away so that Christie would be unable to hear him warning his colleagues that the first of the Press had arrived.

'If you'd like to move your car back to the end of the road, Miss Bradley, there'll be someone along soon to take care of you,' he said, turning back to her. 'Don't cross the tape, please. We don't want the efforts of our rescue workers hampered.'

Christie suppressed a sigh of exasperation. If she did not move fast, she would be corralled into a Press cordon and directed to operate through the 'proper channels'; any chance of some decent pictures, let alone the real story, would be gone. First there would be the standard press conferences: a police spokesman promising the accident was being investigated, a British Rail official expressing deep sorrow at the tragedy and denying all speculation as to its cause. In a few hours the politicians would arrive: an Opposition transport minister would blame the Government's cost-cutting exercises for 'putting lives before cash,' a charge the Government would deny, citing all that they had spent recently on the line in question and promising to set up a fund for the bereaved. Later the celebrities would appear, to hold hands and glean a little sympathetic publicity. If the accident was bad enough, they might even get a Royal or two. It was an established routine, and as always her job was to jolt the politicians and spokesmen out of it and get to the real story. And there always was one.

There was little she could do until Andy arrived; there was no point breaking the rules unless she could get some good pictures. Swiftly she walked back towards the MG, which Dom had parked by the side of the road, fifty metres from the fluttering police tape, and unlocked the boot, extracting a six-pack of lager that she had bought for the party and then forgotten. Handing one to Dom, she tugged the metal ring pull of her own and put the remaining cans down on the pavement, weighing up what to do. She needed to recce the scene to find a good position for the engineers to set up the links so that she could transmit a live piece back to the studio for the Late News at ten.

Christie looked up as the rescue teams suddenly switched on their floodlights, slicing open the darkness around her. She was deeply shocked as she saw the carnage the crash had wrought. It was worse, far worse, than even she had expected, and she fought back tears at the thought of how many lives must have been lost or ruined. Three houses had been all but destroyed, and several others had been untidily severed in two. A bed hung suspended in mid-air, half in and half out of a bedroom. In one living room, she could see the television still playing. With surreal irony it would soon be carrying pictures of the tragedy of which it was a part. Behind the houses, the shattered shells of the train carriages glinted eerily in the unnatural brightness of the arc lights. It seemed she had arrived almost with the rescue services. Certainly there was no sign of any other camera crews or reporters yet, and despite the police presence, the usual

21

security restrictions which came with such disasters were not yet in place.

Suddenly she realised the distant murmuring she had mistaken for wind was the sound of people crying.

Christie turned numbly away from the arc-lights. In a few minutes, she would have to report on the tragedy with clarity and accuracy. She needed a little time to grieve first.

'You a reporter, miss?'

Christie started, and looked at the two teenage boys staring at her with expressions of fascination.

'Something like that.' Christie saw the mingled awe and excitement on their faces, and relented. She tossed them a can of lager each. Time to join the real world and get on with her job.

'Hey, cheers,' the taller of the two commented. 'So who you with then?'

'INN . . . do you know it?'

'Yeah! Get it on our satellite. News, isn't it?'

'That's right.' Christie glanced at the rubble opposite her, still trying to comprehend what had happened. Somehow, this sort of appalling tragedy seemed so out of place in the middle of a quiet suburb like Heathley. She was used to it in Beirut, Sarajevo, Mogadishu. But not here.

The boys followed her line of vision. The taller one sighed. 'Bleedin' mess, ain't it?'

Christie nodded. 'Looks like it. Not that I've been able to see much, yet.'

'Got a great view from my bedroom,' the other boy volunteered suddenly.

Christie regarded him with interest. She had the feeling something was a little out of kilter here. There were too many police here already . . . ahead of the emergency rescue services. Her reporting instincts told her that she was witnessing the result of more than a routine points failure. These two boys might be the way to find out what lay behind it. Christie ducked down into the car. 'Dom, look out for Andy and the other crew for me. The minute they arrive, get them as close as you can for some wide-shots and general views of the area. See what else you can find out, then get back to me with the GVs.'

Christie straightened up and extended her hand to the two boys. 'Christie Bradley, INN. How would you two like to become journalists for the day?'

Moments later, Christie headed towards the police tape, the two boys following closely behind her. She selected a young policeman who had not seen her arrive, nodding towards him politely as she made to lift the police tape.

'Excuse me, miss, you can't do that.'

'Whyever not?' Christie asked indignantly. 'That's my house.'

'Your house, miss?'

'Number Thirty-two,' Christie said, with just the right amount of authority and concern in her voice.

'I'm sorry, miss, but I need to ask you if you can prove that.'

Christie thought rapidly. Before she had a chance to reply, the taller of the two boys scrabbled around in his jacket pocket and produced a piece of paper, which he handed to the policeman. 'The milk bill do you?'

The policeman cast a sceptical glance at it, then nodded and waved them all through. The door of number thirty-two opened, and a startled woman dodged out of the way as the two boys bowled past her, hauling Christie after them. The younger one stopped halfway up the stairs and leaned over the banister. 'It's all right, Mum. She's famous! She's on TV!'

Christie suppressed a laugh and ran up the stairs after the two boys. One look from the boy's bedroom satisfied

23

her that she could not have a better vantage point. She stared down into the garden in disbelief. One of the carriages had cartwheeled down the embankment and come to rest at the end of the garden. Others lay tumbled around the curved road of houses, three of the mangled carriages embedded in the rubble that had once been people's homes. Along the embankment she could see the flares of welding equipment as rescue workers attempted to cut the victims free from the wreckage. Stretchers lay waiting on the grass nearby.

'Need a phone, Christie?'

Christie took the receiver from the younger boy. 'Great. Thanks. Keep an eye out for Andy and Dom, would you, and let them know where I am?'

The boy nodded as Christie began dialling the Newsdesk. 'Ollie. Christie here. What's the latest?'

'Where are you, Christie?'

'Inside the bedroom of one of the houses on the road by the crash. Don't ask why, just send me three hundred pounds. Where's Andy, do you know?'

Ollie did not pause to query Christie's request. 'Just spoke to him, he'll be with you in five. Does he know where to find you?'

'Dom should be seeing to that. He can liaise between us if I'm too caught up. Who else is coming?'

'We've had a few crewing problems,' Ollie said in understatement. 'Should be sorted PDQ.'

'OK. What about links?'

Ollie sighed as he considered the problem of establishing the links truck. Any material Christie shot had to be beamed to the INN building from a van specifically equipped for that purpose, or carried by hand which would take too long. Links had the advantage of providing a mini television transmitting station which could be set up anywhere. Its drawback was that it had to be placed

24

on a high vantage point; if terrain was particularly hilly, it could take two or three links trucks to bounce the signal along from point to point.

'We're working on it,' Ollie replied, in answer to Christie's question. 'They're all out at the moment, covering the byelection. We've got one on its way to you that should be with you within the hour, which should just cover you for the Late News at ten. It'll be tight, but we should do it. We'll try to get the satellite dish down to you for your live two-ways later.'

'Time they get the signal established, the world and his wife are going to be here,' Christie replied in exasperation. 'If you want an exclusive, you'd better get them here in thirty, max. If you need me, you can get me on this number.' She waited until Ollie had noted it down. 'Just get the live crew here as soon as poss. It's going to be a difficult place to establish links.'

'Can you give me a phono before you go?' Ollie said quickly. 'We've newsflashed the details, but you're the first on the scene. Sixty seconds will do fine.'

'You need pictures to tell this story, Ollie, you know that,' Christie retorted. 'If I waste time giving you a phono now, we could lose any chance of some decent shots. Anyway, a phone interview with me doesn't tell you anything you don't know already.'

'It tells us you're there, and the BBC, ITN and CNN aren't,' Ollie said crisply.

'OK, how soon can you be up and running?'

'We're ready to roll.'

'OK, ready when you are,' Christie said, rapidly composing her thoughts. 'Three . . . two . . . one . . . At the crash scene tonight . . .'

Swiftly Christie gave a concise account of the little information she already had, drawing a lightning picture of the scene of the tragedy in a few strong, clear words. As soon as she finished, she signed off with Ollie and put down the telephone. She guessed she would have half an hour before the whole area was declared off limits to the Press, and she didn't intend to waste it.

Christie left the two boys waiting for Andy's arrival and darted downstairs and through the back door into the garden. From here, the view of the crash was even more horrifying. Even while she watched, two firemen carried a covered stretcher down the slope of the embankment to a row of ambulances at the bottom. A waiting ambulance-man directed the two firemen to a back garden which had been commandeered by the rescue services. Three similar shrouded bodies already lay there, blood soaking through the sheeting. Christie turned away, sickened. This was even more brutal than the Clapham train crash had been. God, what had caused such horror?

She heard footsteps on the path behind her, and looked up to see Dom, Andy and Jimmy making their way towards her.

'You're here. Excellent. No trouble getting through?'

'The copper on the gate gave up after Andy started explaining and just let us through,' Dom said. 'I don't think we'll have any trouble now, it's getting far too busy outside. They're stopping everyone else at the end of the road, but I think they've written off Number Thirty-two as a lost cause.'

'Great. OK, let's get going,' Christie said. 'Dom, I'm going to need you to liaise with Ollie for me. As soon as that links truck gets here, you give me a shout. Tell him I need at least two more crews, and we're going to want a lot of back up. We'll go live as soon as we possibly can. Jimmy, you and Dom should cover any pressers that come up.'

She turned to Andy. 'OK, let's you and I go exploring before this whole thing becomes a no-go area. Then we'll have to get to the links truck and get ready to go live with what we've got.' Jimmy and Dom nodded and disappeared up the path back to the house to return to the growing mêlée of journalists, sightseers and police in the road outside. Christie could see dozens of ghoulish spectators already pressing against the cordon established to prevent anyone from reaching the scene of the crash. She turned towards the embankment, edging warily towards the end of the garden, where the nearest carriage lay sprawled on its side. The arc lights bathed the whole area in unnatural daylight. She could hear the hiss of the cutting gear as the rescue workers tried to free those trapped in the wreckage, and the hum of the generators that supplied power to the floodlights. In the distance the night air was filled with the sound of sirens from approaching ambulances.

And screams.

They moved beyond the circle of the arc-lights into the darkness. Low branches whipped at her hair, and she heard Andy curse as he caught his camera in some tangled bushes. Suddenly she ran up against a wire fence. Beyond it, the slope of the embankment towered, seeming far steeper now she was at the bottom of it.

'Can you manage to get up this with your gear?' she asked Andy over her shoulder.

'Should be able to,' Andy grunted. He shrugged his slim shoulders. 'Done worse.'

The two of them inched their way carefully up the slope. The eight carriages sprawled across the embankment to their right. They approached the wreckage nearest to them, and Christie realised that it was not a carriage, but the engine of the train. She gazed at it for a moment, wondering why her senses were instantly alert.

'There's something wrong with the engine,' she whispered after a few seconds. 'It shouldn't look like that.'

27

'Can't see anything funny myself,' Andy commented absently, already lining up the twisted metal in his view-finder. The light from the rescue teams was like daylight here. Andy switched off the small light on top of his camera and paused. 'Seems a bit smaller than the others, though,' he added, straightening away from the eyepiece.

Christie looked at the other carriages, and back towards the engine. Andy was right, it was smaller – almost foreshortened. She left the cameraman filming the rescue teams busy cutting survivors from the wreckage, and sidled forward, keeping to the shadows. No one had told her specifically not to be where she was, but she was in no doubt of the authorities' reaction should she be discovered.

As she moved towards the main carriages, Christie had a sudden vision of what Dante's *Inferno* must have looked like. She felt like a spirit moving invisibly through another world, as she made her way towards the centre of activity. Two carriages loomed, one on either side of her. Groans and cries for help emanated from the tangled metal. Christie stopped, appalled by the feeling of help-lessness that washed over her. All these people dying, and she could do nothing . . . nothing . . . to save them. She closed her eyes, and felt the tears sliding from beneath her lids. Oh God, what a waste. If there were any shady facts behind this terrible tragedy, she owed it to those who were suffering to make sure it was exposed. Resolutely she dashed the tears from her cheeks. She had a job to do. God, but it was hard to remember that in the midst of all this destruction.

Christie blanched as she saw two ambulancemen carry a groaning man out of the scorched metal a few feet from her. As she watched, his head lolled backwards, and he fell silent.

'He's gone,' Andy said behind her, his voice flat and expressionless.

Christie turned, unable to say anything, as Andy continued filming the horrific scene. Rescuers, working quickly and silently, brought more of the dead and injured out of the mangled train. A young woman struggled to sit up as she was lifted from the tangle of seats where she had been trapped and placed on a stretcher. Her face was cut and bruised beyond recognition. Christie put a restraining hand on Andy's arm, but the cameraman had already lowered his lens so that the woman's personal misery would not become fodder for thousands of television viewers.

'Peter? Where's Peter?' she screamed. 'I want Peter!'

An ambulancewoman leant over the stretcher, and took the young woman's hand. 'We'll find him, love, don't you worry,' she said reassuringly. 'Your husband, is he?'

Andy stood up from where he had been filming a tight shot of a teenage couple being helped from one of the carriages. The two looked pale and shaken, but seemed to have escaped with cuts and bruises. Christie wondered how long it would take their emotional scars to heal.

'Let's go,' he said in a low voice, as two rescue officials conferred and nodded in their direction. 'We don't want to get the tape confiscated.'

As they passed the engine on the way back to the garden of Number Thirty-two, they saw a group of rescuers already engaged in lifting it from its precarious position just below the tracks. Andy paused to take a shot of the hoist being fastened around the debris. Two men inspecting the front of the engine turned away, and studied the track itself.

'Follow them,' Christie whispered. 'Something strange is happening here. I know it.'

They edged towards the track, using the activity around

29

the engine as cover. Andy zoomed in on the ground the two men were examining. He heard Christie's intake of breath as she saw the depth of the crater.

'It was definitely an explosion, no doubt about that,' one man said, crouching down at the edge of the crater.

'Bastards,' the other said bitterly. 'What's the point the buggers giving us twenty minutes' warning when they don't tell us which fucking track they've put the device on? It was nothing more than a taunt. Christ, there must have been two hundred people on this train, not to mention those in the houses below.'

The two men moved out of earshot, but not before Christie had Andy record every word.

Chapter Two

■ **DORCHESTER HOTEL, LONDON**
12 March, 8.21 p.m.

'Exactly how do you propose these "opting out" segments will work?'

Ben Wordsworth, Editor of INN, glared at the group of Japanese businessmen sitting impassively around him. He had already explained his proposals for the development of INN in intricate detail. Three times. He tried again.

'It will be a natural progression from what is happening now,' he said, sipping his bourbon and glancing around the hotel lounge for patience, if not inspiration. 'We currently have two channels, carrying domestic and international news. But that's all they do. I intend for them to continue with this diet of mainstream news for twenty of the twenty-four hours a day; on the domestic channel, UK national news, and on the international service, world news.'

'You have spoken of opting out for the other four hours,' the Editor of the Japanese-TV news station said carefully. 'But what, exactly, do you propose to fill them with?'

Ben sighed and gritted his teeth. This was the difficult bit. Why couldn't they just take the money he made for them and run, without knowing every single damned detail of how he was making it? 'For one hour out of every six, both channels would opt out. The UK channel would then take an hour of regional news, fifteen minutes of which would be subdivided into local news. The international channel would take an hour of news of the country it was in – in Spain, for example, they'd take an hour of Spanish news. And into that would go some regional news. CNN's venture with the German ntv station is a precursor to the kind of channel I envisage. But it is only a first step. I intend to go the whole way. In one go.'

The Japanese Editor regarded him with renewed respect. 'You dream big dreams,' he said slowly.

Ben smiled. He always had.

His first dream had been a vision that burned inside him, compelling him forward, no matter what the cost. He wanted to create a twenty-four-hour news station, one that would go one step futher than CNN or the BBC World Service; a news network that would bring supermarket television within the grasp of every viewer. Each would be able to pick up what they wanted, when they wanted, for as long as they wanted. Ben had already stepped into uncharted territory with what he had done for INN so far, but it was not enough. He wanted pay-as-you-view television: at home, a diet of domestic news – national items which covered the whole country, regional items which looked at the news in each county in depth, and local news which covered their own town. Abroad, there would be a mixture of world news, national news, and UK news drawn from the domestic service. It was a heady dream which could be made possible only by drawing on the network of local radio and television stations already in place throughout the world. His vision of a single world network through which all the nations of the planet could talk to each other held him to his path even whilst the rest of the television industry mocked.

He had sold everything he had to raise the money to found INN, including his beloved radio station in Westfordshire, and invested most of his wife's inheritance in the venture into the bargain. But it was still not enough. Much as Ben loathed the idea of having to give up one percentage point of control, he had been forced to trawl the television stations of the world, looking for support. Some of them had eventually given it to him, but guardedly; to find the remaining third of the necessary finance, Ben had been forced to admit three independent backers: the veteran broadcaster Sir Edward Penhaligon, conservative MP Dalmeny de Burgh, and the hotel magnate Harry Foley.

And then his dream had started to come true.

Now he had to persuade his original investors to give him sufficient backing to realize the next phase of his plan.

'Well, Mr Wordsworth, we will consider what you have said,' the Japanese promised, rising and executing a polite half-bow. 'You have not failed us yet. I think we will be able to give you the answer you wish to hear. In time.'

Ben stood and nodded in return. You couldn't rush these people. He smiled as they left. The great thing about the Japs was that, apart from these occasional trips, they took no active part in the running of his company. That was how he liked it. Their money, his control.

For he always thought of INN as his.

Ben left the foyer and headed towards the lift. He glanced at his watch as it rose to the third floor. 8.42. His wife Odile wasn't expecting him home tonight until late, and he planned to make the most of the window of unaccountability he was now afforded for the next few hours. Much as Ben despised Odile, he needed her public support, her impeccable connections, and most of all her father's money. He was not prepared to lose any of it through simple carelessness: he knew that Odile might close her eyes to his indiscretions for the sake of their daughter, but would not stomach them being flaunted to her face.

Ben crept quietly down the corridor and stopped outside his room, checking up and down to make sure he was not being observed. As Editor in Chief of INN, he was too high profile to risk any indiscretion being documented by a gleeful newspaper, particularly in the midst of the most delicate negotiations in his life. Satisfied that no one was watching him, he slid the plastic key through the lock, and cursed as the red light lit up and beeped at him. Christ, getting into your own hotel room these days was more difficult than buying a Lotus with a stolen credit card. What had happened to good, old-fashioned keys? He took the card out and turned it upside down, then re-inserted it. To his relief the green light glowed comfortingly at him, and the door opened with a slight click.

Ben shut it carefully behind him, steadying himself lightly against the door-jamb as he bent awkwardly and slipped off his shoes. Swaying slightly with all the bourbon he had consumed, he padded across the large room, his stockinged feet making no noise on the thick, bilious green carpet.

He paused at the entrance to the adjoining bedroom, and eyed the slender girl on the bed as a stab of desire shot through him. The thin cotton sheet was twisted around her body, exposing one shapely leg in a way that looked both inviting and curiously vulnerable. Ben could just see the tangled blondness of her mound at the top of her thighs, and the soft outline of her full breasts beneath the sheets.

His need became more urgent, and he shuddered with

34

anticipation as he felt his cock grow hard.

'Jesus, baby, am I going to enjoy tonight,' he muttered, unzipping his flies and flinging his jacket on the floor by the kingsize bed. 'And perhaps you will too.' He laughed shortly. 'Although that's by no means essential.'

The girl stirred. 'Ben? Is that you?'

'Sssh, baby, who else wants you this much?' grinned Ben, gripping her slim hand firmly in his and pulling it down on to his cock, so that she could feel how erect he was.

She half sat up, her blonde hair a dusty cloak around her shoulders. 'What time is it?'

'Quarter to nine.'

'Damn. I'm sorry, Ben. I must have fallen asleep after my bath. I didn't expect you back until later.'

'Well, aren't you the lucky one? I'm here early.'

Ben's hand was already beneath the sheet, working its way up the softness of her thighs to the tangle of hairs between them. His third finger slipped quickly inside her, her sleepy murmurs turning instantly to groans. She was already wet, and twisted hungrily against his finger as he pushed himself on top of her, his hard cock rubbing insistently against her soft mound. Suddenly Ben heard a soft knock at the door and pulled away abruptly, his eyes glittering with a mixture of arousal and anticipation.

He leaped off the bed, ignoring the girl's cry of dismay, and crossed quickly to the door. He leant against it and waited.

The knock came again, and a soft voice murmured, 'It's Amy Rose here, sir. From the agency.'

Ben opened the door so swiftly a small brunette nearly fell into the room.

'What kept you?' he muttered, pulling her upright and kicking the door shut with his foot as he lead her through to the bedroom.

The call-girl paused and frowned. 'I've seen her before . . .' she said slowly, nodding at the girl sitting up on the bed, who was now very much awake and clutching the sheet around her naked breasts in alarm. 'Yeah, somewhere . . . now where was it?'

'You don't know her from shit, right?' Ben said, gripping the girl's shoulder. She shrugged and nodded quickly, sensing that this would be a dangerous man to cross.

Ben relaxed and turned towards the bed. 'This, my darling, is Amy Rose. She's your birthday present to me. Amy Rose, I think we'll dispense with introductions on your side, don't you? Now the three of us are going to have a really good time – Christ knows, I'm paying enough.'

Amy Rose eyed the girl speculatively for a moment, then at Ben's impatient sign, shrugged off her coffee-coloured raincoat. Ben grinned sardonically. She must be pretty good at her job if she could afford to turn tricks in a Burberry.

Underneath the raincoat, the call-girl was wearing nothing but a very brief pair of black panties, a matching suspender belt and seamed silk stockings. She was young, not much more than eighteen, Ben calculated with approval; her unsupported breasts were surprisingly high and firm on her small frame, her waist slim above rounded hips and thighs.

She smiled and sashayed towards the bed, her movements assured and provocative. Ben stood aside, his cock rearing hungrily between his legs, as his eyes raked her slender figure. He could see the dark smudge of her mound beneath the opalescent material of her panties, the scent of her arousal filling the air.

'Ben, stop this,' whimpered the girl on the bed. 'I can't. Please, don't ask me to.' Her dark eyes brimmed as she

36

gazed pleadingly at Ben, but his attention was transfixed by the other girl, his eyes devouring her young, supple body as he registered the high, pale breasts, the dark hair spilling down on to her chocolate-tipped nipples; that warm, secret place between her thighs.

'You'll do it, Paragon,' he said shortly, turning to the girl on the bed. 'If you want to present the Early Evening News, you'll do it. Now take her clothes off, and for Christ's sake, look as if you're enjoying it.'

Paragon Fairfax shrunk back against the headboard at the top of the bed. This had definitely not been part of the plan.

She had deliberately set out to seduce Ben Wordsworth, with the sole aim of rising from her current position as one of several fill-in presenters to the slot of main newsanchor for INN's flagship evening show. It should not have been difficult. So far, she had displayed a skill at manipulating men second only to Eva Peron. Her marriage to her aging husband, Harry Foley, meant that she was now extremely wealthy, and it had been his shares in INN that had made her one of the network's newscasters in the first place. Unfortunately Harry could not do any more, and so she had selected Ben Wordsworth as the next appropriate career move. He had apparently accommodated her plans with alacrity.

But suddenly she was not sure who was using whom.

Paragon shrank away as Amy Rose slipped into the bed beside her and blocked Ben from her view. Slowly the call-girl ran her hand over Paragon's left breast and bent her head to suck softly on the pale pink nipple. Paragon gasped despite herself as an unexpected flicker of desire raced through her body. Frantically she pulled away and grasped the sheet closely against herself.

Ben growled and turned away. Paragon breathed a sigh of relief as he disappeared into the main room. Thank

37

God. He'd changed his mind. She leaned against the headboard and closed her eyes. This awful woman would go and she and Ben would make love properly, the way she had meant it to happen. He was just testing her.

Suddenly she felt his hand grasp her right wrist, and yank it round to the headboard. He was breathing heavily, his eyes glittering with a cruel excitement.

'You're going to enjoy this, you bitch, if it takes all night,' he muttered.

'What the hell are you doing? Ben, for God's sake, you're hurting me!' Paragon cried, truly frightened now.

'Help me, you bitch, I'm not paying you to sit and watch!' Ben grunted, glancing up at the call-girl as he panted with a mixture of effort and arousal. If he'd realised it was going to be this much fun, he wouldn't have waited until his fortieth birthday for such a present.

Amy Rose watched a moment longer, then, shrugging her shoulders, took Paragon's other wrist and bound it to the headboard with a second silk tie, as Ben moved towards Paragon's feet. Within minutes she was firmly trussed, able to move slightly but not enough to escape. Ben edged toward the bottom of the bed, surveying Paragon's supine form spreadeagled on the silk sheets with satisfaction. This was one casting couch that she would never forget. Ben could see her cunt glistening wetly, her legs spread wide, her creamy breasts splayed to either side of her chest as she moaned and shuddered. He did not know if it was with fear or arousal, and cared even less.

The call-girl smiled knowingly as she wet her lips with the tip of her tongue and moved slowly across Paragon's body. She had a feeling the girl would prove a willing partner . . . with a little persuasion. She bent her head once more and took Paragon's nipple in her mouth, her little white teeth teasing the sensitive pink tip with quick, darting strokes. With a deft flick, she undid the ties that held her own lace panties together, her glossy chestnut pubic hair springing free, and mounted the other woman. Ben groaned. From his vantage point in an ancient armchair at the foot of the bed he could see the dark pubic hair mingling with the blonde, the high, firm breasts of the call-girl rubbing erotically against the pale pinkness of Paragon's nipples.

Suddenly he could stand it no more, and pulled the call-girl off the bed, thrusting a fistful of notes into her hand.

'Get out,' he panted, mounting Paragon and roughly freeing her hands. Her legs he left bound wide apart. 'And keep your mouth shut.'

He did not even hear the girl leave. Ruthlessly he plunged into Paragon, burying his cock up to the hilt inside her, deliberately trying to hurt her. She would soon learn who was in control. Sweat plastered his hair darkly against his head and trickled down his face as his thighs slammed against hers. Paragon squirmed frantically beneath him, her honey-blonde hair tumbled against the pillows as he pressed her head down with one hand and pounded her body relentlessly with his own powerful thrusts. She arched in pain and desire as he forced himself even deeper into her, screaming his name as she raked her scarlet fingernails across his back.

Abruptly Ben stopped thrusting, and froze.

'What the fuck do you think you're doing?' he hissed. 'You leave a mark on me, and I'll give you something you'll never forget.'

Terrified, Paragon pulled her hands away from his skin as if she had been burnt. She buried them in the small of her back so that she would not be tempted to hold him to her again. Ben saw the fear in her eyes, and a sadistic smile of triumph flitted across his face.

Slowly he resumed his thrusts into her. Her fear had made her go dry, and Ben knew that every movement he made must be hurting her, and that she was too afraid of offending him to let the pain show. He propped himself up on his forearms, and looked at her carefully, consideringly, as if he were studying a mare for sale. That she was physically perfect he could not deny. Her eyes, now tightly squeezed shut so that he should not see the hurt in them, were richly, deeply blue. Her skin was perfect, its ivory creaminess set off to perfection by her chin-length cloud of rich strawberry blonde hair. Her twenty-seven-year-old body was taut and firm, full breasts above a narrow waist, and those perfect legs were always ready to spread wide for him. No wonder he was about to make her one of INN's top presenters. The irony was that he was going to do it anyway, before she decided to screw her way to success.

Abruptly he reached for one of her soft, tanned breasts, and tweaked the pink nipple which was standing out erect and full. Her grimace of pain made him even harder inside her, and he fell on her, his weight across her chest, gripping both breasts in his hands and tightening his hold on them. His fingernails dug into the soft flesh, and thin red half-moons appeared as he pierced her skin. His body shuddered as his climax coursed through him, and he twisted her breasts savagely.

Careless of her feelings, Ben pulled out of her the minute it was over, and sat up on the hotel bed. He leant against the headboard, and reached over to the bedside table to glance at his gold Rolex. 9.20. He wondered absently how the Japanese businessmen were doing.

Paragon slithered off the bed and disappeared into the bathroom. Ben grinned malevolently and switched on the television with the remote control beside him. Automatically he pressed Channel Nine for INN.

He sat bolt upright as he saw Christie Bradley come on to the screen, the twisted wreckage of the train visible in the background behind her.

'Paragon! Where the fuck is my message master?' he screamed, dialling the number of the Newsdesk. She ran back into the bedroom and gestured wordlessly towards his trousers still lying on the floor. Ben reached for the bleep still clipped to his belt and cursed as he rememberd switching it to silent. He yanked on his trousers with one hand as he cradled the telephone between his neck and chin, waiting for Ollie to answer.

■ INN, LONDON
9.22 p.m.

Ollie replaced the telephone with a sigh, shooting his chair backwards and grabbing his coffee from the other end of his desk. It was always like this the moment a big story happened; all the Grown-Ups came dashing into the building to prove how dedicated they were, and because they did not dare be absent in case one of their loyal colleagues stabbed them in the back. In the meantime they made it almost impossible for the poor bastards like him who were actually trying to do their jobs. Every manager had a different opinion and a suggestion, and all expected to be instantly obeyed.

Ollie swigged his coffee and checked his computer to see if any more wire-stories had come through with details about the crash. He had tried earlier to get hold of Wordsworth, without success, since the Editor had not responded to his bleep and had left no message saying where he could be located. Ollie would lay money on the fact that Ben had been screwing around, and he'd double his bet that it was with Paragon.

The News Editor chewed his lip as he scanned the array of television monitors on his desk. INN output was currently showing an interview with an Opposition politician blaming Government cutbacks for the accident, quoting a BR spokesman who had spent the past twelve months criticising Major's plans for privatisation. Ollie could see that their main rivals – ITN, BBC, CNN and one or two others – were all now covering the rail crash in some form or another, although none of them had yet shown any live reports from the scene of the accident.

Above the screens was a monitor with the remote feed, which displayed the picture link to the site of the crash. Christie had just completed a live report in which she had broken the news that a bomb had caused the accident: a report that was as yet unconfirmed by either police or politicians. INN was still ahead of the game.

Their output had switched to other coverage, but in the remote feed monitor Ollie could see Christie standing down from her live two-way. He watched her unhook the microphone from her jacket and call to the crew gathered around the links truck, as she sipped from a bottle of Perrier one of them had just handed to her.

Ollie cursed, a sour taste in his mouth. At Wordworth's insistence, he had despatched one of INN's veteran – and more importantly, as far as the Editor was concerned, male – reporters to the scene of the crash. Bob Carpenter had been given a brief to do a full pull-together of the accident and what had caused it. Ollie was furious; he considered it both unfair and unethical of Ben to allow Bob to bigfoot Christie: coming in over her head after she had already gained a scoop with a piece strong enough to win her an RTS award. He considered the older reporter dishonest and underhand in his dealings, and was well aware of Carpenter's reputation for stealing his colleagues' stories out from under them by pulling rank. But Ollie did not dare to defy openly a direct instruction from the Editor.

He sighed and dialled the portable cellnet telephone in the links van, watching the remote monitor as Christie answered it.

'Great piece, kid,' Ollie said as soon as she picked up the cellnet.

Christie smiled into the camera, aware that Ollie could see her, although INN's viewers were not able to see the remote feed. 'Thanks, Ollie. I'm going to start cutting a piece as soon as Andy and Jimmy get back with the tapes. What's my deadline?'

Ollie grimaced. 'Hey, kid, you aren't going to like this, but I promise you, it isn't my fault.'

Christie's expression grew wary. 'Spill, Ollie.'

'Bob Carpenter's on his way to you now to do the final wrap.'

'Ollie, that's not bloody fair, and you know it,' Christie said angrily, thumping the side of the links truck with the flat of her hand. 'Why should he march in here and use my pictures and my interviews – my scoop – to earn all the kudos? Godamnit Ollie, this is my story!'

'I know, I know,' Ollie groaned. 'Look, Christie, I'm with you all the way on this one. But it's not my decision. What can I do?'

'You can bloody well let me run with my story,' Christie said indignantly. She took a breath and sighed. 'Hey, Ollie, I know it's not down to you. But help me out on this, can't you? I put everything into this story, and I don't want to hand it over to Carpenter so that he can waste it with clichés and the official line.'

'Christie, darling, this is from the Editor himself . . .'

'Ollie . . . please?'

Ollie sighed and glanced at the clock over the monitors. 'It's 9.30 now,' he said slowly. 'The Late News show is on at ten. If you can give me a piece as a standby and

43

Carpenter's story doesn't come in, I've got no choice but to run it, have I?'

He saw Christie grin as she ended the call, and smiled to himself. He knew she understood what he was saying: he would make damned sure the other reporter's package did not find its way to the correct desk in time, if he had to sit on it himself. She had half-an-hour to edit a ten-minute piece together, but if it meant preventing Carpenter from stealing her story, Ollie knew she'd do it. And do it well.

'OK, Ollie, what've you got for me?'

Ollie swung around in his chair and grinned at the news Producer standing behind him. 'Dragged you out of bed, have they?'

Jerry Tallboy rolled his eyes heavenwards, his monkey-like face screwed up in disgust even more than usual. 'Someone's got to play the Indian to all these Chiefs.'

Ollie laughed and shook his head. Jerry was one of his favourite Producers. To him fell the thankless task of putting together the hourly ten-minute headlines, News Update, a poor relation of the main news bulletins with practically no budget of its own. The News Update required constant rewriting and new pictures to keep it seeming fresh, yet was continually fighting the main programmes for crews and editors. Jerry also got landed with most of the Newsflash Specials, since the regular producer of the Early Evening News and the Late News show, Brian Reynolds, hated nothing more than a break-ing story messing up his schedules, and did everything in his power to avoid handling one.

Ollie scratched his stomach absently as he considered the ingredients the news team had already gathered for the ten o'clock show. 'OK. Christie's already there, and she'll give you a ten-minute standby piece,' he said, as Jerry scribbled notes down on his clipboard. 'Bob Carpenter's on his way, but he may not make it in time for your show.

How come you're producing it, anyway? I thought it'd be Brian's territory.'

'He wasn't on today,' Jerry said shortly. 'He's on a Management Orientation Seminar, so I'm producing the Late News all week. What else?'

Ollie dropped the subject. 'You've got live facilities, so you can take an update from Bob as and when he gets there,' he replied. 'And Christie's found the conductress who was on the train; she's a bit battered, but it all adds to the authenticity. You should be able to get a live interview with her, which will be exclusive. Apart from that, Nick's chasing relatives, Archie's covering the hospital where the injured are being taken, and we've got Ginny in-house here digging out footage of train crashes we've known and loved.'

'I'm supposed to make an hour-long news programme out of maybes?' Jerry said, shaking his head in disbelief. 'Never mind, sorry I asked.' He stalked over to the News Update Desk and threw his clipboard down in exasperation, scowling. Every time he was expected to come up with something out of nothing, and every time he managed it. The trouble was, now it was taken for granted he could; there'd be hell to pay if it all went horribly wrong – and he'd get the blame.

The Late News team had already been augmented by various journalists called in by Ollie and Janey on the Newsdesk as soon as they had heard about the crash. Jerry handed out photocopies of his makeshift running order as they gathered around the desk.

'We're on air at 22.00 as usual, which gives us twenty-four minutes,' Jerry said tersely. None of the team balked at his tone; they were used to Jerry's pre-transmission nerves, and his anxiety was never reflected in his programme, which was invariably smooth and professional. 'Forget any other news: we'll just go on the crash unless

45

anything absolutely bloody sensational happens. Ginny, I want you to liaise with Christie and make sure she covers everything in her piece. I'm not putting any money on Carpenter getting there in time. Write me a good, hard news lead-in of a minute or so, and make sure you include the death-toll. Don't let Christie put any figures in her piece, in case it changes before we go on air.'

Ginny Templeton nodded, her chestnut hair swinging below her chin as she wrote Jerry's directives down. 'Do you want a map in the lead-in?' she asked, her mind already three steps ahead with her customary alertness. 'I've already had Lynxie in Graphics put together a locater – most of our viewers won't have a clue where Heathley is, so we'd better show them.'

Jerry nodded thankfully. If he had to get lumbered with this one, which looked like being an all-nighter, at least he had a great team to work with. At twenty-eight, Ginny was one of the top field producers in the business. She had no desire to be in front of the camera; instead, she put everything she had into making the stories she produced as well-researched and accurate as possible. Ginny and Christie were both good friends and an efficient, professional team. Ginny's cool resourcefulness and meticulous attention to detail complemented Christie's innovative, daring reporting, and together they created superb pieces of journalism that few could match. Tonight it would be Ginny's responsibility to make sure the correspondent had all the necessary pictures to reflect each aspect of the story, that the piece was fair and well-balanced, that no crucial element of the report had been missed. She would also order the subtitles to cover interviews, the required graphics, and anything else the reporter needed to keep going. Jerry thought it was a shame Ginny was not as efficient and organised when it came to her love-life.

'OK, Ginny, that sounds good,' Jerry said, making a

note against the list on his clipboard. 'Right, moving on, we'll then go live to Christie for an update, and an interview with the conductress and anyone else still alive who was on that train.' He paused and looked around. 'Let's hope Nick gets some relatives, and Archie some good reaction stuff at the hospital, or we're going to spend a long time twiddling our thumbs.'

'Who's presenting?' Lynxie asked.

Jerry looked up at the graphics artist. 'Charles Silversmith. Oh, and we'll be going from Studio Two instead of the main studio, since the Newsflash team are already up and running there. It'll mean it's a bit of a squash, but it'll save time re-rigging in Studio One. OK, let's go.'

As the team dispersed, Ollie came over to the desk with a small, skinny man wearing a green anorak in tow.

'Jerry, this is Duncan Pink, of the *Railway Enthusiasts' Gazette*. He'll be in the studio for an interview if we need someone to fill.' He winked at Jerry as he lead the pimply man to Make-Up. 'The original train-spotter,' he grinned over his shoulder as Jerry walked away looking harassed.

Five minutes to On-Air, Jerry's expression was close to desperation. He waved his running order under Ollie's nose with disbelief.

'Not a single piece in!' he screamed. 'Five minutes to On-Air and I don't have a frame of picture in the building! I hope that bloody train-spotter of yours has an interesting life-story.'

Jerry marched into the Newsflash control gallery adjoining the newsroom and threw his running order over his left shoulder in despair. There was no point in trying to plan the sequence in which the packages should run: he would just have to take whatever came first. He worked his way along the back of the narrow control room behind the row of seats occupied by his production staff, and squeezed into his place in the corner next to the telephone and computer console. Not for the first time he cursed the designers who had made the newsroom so large at the expense of the gallery.

Directly in front of Jerry, the Programme Director, Muriel Greenwood, scanned the few scripts she did have to work with, and prepared herself for anything. It was Jerry's job to decide what the content of the bulletin would be, but once they were on air, the mechanics of actually putting the programme together would be down to her. The editors rolled the packages, the graphics artists punched up the maps, the journalists began their live two-ways, only at her direct instruction. It was akin to juggling half-a-dozen priceless porcelain ornaments whilst balancing on a greased high-wire. Only more difficult.

To Muriel's right, Kim, the production assistant, counted down the remaining minutes to On-Air. It was her responsibility to make sure the programme ran precisely to time; she would count in and out of the commercial breaks, and ensure that the final credits rolled exactly fifty-nine minutes and fifty seconds after the bulletin started. With so few pre-written scripts, Muriel would rely on Kim's timing to issue the instruction for each package to roll, since many of them required a five-second countdown; working on the principle that the newscaster spoke at a rate of three words per second, Muriel would roll the stories fifteen words before the end of the lead-in. Once they were into each package, Kim would count down to the end of the report, so that Muriel could cue the newscaster to read the next script the moment the pre-recorded piece finished.

'Three minutes to On-Air,' Kim announced, glancing down the gallery at her colleagues. The vision mixer tested her controls with practised sureness, moving her chair as the graphics controller slid into his place on her right.

At the front of the gallery, a bank of forty television monitors flickered and changed. In the centre of the wall of screens, below the clock, the largest monitor displayed INN's current output, which was now a commercial break. The remote feed to its left showed Christie hurriedly easing her microphone beneath her jacket and clipping it to her lapel in preparation for her live two-way. On the top row of screens her cut story was still coming in. Jerry watched it anxiously, praying it would all be in the building before they went on-air. Next to the monitor playing Christie's piece, two other completed packages from Nick and Archie were lined up at the beginning, ready to roll the moment Muriel issued the command. Their frozen first frames shivered in the screens. In the corner of the bank of monitors, the graphics output showed a map of south-east England. The Gatwick to Victoria route had been marked by a dotted line, a tiny orange flame halfway along it representing the site of the explosion. Miniature oblongs indicated the fallen carriages. It was Muriel's task, as the director, to decide which of the many screens at any given time were punched up and trans-mitted to INN's millions of viewers.

'Two minutes thirty, everybody. Two and a half minutes.'

■ HEATHLEY, SUSSEX
9.56 p.m.

At the links truck, Christie tensed as she heard Kim's countdown in her earpiece. She checked over her left shoulder to see what background would be showing behind her when they went on-air. The floodlights illumi-nated the scene of the accident as if it was indeed a film set.

Rescue workers were clearly visible, still cutting the last few victims free from the twisted wreckage of the train. Two ambulancemen side-stepped carefully down the embankment, an elderly woman covered in blood strapped to the stretcher they carried between them. Christie paled as she looked at her, and called out to Andy.

'We can't go on air with her in the background,' she said urgently to the cameraman, a terrible pity in her eyes. 'She's barely alive. You'll have to tighten the shot.'

Muriel's voice sounded in her earpiece.

'Can you hear us, Heathley?'

Christie gave a thumbs-up in affirmation, and she heard Muriel tell the cameraman that she was happy with the look of the shot. Christie turned to face the camera in readiness for her live question-and-answer two-way with Charles back in the studio. She smiled across at Judy Coleridge, the conductress who had somehow survived the horrific accident with no more than cuts and bruises, and who was sitting just out of shot.

'You sure you want to do this, Judy?'

Judy nodded, her battered face pale. 'Got to show them we can keep going, no matter what they do,' she whispered. 'Got to show them.'

Christie was filled with respect for the other woman's courage. After she had given the latest update to the viewers, she would interview Judy live. It would be a superb piece of television, but not one she would have contemplated had not the conductress requested the opportunity to defy the bombers herself.

Christie felt a pulse of excitement as she mentally rehearsed what she would say when they came to her. Nothing gave her a greater buzz than going live on air. For those few eternal, brief minutes, everything depended on her. Millions of viewers would be hanging on her every word, relying on her eyes and ears and mind to interpret a scene which they received only second-hand. And every one of them would be waiting for her to make a mistake. Christie smiled. Just thinking about it gave her a rush of adrenalin that was better than sex. She felt her nipples harden, and the familiar surge of warmth between her legs. If any man could ever make her feel like this, she'd probably agree to marry him on the spot.

■ INN, LONDON
9.58 p.m.

'One minute forty-five to On-Air.'

'Where the hell is Charles?' Jerry yelled from the back of the control room, suddenly realising that the newscaster's chair in the studio was conspicuously vacant. The Floor Manager shrugged his shoulder as he heard Jerry's shouted question through his earphones, glancing around the studio as if he expected to find the absent anchor hiding beneath the desk. Jerry put his head in his hands and closed his eyes. He was putting the final touches to his resignation speech in his head when Charles Silversmith walked calmly on to the studio set, smoothing his artfully grey hair with one immaculately manicured hand.

'Make-Up were a little slow this evening,' he stated coolly, sitting down in his seat and lifting his chin in order to inspect his reflection in his handmirror from all angles. He smiled at himself.

'One minute to transmission. One minute.'

The Floor Manager dived beneath the desk and seized Charles' microphone, weaving it swiftly beneath the newscaster's jacket and clipping it to his tie. Charles shuffled his scripts and checked that the autocue in front of him had been correctly aligned at the beginning of the first story. The scripts were intended merely as a back-up: everything he would say should have been programmed into the autocue, but it always paid to have hard copies in case the cue went down. Charles smiled at the make-up girl as she dashed on to the set to give his forehead a final dusting with an outsize powder puff, and reached once more for his handmirror. Wetting his index finger with his tongue, he smoothed down his eyebrows, smiled at his image and replaced the mirror in the tray beneath his desk.

In the control gallery, Jerry punched the keys of his computer terminal and called up the wire services' latest newsflashes. Reuters, Associated Press, and the Press Association were all running frequent updates on the rail crash. Each time the news agencies unearthed a new piece of information, it was flashed on the wire service to customers around the world. The sombre figure of those killed in the accident now stood at 114, according to AP and Reuters, whilst PA put it at 115. More than ninety people had been injured, at least half of them seriously. Even while he watched, Jerry saw the death-toll reach 118 on all three services.

'Thirty seconds to On-Air,' Kim said tensely.

'Rewrite on story one,' Jerry barked.

Muriel echoed his instruction into the microphone on the desk in front of her. Charles heard the command through his earpiece, and gave a brief thumbs-up without looking towards the camera, to indicate that he had heard. He pulled the pile of scripts on his desk towards him.

'OK. Take the second para, beginning "At least 114 people are thought to have died . . ." Change that to "At least 118 people . . .", updating the death toll.' Jerry paused. 'You'll need to change the recap at the end of the programme to match.'

In the studio, Charles swiftly scribbled the alteration on

his script, whilst the autocue operator made the necessary adjustments on the machine.

'Fourteen . . . thirteen . . . twelve . . .'

Muriel glanced up at the silent monitor in front of her which still showed Christie's package coming in from the links truck at Heathley. Without being able to hear the sound, she was unable to tell if the piece was nearing the end. The package was scheduled to run fifty-five seconds into the programme. It still had to finish coming in and be rewound back to the beginning ready to roll.

'Edit Suite Three, will you be there?' she asked the editor responsible for taping the piece in one of the dozen recording booths.

'Five . . . four . . . three . . .'

'Fifteen seconds to the end of the piece,' the editor replied over the intercom to the gallery. 'Give me a minute and I'll be there.'

'Make it forty-five seconds,' Muriel said.

'On-Air!' Kim called, starting the clock which immediately began counting off the fifty-nine minutes and fifty seconds to the end of the programme.

Charles lent into the camera, his hands clasped in front of him. 'Good evening. The headlines tonight. At least 118 people die in a terrorist attack on a railway line. The IRA says it was responsible . . .'

Muriel waited until the pre-recorded headline shots and rolled to cover Charles' words, then cut back to the newscaster as he introduced the first package.

'At least 118 people died tonight when terrorists blew up a section of track carrying the Gatwick to Victoria Express,' Charles said smoothly, just the right note of concern in his voice. 'Eight carriages from the high-speed train plunged off the track at Heathley in Surrey . . .'

'Take map,' Muriel commanded.

The vision mixer punched up the prepared graphics

map, which filled the screen as Charles described the sequence of events which had lead up to the crash.

'Where's story one?' Jerry shouted, moving forward from the back of the gallery. 'Is it there?'

Muriel glanced up at the monitor and saw Christie's piece being rewound back to the beginning. 'ES3, can you make it?'

'Ten seconds to VTR,' Kim said, glancing at her copy of Charles's script. Every eye in the gallery watched as Christie's video tape recording – VTR – was lined up by the editor in Edit Suite Three.

'Yes or no?' Muriel demanded.

'. . . our reporter, Christie Bradley, was at the scene . . .' said Charles, his expression betraying none of the chaos in the gallery which he could hear through his earpiece.

'It's there!' the editor shouted over the intercom.

'. . . and has this exclusive report,' Charles finished. He heard Muriel tell the vision mixer to punch up Christie's package on to the screen, and sighed with relief as he saw it begin with a GV of the carriages sprawled down the embankment. He sat back in his chair and took a sip of water; her piece was just over eleven minutes long, which meant both he and the control room could take a break whilst it played out. Thank God.

Christie's pictures were the first Ben Wordsworth saw as he walked into the newsroom.

'Jesus,' he breathed, despite himself.

The journalists gathered in the newsroom gazed in silence as the pictures cut to a row of covered corpses lined up in someone's back garden. Andy's expert eye had missed none of the details; he panned from a wide shot of the carriages half-buried in the destroyed row of homes, to a close-up of a baby fist just visible beneath the edge of a sheet, a pink rabbit clutched in the still hand. Christie did not waste words with such powerful pictures telling the tragic story. Even the hardened journalists were shocked out of their normal professional indifference as one horrific picture followed another.

Ollie looked up as Brian Reynolds, the Senior Producer, arrived in the newsroom, panting breathlessly as he reached the newsdesk, his bald head glistening with the obvious exertion of running up two flights of stairs. He paused as he reached the group gathered around the newsroom monitors, and took off his glasses to polish them as he watched the screen.

'Who's producing this programme?' Brian demanded once he had recovered his breath.

Ben turned towards him, his eyes narrowed. 'Brian. Glad you could make it,' he said sardonically. Brian winced.

'Got here as soon as I could,' he said defensively. 'I've been off-roster this week for the Management Orientation Seminar. But I'm here now.'

'So glad to hear it,' Ben drawled. 'I shall rest easy now.'

'I'll take over straight away,' Brian said firmly, with what he hoped was a display of efficient authority. There was no way he was having the Editor witness the fact that his presence was clearly superfluous to the proceedings. These days redundancies were always in the air. He needed to look as busy as possible as soon as possible.

Ben did not bother to answer. He began walking towards his office, and spoke without looking back. 'Ollie. I take it Bob will be there in time for the breakfast update at seven.' It was not a question.

Brian reached across Ollie as soon as the Editor had safely vanished into his office, and picked up the Late News running order on his desk.

'You've got three live broadcasts!' he said in horror. 'Two from the crash scene and one from the hospital!

What if you lose one of them?'

Ollie shrugged and pointed towards the train expert who was sitting next to Charles in the open set of Studio Two. 'We pray he's had an interesting life,' he said.

Brian glared at the unfortunate Duncan Pink, who was sweating uncomfortably beneath the hot lights of the studio and staring out towards the newsroom with the desperate expression Ollie remembered from the journalists trapped in the alcohol-free Arab states during the Gulf War.

'It's too risky,' Brian said with a profound shudder. 'I'm taking over. This has gone on long enough.'

Brian started walking towards the control room. Ollie pressed the intercom which linked the Newsdesk to Jerry in the gallery.

'The eagle has landed,' he murmured into the microphone. 'And it's bald and coming your way.'

Jerry scowled, and leaped off his chair, easing his way behind the production team towards the control room door, wedged permanently open to allow the general assistants to bring updated copy and scripts straight to the programme producer. He took one look at Brian heading towards him and bent to the floor, easing the wedge of paper from beneath the door so that it swung shut. Jerry breathed a sigh of relief for soundproofing as he peered through the glass porthole and saw Brian's face turn an unflattering shade of puce. Firmly he turned his back and leaned against the door, sensing rather than hearing the incoherent ranting on the other side of it.

'You'll never work again!' Brian screamed, apoplectic with rage.

'I've never met a journalist who did anyway,' one of the tape editors muttered under his breath.

'We have been most pleased by the distribution. It seems it has proved more successful than we could have hoped.'

Sir Edward Penhaligon nodded. 'Indeed?'

His guest smiled. 'We can report a ninety-four per cent success rate in the control area, even allowing for error. We now propose extending our operation to the rest of the region as soon as it can be implemented.'

'I see.' Sir Edward looked mildly surprised. 'In that case, we must step up production. You are sure that it can be efficiently and thoroughly administered? There must be no mistakes.'

'That goes without saying,' the other assured him. 'I can foresee no problems, however. In fact, we expect that we shall see considerable improvement in the situation within a year, and a near-total solution of the problem in a decade.'

Sir Edward's second guest leaned forward and gazed intently at him as he broke his silence. 'Of course, your personal profit will be of no mean proportions,' he said quietly, 'Although I know that is not your motive in helping us.'

Sir Edward returned the man's gaze with equanimity. 'As you say,' he commented expressionlessly. He lacked the two Israelis' fervour, but his commitment to the cause was just as strong as theirs.

Sir Edward turned as the club steward approached his ancient leather armchair noiselessly and coughed discreetly into his hand.

'Telephone, Sir Edward,' he murmured, looking almost embarrassed at the modern intrusion into the solid, Victorian establishment.

Sir Edward frowned in irritation as his two guests immediately rose and gathered their papers together, putting them in their briefcases and snapping them shut with an air of finality. He raised his hand to indicate that he wished the steward to hold his call, but the more senior of his two guests smiled and shook his head, forestalling the request, and extended his hand in farewell.

'Please, attend to your business,' he said, in the clipped, perfect English that immediately proclaimed his status as a foreigner. 'There is no need to see us out. I believe we have covered everything, Sir Edward. It was most delightful to see you once more; I do hope we shall meet again soon.'

Sir Edward rose to shake the other man's outstretched hand. His polite smile did not banish the expression of cool appraisal in his grey eyes.

'I am sure we shall,' he said courteously, bowing slightly as his guests left the room.

He sank back into the comfort of his chair, and asked the steward to bring him the telephone with a brief lift of his hand. He reached for his crystal tumbler of Glenfiddich and lifted it to his lips. His expression was unreadable.

At fifty-five, Sir Edward Penhaligon was one of the most powerful men in the country. Substantial family wealth had gained him a place at Eton and then Balliol, even if his mother's background was considered questionable in some quarters, and later instant membership of London's most exclusive clubs. His father's death had given him control of the world's third-largest pharmaceutical company, ChemCo, at the age of twenty-four, but he had preferred to remain a silent partner whilst he pursued his own chosen career in television broadcasting. At the age of thirty he had secured both a position as the BBC's top foreign correspondent and Lady Annabel

Delacourt as his wife; five years later he was presenting and producing his own current affairs programme, and could command the salary of his choice. His distinguished silver hair and patrician features became familiar to a nation who looked to him for comment in times of political upheaval, and support during times of crisis.

By the age of forty-two he had been knighted and widowed, and was the confidante of prime ministers, presidents and royalty alike. Sir Edward's dismay at the passing of Margaret Thatcher as the country's leader reflected his personal friendship with her, as well as his disenchantment with the mediocrity he saw now stalking the highest corridors of power. He leant his support to the Broadcasting Bill, which was aimed at breaking the perceived stranglehold on British news, seeing in the legislation a last chance to revitalise an industry grown lazy and complacent. Deploring what he saw as the BBC's inability to meet the challenges of the future, he had already been searching for an alternative when Ben Wordsworth approached him. Sir Edward agreed to trade his experience, gravitas and some hard cash for a fourteen per cent share in Wordsworth's embryonic television company, and a position as its senior news anchor.

He responded now with his customary calmness to Wordworth's telephone call briefing him on the developing situation at the scene of the train crash. As the steward summoned his driver, Sir Edward finished his drink and completed the *Times* crossword. Shrugging into his dark overcoat, he stepped into the back of the limousine awaiting him.

He was satisfied with the meeting he had just had, despite its somewhat abrupt end. Both his guests had appeared extremely pleased with his product, which was outdoing all expectations. He glanced at his watch. 10.56. A full but rewarding evening.

59

As the driver pulled up outside the steps of the INN building, Sir Edward dismissed the conversation with the two Israelis from his mind. The lights of the newsroom were clearly visible, and he could see silhouettes moving rapidly behind the screened windows on the first floor.

'If you could wait, Denver,' Sir Edward said to the driver as he stepped out of the car, grasping his furled umbrella in his hand.

Denver nodded, and Sir Edward made his way up the steps. The doorman smiled at him and waved him through without bothering to ask for identification.

As he walked into the newsroom, Sir Edward caught the last few bars of the INN signature music, and turned to the nearest television in time to see the credits rolling as the Late News came to an end. He saw Ben waiting by the Newsdesk as the production staff emerged from the control gallery, congratulating each other with relief on the ultimate smooth running of the broadcast. Despite the late arrival of Christie's package, none of the behind-the-scenes chaos had shown on air, to the astonishment of all concerned.

Christie had given INN yet another exclusive when she interviewed the chief ambulanceman live into the programme. His voice had broken and he had been unable to prevent tears filling his eyes as he described how one of the crash victims, a woman seven months pregnant, had gone into premature labour as they lifted her from the train wreckage. The child was alive and had a good chance of survival. Her mother had bled to death beside the track.

Ben nodded at Sir Edward to listen in to the meeting. The newsroom staff gathered together, leaning against their desks and waiting expectantly.

'That was an excellent programme, a bloody good show,' Ben said, looking around him. 'You beat the opposition hollow – none of the other channels have got anywhere near.'

'Christie scooped the lot,' Ollie interrupted smoothly, 'Couldn't have done it without her.'

Ben looked annoyed.

'Absolutely right,' Jerry added, before Ben had a chance to reply. 'She held the show together, and probably pulled the biggest viewing figures of the month with her piece.'

In the face of overwhelming opposition, Ben gave way. 'Tell her well done,' he told Ollie, grudgingly. 'I'll have a word with her when she gets back. She'll need some sleep, I'm sure; Bob can wrap the breakfast piece for her.'

Ollie frowned at Ben's adroit manoeuvring, but kept his silence. He had already escaped with murder; better not to push his luck.

Ben carried on. 'OK. That woman who had the baby,' he said, glancing across the newsroom at Ginny. 'You were Christie's producer this evening, am I right?'

Ginny nodded, the silver hoops in her ears catching the light as she moved. She lifted one braceleted hand and pushed her chestnut hair back from her forehead. 'Not that she needed much help from me, with those live exclusives.'

'Yes. Well, we've had a call from a woman who says she's the dead mother's best friend. Apparently, the girl's parents retired a year ago to live in some remote mountain village in Provence. Needless to say, their house does not have a telephone.'

Ginny hooked one ankle behind the other as she leaned back on the desk behind her. 'I know the area. I think Christie climbs there sometimes.'

'OK. This is obviously going to be the story of the crash – the papers will be full of it tomorrow, and I want you to work on getting to the parents first. They don't even know their daughter was pregnant; she certainly wasn't married.'

Ben turned to the foreign Editor, Sam Hargrave. 'Sam, I'm pulling David Cameron from the story he was working on in Lebanon. I want you to get him on the next flight to Paris.'

Sam frowned in dismay. 'He won't be happy about that.'

'I don't pay him to be happy. I pay him to do his job.'

'He's been working on that story for a month,' Sam objected, his blue eyes angry. 'He's been undercover in Beirut, risking his life to get you an exclusive story that'll be on the front page of every heavyweight paper in the country the day after we broadcast. You can't pull him now.'

Ben scowled. 'This dead girl and her baby will be on the front page tomorrow. David goes to Paris.' He turned to Ollie. 'And I want you to chase up any loose ends here. I want an interview with the best friend, pictures of the baby, the works. But most of all, find me the father.'

He spun on his heel and marched into his office without waiting for any reply. Sir Edward followed him swiftly and shut the door behind him. He gazed at the Editor for a long moment as Ben sank into his black leather chair and put his feet on the surface of the heavy glass slab that topped the desk in front of him.

'Why do you need David Cameron to do this story?' Sir Edward asked quietly. 'Any of the other reporters could do it. Christie Bradley even knows the area. You pull Cameron off the Lebanon drugs piece now, you lose an exclusive, news-making story.'

'Cameron can get there quicker,' Ben shrugged.

'It can only be a matter of hours,' Sir Edward said. 'Why waste a month of work and a major story for that?'

'This story is more important,' Ben said, looking away and playing with the pens on his desk. 'Those few hours could mean the difference between us getting it, and

CNN or the BBC beating us to it.'

'More important?' Sir Edward said, his anger mounting. 'David's about to get you a major exclusive that will *make* the news, not follow the tabloid pack blindly. If you pull him out now, he'll lose it.' He snapped his fingers under Ben's nose. 'He has to stay with the story.'

Ben rose from his chair and leant across the desk. 'This crash is bloody hot news. A hundred and twenty people dead, and one of them a pregnant woman who gave birth by the track. Blood and tears get ratings, Edward, you of all people know that.'

'I also know you don't sell out a correspondent who has spent a month putting a serious piece of journalism together,' Sir Edward retorted sharply. 'Stop playing games.'

'I assure you, this is no game.'

'You're pulling Cameron off the drugs piece because you never wanted it to air in the first place,' Sir Edward said, his voice ominously quiet. 'You don't want serious news reporting. You want cheap, tacky tabloid stories. David's just caught in the middle.'

'If that's what you want to think, it's your prerogative. But this is just as worthwhile.'

Sir Edward laughed shortly. 'You're chasing trash, and you know it. And you're sacrificing a decent news story to get it. I cannot countenance that kind of irresponsible sensationalism.'

'I'm afraid you don't have any choice,' Ben replied, his voice like cold steel. 'David is going to Paris. As Editor, that is my decision, and it's final.'

The two men stood and faced each other across the desk. Sir Edward realised that this had been precisely Ben's aim: to force a showdown between them with the intention of precipitating Sir Edward's resignation, leaving Ben clear to run INN in exactly the way he chose.

Their alliance had always been one of necessity rather than choice, forged when Sir Edward wanted a stake in a major news organisation, and Wordsworth needed the older man's stamp of authority on his embryonic network. Now it had come to an end.

Sir Edward smiled as he left Ben's office. He had no intention of making things easy for the Editor.

Chapter Three

■ ROME – LONDON
12 April, 6.40 a.m.

David Cameron leaned back in his seat and sighed. He glanced at his watch as he saw the 'no smoking' sign blink and go out in front of him, the aircraft settling into its flight. Should be in central London around ten, UK time. Unfortunately.

He kicked off his soft leather shoes and pressed the button in the arm rest to his left, gently easing the seat back. Closing his eyes, he slid his mind into the 'idle' phase he reserved for flying; over the years he had learned to use the dead hours when he was confined to an aeroplane seat to mentally clear the decks in preparation for his arrival at whatever destination he was headed for. As INN's International Affairs Correspondent, David Cameron had grown used to hitting the ground running. And ducking.

He gave a wry smile. He always seemed to end up racing straight from the airport to the middle of a major world crisis, without a pause. There was never time for a de-brief or a leisurely shower and change of clothes before he wandered off to cover a story. This time would be no different. Bullets would already be flying, and it was vital that his mind was tuned to the situation the moment he arrived. Clarity of thought and split-second decision-making could mean the difference between life and death; not just his, but that of his camera crew.

He had only ever made one mistake. His best friend had paid for it with his life.

David forced away the bitter memories that filled his mind, refusing to allow himself to give in to them, and concentrated his thoughts on his more immediate grievance. He resented being pulled from an important news story for one of Ben Wordsworth's PR exercises. He wondered whether there was even a place left for his type of journalistic integrity at the new network Ben was building. Only those who knew him best could have guessed at the intensity of his anger from the calm exterior he presented to the world. His deep-set tiger's eyes still shimmered a soft golden brown. Only the tension in his lean frame betrayed the rage simmering below the surface.

'Sweetie. This champagne is warm. Is this really the best you can do?'

David opened his eyes as his companion's steel-silk voice broke the expensive silence of the First Class cabin. He glanced at the blushing stewardess in the aisle, who stood clutching the bottle of Moët in hand as the other passengers near them looked out of the windows and studied their in-flight guides with commendable earnestness.

'Darling. Have another try, hmmm?' Caryn Kelly tapped the girl's wrist with her slim fingers. 'Perhaps if we didn't dawdle chatting with our friends . . .?'

The girl smiled nervously, and David looked away. Caryn turned to him, flicking her immaculate auburn hair over the shoulders of her Rifat Ozbek dress. 'Thank you for your support,' she murmured, her smile not wavering as her pale blue eyes fixed him with a look of mingled disdain and accusation. She turned away, stifling a sob.

David gazed at the soft curtain of her hair over her face

66

with familiar feelings of guilt and inadequacy. Words rose within him, and died unspoken. He wondered if he would ever be able to salvage some kind of workable relationship with her, without the constant battles, the confrontations, the pain and the tears. A year ago, their relationship had been one of easy camaraderie.

A year ago, Sebastian Kelly had still been alive.

David was aware that Caryn was destroying his life. But then he had destroyed hers, with one single, foolish mistake which he could never undo. Whatever Caryn was, whatever she became, he was responsible for her. He could never give back what he had taken from her or her child, but if it took the rest of his life, he would never stop trying.

He thought back to the bright, outgoing girl whom he had first met when Seb had introduced his new wife to his colleagues with shy pride, and for a fleeting moment he wondered where, and when, she had been lost to this unhappy, brittle socialite. But of course he knew. The girl he remembered had died with his cameraman in a bombed-out church in a tiny village on the outskirts of Sarajevo.

David sighed. He knew only too well that Caryn had buried her hurt and deep pain with the one thing she was certain would never let her down or leave her – money. He glanced at her left hand, the long pink-and-white French manicured nails beating a tattoo on the arm rest. Her wedding finger was bare.

There was so much time, so much distance, between them. He studied her quietly. She looked older than her thirty-three years, although she disguised it well. She was beautifully dressed; the black leather Ozbek outfit that complemented her exquisitely curled auburn hair screamed money, her carefully groomed appearance was a testimony to the many hours she devoted to maintaining its expensive perfection. Her matching diamond Cartier bracelet and watch were discreet and understated, her year-round tan clearly genuine, her make-up expertly applied. Only he knew the price of her fashionably rail-thin figure had been a constant battle with anorexia, a battle she was still fighting.

Yet her groomed perfection repelled him, in some curious way he was loathe to analyse. The symmetrical arched eyebrows, the tinted lashes, the flawless nails, the toned eyeshadow and lipstick . . . it was too perfect. The girl who had once beaten him and Seb at icehockey and slaughtered them at ten-pin bowling had vanished.

And he had done this to her.

He closed his eyes again in despair. He had known of Caryn's desperate need for security and control when he decided to make himself responsible for her, but he had pushed it from his mind, believing that he would be able to satisfy and subdue her terrible craving for solace and for material substance. Instead, the money and social position that he had extended to her had unleashed a demon that seemed determined to make him pay for his mistake with the rest his life.

It was a fair price to ask. A life for a life.

Mingled with his guilt was an overwhelming grief for the loss of his dearest friend. If he could have taken Seb's place, he would have done. After his death, David had spent countless tortured nights staring into the darkness, reliving the past, wondering where he had had the chance to change what had happened, and missed it.

Caryn had accepted his presence and offer of security as her due. She and her son lived in his home in Italy and he provided everything they needed. Except the love of a husband and father. Her attitude towards him veered between hatred and friendship, and it bewildered him. He knew she must hold him responsible for what had happened. She never allowed him to forget it. His life with her was untenable, yet he welcomed the pain she gave him. It could never equal the grief he had caused her in taking from her the man she loved.

David sighed deeply. He had realised almost as soon as he allowed Caryn to move into his home in Frascati that he had made a terrible mistake. He could never give Caryn the companionship, the attention, the approval she clearly needed and deserved. His work had always come first, before his family, before his friends, before himself. No woman would ever matter as much to him as his job did. She had never asked him for anything more than the uneasy and unequal friendship they shared. Yet somehow he knew that it wasn't enough for her. Something was always in the way, something he could not define. It was more than his guilt, or her unspoken accusation. He wondered how they had both loved and lost the same man, yet shared nothing of each other.

Any real affection he had held for her had long since evaporated as the woman he had known faded with each passing day, to be replaced by the hard, bitter creature beside him. But the charade went on, and on the surface, with a measure of success. He sensed Caryn's manic jealousy of every other woman in his life, her terror that he would leave her to fend for herself and she would lose the only financial security she possessed. But she managed all his affairs during the ten months of the year he was on the road away from his home, and there was Sandy to think of. He could not bear to lose him. He had come to mean as much to David as his own son could have done. Every time he looked at Sandy he saw Sebastian, and strangely, instead of being a reproach, it was the only comfort he had. Without Sandy, he would have nothing left to care about.

David thought of the previous evening they had spent

together, sitting at opposite ends of the vast dining-room table, totally unable to communicate. He had stared despairingly into the flames of the candle between them, and for the first time in his life, he had prayed from the depths of his being for a way out.

Caryn made his life hell. But it was he who had put them there.

Aware of his scrutiny, Caryn opened her Louis Vuitton grip and extracted a gold powder compact, discreetly embossed with her initials. She smiled at her reflection. Not bad, considering she would be forty next year. Not that she would ever admit it. To the world at large she was barely thirty-three, and that's the way it would stay. She stole a quick glance at David.

During the year since Sebastian had died, Caryn Kelly had learned the hard way that the wall between herself and David was impenetrable. She knew she had his commitment to care for her, his loyalty and his friendship. But what she wanted was his love. And that was the one thing he would never give her.

In her hurt and anger and pain she had deliberately separated her life from his even whilst they shared the same home, retaining some measure of pride and self-respect against his tacit withdrawal by rejecting him first. The battles he faced at home were far worse than any of those he covered on the road. Deliberately she made their rare times together as destructive as possible, her only revenge against his constant absences and the friendship that would never be enough for her. She subjected him to tirades of abuse, controlling his life, spending his money and preventing him from forming any relationship with another woman, knowing he could never leave her.

Caryn smiled to herself, and snapped her compact shut. David had no way of knowing that she had never cared for Sebastian. It had always been David whom she loved.

The moment Sebastian had introduced David to her, three weeks after their wedding, she had known that it was not her husband she wanted, but this attractive, vulnerable, private man who had seemed to be lost to her forever. She was only too aware that David's sense of honour meant that he would never look at her as anything other than his best friend's wife, yet she loved him with a constant, unyielding passion. She had been consumed with a need for him that had turned her affection for her husband into a simmering resentment, and finally, hatred. She had loathed her child from the moment he was conceived, despising him because he was not David's. She alone knew that her feelings when Sebastian died had not been those of grief but of unutterable release and thankfulness.

And the one way to David had been through his guilt. Only through her grief for a man she had not wanted could she keep the man she loved.

She smiled secretly. That delicious young man was sitting just two seats behind her, across the aisle. She had allowed him to buy her a drink in the airport bar whilst David haggled with the airline officials to reduce the excess baggage charge on her seven matching Vuitton suitcases.

Caryn unbuckled her seatbelt and stood up, smoothing her soft black leather dress down her slim thighs. The scent of Shalimar filled the air as she brushed past the young man. Beneath the five thousand dollar dress and next to the sheer black silk stockings, it was all she wore. She slipped into the curtained alcove of the First Class toilet area, and waited confidently.

Caryn had first slept with another man less than three months after she had married Sebastian. She had realised that David would never be her lover while she was another man's wife, and she had dealt with her pain and despair in the only way she knew how. She made sure neither David nor her husband knew of the hundreds of casual affairs, even though a part of her longed to make David jealous. Sebastian had always been an irrelevancy.

The young man appeared in front of her, as she had known he would, his hard-on already apparent beneath the flimsy white cotton of his trousers. Christ, Caryn thought, he can't be more than twenty. And he wants me. She felt the moisture flood between her legs at the thought. Without taking her eyes from his, she reached out for his hand and placed it on her left breast. His fingers tightened around the nipple, already hard beneath the soft leather. She rotated her mound against his engorged cock exultantly. With a moan of mingled satisfaction and desire, Caryn swiftly opened the toilet door behind her with her other hand, and the two of them tumbled into the confined space.

'I want you to fuck me hard, and fuck me now,' she breathed. A damp sheen of arousal glistened on her forehead and cheeks, and without speaking, the boy knelt down on the floor, a knowing expression on his face as he pushed her back against the tiny steel sink. Caryn felt the taps dig into her buttocks as he worked the clinging dress up to her waist, and gasped as he buried his tongue deep into her dark, wiry bush. The thrill of power turned her on far more than the sex ever could.

'More, harder, faster,' she panted, burying her hands in his thick black hair. Compliantly he worked his tongue around her clitoris, the musky scent of her juices filling the cramped compartment. With one hand he unzipped his trousers, his erect penis springing free, whilst he worked two fingers inside her with practised expertise. Caryn threw her head back, and arched her body, writhing demandingly against his fingers. Quickly the boy withdrew them and slid both his hands under her buttocks and lifted her legs, so that her high-heeled Charles Jourdan shoes rested against the wall opposite.

'You goin' to get it now, rich bitch,' he murmured thickly, his mouth glistening with her juices as he stood up. Pushing his trousers down, he fondled his turgid penis as it reared above his balls, and Caryn shuddered with anticipation at the sight of its angry redness. He grasped her buttocks once more and roughly pulled her down onto its length, burying its shaft deep inside the soft wetness of her cunt. She groaned with pleasure, digging her fingernails into his back, squirming on the narrow sink as she clasped him deep inside her. He thrust hard into her, slamming her against the wall, pushing her legs apart as his own desire mounted inside him.

'Faster! Faster!' she moaned, her cunt slipping and sliding against the rhythmic thrusting of his cock. His head was thrown back now, the dark hair plastered against his scalp, his features flushed and contorted with effort, veins standing out on his forehead. Sweat poured off their bodies as he pumped away at her, the scent of lust mingling with the overpowering Shalimar.

'Now, oh Jesus, now!' Caryn screamed, muffling her own cries with her hand. She felt him come inside her, his hard body bucking and arching against hers, the wetness pouring down her legs to mingle with her own juices as she too shuddered in orgasm.

The two bodies separated, and Caryn smoothed down her dress as the boy zipped up his flies. She smiled as she watched him. The sheer pleasure of leaving the grieving widow behind, if just for a few moments, was almost the best part. She had known him for the gigolo he was the moment he approached her, and he had not disappointed. His performance had been masterful. And she knew he would never tell.

Not that David would ever believe his story for a moment, should he dare to repeat it. After all, she was the epitome of the loyal wife, faithful to her husband's memory. Like Caesar's, she was beyond reproach. She had to be, if she was ever to win David to her.

Caryn manoeuvred past the young man to the door, carefully riffling her hand through her hair as she glanced in the mirror. Resolutely she ignored the aching sense of loss that filled her whenever she thought of David, of how it might be with him.

'In case you were wondering,' she said, ignoring the tears that spilled from her eyes, 'I'm going to be David Cameron's wife. So now we've both fucked him.'

■ ISLINGTON, LONDON
   8.20 a.m.

The shrill of the alarm clock tugged at the edges of Christie's consciousness. With a sigh of disgust she buried her head beneath the pillow in a vain attempt to block its insistent squawk and recapture the disintegrating remnants of her dreams. This might be a lie-in, but it didn't feel like one. Groaning, she capitulated and snaked one arm out from under the duvet to quiet the noise. Typical. That had been the best dream she'd had in months.

Moments later, Christie swung her tanned legs over the side of the bed and sat up, her honey-blonde hair tangled around her shoulders. She knew from experience that if she settled down for just five more minutes, she'd be waking up to the lunchtime news. She switched the radio on, and rebelliously tuned it into Capital. She'd have exactly seven minutes of the latest hits before she re-tuned it to Radio Four for the eight-thirty news headlines.

She smiled as R.E.M. played out, swaying her slim body to the music as she headed towards the shower. With a grimace she set the tap for as hot as she could bear.

74

She was not one of those people for whom a cold shower at the start of the day was an invigorating experience that left them ready to face the rigours of life. As she stepped under the steaming jets she mentally reviewed the day, shuffling her various appointments and commitments in her head. Not that she'd be able to get a great deal done. The Queen was to officially open the INN building, and real news had little chance in the face of that kind of competition. Most PR agents familiar with television news priorities had already deliberately rescheduled their various Press launches this week so as not to clash with the Royal opening, reluctant to sacrifice the chance of INN coverage of their events.

Christie shrugged as she stepped out of the shower and slid into her white bathrobe, towelling her damp hair dry. Royal visits nothwithstanding, she had seven tapes to look through from the previous week's shoot in Brazil, where she had been filming material for a series on the world population explosion. She smiled as she opened the door to her walk-in wardrobe and glanced at her clothes. At least she should get some peace and quiet.

Christie realised her hope had been forlorn as she reviewed the Brazil tapes in the viewing booth half-an-hour later. She glanced at her watch. 9.23. She was fighting an uphill and losing battle to finish logging these tapes before the entire building adjourned for the royal visit.

She shook her head, her hair still damp from the shower, and wondered where the glamour in this job was. You could be first on the scene of a major disaster, blood and misery all around you, and be told by some damn fool producer like Brian Reynolds to 'get the relatives crying.' Or you might spend hours penned behind iron railings outside Number Ten in the coldest street on earth, and receive a surly 'Good morning' from a departing minister for your trouble. Sometimes, as now, you became part of an entire nation's tragedy, recording misery, perfidy and hopelessness, unable to do anything to change it. But glamour? She had yet to see it.

'Darling? Will you be long? Only I have this fashion tape to view and I simply must do it before Ben takes me to lunch.'

Christie started and glanced up as Victoria Lawrence tapped one elegant Maud Frizon shoe on the coffee-stained carpet and looked at her watch. Christie sighed. Victoria was forty-something, icily beautiful and INN's top female newsanchor. She was also extraordinarily vain, terrified of growing old, and very practised at getting her own way.

'Just finishing up, Victoria,' Christie said, a resigned expression on her face. She knew from experience that she would get no more work done with Victoria hovering beside her.

'Lovely suit, darling. Ungaro?'

Victoria felt the pink sleeve of Christie's suit with expert hands, and Christie nodded, unsurprised. Designer clothes were Victoria's Mastermind subject, and she rarely guessed wrongly. The soft wool suit from Ungaro's new spring range was the most extravagant purchase Christie had ever made, and she felt a delicious thrill of guilt every time she slithered into the outfit.

Christie smiled. Her French godmother maintained that it was far more economic to spend a fortune on clothes before one had caught one's man, than on one's trousseau afterwards, when it no longer mattered. How easily the French managed to reconcile femininity with feminism.

Victoria saw Christie smile and frowned. 'Mmm. I thought of getting one myself, then I decided no. Simply not me, darling.'

Christie's face was a picture of innocence as Victoria sat

down in the seat she had just vacated. 'Too young for you, I suppose?' she said sweetly, running for cover.

'OK, you get to put them all in order,' Ginny said, as Christie collided into her and sent a dozen tapes flying in all directions.

Christie laughed, and bent to pick up the cassettes. 'I'm sorry. Blame Victoria. I don't know what it is about her, but she always manages to make me feel about twelve years old.'

'Tell me about it.' Ginny leant against the corridor wall, as Christie restacked the tapes in her arms. 'I'm determined to put a worm in her knickers before I leave this company.'

Christie giggled. 'Promise you'll tell me when, or I'll report you to the RSPCA.'

'It's a deal.'

Christie tapped the block of cassettes with her finger. 'What're all these, anyway?'

Ginny rolled her dark eyes heavenward. 'Don't you start. These are the most important tapes in the building.'

'Let me guess. The secret love tapes between Prince Philip and his French mistress? Something interesting to put into Major's obit? Better yet, Ben Wordsworth, aged seven, in the Christmas panto?'

'Nearly, but not quite. These tapes are all of this building being erected, from a hole in the ground to its current cult status.'

'Fascinating. What on earth for?'

'The Queen, lucky soul, is going to receive a ten-minute piece on the establishing of the new INN HQ. Care of yours truly.'

'You get all the best jobs,' Christie smiled.

'God, that reminds me. Brian Reynolds is looking for you, and judging by his evil glint of satisfaction, it isn't going to be good news.' Ginny arched one eyebrow in query. 'So what have you done to upset our illustrious Executive Producer?'

Christie shook her head. 'You tell me. By the way, you seeing Nick tonight?'

Ginny blushed. 'Mmmm. Why?'

'Just wondering . . .'

'Yeah, yeah. I could ask you about . . .'

'Don't you have to do something with those tapes?'

Ginny glanced at the clock on the wall and gasped. 'Oh, Christ! I have to do this by two p.m. That gives me four hours to view and cut fourteen tapes! Go away.' Ginny shook her hands in Christie's direction and performed a standing start that Ben Johnson would have found hard to beat, disappearing into one of the nearby edit booths.

Christie smiled and headed towards the newsroom, staving off the inevitable meeting with Brian Reynolds. She slid into her seat at the bank of reporters' desks, which had been situated nearest to the atrium and gained what little natural light managed to filter into the building. With inspirational genius, the newsroom designers had put the writers and producers – troglodytes who spent all their waking hours incarcerated in the building – as far away from daylight as possible on the opposite side of the newsroom, whilst the reporters – who were usually out of the building anyway – had the best seats. The more cynical claimed that the producers had been stationed furthest from the doors in a deliberate ploy to prevent them ever finding a way out of the building for fear they would never come back.

Christie logged into the computer, and called up the latest wire stories. She smiled at the welcoming message which immediately flashed in the top right hand side of her screen. It was from Ollie. He had never missed a day. Another warning to stay away from Brian Reynolds followed his friendly greeting. Christie frowned. She did not trust the devious Executive Producer for a moment, and had no doubt that Brian was scheming to balance out the series of coups she had achieved since the Heathley rail crash. Like many men in the newsroom, Brian Reynolds resented a successful woman, particularly one who looked as if she could grace the cover of *Vogue* as easily as a Beirut suburb. Christie shrugged. She would find out what he was up to soon enough.

Christie glanced down at the scene in the atrium, and smiled at the activity. Two floors below, the News Mall had been roped off, and a bevy of caterers were busy establishing a long buffet table at one end. All but the souvenir shops had been closed, and a small podium had been erected where Ben Wordsworth's cardboard statue usually graced the hall. She could smell the fresh paint that had been used to redecorate the areas of the building which would be used for the opening.

Christie checked her watch. She still had a few hours. Entering the computer, she called up her notes on the population story, and swiftly began to write the script that would accompany the tapes she had managed to view earlier that morning, pausing occasionally to collect her thoughts. She knew that her piece on the situation in Latin America would result in hundreds of calls from Catholics who resented any suggestion that the Pope's ban on artificial birth control might be creating a demographic time-bomb. She intended to balance that by including a lengthy interview from an eloquent Cardinal to whom she had spoken, who had explained that if the Church did not at least set high ideals, there would be nothing to aim for. Even so, the story would be controversial, but that was the way she liked it. Christie dreaded the day no one complained about her work, for that would be the day no one noticed it.

She paused in her writing, searching for the right words

to encapsulate the Cardinal's general attitude, and flipped open her notebook to the log she had done of his interview. Suddenly she realised that something warm and wet was sliding insistently up her inner thigh. Christie froze for a moment, then shot her chair back and leapt up.

'What the hell was that?' she exclaimed in disbelief.

A shadowy form appeared from beneath her desk. 'Terribly sorry, ma'am,' a flustered policeman apologised, hauling his Alsation to heel. 'Just checking for suspicious packages before Her Majesty arrives. No need to be alarmed.'

Christie dissolved into giggles as the policeman shot away, his cheeks flaming scarlet.

'Don't tell me. Thought it was your lucky day?'

Christie shook her head as Archie Michaels leant against her desk, his body shaking with silent laughter. 'It'd be the best offer I've ever had in this place,' she smiled, unaware that most of the men at INN, including Archie, would have given half a year's salary to change places with the Alsatian. None of them had ever dared to risk her warm, easy friendship by making unwanted overtures, much as they might desire her.

Archie stood and gazed over the atrium railing next to Christie's desk, his expression sardonic as he watched the activity below.

'You got any idea how much this cost?' the young reporter asked over his shoulder.

'Archie. You didn't hack into Ben's personal file again?'

Archie grinned. He was as renowned for his computer abilities as for his reporting skills, which were significant in themselves. 'You might say that, Christie, but I couldn't possibly comment.'

'Okay, you two, out with it. What gives?'

Christie and Archie turned as Nick Makepiece, another of INN's young, talented reporters slid into his place at

80

the desk. 'Oh, we're all coming out of the woodwork for the royal visit, are we?'

'Something like that.'

Christie smiled at her colleague in welcome, then her face grew serious. 'How was Johannesburg?'

'Fine.'

Christie saw the pain in Nick's blue eyes at the memory of the story from which he had just returned. He had spent three harrowing weeks in the townships on the outskirts of South Africa's largest city, recording the latest outbreak in the country's cycle of violence. The pieces he had sent back had been vivid reflections of the unbridgeable divisions which had arisen between the black factions since the whites had agreed to the principle of black government. Nick had also demonstrated considerable personal courage in his coverage. One Australian journalist had been killed already and four Western correspondents had been seriously injured in the conflict between the rival Inkhata movement and the ANC.

Christie and Archie were both well aware of the surreal disjointedness every reporter experienced when they returned from such a situation to the banal normality of the newsroom, and quickly grasped Nick's unwillingness to talk about it. Christie gave his shoulder a quick squeeze of sympathy and reassurance, and was rewarded by a warm smile.

'OK, here's the shopping list,' Archie said, deliberately lightening the atmosphere. 'If you don't want to hear it . . .'

Nick and Christie grinned at each other. 'OK, we want it. Spill, Archie.'

'You're sure? OK. Repainting the building along the corridors where HM will walk – £15,000. Putting glass windows in the doors along said corridors, for security reasons – £10,500. Catering for HM and select few –

£40,000 including champagne. Dom Perignon, naturally.' Arnie looked up at his captive audience. 'Oh, and you'll love this one. Cost of flying David Cameron back home, first class, so HM can have the thrill of meeting our senior war correspondent – £870. And the same again for Sebastian's wife.'

Christie remembered the vital, charming man who had been killed a little over a year ago in the terrible war that had consumed Sarajevo. Every journalist at INN had been shocked by the tragic accident that had claimed the life of one of their most talented cameramen. He had simply been in the wrong place at the wrong time, attempting a rendezvous with David when the church in which he was sheltering had received a direct hit from an artillery barrage.

'I still miss him,' Christie murmured. 'Think how his wife must feel. She must be devastated.'

'I doubt it,' Archie said. 'You don't know Caryn Kelly. I'm sure she has found consolation elsewhere by now.'

'With David?' Nick asked.

Archie shook his head. 'No. He and Sebastian were very close. Mind you, I'm sure she wouldn't mind trying.'

'Talk of the devil,' said Nick. 'The merry widow herself.'

The three of them leaned over the atrium rail as David and Caryn swept in through the revolving glass door below. Christie looked surprised. 'That's Sebastian's wife?'

'Don't worry, you'll be OK,' Archie said. 'She only eats men.'

'Archie. You don't know what she's going through.' Christie said reprovingly. 'Sebastian loved her very much.'

'Ah, but did she love him?' Archie said.

Christie watched silently as the couple made their way

along the corridor towards the lift. Although she had never met Sebastian's wife, since they did not operate in the same orbit, she had known Sebastian to be an intelligent man of taste, style and integrity. The woman beside David was not what she had expected Caryn Kelly to be. Christie frowned. She was not sure exactly what she had anticipated, but knew it was not this immaculate, brittle fashionplate. There seemed to be no substance behind the image. She wondered why David had decided to take responsibility for her after Sebastian had died.

'Now there's an unhappy man,' Nick observed.

'I'm not surprised,' Archie said, as the couple vanished from view. 'He still hasn't got over what happened to Seb. And thanks to our dear Ben, not only did David get yanked off the drug story he was chasing in Lebanon last month, so that he could chase that train-baby's grandparents, but he missed an exclusive with Gaddaffi to get dragged to London for this shindig. No wonder he's fed up.'

'Aren't we all,' Nick grimaced from behind his computer. 'Bloody Royals and their annus horribilis. Thanks to Ben, mine isn't that good right now.'

'They're not all bad,' Archie said thoughtfully. 'I'd kill for a night with Sarah. Mmmm. Drop dead gorgeous.'

'She was always too intelligent to be royal,' Nick said. 'Have to have a frontal lobotomy to join that family. The only time I ever feel sorry for them is when I consider their agony at having to attend the Royal Variety Show.'

Christie laughed, still leaning on the atrium rail and watching the activity in the News Mall. She missed the appraising glance David cast in her direction as he crossed the newsroom towards the Editor's office, and the expression of mingled longing and hopelessness that filled his eyes as he saw the three friends casually chatting and laughing around the reporters' desk.

Ginny materialised from an edit booth and planted a kiss on the top of Nick's head, winding her arms around his shoulders with easy affection.

'Enough of that, you two,' Christie laughed. 'Don't you get enough sex at home?'

Nick blushed, embarrassed by the good-natured teasing, and slid away from Ginny's embrace. 'I thought you were supposed to be in mid-panic about that piece you're editing?' he asked Ginny gruffly.

Ginny smiled. 'I've got a piece of gossip too delicious to wait,' she said. 'In fact, Archie, I'm surprised that you, as the arch-exponent of scandal, haven't beaten me to it, but if you had, you wouldn't all be sitting here.'

Archie assumed an offended air.

Nick laughed. 'Don't tell me, Bob Carpenter and that PA . . . what's her name? . . . oh yes, Annie . . . are having it off again in the Green Room?'

'Old news, Nick, my darling, that was last week. No, if you tune in your monitors to Studio Three, you'll see what I mean.'

As one, Christie, Arnie and Nick turned to the small television screens, which were bolted to each desk in case anyone should dare to make off with them, and punched up the in-house channel. They exchanged looks of wicked interest as Victoria Lawrence appeared sitting at the Early Evening News desk wearing an expression of pure venom. Next to her was Paragon Fairfax, looking, by contrast, inordinately smug.

'Paragon looks like the cat that's got the cream,' Ginny observed.

'More like the cat that's just creamed, judging by the corresponding smile on Wordsworth's face this morning,' Archie corrected.

'I give up. I'm never going to get any work done this morning,' Christie said, sighing and logging out of her computer. 'I can't just sit here, I'm going down to the gallery to see what's going on.'

The other three grinned and followed as Christie got up from her desk and made her way towards the lifts. Swiftly they descended to the ground floor, where the main studio was situated. The smaller set in the newsroom was used only for the News Updates and any emergency newsflashes. INN's main lunchtime and evening programmes were presented from the larger, more flexible studio in the basement. Several different sets were stored there, and rearranged for each show. The breakfast and lunchtime programmes had a single presenter, and the same desk was used for both. From one side, for the morning broadcast, it was a dusky pink, used with a matching curtain representing the London skyline, which was hung behind the presenter. Facing the other way for the midday bulletin, the desk was a pale blue, with a corresponding curtain. On the opposite side of the studio, a large, deep blue desk was used for the double newsanchor Early Evening News programme and the Late News show. Dozens of thick cables snaked across the floor, many of them taped into place, whilst suspended from the high ceiling were numerous lights and overhead cameras. When they were on air, one of the Floor Manager's many duties was to shepherd guests to the right desk, negotiating a safe path through the maze of cables and floor cameras.

Paragon and Victoria were still seated at the double desk when the posse from the newsroom arrived in the gallery next-door to the studio. The harassed Floor Manager looked at his watch, then called out, 'Once more, Victoria, then we'll have to close. It's already eleven-fifteen. We'll be in the way of the lunchtime pre-record interview from Nairobi if we don't get a move on.'

Victoria smiled obligingly. 'Tony, sweetie, I'm so sorry. It's just terribly difficult when one isn't working with a professional. I'll try to cover for her, and we'll get it right this time.'

Paragon glowered, but prudently said nothing. Turning towards the camera, she started reading her script from the autocue. Although the words were, in reality, upside down and below the camera lens, a mirror reflected the autocue so that to the newscaster the words appeared to be in the lens itself. The device enabled the presenter to talk directly to the camera, whilst the viewer saw nothing. The newscaster regulated the speed of the words with a foot peddle beneath the desk.

'Students wielding Molotov cocktails gathered outside the American Embassy . . . centre . . . in . . . Kwanju . . . this . . . morning . . .' Paragon stopped and wailed. 'Tony, my autocue is going too slowly.'

'Oh sorry, darling, my foot must have slipped on the peddle,' Victoria apologised. 'And we haven't got time for another screen test. Terribly sorry, sweetie.'

'Not to worry,' said Ben Wordsworth, materialising from the shadows. 'I've seen enough. Paragon, you and Victoria can present the show tomorrow. We'll take it from there. Victoria, I'm afraid we'll have to cancel lunch. Maybe next week. I've still got a few things I need to discuss with Paragon.'

Ben swept out, a triumphant Paragon in his wake. Victoria stood up stiffly, smoothing her expensive crimson suit with shaking fingers.

'Not so much *haute couture* as *haute* pissed off,' Arnie said irreverently from the gallery. In the studio, Victoria heard him over the intercom and frowned, before remembering that it gave you wrinkles and hurriedly straightening out her face.

'Doesn't this just fill you with patriotic fervour?' Ollie muttered, joining the entire staff of INN as they trooped

86

into the News Mall in anticipation of the Royal arrival. 'I just pray none of the Royal Family choose now to peg out. Christ knows where the key to the Obit Box is.'

Philip Cunningham looked anxious. 'I don't even know where the Obit Box itself is.'

Ollie regarded Philip disparagingly. He had no respect for the twenty-seven-year-old Executive Foreign Editor, who had been appointed to his current position simply because he lacked the experience or courage to present any opposition to the decisions made by the Executive Producer, Brian Reynolds. Cunningham didn't even put up a fight. What should have been one of the most powerful jobs in television was reduced to rubber-stamp approval of Brian's directives, whilst Cunningham spent all his time constantly fighting to keep his head above the shark-infested political waters.

'Try looking behind the bar,' Ollie commented dryly. The in-house bar was always the first place to find any reporter who had gone AWOL; the second was Aristotle's, the wine-bar across the road. Ollie grinned. Although the Obit Box was not actually situated in the bar, it would have been a more logical, not to say convenient, place to put it.

The Box was so named for its contents: pre-edited obituaries of the most prominent Royals and politicians, plus the accessories deemed essential in the event of a National Tragedy. These included black blouses (sizes 12 and 14) for female newscasters who might have come to work inappropriately dressed, and black ties and jackets (40 to 44) for the men. There was even a record of the National Anthem, just in case everything else went horribly wrong. The latest listing currently consisted of five Category One VIPs: the Queen, the Queen Mother, the Duke of Edinburgh, the Prince of Wales and (officially) the estranged Princess of Wales.

Along with the remainder of the Royals and the President of the United States, the Prime Minister was only Category Two. In the event of the death of one of the Category One VIPs, INN's usual television schedule would be abandoned, and the network would immediately start broadcasting the relevant obituary whilst it positioned itself to cover the breaking story. The only problem was that the obits continually needed updating, and given the demands of daily news and the scarcity of editors, the last time this had been done was just after Princess Eugenie was born.

'What will you say if Her Majesty stops by the News Update desk?' Philip asked Jerry, who was standing behind him eyeing the proceedings with distaste.

'The way staffing is going in this place, I'll probably ask her if she'd like to write a few stories,' Jerry replied mournfully.

Before Philip had time to comment on this unseemly show of company disloyalty, the Queen arrived with a suitable fanfare of camera flashbulbs from the Press waiting outside INN's front door. Sir Edward Penhaligon escorted her into the building, chatting quietly with the ease of long friendship as he lead her past the crowd of journalists. Ben Wordsworth trailed impotently behind him as the Queen was introduced to the various news-anchors and correspondents who were considered worthy of such attention. Brian Reynolds had already given the selected few a special name tag, and instructed them to stand in pre-ordained positions, so that they could be 'casually' introduced to the Queen in a manner considered daringly informal. Amongst the chosen few were David Cameron, as INN's top war correspondent, and Caryn, the widow of the tragic Sebastian Kelly. As soon as the introductions were completed, the Queen was whisked into the Executive Boardroom for lunch, whilst her loyal subjects took their chances with the limp buffet set out in the atrium.

'Ah, fish *goujons* again, I see,' said Nick. 'Where would we be without fish *goujons*?'

'Don't tempt me to tell you,' Christie said, laughing. 'D'you fancy nipping round the corner for a quick coffee? I'd like to have a chat to you about Somalia – I'm supposed to be going back there again in a few weeks to do a follow up, now that the US marines have finally left.'

'Sure. I'd like a chat anyway,' Nick said, his shy smile belied by the serious expression in his eyes. 'Ginny and me . . . well, it's not really working any more.' He looked down at his slim hands. 'It's not her fault. It's mine. I know she's your friend too, and I'd be the last person to hurt her. But . . .'

'Christie, there you are. I've been looking all over for you!'

Christie turned and rolled her eyes heavenwards as Brian Reynolds panted up to her, two sticky children in tow. 'I wondered if you'd look after Tarquin and Ashley for me. They came to see the Queen – Ashley presented the bouquet, you know – only now my wife seems to have wandered off . . .'

Brian paused as he saw the look on Christie's face. 'Ah, perhaps you're busy,' he amended, wisely thinking the better of continuing. 'I'll see you in the lookahead meeting then. Got an important story idea to discuss. Ah, well then. No, Tarquin, you can't touch the satellite dish. Just because, that's why. Oh, God, now look what you've done.' Hastily Brian replaced the newly-collapsible antennae and tugged his monsters away from the dish on display. Christie and Nick watched him dashing after a woman in a long dirndl skirt that did not quite cover her unshaven legs, her straggly brown hair lying limply down her shoulders.

'Another time, Christie,' Nick said, already regretting his half-confidence, and moving away. Christie nodded, understanding his mood, and slipped behind the rope partitioning the Italian restaurant off from the rest of the News Mall. She sat down at one of the small tables scattered in front of Luigi's, and gazed absently at the mobile swinging gently down the twelve floors of the atrium. She had already sensed something was wrong between Ginny and Nick, but being good friends with both of them, had been reluctant to interfere. Now she wondered what had gone wrong.

Christie sighed. Was it true that it was better to have loved and lost, than never to have loved at all? She had a feeling it was the last great con in a game that no one ever seemed to win. Suddenly Christie wished she could experience that overpowering feeling of love, just for a moment: that crazy, star-dust magic that seemed to send lovers into a different dimension, where they could see and hear the world around them, but did not really communicate with anyone except each other. To be that overflowing with happiness and expectation of the joys the future would bring, that certain that the whole world had been created just for the two of you . . . surely that experience of love would be worth the risk of losing it, just for the moments when you held it in your grasp?

Christie thought of her last boyfriend with a feeling of regret. He had been a good friend, and a good lover, but she had never been in love with him. Like all her boyfriends, he had never demanded that secret self which she knew was within her to give, if only someone would ask the right question.

But perhaps her dream of an overwhelming, all-encompassing love did not exist in reality. Dreams, dreams.

Yet she knew she would settle for nothing less.

90

Christie shook herself, surprised at the sudden loneliness and melancholy which had engulfed her. Usually her job gave her all the stimulation and reward she needed, and what free time she did have was always brimful with friends, parties, and a hectic social schedule. She did not have the time for an all-consuming relationship, and, as with everything in her life, she had refused to compromise her job by trying to have half of both.

'You look like you've found a peaceful corner, in the midst of this chaos. Do you mind if I hide with you, or would that be intruding?'

Christie started, and looked up. David Cameron's eyes sparkled, and Christie responded to their irresistible urging to smile.

'Please, I would love some company,' she said warmly. David pulled out one of the wrought iron chairs and slid gracefully into it. 'I'm avoiding sticky children and producers on the warpath. What's your excuse?'

David's eyes clouded for a moment, then he grinned boyishly at her. 'Oh, I'm just playing hookey,' he laughed. 'I'd had enough of being with the Grown-Ups and Prefects. I'd much rather be flying my model airplane or goin' fishin', but that's strictly off the record.'

Christie composed her face into mock-seriousness. 'You're secret's safe with me,' she said, relieved at the diversion from her melancholy thoughts. 'I could do with a few lessons myself. I'm a rotten pilot.'

'You fly?'

'In a manner of speaking,' Christie laughed. 'A Nikko SkyAce, most of the time.'

'But you're a girl,' David said indignantly, making a moue of disgust. 'Girls don't fly planes.' He sighed and shrugged his shoulders in resignation. 'There's only one thing for it. I'll have to marry you.'

'I wouldn't go down on one knee just yet,' Christie

91

smiled. 'It's my brother's, really, but he lets me have a go when I go home for the weekend. I keep on breaking off the propeller, so I have to go to Harrods and buy a few spares before I go down to Sussex.'

'And I thought it was only me,' David said with exaggerated relief. 'I gave up on the undercarriage a long time ago – where I live, it's just ploughed fields, no grass for a soft landing, so it's hopeless. The best bit's when I get to strafe the goats in the field next door . . . you should try it sometime.'

'I'll have to remember that,' Christie said.

The two of them smiled in understanding and complicity. Christie realised with surprise that she felt totally at ease with David, as if they shared a long friendship that stretched back to their childhood.

David grinned and extended his hand with mock gravity. 'But how forward of me. We haven't been introduced. I'm David Cameron.'

Christie took his hand, feeling a tingle of excitement that she quickly suppressed. Slow down, she reminded herself. 'Christie Bradley.'

David recognised her the moment she said her name, and smiled ruefully. He had not expected this stunning woman to be a reporter, much less one of INN's most talented correspondents. Mentally he reassessed her, kicking himself for the chauvinistic assumption that she must be a presenter or somebody's wife. 'Of course. You look a little different away from the battlefield.'

Christie laughed. 'So my mother always says.'

'Wise woman.'

'Very. David, do you realise how strange it is that we've worked for the same company for several years and never even met?'

'It's nice to meet the person behind the screen image, even if I don't recognise her,' David smiled. 'I don't get over here much, except when I have to declare war on Ben Wordsworth. I don't really have much time to myself. Always seem to be being shot at, bombed and generally in the shit.' He shrugged. 'And that's just at home.'

Christie laughed again. God, I've never met a man who made me laugh so much, so quickly. He's so easy to be with. She gave herself a mental shake. Don't get carried away. You've only just met the man. But there was no harm in looking . . . Christie felt the guilty thrill of a child peeking at unwrapped Christmas presents two weeks early, and hugged the sensation to herself. She could feel the warmth of his leg against hers, and treated herself to a sidelong glance. David Cameron was undoubtedly the most attractive man she had ever met. His dark brown hair curled softly into his strange gold-brown eyes, his smile was warm and endearingly crooked, his body lean beneath the soft linen suit he was wearing. He had an air of vulnerability about him that belied his reputation as a tough, fearless war correspondent. His eyes were shadowed with unhappy secrets, and she felt an impulsive need to reach out and shelter him.

But wasn't that always the attraction of dangerous man?

She felt David's eyes upon her, and looked away, feeling unusually self-conscious. For a moment, she wondered if he felt the attraction that pulled her towards him. She sensed his gaze travelling over her, and pushed her hair away from her forehead to break the spell. David shook himself, and smiled.

'Tell me, your last trip to Somalia,' he said, a touch too casually. 'It was an amazing piece of journalism. I always find that sort of situation overwhelming. How did you deal with it?'

Is he changing the subject deliberately? Christie wondered. 'It was very difficult, literally and emotionally,' she said, mentally changing gear. She admired David's work and welcomed the chance to discuss what had been one of her most demanding assignments with another professional of his calibre. 'We nearly lost the exclusive to the BBC – we would have done, if Sam Hargrave hadn't forced the issue with Brian Reynolds, and got us to take it straight to Ben.'

'I heard something about that at the time,' David replied, his eyes never leaving hers. 'They wanted you to ship the piece out, rather than bird it, simply to save the cost of a satellite, isn't that right?'

'It was crazy,' Christie said, shaking her head. 'You would have thought that after the US went in over Christmas, Brian and Philip would have realised that Somalia is still a good story. We should have taken a full edit pack with two BVU 75s in with us, so that we could edit the piece there, but Philip refused to sanction the cost of the excess baggage for the gear.'

David frowned. 'They never seem to understand that you have to spend money sometimes to get a good story. If you have a rival network breathing down your neck, you need to be able to get a story on air as soon as possible.'

'Tell me about it. We didn't even have a camera playback adaptor, so that we could rough cut the raw material to give them highlights to edit down back in London.'

'You mean you had to ship back every single tape you shot? That's a hell of a lot of tapes for some poor sod to look through back in London.'

Christie nodded. 'I hate doing it that way. Apart from the hours wasted there, it means I have virtually no control over which pictures get used to cover my track.'

'Always the way.' David leant forward, his elbows on the glass-topped table in front of him. 'So where were you trying to feed from anyway?'

Christie looked up, and their eyes met. Suddenly she felt a flicker of excitement and desire, and looked away in confusion. 'Nairobi. Not that we could feed it from there, since Philip refused to allow us to book a satellite.'

David smiled as Christie ran her hand through her hair in a self-conscious gesture. 'So how did you get it past him?'

'I joined forces with a reporter for the *Daily Mail*, who was stuck in Nairobi, trying to get on a Red Cross airlift to Mogadishu. I promised her a place on the plane with me, if she got my tapes back to Ginny, who'd stay in Nairobi.'

'You got that past the BBC?'

Christie laughed, her uncertainty vanishing. 'I simply did a piece-to-camera two days into the week-long shoot, voiced the script and sent the *Daily Mail* girl back with the pictures. That fooled the BBC, who thought we'd have to wait until we came out of Nairobi at the end of the week, and delayed their filming accordingly.'

David stared at Christie with admiration. To his initial attraction to her was added a deep respect for her as a journalist. 'So how did Ginny persuade the Foreign Desk to bird the piece out?'

'Ah. Well, there's nothing like going straight to Ben Wordsworth and telling him his Foreign and News Editors are about to let the BBC slip straight through the net and scoop his network.'

'A girl after my own heart,' David smiled. 'Tell me, do you think the US operation has made any real difference to the situation there?'

Christie's face clouded with the memories. 'God, per-haps, but it's still so damned terrible. I had to fight the urge to take every child I saw home with me. It was the most difficult story I've ever filmed; those images never go away, not really.' She shook her head to clear it. 'Yet somehow you go on and film the story, and focus on the swollen bellies, and the ancient, young faces crawling with flies, and for a few minutes, people back home might feel a little guilty.'

'What you do *is* important,' David said quietly. 'Without us, no one would ever care. It took Michael Buerke to bring Ethiopia to the fore, and I'm damned sure America wouldn't have intervened in Somalia if it hadn't been for Brent Sadler's documentary on CNN, which lifted the lid on what was happening there.'

Christie sighed. 'Do we really do any good? How long does anyone remember before it's yesterday's news, and they move on to a more fashionable crisis?'

'You can't think like that, or you'll never survive,' David said, leaning forward and resting his hand on hers without thinking. Both of them felt the charge of electricity that sped through them at the touch, and their eyes locked. Christie realised that the powerful attraction she felt for him was reflected in his own eyes, and her pulse raced.

Slowly Christie eased her hand away from his, a half-smile on her lips. She had met too many correspondents who left a trail of broken hearts behind them. Exciting though it might be, a love affair with David Cameron was courting danger. As if he could read her mind, David smiled ruefully and twisted the gold signet ring on his right hand.

He knew what was happening. But for him, it came too late. He had nothing left to give.

'David! There you are. Keeping busy with the staff, I see.'

Christie looked up as Caryn Kelly swept up to the table and slammed her black Chanel bag on to the glass-and-wrought-iron table. Caryn coolly returned her gaze. 'I came to find David,' she stated possessively, marking out her territory without delay.

Christie extended her hand in greeting, but Caryn had already turned away. She slipped her arm through David's as he stood up to meet her. 'I'm sure you've been soaking up the hero's tales of war. David has a very wide fan club, you know. I'm just lucky he spares so much of his precious time for me. He's so loyal.'

Was Caryn warning her away? Perhaps Archie was wrong and there was something between them. Christie glanced at David again. No. The expression she read in his eyes was not one of love. Just of sadness.

'Of course, he knows I couldn't do without him,' Caryn laughed, the smile on her lips failing to reach her eyes. 'Lovely to meet you, sweetie. Sorry we have to dash.'

David glanced back over his shoulder at Christie as he followed Caryn. She was already heading for Sir Edward Penhaligon with a sense of purpose. Christie gave herself a mental shake. You deserved that, she thought ruefully. She needs him more than you do. Leave well alone.

Christie made her way back to the lift and re-entered the newsroom, where some semblance of normality had at last been restored now that the Queen had left the building. She glanced at her watch. 3.47. She had missed the lookahead meeting. Brian would be even more diffi-cult to deal with now. As she walked wearily past the Foreign Desk, Janey put her telephone call on hold and called her over.

'Christie, someone called Marina has been trying to reach you,' Janey said, searching through a heap of papers on her desk. 'Ah yes. Here's the number. Can you call her back?' Janey smiled, picking up her telephone again, and waved as Christie walked away. 'Hope it's good news. Ah yes, hello Andy, sorry to keep you . . .'

Christie raised her eyebrows in surprise as she glanced at the piece of paper. She recognised the overseas code, but could not place the name. Swiftly she dialled the number, but the line was engaged.

She shrugged and slipped the piece of paper into her notebook. One more call to remember to make. Damn, she still had that CARE spokesman to talk to about the piece she was doing in Rio. She needed some statistics on the number of children forced to sleep rough in the city's streets, left to fend for themselves at the age of five or six. Christie walked towards the Executive Producer's office, resigning herself to the inevitable. She already had that excellent interview with the ten-year-old girl who had given birth to twins. Put it with the reactionary Spanish priest who insisted the use of condoms were a mortal sin, and she'd have a good piece.

'Ah, Christie. Just the person. Could I have a word?' Brian asked unctuously, appearing suddenly from his glassed-in office at the edge of the newsroom.

'Sorry I'm late, Brian. Got held up.'

'Indeed. Well, you weren't the only one, so I cancelled the lookahead. Anyway, I just need a quick chat with you about a story, and then I'll let you get back to whatever you were doing.' His tone suggested that it was probably filing her nails.

Reluctantly Christie followed him into his office, and eyed the neat piles of paper on his desk with irrational annoyance. Unlike almost every other journalist, Brian had no untidy profusion of newspaper clippings, half-developed story ideas, and wire copy strewn across his desk. Idly Christie wondered if he made love in the same clinical way as he composed a news bulletin.

'Ben's come up with a wonderful idea, and I think it's a great opportunity for you,' Brian said carefully.

Christie groaned inwardly. Brian's great opportunities tended to herald a new series of cutbacks or something equally unpalatable. She wondered if he was about to ditch the rest of her population explosion series.

'Ben wants us to concentrate on some human interest stories, things that wring the viewers' hearts and get them tuning in to find out the latest,' Brian said.

Christie maintained a diplomatic silence.

'Well, anyway. We thought we'd start with a transplant kid, you know, follow a child through from the wait to the op. itself. Do a piece a week on how it's going, the false alarms, dialysis, trying to find a donor, the whole works.'

'Why are you telling me this?' Christie said, knowing the answer before she spoke.

'Ben wants you to do it,' Brian replied complacently, pleased he had an excuse to annoy her. 'He feels it needs a woman's touch.'

'You don't need me to do this,' Christie said, controlling her anger with difficulty. 'Give it to one of the trainees – Dom Ryan would be perfect. All he has to do is film the child once a week and pull it together. You know if I do it, it'll take me out of the frame for any foreign assignments for months.'

Brian smiled.

Christie stood up abruptly, and walked out of his office, not trusting herself to say anything more. She was damned if she would give Brian Reynolds the satisfaction of seeing her lose her temper. She hated this kind of sob story, and thought with frustration of the projected return trip to Somalia which would have to be postponed or reassigned to another correspondent. For all its trumpeted equal opportunities programmes, INN was riddled with the kind of chauvinism which said pretty woman were allowed in two places only: the newscaster's chair and the bedroom. The news arena was reserved for men.

Fine. If they wanted heart-jerking footage and tears before bedtime, she would damn well give it to them.

Chapter Four

Denzil Calhoun climbed heavily out of the black cab into the crisp darkness, and fumbled in his overcoat pocket for a ten-pound note, which he fished out and gave to the driver. He readjusted his trouser belt around his overflowing belly, and walked with the assurance of a man used to power towards the entrance of Annabel's. Two doormen leaped to attention as he arrived, and made way for him to pass down the narrow steps into the nightclub. Calhoun shrugged off his damp Burberry and handed it to one of the lackeys standing inside the red-carpeted interior. With a smile of satisfaction, he manoeuvred his bulk along the narrow entrance hall towards the steward ticking off club members in a large, gilt book. In front of him, two men were being discreetly informed that their cream trousers were unsuitable for admittance to the establishment, no matter how well-pressed the garments were, or how intimately their wearers knew Rod Stewart.

Calhoun gave his name with the careless confidence of a longtime member. He knew both Sir James Goldsmith, Lady Annabel's second husband, and his predecessor, Mark Birley. As owner of the world's largest media conglomeration, Calhoun News Group, he was on first name terms with all the significant men in industry, as

100

well as having an address book that read like a Hollywood *Who's Who*.

'Ah, Mr Calhoun, sir,' the steward murmured, adopting the reverent tone reserved for the club's most favoured members. 'Sir Edward mentioned that you would be meeting him, and asked me to escort you to his table.'

Calhoun grunted. 'Hope he's got a good bottle of Taittinger waiting,' he growled good-humouredly.

The steward disappeared into the maze of secluded tables, and Calhoun struggled to steer his massive girth through the narrow aisles after him. He paused as he recognised one of his favourite leader writers sitting at a table nearby, deep in conversation with an attractive blonde.

'Loved the column, Roberts,' Calhoun said, his beady eyes glinting in the doughy rolls of his face. 'When are you going to agree to write for me?'

Andrew Roberts smiled easily. 'When you can afford me.'

Calhoun guffawed. Shaking his head in amusement, he moved on, scanning the tables as he passed. The subdued lighting and expensive red velvet furnishings gave the club a discreet atmosphere that, at this time of day, suggested a don's common room rather than a fashionable and exclusive London nightspot. Calhoun knew that as much business was done in places like this as in the city's offices, if not more. If Stringfellow's was the club for the pop celebrities and starlet wannabes, Annabel's was the haunt of the men with the real power, those moguls who stayed out of the limelight but controlled events from behind the scenes. Many of them made more money in a week than the headline stars made in a year, and daily they controlled fortunes in excess of some countries' Gross National Product.

The groupies here were not teenagers, but the failing,

ailing businessmen whose ditsy escorts were not super-models but secretaries, and who hung around the men of success with their legs spread as wide as any movie starlet hungry for a part.

Calhoun felt the flood of power wash through him. Balding and ugly he might be, but he could have every woman here if he just lifted his little finger.

Denzil Calhoun already owned a vast empire of newspapers, publishing companies and a sizeable chunk of the record industry, amongst other things.

Plus two prime UK papers.

The right-wing *Daily Chronicle* successfully competed with heavies such as the *Guardian* and the *Independent*, and the equally reactionary *Daily Ethic*, which stooped to conquer, had a readership that already outnumbered both the *Sun* and the *Daily Mirror*. Together with their Sunday stablemates, the papers contributed in no small way to the thinking of the nation, and a favourable piece could make today's nobody into tomorrow's star. One bad review could turn an overnight success into the has-been of yesteryear. It was no wonder Denzil Calhoun at fifty-three felt pleased with life.

The one thing he did not have was a television station.

'Sir Edward, good to see you,' Calhoun boomed, finally locating Penhaligon's table.

Penhaligon rose gracefully and shook hands, betraying none of his distaste as the sweaty paw grasped his fingers.

'Mr Calhoun, good of you to come at such short notice. Champagne?' Penhaligon lifted his hand to a waiter standing in the shadows, and the man whipped forward and filled the waiting glass.

'It's Denzil, please,' Calhoun urged cheerfully. 'How could I resist a phone call like yours? Full of cloak and dagger.'

Penhaligon arched one eyebrow and inclined his head in

a gesture of acknowledgement. Calhoun sipped his champagne appreciatively, and sat back comfortably in the deep red velvet chair. He was fascinated to learn what had prompted Penhaligon to summon one of the few men able to wield as much media power as Penhaligon himself for a private conversation well away from their respective business establishments, but he knew that Penhaligon would broach the subject in his own good time. Calhoun was prepared to wait.

Penhaligon swirled the unfamiliar taste of being forced to do the running around his mouth along with his scotch. Nothing would have induced him to drink champagne. He eyed Calhoun reflectively as the other man slugged back a hefty measure of Taittinger. They were unlikely companions. Calhoun's Afrikaner outspokenness and uncouth behaviour could not have been more different from Penhaligon's reserved good manners and essentially English breeding, but they shared one thing in common: power. And both knew how to use it.

'I understand congratulations are in order,' Penhaligon said in measured tones.

'The independent radio? Yes, a pleasing acquisition,' Calhoun answered.

He sipped his drink and waited for the next step in the complicated dance which would eventually lead up to the subject of the evening. It was not his style, but it gave him the chance to observe the man before him in action, and anything he learnt could be useful when it came down to the hard brass tacks of negotiating. He had no doubt that negotiating was the purpose of the meeting.

'But not as pleasing as a television station would have been?'

Penhaligon smiled inwardly at the other man's start of surprise. He was well aware that Calhoun had been expecting the usual series of feints and parries before

Penhaligon made his move, and deliberately chose to wrongfoot him by getting straight to the point.

Calhoun grunted, narrowing his eyes. 'No, not as pleasant,' he agreed guardedly. For the first time a trace of his native South African accent appeared in his voice, as it often tended to when his mind was on business rather than social manners.

'I gather you plan to compete with ITN when their news franchise comes up for renewal?' Penhaligon stated calmly, swirling his scotch in his tumbler before draining the glass.

'It's no secret,' Calhoun replied defensively. 'They're very vulnerable, particularly after the takeover last year. Change has been in the air since the other ITV companies had their cosy monopoly reduced to rubble by the Broadcasting Bill. It'll be a free-for-all next time round.'

'Another of the same. No ice,' Penhaligon said to the waiter behind him, without looking over his shoulder. He glanced at Calhoun. 'The challenge for Channel Three's news franchise is a long way away yet. And things move quickly these days. It could be a long wait.'

Calhoun deliberately chose not to reply, his mind racing as he tried to predict Penhaligon's next move. Slowly he produced a large Havana and sliced its end with a solid gold guillotine.

Penhaligon suppressed the urge to shudder at the initial 'C' picked out in diamonds. 'You're aware, of course, that Ben Wordsworth is still determined to create what he graphically describes as supermarket television. In fact, he is very close to getting agreement from a number of backers.'

Calhoun did not miss the casual tone Penhaligon used. Swiftly he picked up the apparent change of subject as if the topic had been the INN Editor all along. 'Yourself amongst them,' he said smoothly, drawing hard on his cigar and exhaling a soft curl of smoke.

'Myself amongst them,' Penhaligon confirmed easily. Suddenly he tired of the cat and mouse game and leant forward, his silver hair catching pinpoints of light as he moved from the shadows.

'When I agreed to back Wordsworth two years ago, it was in exchange for several things. Control. Power. Editorial veto. Wordsworth hasn't delivered. I'm beginning to wonder if that means the agreement has been declared null and void.' He paused, assessing Calhoun's reaction. Silently he congratulated the other man, who did not betray a flicker of his inevitable surprise.

'So what's changed?' Calhoun asked, his expression unreadable. His mind raced. Penhaligon's defection to INN had caused a major stir in the media world, the ripples of which were still subsiding. If he had summoned Calhoun to tell him the honeymoon was over, the newspaper editor would be more than pleased to proclaim the good news that Wordsworth was on the way out. Calhoun owed the INN Editor a few, and it seemed payback time was coming.

'Wordsworth is a man possessed, and I think a little exorcism is in order,' Penhaligon said with no trace of a smile. 'As you know, he initially came to me for money and my imprimatur. The idea was to start a global network in direct competition with CNN and the BBC World Service TV, and once it was up and running, to then take it one step further, incorporating regional and local news into the melting pot.'

'But you knew that when you joined Ben,' Calhoun said impatiently. 'Why are you running back to mother now?'

Penhaligon flinched at the barb. 'Because my partner is playing around,' he said bitterly. 'Why else do you go back home?'

Calhoun mentally reviewed the press cuttings on INN and Penhaligon which he had had his secretary dig out for him as soon as he received the unexpected summons to Annabel's. In not one of them had he found any mention of a rift between the Editor, Ben Wordsworth, and his top anchor. On the contrary, the cuttings had been full of the success of INN, and its imminent dive into the uncharted waters of select-a-vision. A third of the company was already owned by an array of foreign television broadcasters, and more were lining up in the street, desperate for a piece of the action. He also knew what the cuttings did not say: that over four hundred affiliates were about to sign, if they had not already done so, on the dotted line, giving INN true world exposure and participation in the politics of almost every significant country in the world. Ben Wordsworth – and with him Penhaligon – was about to become very, very powerful. They would make Ted Turner's CNN look like Blue Peter. So what was the problem?

Penhaligon crossed one elegant leg over the other, and sat back, waiting. Two girls swathed in form-fitting lycra sashayed past their table. Calhoun's eyes followed them wolfishly towards the tiny dance floor, where several ill-matched couples swayed in an approximation of 1970s Travolta gyrations. No one had ever told the music maestros of Annabel's that Abba was out and House was in. Even if they had, it would probably be several decades before the club was ready for it.

'It's being said that Mickey Mouse wears an INN watch,' Penhaligon said dryly as Calhoun's eyes returned to their natural orbit. 'At breakfast time I'm happy for GMTV to concentrate on the 'F' factor and the latest round of Oscar winners. It's what the viewers want, and GMTV has never set out to be anything other than a magazine programme. But not INN. That was never the

106

aim, and it cannot be now. Not if it's to remain a news channel. If you want entertainment, sex, drugs, rock-and-roll, fine. But not on my news programme. This was meant to be a hard news channel, and I want it to stay that way.'

'No one ever lost money underestimating the taste of the viewer,' Calhoun said laconically. He had heard the quality-versus-money argument so many times, he was immune to it now. But he had not missed Penhaligon's unconscious use of the word 'my.'

'INN is about to launch itself as the world's biggest ever TV party-line,' Penhaligon said, with such intensity Calhoun dropped his laissez-faire attitude and sat up to listen. 'As soon as Wordsworth's deals are finalised, every country in the world will have access to a television news channel that not only gives them the international news, as CNN already does, but the news of their own country – like ITN in the UK, like ABC and CBS in America, like ZDF in Germany. And then, so that their cup really runneth over, INN will give the local news, the school fêtes and train delays, throughout the world. In other words, every kind of news you could want will be there, on one channel, for the taking. All you'll have to do is switch it on.'

Calhoun frowned as the implications of what Penhaligon was saying finally registered. Suddenly he wondered where he had been for the last two years. Wordsworth had touted his vision around the media world, and they had all failed to see it.

If Wordsworth pulled it off – and there was no reason to suppose he would not – it would mean that INN would have everything on one channel. Everyone would want to watch it. It could put half the other news agencies in the world out of business, if not all of them, giving INN the voice of the planet. Every politician and terrorist would put their point of view on INN first. Every opposition spokesman would answer back on INN at once. It would be world politics in action, and the world would want to watch. The power of the network would be dizzying.

Penhaligon slammed his tumbler down on the table. 'And Wordsworth is about to throw it all away. His idea is right, but his news values are all wrong. If he takes INN any further down the road he is currently mapping out, it will turn the network into a cross between MTV and a problem talk show, and we'll be laughed out of town. If INN is to be taken seriously, it has to live, eat, breathe, and dream hard news.'

'You own fifteen per cent of the company,' Calhoun said, waving his arm in the air in a dismissive gesture. 'You're the face of INN, and Wordsworth knows it. If you want control, take it.'

Penhaligon smiled, slowly and with the triumph of someone who has just heard the right answer after hours of coaching.

'I intend to,' he said.

■ KENT
1 May, 7.15 p.m.

Odile Wordsworth gazed absently at her reflection in the mirror. Consideringly she held a pair of drop pearl earrings up next to her cheek and, frowning slightly, tilted her head to the side, so that the earrings dangled gently in the hollow of her neck. No, not the pearls, she decided, replacing them on the velvet-lined tray in front of her. Thoughtfully she selected two blood-red ruby stones, and screwed them into her ears, sitting back to survey the effect. Perfect. The glowing stones flashed fire against the rich brown of her hair, and giving her an oddly timeless appearance which was enhanced by the antique burgundy crepe-de-chine Caillot dress she was wearing. It had belonged to her grandmother: the French grandmother, naturally. No Englishwoman would have had such an elegant gown in her wardrobe.

Odile rose gracefully, and moved to the full-length cheval glass at the end of her dressing room. The crepe-de-chine rustled as she walked, exuding a faint scent of roses from long-dead parties. For a moment, she regarded her reflection in the burnished glass with detached scrutiny; her figure was still willowy, her waist a generous twelve inches slimmer than the curve of her hips. She caught her hair with a quick, practised movement, and swiftly twisted its chestnut length into a neat chignon at the nape of her slender neck. Odile smiled at her reflection. Her appearance was one of classic elegance, deliberately chosen to stand out from the Lacroix and Alaïa outfits that would throng the party.

Odile shrugged. However stunning she looked, she doubted Ben would notice.

'Oh Mother, surely you're not going down in that?'

Odile paused at the top of the great curved staircase and glanced at her fifteen-year-old daughter. 'Why not, Lucille?'

'I'd have thought that was obvious. You'll embarrass Daddy. Everyone'll think he can't afford to buy you anything new.'

Odile smiled. 'You, young lady, have a great deal to learn about style.'

She turned to go downstairs, one slim foot already on the top step. Suddenly Lucy's appearance registered, and she whirled back. 'What on earth are you wearing? I don't remember giving you permission to join us this evening.'

'Daddy said I could come,' Lucy retorted defiantly.

Odile sighed. She was obviously wasting the exorbitant

109

amount of money she spent on her daughter's select Swiss finishing school. In matters of fashion, Lucy was one hundred per cent her father's child. And having also inherited a good dose of his manipulative talents, she could twist him around her little finger.

Odile watched as Lucy shrugged the red leather dress down her voluptuous curves so that it just reached the top of her thighs as a sop to decency and her mother's outrage. Before she could object further, Lucy fled down the stairs, her thick black wool stockings failing dismally to hide her shapely legs. Odile made a mental note to ensure that Lucy was returned post-haste to her bedroom before some unfortunate man was tempted into indiscretion by her daughter's attractive but under-age charms.

She could hear Ben shouting apoplectically at the caterers downstairs, and mentally she prepared herself for the chaos awaiting her as she descended the staircase.

'Where the fuck have you been?' Ben snarled as she reached the marbled entrance hall. 'Luigi's have forgotten the champagne, the cook has eloped with some damned vicar, and the Agency have sent some dimwitted Frenchman instead.'

Odile's elegant eyebrows arched at the insult to her countrymen. 'Anything else?'

'Since you ask, yes. I haven't even seen the bloody flower arrangers, and they should have been here two hours ago. And Perpetua disappeared into the shrubbery to look for mint and hasn't been seen since.'

'Is that all?' Odile murmured.

She turned as a harassed man darted into the hall, his chef's hat borne aloft before him like a standard into battle. 'Madame, Madame, zer eez no hot!' he shrieked, grasping her sleeve. 'Eef zer eez no hot, zer eez no cookeeng!'

'Sounds like a fucking extra from '*Allo* '*Allo*,' Ben muttered, storming off.

Lucy poked her head around the open French windows as Odile disentangled herself from the sobbing Frenchman. 'Mother. Thought you'd like to know. The swimming pool's pink. Personally, I think it looks better that way.'

'OK, lady, where d'you want the flowers puttin'? We've been chasin' 'alfway round the country lookin' for your 'ouse. Don't you have no bleedin' signs in Kent then?'

'Over to you, Mother,' Lucy said, disappearing from view.

The florist leant back against the cream walls of the hall and waited happily for Odile to have hysterics. He was disappointed. Odile strode through the hall, mentally rolling up her sleeves. It was always like this. She knew that, by the time her guests arrived, she would have achieved a measure of ordered serenity. Somehow, she always did.

By 7.57, the electricity had been restored, and the cook was happily brooding over forty cheese-and-asparagus souffles which were blooming in the large oven. A dozen crates of champagne had been delivered by the local off-licence, whose owner had gone on a three-day bender with the unexpected profits. The tired-looking flowers had been revived with a small dose of TLC and a large tip to the florist, who miraculously rediscovered his green fingers and brought the wilting blooms around. Indeed, such was his benevolence upon receipt of several crisp notes that he was even happy to distribute the flowers artistically around the house.

Lucy winked at the florist as he retired discreetly to the bottom of the garden with two bottles of champagne. He disappeared into the shrubbery with Perpetua, whose arms were still full of mint. Lucy darted over to the incandescent swimming pool and dipped one long tress of heavily bleached hair into the water to check the chemical reaction. Delighted with the vivid green result, she rapidly dunked her whole head in and emerged with emerald hair. Horrified, Odile threw a cocktail of all the chemicals she could find in the poolshed into the water, and prayed that the pink would vanish before the poolman got back from his holiday.

'Sweetie! So good to see you again. And what a charming little dress. You must tell me where you got it.'

Odile hid one pink hand behind her back as Victoria swept into the house and shrugged off her mink wrap. She handed it to the waiting valet with a conspiratorial smile. 'I know one shouldn't really wear them anymore, but I so loathe anything artificial, don't you?' she said in a loud stage whisper, kissing the air on either side of Odile's head.

'Funny. We were just talking about you,' Lucy said gaily, sauntering through the french windows as she towelled her hair.

Odile froze, unable to decide between laughing off the jokes of adolescence or pretending she had not understood. Her concern was wasted. Victoria had eaten bigger things for canapés.

'Darling! You look like a traffic light,' she trilled with saccharine sweetness, giving Lucy's emerald hair and scarlet dress a quick once-over. 'Only upside down.'

Lucy scowled.

Hastily Odile moved on. 'What a splendid gown,' she enthused, carefully steering Victoria towards the main room, wondering where the hell Ben had got to. It was not like him to be absent just as half the known media world was about to invade their home.

Victoria smoothed the sculpted black velvet gown

112

down her thighs. 'One has to keep one's figure so carefully, if one is to carry off a dress like this,' she said complacently. 'I'm so lucky, I never seem to put on an ounce.'

Odile smiled politely as Victoria smugly ran her fingers around the pearl and diamante halter-neck collar of the dress. Privately she thought Victoria's wafer-thin body would be infinitely more attractive with a few curves.

'So where is the birthday boy then?' Victoria asked coyly, looking around her. 'Doesn't he want a birthday kiss?'

'Ben's already had plenty of those,' Morgan de Burgh said dryly from behind her.

Victoria whipped around, and stared nonplussed at the woman who had just entered the main reception room.

'Morgan, darling. No Dalmeny?' Odile asked swiftly, greeting her guest.

'He'll be along later. Finishing up some rather dull business at the House, I'm afraid.'

Victoria started. So this was Dalmeny de Burgh's wife. Expertly she assessed the blue silk Lagerfeld trouser suit in front of her. Several thousand pounds, easy, she thought quickly, and the handmade Lilibet Devereaux shoes half as much again – and that was if you were lucky enough to be admitted to the exclusive group of a few dozen obscenely rich and famous women whom Ms Devereaux chose to take as clients. Victoria had tried several times to be included in their number without success. Rather obviously expensive for the wife of a Tory MP, given the Prime Minister's fetish for a classless society – even if her husband was one of the richest men in England. Pretty few M & S checkout girls wandering around the tills in Lagerfeld.

Morgan submitted to the scrutiny with amusement, calmly drawing an amber cigarette holder from her clasp

113

bag and inserting a Marlboro. Lazily she drew on the cigarette as she threw her shingled blonde head backwards. She resembled nothing so much as a twenties fashion lithograph, all slim, boyish lines and expensive idleness. Victoria watched, fascinated, coveting the other woman's poise and ultra-chic sharpness.

She followed Morgan's gaze as Dalmeny de Burgh entered the room. No man should be allowed to be that extravagantly handsome as well as successful, intelligent and rich. Some women just got handed life on a plate.

Odile noticed with relief that Ben was now in place at the front entrance hall, welcoming a clutch of guests – why was it that guests were like buses, none for ages, and then they all arrived at once? She joined him swiftly as Sir Edward Penhaligon arrived.

'Splendidly done, as always, my dear,' Sir Edward murmured softly, taking her elbow. 'How you create such beauty out of chaos, I have no idea. That husband of yours doesn't realise what an asset he has in you.'

Sir Edward glanced around the room. He was well aware that it was only Odile's exquisite taste that redeemed Ben's tendency to flashy opulence and subdued it to a stylish, if not understated, simplicity. She had managed to prevent Ben from converting the vast, red-bricked house into a mock-Tudor mansion, insisting that if their home had to be modern, it would not pretend to be otherwise. Brought up in an ancient chateau in deepest Provence, there was nothing Odile loathed more than fake leaded windowpanes and imported antique fireplaces. Instead, the house was decorated in neutral tones – beige carpets, soft creamy walls, taupe curtains – set off by sudden strokes of dark grey furnishings. In each room of the house, one colour was allowed to take precedence: lemon cushions and saffron Aubusson rugs in one room, malachite candlesticks and deep, olive green lamps in another. In the main reception room, Odile had deliberately mixed her extensive collection of first editions with cheap paperbacks, the books piled haphazardly together on the shelves, so that the untidiness and uneven splash of colour brought the room to life without disturbing the simplicity of design.

'Excuse me, my dear, I wonder if I might have a word with Edward?' Odile turned as Sir Joseph Bower, one of television's most senior figures, approached them. 'But of course. Please, I was just about to leave.'

The two men inclined their heads courteously and Odile left them in the breakfast room, crossing the hall and emerging on to the veranda. She glanced back at the sprawling house with a smile. It was the gardens that had captured her heart.

Set in the midst of the Kent countryside, the house was flanked on either side by undulating woods of slim silver birches and copper beeches. A lengthy gravel drive lead up from the main gate to the house, clipped green lawns flowing from either side until they merged into the edge of the woods, now ablaze with a riot of spring daffodils. Odile did much of the gardening herself, allowing the estate to verge on the edge of incipient wildness, giving it a character unequalled even in this beautiful part of Kent. Behind the house, the swimming pool was concealed by yew hedges, and next to it, it was just possible to see the top of the tennis court fencing above a line of cedars.

Odile glanced at the swimming pool, now reassuringly un-pink, and took a deep breath of the early evening air. It was surprisingly mild for early May, a chill breeze ruffling against her bare arms, but not enough to make her shiver. Together with autumn, this was her favourite time of the year; emerging from the bleak snows of January and February, sloughing off the depressing March drizzle, but still waiting with anticipation for the warm summer days, and long, relaxed evenings.

'Odile! You look very fey tonight,' Christie exclaimed, crossing the damp lawn to meet Odile on the terrace. 'You look stunning as always. I wish I knew how you do it.'

'Christie, how lovely to see you. It's been far too long. I was just reciting a little Keats to myself . . . what I can remember of it.'

Christie smiled, and glanced around her. 'Yes, I can see why. This is such a beautiful place, particularly at this time of year.'

'I always prefer it. Somehow the anticipation of summer is always better than the reality, when it comes.'

Christie laughed. 'Ah yes. That's why all the best poets die young, before they have had time to be disappointed.'

'You have a Celtic soul,' Odile said, shaking her head. 'You shouldn't be a journalist. Such a waste!'

'Don't let Ben hear you say that. He might just agree,' Christie said, linking her arm through Odile's as they made their way across the terrace back towards the house.

The rooms were already thronged with people. A hundred and fifty people had been invited to celebrate the fortieth birthday of the Editor of INN, and all but a few had accepted with alacrity. It was a media event, and everyone wanted to be a part of it. Apart from the more senior members of INN, the other news networks were well represented, with a handful of well-known actors and musicians thrown in. The paparazzi hung about near the entrance of the drive, waiting to take pictures of the rich and famous as they arrived. One or two of the more enterprising had already started slinking up through the garden, with a measure of stealth that would put the SAS to shame.

Victoria fiddled with a wrought-iron curlicue on an art

deco lampstand which Odile had bought in exchange for her soul from an antique dealer in Islington's fashionable Camden Passage. She was unhappily sandwiched between Brian Reynolds and Bob Carpenter. Bob was INN's oldest and most disreputable correspondent. Unfortunately, he had recently been awarded an OBE, probably because everyone at ITN and the BBC already had one, which made it extremely difficult for Ben to sack him, much as he might like to. Victoria sighed, trying to decide which was worse: yet another anecdote from the Executive Producer about Tarquin and Ashley, or Bob's latest account of his presentation at the Palace. Some choice.

She scowled as she saw Julia Somerville enter the room, every man's eyes following the newscaster with a mixture of admiration and respect. Julia was Victoria's personal *bête noire*, always just that little bit more famous, just that little bit more stylish. Victoria loathed the constant references to herself as 'the second Julia Somerville' by the tabloids. When would Julia Somerville be written about as 'an older Victoria Lawrence'?

Behind her, Sir Joseph Bower was already deep in conversation with Penhaligon, discussing the prospects for the beleaguered Channel Five, if indeed any remained. Victoria watched as the portly Sir Joseph gestured discreetly in Ben Wordsworth's direction with his crystal tumbler of scotch. Automatically Victoria followed the movement, turning in time to see Wordsworth welcome Paragon Fairfax as she sashayed provocatively into the room, fully aware that all eyes were on her.

Victoria froze, rooted to the spot with horror. She felt an unbecoming flush mount in her cheeks, and spread across her chest, as she gazed at Paragon in dismay. Suddenly the room fell quiet, as if anticipating one of those classic scenes which they would forever after claim as having happened when they were there. Paragon's

117

elderly husband, the hotel magnate Harry Foley, fluttered helplessly behind his show-stealing wife. Victoria was not sure which she hated most: the embarrassed sympathy or the polite attempts not to laugh which she saw reflected all around her.

Lucy broke the silence, striding forward into the centre of the frozen tableau and hugging her father.

'Daddy, I love it,' she cried, laughter convulsing her. 'You've got the newscasters to come in uniform!'

Victoria stared at Paragon's dress. Oh God. They were both wearing the exclusive and expensive Hamnett design. None knew better than she how much it had cost. Paragon's shapely curves filled the velvet sheath, her ripe breasts swelling provocatively below the glittering choker, her tanned shoulders giving the halter-neck a rich, tawny frame. Her clouds of strawberry blonde hair rippled on to her shoulders, and Paragon lifted one manicured hand casually to lift it backwards, as she stood gazing at Victoria with undismayed surprise. One swift glance at Victoria's narrow, pale shoulders, her small breasts which failed dismally to fulfil the gown's potential, her stiffly coiffeured, iced-charcoal hair, and Paragon had known the battle was won. Victoria's unhappy choice only enhanced her own gloriously young, vibrant appearance. She smiled sweetly.

'What wonderful taste, Victoria,' she said pleasantly. 'Isn't it amazing how a designer can leave room for such interpretation in a dress?'

Victoria swallowed hard, mortified and appalled. She prayed none of the paparazzi would get to hear of it, but held out little hope. Already, she was sure, the phone lines back to Fleet Street . . . or was it Docklands now? . . . would be buzzing with the delicious titbit of gossip. She envied Odile her inimitable chic, Morgan her bank balance, Christie her style, which would ensure none of them ever had to face such humiliation. Wordlessly she turned away.

'She hasn't the character to carry it off,' Philip Cunningham murmured quietly beside her. 'It takes an older woman's poise to lift that dress from obviousness to elegance.'

He smiled at her comfortingly, his pale blonde hair flopping into his watery blue eyes. Victoria looked at him consideringly. Swiftly she assessed this new turn of events. Like most of the newsroom, she had always ignored the ineffectual Executive Foreign Editor, assuming Brian Reynolds and Ben Wordsworth pulled his strings too effectively for him to be worth cultivating. But perhaps now was as good a time as any to discuss increasing her allocation of foreign assignments.

Victoria glanced back again at Julia Somerville, who was chatting casually to Christie as the two of them walked out towards the pool, glasses in hand. Yes, what she needed was credibility, a few serious stories reported on location to give her some gravitas. She did not want to be just a face, a clothes horse for INN, particularly with so many lissome beauties lining up to take her place.

She took Philip's arm firmly with one hand, and picked up a glass of champagne with the other from a passing waiter.

'Now,' she said brightly, propelling Philip before her, 'Let's talk about you.'

■ 11.59 p.m.

Ginny sat down on the low brick wall near the pool and leaned back against the small stone urn at the end of it. She listened as the village clock chimed the hour in the distance. Twelve o'clock tonight and all's well. All's well.

She smiled sadly at the irony of her thoughts.

Christie lifted two full glasses of champagne from a passing waiter and crossed the terrace towards Ginny. She handed one to her and sat cross-legged beside her, unaware of the casual gracefulness with which she carried out the simple movement. Her Arabian white silk trousers hung in elegant folds as she eased one cream slippered foot beneath the other.

'OK, Ginny, spill.'

Ginny sighed. 'How did you know?'

Christie smiled. 'I always do.'

'Is it really that obvious?'

'Don't worry, only to me. It's Nick, isn't it?'

'Oh Christie, I'm so useless with men,' Ginny wailed. 'I always seem to fall for the wrong ones. How can I be so good at organising everyone else and so hopeless with my love-life?'

'But you seemed so happy together. What happened?'

Ginny took a sip of her champagne. 'I don't know. I wish I did. I'd almost think he's found another woman, only I haven't seen any signs of it.' She sighed again. 'We just seem to have drifted apart. We have been living together for more than a year. Maybe he's had enough.'

'Have you?'

'Me? No, I'm terrified he'll leave me. I don't want us to split up. But what can I do if that's what he wants? I just wish I knew why, that's all. Has he said anything to you?'

Christie earnestly vowed never to let any of her friends go out with each other again, if this was the position she ended up in. 'About what's wrong between you?' she temporised, hoping she was not going to end up as a confidante on both sides of the fence. 'No. But surely he'd talk to you first, anyway?'

'Don't they always say you're the last to know?' Ginny said, peering into her glass, which was dangerously close

120

to empty. 'Christie, have you ever been in love?'

A picture of David Cameron suddenly filled Christie's mind. Annoyed at herself, she dismissed it.

'No,' she murmured, almost to herself.

'Keep it that way,' Ginny said mournfully. 'It makes you suspicious, afraid and jealous, and it bloody hurts.'

Christie reached out her hand and touched her friend's arm sympathetically. 'Look, Ginny, why don't you talk to him? Find out what's on his mind,' she suggested. 'At least you'll know where you stand.'

'Yes, you're right. It has to be better than not knowing. God, why do I do it? I want a man in my life, not in my house. Never again.'

Christie laughed. 'Sure. Until the next time.'

'No, I mean it. This was love, and I'm not doing it again.'

'Excuse me . . .?'

Christie turned and smiled at the grey-haired old gentleman she recognised at Paragon Fairfax's husband. 'Mr Foley, hello. Can we help you?'

'Miss Bradley, how kind. I was just looking for our hostess, to say goodbye. You wouldn't know where she is, would you?'

Ginny stood up, the half-dozen antique silver bangles at her wrists clanking melodiously. 'She was at the other side of the house a few moments ago, trying to find her daughter,' she smiled. 'Let me show you . . . I was just on my way to get another drink anyway.'

Harry Foley smiled his gratitude, and nodded courteously to Christie as he followed Ginny around the side of the house. He did not like to admit he was also looking for his wife, whom he had not seen since her dramatic entrance several hours ago.

Christie stood up slowly and placed her empty glass on the low wall. She smiled sadly as Ginny escorted Harry

121

Foley across the terrace, wondering how two successful, intelligent people could both make such mistakes in their romantic liaisons. She wondered how well the old man knew his new young wife. With a flash of sudden insight she realised that he probably understood her extremely well.

Whereas Ginny . . . Christie sighed. She had so hoped that her friend's relationship with Nick would work out. Ginny had such a tendency to fall deeply and passionately in love with out-and-out bastards who hurt her again and again. Nick had seemed the perfect answer. But obviously that was not the case.

On a sudden impulse Christie decided to talk to Nick. Perhaps it was not as irrevocable as Ginny feared . . . maybe she could somehow help. Christie remembered seeing him earlier making his way along the path towards the tennis courts, and set off in that direction.

She could see that the party was in the final stages of disintegration. The more famous guests such as Julia Somerville had long since left, leaving a hard core of determined party-goers. Most were either in drunken, flirtatious conversations with people with whom they had most definitely not arrived, or desperately looking for those with whom they had. Giggles came from the poolhut on the other side of the water, and Christie thought she recognised Dalmeny de Burgh's rich laugh. A man in shirt-tails staggered past her, and slumped into a corner beneath the shade of a large camellia. All around were empty lipsticked glasses and cigarette ends.

The two figures on the tennis court had obviously not heard her approach. Christie moved towards the three-sided wooden hut at the side of the court, which was more usually used for watching the grudge matches Ben liked to play with his rivals. As the scene came into focus, Christie froze, utterly shocked.

122

Both were naked. A tangled heap of clothes scattered around the nearest edge of the tennis court bore witness to the urgent need for one another that had obviously overcome any sense of discretion or self-preservation.

Christie stared, aghast, unable to move, as she watched Nick plunge deep into his partner, his thighs pumping hard and fast against the body beneath him. His dull blonde hair was wet with sweat, droplets glistening on his naked body as he worked with rhythmic concentration. Christie could see his chest heaving with effort as, below him, his partner moaned. Oblivious to Christie, Nick withdrew his cock almost to the tip, then gathering himself, his face flushed and frowning with the effort, plunged once more into his willing lover. Christie saw him lift his forearm to his lips, biting down on his own flesh until it bled, as if to suppress his scream of pleasure. His eyes were closed, his head thrown back, his hair hanging wetly down his shoulders. His nipples stood out, stiffened by the breeze, and he rose up above his prone lover, whose face was buried in the rug as Nick thrust from behind.

Christie's hand flew to her mouth as she saw Nick reach forward to his lover's head and caress the brown curls with unconscious tenderness, as the two curled together for a final still moment before rearing as their orgasms convulsed them.

Nick screamed, and thrust, and screamed again. 'Yes! Oh God, yes! Please, yes, yes, yes!'

They bucked as their climax raced through them, and then abruptly their bodies quietened and separated and they folded into one another's embrace, stroking each other softly, exchanging quick, exhausted kisses. Christie could hear Nick murmuring, 'I love you, love you, oh how I love you,' over and over again, like a mantra.

Silently she backed away, the spell which had held her

123

in its thrall breaking as the writhing couple breathed slower, and finally became still. Her heart clenched in horror as she turned and fled from the tennis court, tears of shock and unhappiness spilling from her eyes as she reached the path and flung herself against the tall oak that stood at the entrance to the court, clinging to it for support. Ginny had been wrong. Nick did have someone else.

Ginny's own brother.

■ 2 MAY, 00.45 a.m.

Ben glanced surreptitiously at the clock on the mantel-piece below the Monet in the drawing room – a gift from Odile's father when Lucy was born – and wondered how long he could reasonably be expected to enjoy his own birthday party. Quarter to one. They were left now with the diehards, the people who would tumble at dawn into their Jaguars and Lagondas and the occasional battered Volvo Estate . . . the nanny finds it so much easier to drive, darling, and the insurance is so much cheaper . . . and weave drunkenly down the winding country lanes, neatly sandwiched between the police shift changes so that they were rarely, if ever, breathalysed.

It had indubitably been a success, and Ben measured real success in terms of venomous envy per square metre, relishing his status as the most hated man in television. He craved recognition like a drug. He smiled in gleeful satisfaction. ITN's new Chief Executive had actually congratulated him on his newly-won BAFTA for Best News Actuality, INN's first. The bronze cyclops head with its one eye now watched him balefully from a high shelf in his office. It was a gracious if difficult thing to do, given that ITN had come to look on the award as their own, having won it four out of five times in the previous years. The BBC's Director General had not attended, or sent word of congratulation. Ben liked that. The one thing sweeter than praise from one's rivals was their refusal to do so as one climbed over them.

Behind him, GMTV's News Editor, Nigel Hancock, lay in an exhausted sleep on the white leather sofa, one hand still clutching a fat cigar. Nigel's dapper black monk shoes with their silver buckles gleamed as Ben opened the heavy peach damask curtains to let the moonlight stream in. GMTV had replaced TV-AM at the beginning of the year, when the franchise changes had been implemented, and Nigel had succeeded against all the odds in giving the morning show some semblance of a news service, kicking off with a major scoop when he got the first television pictures of the estranged Princess of Wales in her bikini on holiday in the Caribbean. Ben was pleased with the way their earlier conversation had gone; a deal between GMTV and INN over coverage could only benefit both of them. Wooing, schmoozing, bargaining, tempting, intimidating – making deals. There was nothing he liked more; it was better than sex, even with such skilled experts as Paragon. Ben was less happy with a passing comment Nigel had let slip about INN's Latin America correspondent, Peter Princer, which suggested that Princer was involved in some deal which was definitely not to INN's advantage. Mentally Ben resolved to speak to his Executive Producer, Brian Reynolds, in the morning.

Thinking of Paragon, Ben felt a dull ache in the region of his groin, and frowned sulkily. It was his bloody birthday, and everyone seemed to be getting it except him. He'd already had to boot his PA and her boyfriend out of the maid's bedroom – God knew what Perpetua would say if she found out. His cock needed some imminent attention, and for a moment he wondered if he dared get Paragon in here and down on her knees in front of him. She had the wettest, warmest throat and the most talented tongue he'd ever had suck him off. With frustration he remembered that her antique husband, having finally located his wife, was about to take her home for Horlicks and a hot-water bottle. He cursed at the thought of that erotic, second skin of a dress going to waste. It had cost him enough when he bought it for her, and he'd have paid double if he'd known that frigid bitch Victoria was going to turn up in the same outfit. He smiled evilly. Thank God both he and Paragon were safely married, and not to each other: he did not trust himself to be able to say No to her when she had his cock in her luscious mouth, and Christ knew what she'd ask for if she thought he was available. He pitied Harry, the poor sod. God knows why he'd married a piece like Paragon; he just hoped Harry didn't expect fidelity as part of the deal. It was easy to see, however, why Paragon had married Harry. After all, Harry Foley owned twelve per cent of INN.

Ben stepped away from the window, idly wondering who were the dishevelled couple now making their way back across the lawn from the direction of the tennis court. Carefully he moved around Nigel, still happily asleep, and crossed the marbled hall towards the main reception room. As he did so, he noticed Lucy in the shadows of the stairwell, and recognised the slightly shifty face of Bob Carpenter beside her.

'Isn't it about time you were in bed, young lady?' he said grumpily. Guiltily Bob shied away from Lucy as if she were radioactive.

'Whose did you have in mind?' Lucy responded irreverently, longingly thinking of the delectable Dalmeny de Burgh. Bugger his wife. Some sixth sense had sent Morgan straight to the poolhut, just as Dalmeny was sucking Lucy's full, eager breast and inserting one expert hand into her flimsy lace panties. Morgan hadn't found them, but Dalmeny had been put off his stroke by the fear that even his complaisant wife might not forgive infidelity with a fifteen-year-old, and that one word to the wise – or, more accurately, the tabloids – would bring his promising career as an MP to a shuddering halt. Lucy had been left panting, aroused and frustrated as Dalmeny had hastily buttoned his flies and vanished towards the safer waters of polite conversation with Charles Silversmith's unprepossessing wife.

Ben's eye glinted dangerously, and reluctantly Lucy moved away from Bob Carpenter. This was not going to be her lucky night, and, now as grumpy as her father – for exactly the same reasons if she did but know it – she sulkily moved up the staircase.

Ben walked into the main room as Odile and Harry strolled through the French windows, heading for the carpark behind the pool. Paragon trailed disconsolately in the rear, the velvet hem of her dress skimming the puddles of water which had gathered in the crazy paving around the tiled edge of the pool. She glanced at Ben hungrily, her dark eyes reflecting her equally urgent need for satisfaction, and lasciviously she licked her lips and ran her hand down her flat stomach to the slight roundness of the mound beneath.

Suddenly Perpetua lurched out of the tall rhododendron bushes at the side of the pool, crushed mint sticking to her white apron, her black dress crumpled, her neat black stockings torn. A beatific smile testified to the pleasant hours she had spent with the florist and two bottles of vintage champagne.

Ben could see exactly what was going to happen, but seemed powerless to stop it. Paragon remained oblivious to it for a few more vital seconds. Suddenly Ben's expression registered and she turned just as Perpetua stumbled drunkenly in her direction. Too shocked even to cry out, Paragon fell backwards into the pool as the maid passed out on the tiles.

Odile heard the splash and rushed back towards the pool in horror. The gallant florist, unhurriedly arranging his clothes as he too emerged from the rhododendrons, dived into the pool with a flourish and grasped Paragon's dress as she went under for the third time, skilfully managing to undo the flimsy fastening of the halter-neck as he struck out towards the steps. One cinnamon-tipped nipple and full creamy breast was exposed as Paragon flailed hopelessly, hampered by her constricting dress and the enthusiastic grasp of her rescuer. Christie and Odile leant forward to haul her out as the florist reluctantly loosened his grip.

Spluttering and shivering, Paragon staggered to the low wall at the edge of the pool and sat down, still too stunned to utter a word. Ben watched in disbelief as an excited photographer leapt from the rhododendron, which was beginning to seem like Picadilly Circus. How many more people were going to emerge from the bloody bushes, for Christ's sake?

'Get that damned snapper out of here!' Ben yelled in irritation. All he needed was Paragon's tits splashed across some Sunday paper. His cock hardened rebelliously in his trousers, and he wished he could suck that provocative nipple and fuck her until she screamed for him to stop. Too late he saw the flash of a bulb, and the photographer leaping athletically back through the bushes, having got his scoop.

Paragon stood up like an avenging Venus, and pointed towards the sprinting figure.

'Well don't just stand there!' she screamed majestically. 'Go after him!'

Obligingly the florist shook himself like a wet dog and turned in hot pursuit, unable to believe the time he was having.

Ben rolled his eyes heavenwards. Just as you thought things couldn't get any worse, they had a way of completely fucking you up.

Behind him, Christie moved away from the treacherously slippery edge of the pool, pushing the crimson silk sleeves of her shirt up her arms, where they had been soaked in rescuing Paragon. She smiled. Somehow she could not help thinking there was some fairness in the world after all. She glanced at her watch. God, it was after three. She'd better call for a taxi, or she'd never get home.

Christie felt a light touch on her shoulder, and turned absently, still fascinated by the drama unfolding in front of her.

'I was wondering,' David Cameron said, his tiger's eyes boring into Christie's, 'If you'd like a lift home.'

Chapter Five

The electricity between them was palpable.

Christie climbed on to the back of David's Harley Davidson, heedless of her expensive silk trousers as she swung her leg over the back of the motorbike. David patted the gleaming turquoise tank with affection as she slid into the seat behind him.

'Belongs to my brother,' he said, with an endearing note of boyish envy in his voice. 'He lets me borrow it whenever I'm in the country. Wish it was mine.'

Christie smiled inwardly. He sounded like a small boy gazing longingly at his big brother's bicycle.

David reached awkwardly around the handlebars and picked up two helmets from the ground where he had left them, handing one to Christie, and expertly pulling the other down over his head.

'You must have been pretty sure,' Christie murmured. 'You knew to bring two.'

David laughed, but did not reply, clipping the strap beneath his chin in a swift, practised movement. He leant forward and inserted the key in the ignition, waiting for a few moments as the engine throbbed into life.

Christie turned the shining black crash-helmet in her hand, admiring its sinister sleekness, relishing the threat of

130

danger and risk which it embodied. Almost more than the motorbike itself, it summoned thoughts of speed, chance and untamed energy, and Christie was surprised at the surge of sexual excitement which pulsed through her. She leant against David's broad back, her nipples straining against the flimsy red silk of her top, burning against his rough cotton shirt. Unconsciously her thighs tightened against his legs as he twisted around towards her.

'Cold?'

'No, I'm fine,' Christie smiled. 'You?'

'Not any more.'

Swiftly Christie pulled the helmet down over her head, tucking the stray wisps of her blonde hair out of her eyes as she closed the visor. In the distance she could still hear the sounds of the party. David's chest felt warm and hard beneath her fingers as she put her arms around him, and he placed one hand over hers in a gesture of reassurance.

'Hold on tight,' David called over his shoulder, his voice muffled by the helmet. 'I don't want to lose you now.'

Christie nodded and tightened her grip.

David kicked back the stand and twisted the throttle in his hand. The Harley reared dangerously, spinning gravel beneath its wide rear wheel, as David eased the proud machine around Ben's Porsche, still slewed haphazardly in the centre of the drive.

Christie hugged herself forward against the comforting solidity of David's back, closing her mind down to everything but her reeling senses as she inhaled the freshness of newly turned earth and the scent of early irises that crowded the verge at the entrance to the drive. The earlier breeze had died down, leaving behind it a cool stillness, and the only sound she could hear apart from the throbbing of the motorbike was the hammering of her own heart. Moonlight gleamed on the trees and the empty

131

road, and the frantic dizziness of the party seemed a world away as they roared down the country lanes. David's warmth and closeness enveloped her as they sped along, her hair escaping from the helmet to be whipped by the wind as they carved through the night. It was as if they were the only two people left on an alien world, the first fingers of dawn pinking the grey night over the fields.

It was only then that Christie had realised she hadn't the faintest idea where they were going.

They rode along the deserted lanes for an hour, the silver night gradually dissolving under the soft pink hues of dawn. In that timeless moment of half-light before the break of day, David slowed the powerful machine and turned away from the road down a narrow track, half-hidden from view. He eased the Harley along the rutted path for five minutes, and finally drew to a halt beside a dilapidated five-bar gate at the edge of a field. He turned the engine off and the machine lapsed into silence. David kicked the stand down and dismounted. He turned to help Christie down, and the two of them drew off their helmets and laid them on the seat of the motorbike.

They stood side by side, not touching, gazing out across the field as the dew gleamed in the chill early morning light. Birdsong shivered the crisp air, and here and there Christie saw the long grass rustle with the movement of invisible creatures. Once a fieldmouse broke cover and scurried across a patch of furled dandelions. Gradually soft gold and intense orange striped the grey sky, and the breeze rippled the heads of the tall grasses, caressing the blue speedwells as they bent before it.

'I was born near here,' David whispered eventually. 'It soothes my soul like nothing else can, but it tears me apart too. It's like being shown something I can never have.'

He turned to gaze into Christie's emerald eyes, the trust

and warmth in them knifing his heart. 'I'm sorry,' he said softly. 'I shouldn't be here with you. There's nothing I can give you. I have nothing left to give.'

Christie watched the pale sunshine gilding his face, his rich brown hair glinting with auburn and chestnut highlights as the new day caught and played with it. His eyes shimmered with unspoken feelings and unsaid words. 'You have yourself,' she said.

'No,' David answered, turning away so that she saw only his strong back silhouetted against the early morning. 'Not any more. Not even that.'

Christie struggled to navigate her way around the unfamiliar landscape he represented. Everywhere she turned deep chasms yawned before her, as she searched for the words to soothe this man's unhappy, grieving soul without knowing why she did so. She knew only that she yearned to give something of herself to him, even whilst she realised that her feelings for him could destroy her own carefully husbanded independence.

Slowly, infinitely slowly, Christie eased herself into the space between his hard, warm body and the wooden gate where he rested one hand as he stared unseeingly across the dipping grasses to a valley in the distance. He looked down at her as she raised her face to his, and saw his own reflection in the opaque green depths of her eyes. Her dishevelled hair framed the smooth planes of her face, and her lips were slightly parted as she watched him intently. She leant upwards and forward, the gauzy crimson fabric of her blouse whispering against his shirt. With deliberate slowness she raised herself on tiptoe, and put one hand behind his head, her fingers grazing the soft downy hair on the nape of his neck. Christie felt him shiver at her touch, and he closed his eyes to shut out her image, desperately summoning the resolution to move away from the silken body in front of him.

133

Unwillingly he found himself crushing her between the gate and his chest. He knew what was happening, knew that he should not let it happen; knew, too, that he wanted it to happen more than anything else in the world.

Christie leant forwards and her lips touched his. He felt the softness of her mouth, and his teeth grazed her as he opened his lips against hers. He inhaled the scent of her hair as his arms reached around her, and her body yielded to his as she curled into him. Unable to hold himself back any longer, he gave himself to her kiss, tasting the champagne sweetness of her mouth on his tongue, feeling the gentleness of her face against his cheek. Unconsciously his left hand moved upwards and buried itself in the thick mass of her hair, holding her against him even as she held his head in her hand. His right hand found her left, and their fingers clasped. Slowly Christie opened her eyes, and they drew apart, gazing at each other wordlessly.

The moment ended, and both turned slowly back towards the road. Still holding her hand, David lead her to the Harley, and the two of them silently pulled their helmets back on and remounted the glistening machine.

It was after six o'clock by the time David dropped Christie off at her flat in Islington. The rest of the journey had been passed in companionable silence, neither needing to speak, as they drove quickly and surely into the still-sleeping city, the clink of milk-bottles replacing the soft soughing of the trees. Christie knew she would always remember every shadow, every fleeting expression, that passed across his face as he gently touched her cheek, then left without kissing her, without saying goodbye.

Angry at herself for letting him reach her, and angry at him for being able to breach her defences, Christie did not know whether to laugh or cry.

Mickey zoomed the camera in for a close up, his fingers working automatically as he pressed his eye even tighter against the padded viewfinder. Through it he could see the moisture on the child's pale face, the purple shadows beneath his eyes, the lines in his forehead etched by pain and incomprehension.

'Is it hard, being so brave?' Christie asked.

Patrick smiled at her as she hunkered down on the floor beside his bed, trying to put him at his ease. 'The nurses say I'm the best boy they've ever had,' he said with pride. He did not even glance towards the camera, disregarding its intrusion with the careless confidence of a seasoned veteran, pointing instead down the ward. 'But Lucy Miles is braver'n me,' he confided honestly. 'They chopped her leg off, and she didn't even cry.'

Christie was angry with her own weakness as her eyes pricked with tears. She looked away from the five-year-old boy in the bed, his slim hand lying trustingly in hers, trying to analyse the effect this story was having on her emotions. It was the first time she had ever had to deal with such a personal story so closely, and her own involvement terrified her. Christie had covered death and suffering in so many hideous forms as a war-correspondent, and whilst she had always cared, the world's tragedies had never managed to break through to touch her soul the way this tiny mite did. What had happened to her professional detachment? Why had this child stirred such feelings in her?

Behind her, she heard his mother stifle a sob and look away. Patrick glanced above Christie's head and smiled

135

reassuringly, an oddly adult expression on his young face.

'Mummy gets upset, you see,' he confided. 'So I have to look after her. Daddy went to heaven and there's only me left. But I'm big, so I can help now.'

Christie gave Patrick's hand a quick squeeze, thinking hopelessly how lost he looked in the vast hospital bed. The brightness of the coloured pictures painted around the children's ward seemed only to emphasize the fragility of its patients. She turned back to Mickey Beaumann, quietly shooting some covering shots with a careful precision that was at odds with his audacious grin and schoolboy humour. With professional expertise he completed a pan across from the child's I.V. line to the pile of toys jumbled on the foot of his bed.

'OK, Mickey, I think that's it,' she said, hoping he would not see her unshed tears. It was hard enough being a woman in the male-dominated world of television news, without reinforcing stereotypes. 'Let's do the two-shot, then a quick noddy, before we set up the interview with Jenny.'

Mickey gave her the thumbs up and lifted the heavy camera from the tripod. Christie unhooked the microphone clipped to her pale apple-green jacket, so that the wires would not trail in shot, and turned back to Patrick.

'OK, soldier, you know this bit, don't you,' she said, with a conspiratorial smile at the little boy.

'I mustn't say anything, and you talk to me about my breakfast,' Patrick replied enthusiastically.

Over the four weeks since Christie had begun the transplant series with Jenny Strand and her son, Patrick had grown used to the paraphernalia of television, accepting it as a natural part of the mysterious but infinitely fascinating adult world. Christie and Mickey had made him an honourary employee of INN, although perhaps honour wasn't the right word to use in the context of anything to do with Ben Wordsworth, Christie thought cynically. Mickey had let Patrick gaze enthralled through the viewfinder of his camera, and taught him how to zoom in and out, letting the child handle the controls himself – a privilege that had not even been granted to Christie. The lanky cameraman even got Security to make Patrick a laminated Press pass with a still picture of the little boy which he'd got Graphics to lift from an earlier interview. Before Patrick had been confined to bed, Christie had even taken him around the INN building, and he had been fascinated by the cameras, the studios, the pulsing excitement of the busy newsroom.

Christie started talking quietly, whilst behind her Mickey filmed the back of her head, and Patrick's studious expression. The twoshot would be used when Christie wanted to jump between different clips of Patrick's interview by inserting a question. It would form a bridge between two different parts of the sound bite without having to use a clumsy jump-cut, which was rather like letting the viewer see the magician's hand.

'So, you had Harvest Crunch with extra banana on the top, then five Marmite soldiers. Five soldiers! You won't fit in that bed soon.'

Patrick giggled, then clapped a dimpled hand over his mouth, his eyes wide with mischief.

Christie stood up and laughed. 'It's all right, you can talk now,' she said, reaching forward to unclip the other tiny microphone from Patrick's Mutant Ninja Turtle pyjamas. She felt the warmth of the tiny body as she did so, and longed to gather the child in her arms and imbue him with some of her health and strength. She wondered how much worse it must be for Jenny, standing stoically beside the window, gazing into the May sunshine and wondering if her son would ever see another spring.

'Right, pickle, you stay right there while I do. . .'

'The noddy!' Patrick shrieked for her, collapsing into more giggles. His dark eyes shone, and for once there were roses in his pale, clammy cheeks. 'And Big Ears, and Tessie Bear!' he added, rolling about on the bed. Christie could not help but respond to his infectious laughter as Patrick repeated their favourite joke. Only two people had ever made her laugh so spontaneously, with such *joie de vivre*. One of them was this child who was dying from kidney failure. The other was David.

Resolutely she clamped down on the memory of David's eyes as he had looked at her, the feel of his finger as he touched her cheek in a gesture full of longing and sadness, the scent of him as he leant forward as if to kiss her, before pulling away abruptly and disappearing into the early dawn. That had been a full three weeks ago, and she had not heard from him since.

She shook herself. Of course she had not heard from him. He was still in too much pain to be free to come to her.

'Move the chair a couple of feet back, could you, Christie, otherwise the light from the window casts a shadow across your face,' Mickey said, moving the camera round the bed and lining it up to focus on Christie, who sat down in the informal basket chair the hospital provided for children's visitors.

'That OK?'

Christie angled herself away from the bright patch of sunlight which fell on to the worn lino of the floor, and straightened her jacket. A slight breeze blew in through the two-inch gap at the bottom of the old, wooden frame, carrying with it the fragrance of cherry-blossom from the gnarled old tree outside.

'Perfect. Okeydoke, Patrick, no more giggles or Christie will get into trouble,' Mickey joked, winking broadly as Patrick bounced on the bed, rattling the IV tube against its frame.

Christie composed her face into seriousness, then tilted it to one side, nodding as if she was listening attentively to something that was being said to her. After a moment or two, she moved her head back the other way, pausing as if to get a particularly important piece of information. The noddy provided her with an alternative shot to use when she was gluing the interview together, and would look as if there had been two cameras during the shoot, one focused on Patrick, the other on her reaction to the interview.

'OK, we've got enough,' Mickey said, switching off the camera after he'd taped thirty seconds.

Swiftly he lifted the battery off the back of the camera, and searched for a new one in his equipment bag. The size of a paperback novel, and a good deal heavier, camera batteries only lasted for twenty minutes and were ardent devotees of Murphy's Law, always running out just when the shot of the year happened in front of you. Mickey had learned from bitter experience to keep a spare with him, rather than waste precious minutes running back to the crew car to get one and possibly missing an exclusive.

'Jenny, are you ready for the interview now?' Christie asked.

Patrick's mother turned from the window as Christie gently touched her shoulder. The expression on her face was one of weary resolution, her eyes tired, but undefeated. She smiled ruefully and smoothed the skirt of her only presentable outfit, a crumpled and dated dove-grey wool suit that was too heavy for the warm weather.

'As ready as I'll ever be,' Jenny said. 'Where do you want me?'

Christie turned to Mickey and lifted one eyebrow in question as he looked up from the camera eyepiece, his

139

gingery hair flopping forward over his eyes. 'Is there a sofa somewhere?' he asked consideringly. 'Make a bit of a contrast to all the hospital pictures.'

'Well, there's the day-room,' Jenny said doubtfully. 'You could use that, I suppose.'

'Sounds fine,' Mickey said. 'I'll just check it out, be back in a mo.'

Jenny leant against the chipped window-frame as Mickey sprinted out, and stared with apparent fascination at the peeling wood. She sighed, pressing her forehead against the cool pane, and Christie saw the infinite weariness in the unhappy slump of her shoulders.

'He's not going to live much longer,' she said, so softly Christie could barely catch the words.

'You can't say that, Jenny,' Christie whispered. 'You musn't ever think that. We can't give up hope now.'

'It's true,' Jenny said bleakly. 'I have to face it. I'm his only hope now. They wouldn't be taking my kidney if they thought there was any chance of finding another donor before . . . before it's too late. I just wish I was a closer match.'

Christie thought back over the past few weeks of disappointment and increasing desperation. When she had met Jenny and Patrick, her cool determination to do a thorough, professional job and give Ben Wordsworth the human drama and tragedy he wanted had been quickly overwhelmed by her own surprisingly strong emotions. Her angry resolve to get a good story and shoot some award-winning footage was replaced by a desire to actually help the child. Perhaps the publicity would help him jump the queue on the donor waiting list.

Christie's sense of fair play had evaporated; suddenly she did not care about the other patients still on the waiting list, only about Patrick.

There was nothing she could say to Jenny to comfort

her, she thought with frustration. How could you help a mother who was about to lose her only child? She had already lost her husband in a car crash two years after Patrick was born. How much more was one person expected to cope with?

As Christie climbed into the battered crew car at the end of Jenny's interview, she considered how petty her troubles ought to seem, when she compared them with the tribulations of the brave woman she had just left.

But somehow the thought did not help quell the mingled anger and dismay she felt whenever she thought of David.

■ INN, LONDON
12.45 p.m.

'Heads you fuck her, tails I do,' said Archie, grinning mischievously into Jimmy's eyes.

'You're the one with all the charm,' the cameraman replied mockingly. 'I dare you.'

'If you two don't make up your minds soon, it'll be too late,' Ollie retorted with some asperity. 'Someone's got to get her out of there, or we'll never hear what's going on.'

'Oh, all right then, but I shall expect a full report later,' Archie said, pocketing the coin and rolling his eyes heavenward. 'Why I get stuck with all the lousy jobs when it's your idea, I don't know.'

'That's easy,' said Janey, making all three men jump in alarm, materialising behind them as they hovered furtively outside the Editor's office. 'You're the only one silly enough to agree.'

Janey paused, suddenly noticing the conspiratorial atmosphere as they hugged the wall like second rate spies in a third rate movie. 'OK, what are you up to?' she asked.

141

'When a reporter, a cameraman and a News Editor get together, angels tremble and the saints close their eyes.'

'I thought I left you minding the Newsdesk?' Ollie asked with a feeble attempt at authority. The best form of defence was attack.

'Yeah, well, bloody Tommy has gone AWOL again, and his wife's in Reception looking for him. I thought I'd better warn him, though the two-timing bugger doesn't deserve it. I'd like to slap his face for him – both of them.'

Ollie scowled. 'Great. So no one's on Assignments, yet again. How the hell are we ever going to get any crews sent anywhere if Tommy's not there to send them?'

'You're not there either,' Janey observed accurately.

'Tommy's in the editing suite with Polly-Anna,' Archie hissed, motioning her away from the door with his hand. 'For Christ's sake, get to him before his wife does. Now go away, you're interrupting a very important mission.'

Janey threw her plump arms into the air in exasperation, a hundred bangles chiming on her arms and setting the three men into renewed nervous frenzy. They watched her make her way back to the lift, before looking carefully along both ways of the corridor as if auditioning for a remake of *Return of the Pink Panther*. Archie knocked on the door.

Ben's tight-lipped secretary looked up as Archie walked into the Editor's outer office, a ready-made expression of disapproval on the angular planes of her pallid face. When she saw Archie's impish grin her expression softened. He was one of her favourites; few women could resist the reporter's genuine charm, which was the essence of his success. Archie simply loved women, and they loved him loving them. One limpid gaze and a flash of the Tom Cruise smile, and most women melted. Lisa was no exception.

'Archie!' she said warmly, a pink blush suffusing her

142

cheeks and making her look almost attractive. 'What are you doing up here? Ben's busy at the moment, and I think he'll be quite a while.'

Archie smiled suggestively, and did not let his eyes leave hers. 'It wasn't Ben I came to see,' he said, perching on the edge of her desk, inches away from her.

Lisa dropped her eyes and started shuffling papers around her desk in delicious confusion. She stole a secret glance at Archie's leg swinging gently beside her, and glimpsed the undisguised bulge in his trousers, a surge of excitement flickering through her. She had spent so many sleepless and frustrated nights dreaming that Archie Michaels would notice her, whilst he had remained apparently oblivious to her charms. Now he was here, talking to her.

Archie hid a grin as he saw the tell-tale blush and quick, coy glance towards his crotch, and mentally continued undressing Christie Bradley in his head. Lisa thought this bloody incredible hard-on was for her? Jesus. Well, if he was going to complete Operation Decoy successfully, he'd better not disillusion her.

'I was wondering . . . fancy a coffee?' Archie suggested, allowing his eyes to linger just a little too long on Lisa's cleavage.

She twisted a gold chain at her neck with self-conscious embarrassment and nodded, obviously not trusting herself to speak. Archie deliberately let his eyes follow her as she rose, smoothing her unattractive mousy hair, and scrabbled out from behind her desk. His hand grazed her shoulder as he followed her down the corridor to the pantry, a ten-foot square, windowless room at the end of every floor.

Archie knew from experience that the door locked.

He watched Lisa's slim figure as she wiggled with nervous excitement towards the tiny room, and he noticed with amusement that almost every woman became attractive if you made her believe she was. Already Lisa's walk had a more confident lilt to it, and her eyes as she turned shyly back to him when she reached the door were full of unconscious sensuality. Her lips were parted and moist; her breathing shallow. He watched with interest as her small, pert breasts rose and fell beneath the insubstantial white cotton of her blouse. Perhaps this mission might be more pleasurable than he'd imagined.

As soon as they saw Lisa and Archie shut the door of the coffee pantry, Jimmy and Ollie whipped out of the cleaning cupboard and into the empty office. Through the imposing oak door leading to Ben's inner sanctum they could hear muffled voices, and quickly Jimmy reached across the desk and switched on the intercom.

Immediately they heard a buzz and Ben's impatient voice. 'Yes, Lisa?'

The two men froze. Over the open line they could hear a silence, then Ben's voice mutter, 'Oh, never mind.' Both men breathed a sigh of relief. Keeping a wary eye out for Lisa's return, Jimmy carefully perched on a filing cabinet near the corridor. Ollie took up his position outside Ben's door: it would be his job to bluff Ben for the few vital seconds it took Jimmy to switch off the intercom if the Editor should open the door unexpectedly. He fiddled with the volume control until they could both clearly hear the conversation taking place inside the office.

'How did you know about this?' Jimmy whispered to Ollie.

'Sssh! From the travel office. They had to fly Princer back from Rio when Ben decided to give him a going over. I asked around and got the gen; then Archie hacked into Ben's computer.' He nodded towards the main door. 'Check Lisa's still busy, then shut up and listen!'

Jimmy stood up and stuck his head out into the

144

corridor. From the direction of the coffee pantry he heard unmistakeable sighs and groans, then a little squeal of pleasure. Archie'd made it, as usual, lucky bugger. Jimmy was suddenly confused by the similar sounds coming from the opposite direction, until he remembered Polly-Anna and Assignments. Someone can't spell, he thought sardonically. They mean Assignations. Softly he shut the door and came back into the room.

'OK!' he whispered. 'All systems go!'

Ollie motioned to him to be quiet. Through the intercom they could hear the shuffle of papers and the squeak of seats being eased around nervous bottoms.

Inside the large, quiet office, Ben looked up from his glass desk and frowned at Peter Princer, who was sitting jauntily on the swivel chair opposite him. Behind him sat his Union representative, Chris Keele, stoically maintaining an expression of disbelief in the capitalist system of justice. Ranged against the wall on the far side of the office below the tinted glass window were the remaining press-ganged members of the kangaroo court. The newly-won BAFTA statue glowered down at them. Brian Reynolds, already sweating in the uncomfortable heat Ben maintained in his office, mopped his brow and looked out over the grimy rooftops. Fervently he hoped he would not have to take any part in the proceedings other than as a silent witness.

Next to Brian, the Head of Bureaux, Robin Fernly, scribbled down notes of the proceedings and prayed that no one would remember Peter Princer had been his choice as Latin America correspondent. He hated being responsible for all INN's foreign bureaux. It just meant he got bollocked in five different languages instead of one.

'Everybody happy?' Ben said grimly. No one was, but the question had not required an answer.

145

'Peter, this is the beginning of a disciplinary procedure after our inquiries discovered that you have been involved in the unauthorised sale of INN material to Brazil's Globo TV, and the private offering of material to an independent production company working for the World News Service.'

Robin struggled to get the words down as Ben spoke, wishing earnestly that they had been allowed to have a secretary present. He wasn't a bloody court stenographer, for Christ's sake, and his shorthand definitely wasn't short.

'On what basis do you make these allegations?' Chris Keele, the Union man, demanded belligerently. In his centre-stage seat, Peter remained silent, a mocking smile hovering just out of sight around his lips.

Ben ignored the interruption. 'I'll begin the procedure of summarising the results of our inquiry,' he said smoothly.

'On January thirty-first this year, you interviewed Fidel Castro in Havana. You offered that interview to the INN Foreign Desk, but Brian Reynolds, who was acting Foreign Editor that day, told you it wasn't wanted.'

Brian winced at the unspoken accusation, and a red stain spread across his gleaming head as he blushed furiously. Sam Hargrave, the Foreign Desk Editor, had been in Iraq overseeing the coverage of the Allied strike against Saddam Hussein that had accompanied the change of US Presidents, and Brian had been asked to stand-in for him on the Desk. Brian was a natural accountant: the newsroom joked that he'd been born with a calculator in his hand and made love to his wife by numbers. But Brian Reynolds was not a newsman. Live news coverage was not his forte, his definition of live including anything that had not been on his list at the 8.10 meeting in the morning. When he had received Peter's excited call about

Fidel Castro half-an-hour before the Early Evening News, he had told him it was too short notice for him to run it that day, and it would have to wait until later in the week. Brian liked his running order the way it already was, the stories mapped out and settled two hours ahead of transmission time, and saw no reason to change it to accommodate breaking news.

It had been a serious mistake, as Ben pointed out in no uncertain terms when he eventually saw the exclusive interview, by now hopelessly outdated and already syndicated around the world by rival networks. Brian knew he was on probation after the embarrassing faux pas, and he felt his underarms dampen at the thought. The most heinous crime in Ben Wordsworth's book was giving the opposition an inch. Brian had handed them a bloody yard.

Peter eyed Brian malevolently as Ben continued. 'The tape was then offered to Globo TV in Rio de Janeiro. They expressed interest and a tape was prepared by your multi-tech, Claudio Farago, containing the interview and some pictures of Cuban military manoeuvres. The tape was shipped from Cuba to Rio via WNS's office in Havana. It was collected in Rio by Globo who edited and transmitted it. They later sold the material to a number of networks around the world, including CNN and the BBC.'

Ben's eyes bored like gimlets into Peter's, the latter dropping his gaze and staring across the room. He became transfixed by the sight of Robin, who was shaking his aching hand in an agony of cramp. Ben turned and looked at his whimpering lackey, who was now blowing on his fingers like an inky-fingered schoolboy in the middle of an exam.

'Trouble keeping up, Robin?' he asked sardonically, raising one dark eyebrow.

147

Robin looked up fearfully, and hid the offending hand behind his back. 'No, no, nothing. Just a problem with my biro,' he apologised.

'Here, have my pen,' Peter said easily, opening his jacket and smoothly extracting a gold Parker. 'That should make it easier,' he added, calmly recrossing his legs and gazing expectantly across the desk at Ben. There was not even the slightest glimmer of concern on his tanned, mobile face. Looking at him, Brian envied him his sanguine expression. He wished for the hundredth time that Ben did not always insist on a witness for these ritual humiliations, and that if there had to be one, it could be anybody but him.

'If we can continue?' Ben asked into the tense silence, broken only by the sound of Robin's borrowed pen scratching as he desperately tried to keep up. 'Four weeks later, you invoiced Globo TV for the use of the material on INN's headed notepaper. You told them to pay ten thousand US dollars into the bank account of Peter Princer/INN.'

The Union man sat up as if feeling he ought at least make a token effort at protest at this juncture. 'I hope you have proof of all these allegations,' he said darkly, trying to convey a suggestion of serious repercussions should they be proved to be false. He failed.

'At no time had you any authority for this,' Ben stated calmly. 'You had not consulted INN in London in any way. With your experience, you would know that such deals would have to be done with agreement from London, because – for one thing – INN does not have a two-way affiliation with Globo TV.' Ben scowled. It was just the kind of scam he might have pulled himself in the early days, and he resented Princer's impudence all the more. 'Despite this you sent off the invoice, and were duly paid ten thousand dollars. INN have yet to see the money, but your wife is very happy with her new open-topped Mercedes.'

For the first time, Peter showed an interest in the proceedings. 'You have my accounts book,' he said calmly. 'It shows ten thousand dollars was to be credited to Claudio's company. We owed them the cash.'

'That's not what Farago says,' Ben flashed back. 'He says he's owed nothing. So why were they to receive ten thousand dollars? You have been caught with your hand in the washing powder, trying to launder the money through Farago.'

Peter was silent. Robin fervently hoped it would be one of those pregnant pauses which would give his shorthand time to get up to the washing powder. He was still on the wife's Mercedes.

'And now we get to the famous tape,' Ben said, with the air of a leopard moving in for the kill.

Ollie could not resist moving forward towards the intercom. Rumours about the Princer stitch-up had been passed around the building quicker than a choirboy in a monastery. He already knew that some double-crossing freelance in Rio with a major grudge against Princer had filmed him in the middle of an illicit deal. Being first with the real story would give Ollie unprecedented street-cred in the newsroom. There was only one thing more important than news at INN: gossip.

'The tape clearly shows you discussing the sale of a clip reel of INN pictures, for resale to WNS. You've seen the tape. Give me one good reason why I should not fire you now.'

Ben's voice was unremitting. He had paid lip-service to the idea of a fair hearing, and now he was taking the velvet gloves off.

Princer laughed uneasily. 'That tape was a wind-up,' he said unconvincingly. 'We were just playing along. Why else would we make the deal in broad daylight on a balcony with a good view from half a dozen windows?'

'Why indeed,' said Ben grimly. 'I don't fucking believe you, you double-crossing bastard. Oh, for fuck's sake, Robin, you don't have to write that down.'

Robin dropped his pen, leaving a large, spreading ink stain on the thick beige carpet. Surreptitiously he moved his left foot to cover it, fumbling around for the pen as quietly as possible.

Princer still maintained his air of unruffled calm. 'That reminds me, Ben,' he said nonchalantly. 'I meant to have a word with you. About the krugerrands.'

The silence in the office lasted so long Ollie bent forward and fiddled with the volume control. Suddenly he heard the scraping of chairs, and leapt back as if he had been scalded.

'They're coming out,' he hissed frantically. 'Leg it, Jimmy!'

The two men scuttled out of the office, only just reaching the sanctuary of the cleaning cupboard as the Union man opened Ben's office door and fled thankfully down the corridor, closely followed by a relieved Brian Reynolds. Robin stood hesitantly in the doorway.

'You definitely don't want me to write this down?' he asked nervously.

He was rewarded by an uncompromising glare, and hurriedly backed out of the office, swiftly followed by his notebook as Ben hurled it into the corridor. In the stuffy darkness of the cupboard, Jimmy eased his way around a mop handle threatening to do what no one else would dare. Ollie groaned as the cameraman's elbow found his jaw.

'What you doing down there, anyway?' Jimmy asked defensively.

'Watching through the keyhole, what does it look like?'

'You're not going back, for God's sake?'

'Don't you want to know how Princer's got the drop on our illustrious leader?' Ollie asked.

'Not really,' Jimmy muttered, but followed Ollie's large and dusty rear out of the cupboard. Suddenly Ollie went into reverse, and Jimmy found himself unceremoniously bundled back into the cupboard. Ollie held the door shut, his fingers trembling. Along the corridor they could hear the slam of Ben's oak door. Easing the door open a crack, Ollie saw Peter Princer sauntering casually towards the lift, whistling 'Dixie' tunelessly as he imagined a hundred and one different ways to disembowel the miserable sod who'd shopped him.

Abruptly, the cupboard door opened. The two men shut their eyes in a futile attempt to escape the humiliation and impossibility of explaining their position. Jimmy winced at the impending cliché of being caught in a broom-cupboard. Carry on Television. Oh God. He waited in an agony of embarrassment for the guffaw of laughter. He'd be a laughing stock in the crew room. He'd never make it with that stunning new piece in the Press Office. Ollie and his fucking bright ideas. Beside him the News Editor froze in the half-crouched position he had adopted when he shut the door. Humiliatior. was not new to him, but he'd never been caught with a man before. Shit! It'd be round the building in milliseconds. The silence terrified them as they imagined Ben Wordsworth staring down at them, but not knowing was worse. Quietly both men opened half an eye to see a bemused black face looking inquiringly but unsurprised at them.

'Sorry, Mo,' Ollie apologised sheepishly. 'Contact lens. Bugger to find. . .'

Jerry Tallboy glared as Sam Hargrave hurried into the meeting ten minutes late.

'This is a two-thirty meeting,' he said tightly.

'Sorry, Jerry,' Sam said unrepentantly. 'I was learning my lines.'

If the Producer noticed the sarcasm, he did not let it show. With an offended air he picked up the 14.30 running order and looked around the room. The News Update team doodled on their copies and tried to look interested and inspired, failing dismally. At the end of the table, the graphics designer assigned to the headlines grimaced as she perused the list. Only the weathergirl, Suki, looked fascinated by what Jerry was about to say, but then, she had to. She was his wife.

'Right, now we've got an extra five minutes on the four o'clock Update because the NewsMaker Interview segment ran short. It seems the Anti-Christ didn't have a lot to teach INN. That'll teach him to take on the experts.' Jerry's face did not show a flicker of a smile, but they all heard the lilt in his voice and grinned. Most of the Producer's deadpan comments were like this, and his team had learned to listen hard to detect which were the jokes.

'On the Jehovah's witness whose wife died when he refused to let her have a blood transfusion: Nick Makepiece has got an exclusive interview, which we managed to hold back from the Lunchtime show, but for Christ's sake don't tell them. This is its first airing, so I want to give it plenty, OK, Ginny?'

Ginny hid a smile, and nodded as she scrawled in the margin beside the story, slugged 'Jehovah.' She noticed 'Pope' was the next story, and wondered if they were turning into the Sunday God Slot.

'Serves him right, anyway,' Jerry added feelingly. 'Now he's got the kids to look after.'

Lynxie, the Graphics girl, looked up as Jerry prepared to move on to the next story. 'What do you want as a window?' she asked. 'A slide of the bloke, or something to do with blood?'

Jerry paused, considering the picture which would appear over the shoulder of the newscaster, like a window superimposed on the newsroom background.

'I'll come back to the windows later,' he decided after a moment. He glanced towards the assembled group of story producers. 'Now, Rich, at the moment I've got the Pope's illness as the second story, but if he pops off we'll have to go into Operation OpenEnder and drop everything else. I want you to find his obit, and dig out the Easter pictures from last month – the St Peter's Square address, his last meeting with the Archbishop of Canterbury, Catholic marches in Eastern Europe. . .'

'A sort of Pope-pourri?' Rich asked, a neutral expression on his face.

'I'll make the jokes around here,' Jerry answered with a quick grin. 'Talking of which. . .'

Charles Silversmith opened the door and made his entrance unhurriedly. Sam looked relieved that he was not the last one in. Jerry looked thunderous, but did not dare say anything. The newscaster was currently one of Ben's golden boys, and Jerry had no wish to tangle with the Editor after the Princer episode that morning, which had travelled around the newsroom faster than herpes.

Swiftly Jerry ran through the rest of the day's stories, allocating them amongst the three item producers who had been rostered on the News Updates that day. Each would be responsible for writing the lead-in to their stories, ensuring the reporters finished their packages on time, and checking all the necessary maps and graphics

153

had been ordered and – more importantly – completed by the somewhat unreliable graphics Department.

'OK, any questions?' Jerry asked when he had finished outlining the day's stories.

'Are we sure about the Colombia drugs story?' Rich asked, a frown on his face as he doodled in the margin of his running order. 'Do you want me to get it legalled by the lawyers?'

'Don't worry about being moral or legal,' Jerry replied carelessly. 'They're a long way away. Anyway, they're foreign.'

'How long do you want?' Rich asked. It was a ritual question. Jerry's answer never varied.

'I'll have to do some sums, but one minute fifteen sounds good,' Jerry answered. 'Just get cracking. We'll worry about the editorial content later.'

Sam looked up from his list of foreign stories, and wondered for the hundredth time why he bothered turning up at the meeting. 'Nothing to add from us,' he said. 'But just to let you know, we'll be able to feed direct out of Beirut from Monday. Our dish is up and running.'

'What will we have to feed?' Jerry asked incredulously.

'What does that matter?' Sam said, feelingly. 'Ben wanted live feed capability, and he's got it. Shame all the hostages are out now.'

Jerry sighed and stood up, leading the unenthusiastic shuffle out of the meeting room back to his desk. He leant across the News Update table and fiddled with the monitor until he picked up the outgoing signal from the building. The trouble with twenty-four hour news, he reflected, was that it was on twenty-four hours a day. Methodically he opened his desk drawer, and extracted a thick nubbly beige Marks and Spencer cardigan. Whatever the weather, which was a somewhat irrelevant consideration in the icy air-conditioned building, Jerry ritually put on the cardigan at three o'clock after the meeting. The rest of the newsroom set their watches by him.

Jerry sat down at his desk and looked around with a puzzled air. Suddenly a glow of enlightenment spread across his face.

'I knew there was something missing,' he said accusingly. 'Some bugger's nicked my keyboard.'

■ 5.20 p.m.

Christie walked wearily into the newsroom and slung her Billingham bag defeatedly into the chair next to her desk. Slowly she pulled out her own chair and sank into it, burying her head in her hands. The image of Patrick's face haunted her. She logged into her computer without enthusiasm, and immediately a message flashed up onto the screen. Christie returned Ollie's customary greeting, intrigued by his reference to krugerrands, and read the impatient summons from Ginny that followed it.

'Where do you want me to meet you?' she typed back.

Moments later, Ginny's return message appeared. Christie smiled and finished scanning the latest breaking stories on the wires, which included violent clashes in Israel's Gaza strip and a man charged with sodomising a cat on a moving tube-train. Wrestling with the mental images – the Central Line would never seem the same again – she stood up, and made her way back towards the lift. She headed for the canteen, which had been carefully situated two floors below the newsroom next to the atrium. That way the designers made sure everyone had the benefit of the noisome smells emanating from the kitchen. It had its blessings, however: it was never difficult to work out which days curry was on, and avoid them accordingly.

Ginny was already waiting at one of the pink tables, her face glowing with suppressed excitement. She pushed a cup of tea across at Christie, the brackish liquid slopping out into the saucer. Resignedly Christie poured the overflow back into the cup. You did not have to work long at INN before learning to take what you could get when you got it.

'Don't you ever wish life would give you a nice surprise?' Christie said mournfully as she tasted the tea.

Ginny grinned smugly.

Christie shook her head with a smile. 'Don't tell me, you and Nick are back together.'

Christie tried to sound impartial as she mentioned Nick's name, but it was difficult. She could not erase the image of Nick on the tennis court as he made love to Ginny's brother, Jack.

Christie had gone out of her way to avoid Nick since Ben's party. She was not bothered by his sexual preferences; but his deception of both Ginny and herself, and her own utter obliviousness to a vital part of his character, made her question her own perception. Suddenly everything they had shared was filmed with a patina of deceit. Christie felt as if her friendship had been tested and found wanting, and had spent several sleepless nights wondering if she had failed Nick.

'Much better than that,' Ginny answered, her dark eyes sparkling. 'I'm in love, really in love this time. Oh, Christie, he's so wonderful.'

Christie tried to look enthusiastic, but inwardly quailed. An opener like that always meant trouble with Ginny.

'OK, give me the gen.,' she said, rolling her eyes heavenward and mentally taking a deep breath.

Ginny looked surreptitiously over Christie's shoulder and nodded significantly. Christie turned round carefully, and saw Charles Silversmith carefully extracting an Earl Grey teabag from his briefcase, which he inserted pedantically into the cup of hot water in front of him. Ostentatiously he shot his cuffs, revealing gold cufflinks engraved with the crest of an Oxford college he had never even visited. Not a hair of his artfully greyed head was out of place. Fleetingly Christie wondered whether he maintained his groomed perfection in the sack.

'Oh Ginny, not Charles,' she said wearily. 'You know what he's like, he's had every PA in the building. You can't fall in love with him, please! I can't stand the strain, even if you can.'

'But he's not really like that,' Ginny said earnestly. 'He says it's never been like this with anyone else.'

Christie gave a sad laugh. 'Ginny, you've helped me pick up the pieces of half-a-dozen broken hearts in the Press Office. Are you crazy?'

'Of course.' Ginny looked troubled for a moment, then a dreamy smile of rememberance curved her lips. 'Christie, he knows exactly what a woman wants, and how to give it to her. I came four times last night, without even trying.'

Christie sighed. 'He should be good. He's had enough practise.'

Ginny laughed. 'Witch! Don't be so jealous. I don't think I ever had a multiple orgasm in a whole year with Nick.'

Christie winced, hating the invisible wall which had sprung up between them since she had seen Nick. However much she wanted to tell Ginny, she could not be responsible for destroying her image of both her brother and the man she had lived with for a year. But the unspoken words hovered between them, creating a barrier

157

which Christie could almost see. She sighed. It must be like this if you were unfaithful to your partner, even if they never found out. The wall of silence would separate you as much as the betrayal.

'But Ginny, he's married. Very. Happily. With two children. Off limits, Ginny. *Verboten.*'

Ginny looked crestfallen, but undeterred. 'OK, what about David?' she replied defiantly, trying to change the subject. 'Don't think I didn't see you racing off into the sunset with him after Ben's party.'

Christie laughed. '*Touché.*' She shook her head, unable to hide the chagrin in her voice. 'Not that anything happened.'

Ginny smiled. 'It will, it will.' She reached out and touched Christie's hand. 'You've just got to give him time, that's all. He's still terribly cut up about Sebastian. They were very close. They'd known each other for years, and always worked together. It was more than just losing a friend to David.'

'I know. But what about Caryn?'

'He feels he owes her, I suppose, because he was the last person to be with Seb, and maybe he feels responsible for her. But I don't think there's anything more to it than that.'

'Perhaps you're right,' Christie said doubtfully.

'Trust me.' Ginny gave a wicked grin. 'Hey, now I know why you're so jealous.'

'I give up,' Christie said, shaking her head. 'I'm going before you lead me astray.'

Christie left Ginny still making significant eye-contact with Charles, and returned to the newsroom. She slipped into the viewing booth, pushing her hair back away from her forehead. Maybe Ginny was right. Maybe she was jealous. However much -she tried, she couldn't erase David from her mind.

She sighed. He had obviously forgotten her. He had made that all too clear by his complete silence during the past three weeks.

She turned her mind back to Patrick. She had one more piece to cut, the last she would be doing before his operation, which was scheduled for the following Tuesday, in five days' time. As she slotted the first tape into the machine and twirled the control button to line it up, she wondered how Jenny Strand's preliminary tests had gone that morning. She picked up the telephone and punched the hospital's number.

She had no way of knowing that David was dialling her extension as she did so.

'I'm afraid her line's engaged, sir, can I take a message?' the girl on the switchboard said.

'No,' David said quietly, the overseas crackle distorting his voice. 'No message.'

Chapter Six

The pungent smell of cinnamon and cloves was overpowering.

Marina Mehdi paused for a moment, stopping to inhale the rich, exotic fragrance of the spice souk. This was her favourite part of the ancient market that was the hub of East Jerusalem. Large open sacks of spices, their rough hessian edges folded down the better to expose their harvest, bulged out into the already crowded streets, almost blocking the narrow passageways. She dipped her hand into a sack of saffron, running the bright crocus yellow powder through her fingers, watching it cling to them like pollen to a bee's wing. Ginger, ochre, oregano, turmeric; slowly she recited the names like a litany of forgotten treasures. She had been away too long.

A large Arab woman thrust her way past Marina, her black cloak flapping against the cool stone of the wall. She snapped one fat, brown stained hand under Marina's nose, cursing volubly, spittle visible on her squashed upper lip. Still muttering, she disappeared into the tumult of the crowd. Marina moved reluctantly away from the spice souk, and made her way down the close, crowded streets, the arched alleyways linking and relinking, always interconnected like a maze. She plunged down a narrow

160

cobbled passageway, the walls on either side leaning inwards, casting a slim shadow on one side. A riot of stalls clustered along the edges of the alley, their wares spread in brightly coloured disarray across rickety tables. Carpets covered the hot dusty pavements, and brass cooking utensils gleamed in the unrelenting sun. Olive-wood carvings were crowded together on a dingy blanket, hand-crafted mother-of-pearl objects thrust seemingly at random into their midst.

The rank smell of a thousand unwashed bodies mingled with the sickly sweet odour of the uncovered meat on display, haunches hanging on unclean hooks, quickly rotting in the intense heat. Rough sacks of countless vegetables and nuts jostled for prominence, rice and grain spilling out on to the cobbles to be trampled in the grime by countless passing slippered feet. Bangles glittered on every wrist, chickens squawked as they flitted beneath tables and around impatient legs, a choking dust rose and filled the air. Arab men, their heads wrapped around with the distinctive black- or red-and-white checked *keffiyehs*, thrust impatiently past flocks of women, whose *chadors* hid everything but their sallow faces and large, liquid brown eyes.

Marina stopped for a moment beside a stall displaying bales of dazzling material, turquoise threaded with gold, shocking pink stripes, orange and green discs. Raw silks and cheap bedouin goods were piled high on carpets smelling of goats. Slowly she fingered the black and silver gauze which had caught her attention, enjoying the sensuous feel of the material against her skin.

The wizened Arab woman behind the stall peered out from her crimson headscarf, the concealing material wrapped tightly around her face and neck. The beady eyes conveyed unspoken disapproval at Marina's blatant Western dress.

161

'How much?' Marina asked in Arabic.

'Three hundred shekels,' the woman grunted, exhibiting two blackened stumps instead of teeth.

Marina made to move away from the stall in disgust, hampered slightly by a fat woman bearing a basket of three-day-old chicks who stood beside her.

'To you, two hundred and seventy-five,' the woman countered.

'Two hundred and twenty, not a shekel more.'

'Two hundred and sixty.'

'Two hundred and forty.'

The woman paused, savouring the idiosyncratic pleasure of bartering. She despised the stupid Western tourists, who rarely bothered to quibble over any price she quoted. They just wanted to claim their souvenir of the dangers they had faced plunging into the unpredictable soup of the Arab market, and return triumphantly to their safe suburban homes, their prize consigned to some dusty corner. The few who contested her outrageous demands did so half-heartedly, and often walked away unaware that they were supposed to argue the ridiculous price down with her. It took all the fun out of it. This girl might be obscenely dressed, displaying her plump figure and friendly smile so that every man could see his fill, but at least she knew how to play the game.

'Two hundred and fifty, and you're robbing me blind. I'm a fool to myself, letting it go at such a price.'

Marina nodded, satisfied, and handed over the money as the old woman carefully wrapped the scarf, her gnarled arthritic hands surprisingly deft. She eased her way around the chicken woman, and thrust a path through the crowds gathered around a glittering display of gold rings, bracelets, necklaces, and earrings.

A familiar, half-forgotten aroma assailed her nostrils, and hungrily she stopped by an antique cart to buy a

162

falafel from the angry man slouching against it. Slowly she savoured the taste of the warm pitta bread, stuffed with a deep fried mush of chick-peas, cold chips, hoummos and salad. It was a taste she had been unable to recapture anywhere else in the world, a taste unique to the Arab quarter of Jerusalem. With a hidden grin she recalled the rumour that had swept through the occupied territories in 1987 at the start of the Palestinian uprising against the Israelis that became known as the Intifada. Determined to fight the Israelis anyway they could, it was said the rebellious young Palestinians had ejaculated into the hoummos as they stirred it for the hated Jewish enemy. Even if it was not true, she reflected, the mere idea had ruined the Israelis' favoured treat for them.

Marina licked her fingers, and quickened her step as she weaved her way through the crush of people gathering near the ancient Jaffa gate. It was nearing midday, and the marketplace was only open until lunchtime as part of the economic boycott of Israel, another facet of the Intifada which seemed to rule their days. In the years she had been away, the Palestinian struggle against those they saw as their oppressors had not diminished. The number of Israelis stabbed or stoned by the Palestinians had risen disturbingly in recent months, as had the bitter reprisals by the beleaguered Israeli security forces. This was a fight that bit deep into the soul of every man, woman and child who existed in the ancient lands of Palestine, Jews and Arabs alike. In this war, there was no such thing as a civilian. There was no such thing as mercy. There was no such thing as peace.

A border guard pinched Marina's arm roughly, and nodded his head for her to move on. She glanced at his uniform, disorientated for a brief moment, before remembering that Jerusalem was still officially a front-line. Border guards patrolled this area. Shaking herself free

163

from his grasp, she darted out into the road, colliding head-on with a handsome Western man climbing out of a taxi. Marina dropped her parcel in her confusion, suddenly dizzy at the intrusion of this cool European in the midst of the impassioned ferment she had just left. Conflicting images, past and present, jarred. As if sensing her turmoil, the man bent down and picked up her package for her, returning it with an engaging smile.

'*Shukran*,' she panted breathlessly, automatically reverting to the Arabic. It was in her blood, stripping away what had seemed such a deep layer of Western civilisation until now.

'*Ahlan wa sahlan*,' the man replied politely. He smiled in an understanding he could not possibly have, and nodded towards the taxi he had just vacated.

Marina shook her head, and instead swiftly ran to the other side of the road, where an Arab service taxi was waiting. Its Palestinian number plates distinguished it from the Israeli cars, which were rarely seen in the volatile Arab quarter for fear of stoning. The service taxis took up to a dozen passengers, dropping them off at destinations roughly along the same route, and despite their distinctive plates, were safe enough in Jewish areas. There was no way she could afford the luxury of an individual taxi. Marina spoke to the driver, then piled into the ramshackle vehicle. A heavily veiled woman climbed in beside her, plumping herself firmly down on the sticky, hot plastic seat. The driver slowly moved away, his horn blaring as a bevy of children surrounded the car, laughing and screaming raucously.

The taxi drew to a halt outside the entrance to the charity care organisation for the Palestinian population in Israel, the World Relief Agency for Palestine Refugees, WRAPR. Marina climbed out, silently cursing the Arab woman beside her who refused to budge, stolidly staring into space as Marina, puffing with exertion, eased her way around her. It was not the first time she had been on the receiving end of open hostility from the same Arabs she was trying to help, particularly from the women, and she was beginning to realise that simply by dressing in Western clothes she was deemed to have sold out to the Great Satan, America. She belonged to both sides, and to neither.

'*Marhaba*,' Mohammed grinned as Marina walked into her office. 'You look like you had a hard day.'

'Hello to you too,' Marina answered with mock-irritation. 'Some friend you are, calling me in on my day off.'

Mohammed sighed. 'What can I do?' he asked, lifting his shoulders. 'Someone has to go to Gaza, particularly with this latest incident. They know you, they trust you. We need you there, to calm the situation. Farouk would only inflame it.'

Marina shook her head ruefully at the mention of the WRAPR field assistant's name. Farouk was old enough to remember the 1967 invasion, when Israel had seized the initiative from a hostile but impotent Arab world, attacking Egypt and annexing the Gaza Strip and the West Bank territories in what became known as the Six Day War. In less than a hundred and fifty hours, Farouk's parents had become displaced refugees for the second time in a generation, part of half a million Arabs rendered homeless, caught in the middle of a war they did not understand, but which destroyed the very fabric of their lives. Again.

They had already run once, when the State of Israel had been created in 1948 by a world choked with guilt from the Holocaust and keen to deflect the Jewish problem far away from the doorstep of a weary, exhausted Europe. Now they were forced to run again. This time they had

165

settled in southern Lebanon, hoping that if they had to leave again, it would be to return home.

They did not have to run again. Instead, they died in Lebanon, refugees in an alien land, shot by their own people when they were caught in a random exchange of fire between Palestinian forces and the Israeli army, which had invaded Lebanon in 1982 in an attempt to defeat the PLO and end the deadly terrorist attacks that had claimed yet more lives.

Farouk had survived. So too had his bitter and lasting hatred for the Israelis whom he held responsible for his parents' deaths. He had returned to Israel, resolving to fight from the inside, and joined WRAPR to help those Palestinians who were determined to remain in lands they saw as their own despite the Israeli occupation of the territories. Farouk's corroding bitterness had not subsided. Mohammed was right; his presence in the Gaza refugee camp would only make the tense situation worse.

What Farouk had never comprehended was that the Israeli victors were just as much victims as the Arabs they defeated.

Driven to the brink of extinction by the Nazis, an unwanted problem to the Allies, the Jewish race had been and was still being forced to fight for its very survival in the midst of an Arab world that had vowed to annihilate it. The Holocaust had taught the Israelis one lesson, and they had learned it well.

Only the strongest survived.

'I only heard a little of the BBC World Service on the radio this morning,' Marina answered, picking up a sheaf of papers from her desk as she sat down. 'What's the latest?'

Mohammed shrugged as he leant across the overflowing filing cabinet, and pressed the television on. Nothing happened. With a curse, he leant around the dusty screen and rattled the back. A box file, so full it would not even close, fell off the shelf below the television. Automatically Marina knelt down and started piling the closely written pieces of paper back into the box. Along its spine, in felt-tip pen, were the words 'Schools Closed 1992–3'. She replaced it in its slot beside the dozen other box files that told their own story of the Palestinian Intifada. Collaborators. Incursions. Demolitions. Detained. Curfew. Casualties. The history of a people with nothing left but their collective memory. And it was long.

Suddenly the tiny screen flickered into life as Mohammed jammed a screwdriver into the plug socket. One skinny arm reached around to jiggle the tuning button as he fiddled with the screwdriver, and a snowy picture appeared out of the static. Marina recognised the INN ident burned into the bottom left-hand corner of the picture. A glossy woman of about twenty-seven filled the screen, a picture of the European Community flag over her right shoulder as she mouthed words soundlessly.

'. . . the meeting next week,' the woman said fluidly, as Mohammed found the volume, and returned to his seat to watch the rest of the broadcast.

A map of Israel and the occupied territories replaced the blue flag with its twelve gold stars, and the woman looked down at the pile of scripts on her desk. It was a cosmetic movement: every word she read was from the autocue in front of her, but by looking down she added an air of authority and immediacy.

'Four Palestinian youths and an Israeli soldier died today during a third successive day of rioting in Israel's occupied Gaza Strip. The fighting followed the stabbing of a fifteen-year-old Israeli girl on Monday by two Palestinian men. David Cameron has more.'

Abruptly the screen cut to a young boy of no more than sixteen, a stone grasped firmly in his right hand as he

167

prepared to throw it at a group of Israeli soldiers no more than one or two years older than he, carefully advancing down the dusty street. Marina recognised the tiny village of Dar el-Baran, where the WRAPR Health Clinic catered to the thousands of Palestinians crowded into the makeshift refugee camp. Numbed by the violence she watched unfolding before her, as a motley army of youths charged the weary, conscripted Israeli boy-soldiers, she barely listened to the deep, precise tones of the reporter as he described the scene. A barrage of tear-gas containers forced the surging teenagers back to the meagre shelter of the doorways near where the INN cameraman must have been filming, filling the screen with cloudy swirls of gas and angry, screaming faces running with tears, eyes scrunched up in pain.

'War veterans at five and six years old, these children are never too young to learn how to hate . . .' said the reporter, as the cameraman zoomed in on a child of about five, standing in the shelter of a doorway, a large stone clutched in his skinny hand. His mouth was screwed up in a grimace of anger and frustration generations old, and suddenly he lurched into the street, throwing his meagre weight behind his hand as he jerked his arm up and pitched the stone at an Israeli soldier. The rock was accurately aimed but fell far short. Transfixed by his own daring, the little boy stood motionless in the middle of the street. The boy-soldier heard the clatter as the stone fell and started in alarm, whipping round to face the direction from which the danger seemed to be threatening. Automatically the terrified young Israeli sprayed a rash of rubber bullets towards the child as he turned. The little boy was spun backwards and fell without a single cry.

Abruptly the reporter's face loomed in the screen. With a faint start Marina recognised him as the man she had bumped into as she left the Arab souk. He looked tired; his sleeveless safari jacket was dusty, the hand that clasped

168

a microphone bruised, one finger bearing the crimson line that bespoke his proximity to the fighting.

'Since its beginning in 1987, the Palestinian Intifada has become known in Arab circles as *atfal al-hadara* – Children of the Stones. It is aptly named, for in this brutal and bloody war, it is the teenagers and now even the children who are caught up in the hatred and end up paying its terrible price. David Cameron, INN, Gaza.'

Marina turned towards Mohammed, her eyes bright with anger and an ancient heartache. 'I think it's time I left,' she said, and turned off the television set.

■ 2.00 p.m.

During the long two-hour drive from the WRAPR office in Jerusalem to the Gaza Strip, Marina's thoughts returned again and again to the image of the child she had just seen, his face contorted with an all-consuming hatred. It was impossible to be Palestinian and not understand the tragedy of a people without homes, land, or rights, ignored and neglected by a world too busy feeling guilty about the Jews. Marina shook her head. Surely the Israelis, of all peoples in the world, should understand what it was to be persecuted? Yet now, still fighting for their survival, it was as if they pursued the Palestinians with the same relentless determination that had been shown to their race just fifty years before. Even knowing the Israelis had no choice, it was still hard to accept. The Jewish diaspora had simply been replaced by a Palestinian one.

Marina's own upbringing had been far from typical. Unusually for an Arab daughter, she had been allowed the freedom to wear whatever Western dress she chose, and to go out unaccompanied, although never with a man. Her father protected her from her three brothers' more conservative views, and insisted on giving her an education against the wishes of her mother, who was convinced that her daughter's chances of marriage had been ruined by it. Marina far outstripped her three brothers by the time she was sixteen, and at seventeen applied to the English University of Oxford, encouraged by her father, who was determined to see Marina succeed. She was quickly accepted on a scholarship, rewarding her college's confidence in her with a First in Law three years later.

It was her beloved father's death the previous Christmas that had caused her to throw up a promising career as a barrister at Lincoln's Inn to return to take care of her mother. WRAPR had been looking for a lawyer to defend the thousands of Palestinians accused of crimes against Israel, and in the six months she had been with them, Marina had experienced more fulfilment and more frustration than in the whole time she had spent in London.

Marina shook her head so that her dark curls bounced around her shoulders, and leant on one plump hand, the fingernails bitten down to the quicks, as she peered out of the car window. It had been a difficult decision, but once she had made up her mind to return to her country, she realised that it was the only decision she could have made.

Having experienced the freedom of the West, it had been even harder to accept that nothing had really changed for the Palestinian people with whom she identified even more strongly than before. She frowned. The West had gone to war for Kuwait when Iraq had invaded the small country in 1990, yet the UN Resolutions 242 and 338 demanding Israel's withdrawal from the Occupied Territories had been standing for decades, and the world shut its eyes, unwilling to enforce them. The Palestinians were literally a forgotten people.

Marina cleared her thoughts as the taxi arrived at Dar el-Baran. She was shocked to see everything exactly the same as it had been on her last visit. Somehow she had expected the violence to have left its indelible imprint on the crowded camp. She noticed there were new piles of rubble where the Israelis had demolished the homes of agitators whom they deemed security threats. They were barred from rebuilding on the site on pain of imprisonment. In a place as crowded as this, it was a doubly bitter blow. But there was little other sign of the riots which had filled the television screens for the last three days.

Marina climbed out of the WRAPR taxi, and told the driver to wait. She made her way around the piles of stones littering the narrow, unpaved dirt road, finding her way unerringly around the chaotic streets. Many of the homes were still the one-roomed concrete huts that had replaced the tents of those first refugees, fleeing in 1948. Additions required permits, almost impossible to obtain. Those householders who risked building an extra room to contain their overflowing families were liable to have the whole house demolished as a reprisal. Dark-eyed children peered up at Marina from the shelter of doorways, their clothes grey and torn, their faces smeared by dirt, food and tears. As they overcame their shyness, they emerged from the rubble, the doorsteps, the piles of rubbish that filled the streets, to throng around Marina, slipping shy hands into hers as they followed her.

Pursued by children, Marina walked down the cleared path towards the WRAPR health clinic, avoiding the open sewers which reeked of rotting meat and excrement. There were no drains; in the winter rains, the water just rose and flooded the entire area. She poked her head around the door and called out. A small man with tired eyes appeared from behind an inner door.

'*Marhaba*, Ahmed,' Marina smiled, disengaging herself from the tiny hands holding her skirts and shutting the door to the street behind her.

'*Marhaba, Marhaba,*' Ahmed replied, pulling a chair forward and settling himself behind the large veneered desk in the centre of the tiny room which served as his office. 'It is very good to see you again. You are well, I hope?'

Marina sat down on the metal upright chair. 'Very well, thank you. But you look tired, Ahmed. It has been a difficult week for you?'

Ahmed shrugged his shoulders expressively. 'It is always a difficult week for us. But one day things will change, *inshallah.*'

'*Inshallah,*' Marina murmured. For the Palestinians, everything was always in God's hands. What else was there?

Ahmed stood up again, and called through the door at the back of his office. Marina saw the piles of paper piled up on his desk, and once again felt sorry for the camp leader. To him fell the responsibility of overseeing the five thousand inhabitants of Dar el-Baran; he was the ombudsman, arbitrator, negotiator and general fall guy. It was to him everyone came with their problems, from imprisoned relatives to a shortage of nappies, expecting him to solve everything. It was an impossible mandate, one he could not hope to fulfil.

A young boy appeared in the doorway, bearing a tray with two glasses of hot, sweet tea, which he set down on the desk between Ahmed and Marina.

'*Shukran jezilan,*' Marina said in thanks.

'*Ahlan wa sahlan,*' the boy replied automatically.

Marina turned to Ahmed, who had placed a pair of wire-rimmed spectacles on his nose, the left arm wrapped around with sticky-tape to keep it in place. 'So, what do you have for me?' she asked.

Ahmed shuffled through a sheaf of papers. 'Every time, it gets more difficult,' he said. 'So few have permits to leave Gaza, and those who do cannot go now because of the curfew. There is no work here, so they have nothing to do and no money. Tempers rise, anger erupts. What can I do?'

Marina nodded in silent understanding. Every Palestinian had an identity card, without which it was impossible to leave the Occupied Territories to find work in Israel. The West Bankers and Gazans had orange or pink ones; those in Jerusalem had blue. But anyone who had ever been imprisoned or even arrested for 'security offences' – which might mean being in the wrong place at the wrong time when there was a security sweep – forfeited the right to hold an ordinary ID card. Instead they were given green ones, which meant they could not leave their own areas. If they were subsequently arrested or stopped, and the Israelis saw the green ID card, they were liable to get beaten up and re-imprisoned. Much of Marina's casework was taken up by green card holders. That card was the death knell to hope: holding such a card meant there would be no travel permit, no travel permit meant no work, for there were no jobs in the Occupied Territories. No work meant no money, no life, no hope.

Part of the problem of unemployment was of their own making. The Palestinian uprising in 1987, the beginning of the Intifada, had aggravated the situation. As part of their protest, many Palestinians had stopped working in Israel. Over the last two years, however, gradually they had been forced to return to work. They had no choice: it was either that or starve. But as Eastern Europe collapsed, the influx of Russian and European Jews to Israel meant there were now even fewer jobs available for Palestinians anyway.

Every time there was a security incident, the Israelis slapped a curfew on the camps, preventing anyone from entering or leaving. The inhabitants, cooped up, angry, expressed their frustration in the only way left to them: violence.

'So many of our people are so young, and so angry,' Ahmed said, pushing his spectacles up his nose. 'They have known no other life but this, and they are frustrated, desperate. Sixty per cent of the people here in Dar el-Baran are under fourteen. Sixty per cent! No wonder the Jews are so afraid of us. We are a time-bomb ticking away in their own back room. I almost pity them.'

A knock at the outside door disturbed Marina's depressed thoughts. Three young men filed silently through the door, murmuring greetings to Marina, and sitting quietly on the group of chairs lined up against the wall for just this purpose. Marina was used to such arrivals; with nothing else to do, to these youths her presence was an event of note, and inevitably attracted attention.

'We are growing so fast,' Ahmed continued, almost to himself. 'Twenty years ago, we were twenty per cent less. Every year there are more of us, and the new generation will be stronger.'

'Stronger?' Marina queried.

Ahmed nodded, a timeless patience in his tired eyes. 'Empires rise and fall,' he said. 'Rome, Greece, the British Empire. No-one thought the Soviet Union would fall, but look now. We can wait, we are a patient people. We wait. Then things will change.'

One of the boys sitting smoking at the back of the room pulled his chair forward, leaning his elbows on his knees. 'Our children are our weapon!' he declared, the light of fanaticism in his eyes. 'We will fight by growing more, growing faster, having more children. We will outnumber the Jews, and then, we will take back our land.'

It was the weapon the Israelis feared the most, the reason they summoned Jews from all over the world to return to the Promised Land. They did not dare to give the Palestinians room to expand. The average Palestinian family had seven children, but some Moslem families were as many as twenty strong. The cost was high, but the Palestinians were prepared to pay it.

Marina stood up. 'It is time I saw the clinic,' she said. 'I will be back soon, Ahmed.'

'*Inshallah*,' he returned, standing and courteously opening the connecting door to the health clinic. '*Ma salema.*'

'Goodbye, *ma salema*,' she answered.

The health clinic was dilapidated but clean. A spartan mother-and-baby unit held four iron beds, and an ancient but still functioning pair of baby scales. Faded posters sellotaped to the walls proclaimed the benefits of breast feeding, and offered advice on inoculations, purifying water and vitamin supplements. A perspex partition separated the unit from the plastic desk and battered filing cabinet that served as a Family Planning office. As usual, it was unoccupied. The older generation and the less educated were reluctant to use birth control, which some believed was against the teachings of Islam. The younger generation, who might be more open to the idea, generally sided with the view of the young man in Ahmed's office. Children were their weapon, the more, the better. It was ironic: birth control was the only area of the health clinic funded by the Israelis, and the only area undersubscribed.

A connecting door from the mother-and-baby unit led into a badly lit corridor, greenish paint peeling from the walls, the grime of decades ground into the floor. At the end it opened into a wide area, with half a dozen cubicles containing beds, curtained off with material that had once been pink and white, and was now a uniform grey. This was the casualty area, quiet now, but the evidence of its recent use was clear in the pile of bloodstained sheets and bandages in a corner, awaiting cleaning. It had once been the infectious diseases unit, before the Intifada. Since then

175

it had been kept busy with stabbings, bullet wounds, ribs and skulls broken from beatings.

A nurse came out of the doctor's office, which was next to the Casualty ward. She smiled when she saw Marina, and motioned for her to come inside.

'Marina, it has been a while since you visited us,' she said. 'We have been busy, but – praise Allah! – it is quiet now.'

Marina looked around the barren room, with its bare desk and half-empty bookcase. In one corner was a brand new cabinet, a heavy padlock linking two ends of a strong chain fastened around it. The nurse noticed her look of surprise.

'Our new drugs cabinet,' she said, with a note of pride in her voice. 'Doctor Joseph brought them with him. You haven't met Doctor Joseph, have you? He joined us three years ago, but spends a lot of his time on his rounds at the other camps.'

'No, I haven't, although I have heard a lot about him,' Marina answered, perching herself casually on the desk. 'Tell me, Afnan, why are there so few in the baby unit? Usually it's full at this time of day.'

Afnan shrugged. 'Maybe they are finally seeing the sense of our point of view,' she said. 'They have trouble feeding the children they do have, without having more mouths. We have had very few infants recently, now that I think about it.'

Marina frowned. After what she had just heard, she was surprised. 'Do you have any figures?' she asked, intrigued.

'Not for Dar el-Baran alone,' the nurse replied. 'But I can give you the total figures for the district, which is made up of around ten camps roughly the same size as this one.' She crossed to the bookshelf, and pulled down a black ring-file. Opening it on the desk, she ran her finger down a list of entries, until she came to the one she was looking for. 'There you are,' she said with satisfaction. 'The total populations for this area going back to the end of 1987, and the birth-rate. Which do you want?'

Marina thought for a moment. 'What's the current population?'

'Well, we only have the figures for last year, ending in December 1992. But then it was just over sixty thousand – 61,649, to be exact.'

'And what was it at the end of 1987?' Marina asked, scribbling down the figures in her notebook.

'52,678,' the nurse answered after a pause.

Marina did some swift calculations, her sharp lawyer's brain adding the figures rapidly. 'That's an overall increase of seventeen per cent in five years!' she said, astonished. 'No wonder the Israelis are alarmed. Ahmed is right. They have a demographic time-bomb ticking away beneath them.'

The nurse nodded, not understanding, but glad she had pleased Marina. 'Do you want the birth-rate as well?' she asked, eager to capitalise on her success.

'Just read me the figures, and I'll write them down,' Marina said, not sure where all this was leading, but some instinct telling her to pursue it.

'During 1988 – 2,099. In 1989 – 2,191. For 1990 – 2,279. You do realise this is the total number of births, don't you? Some of these infants were stillborn, or died very young.'

Marina nodded, and the nurse continued. '1991 – 1,185. And the latest figures we have, for 1992, 1,208.'

Marina paused in her scribbling, and stared at the figures. 'Up until 1991, the rate was around two thousand or so,' she said in puzzlement. 'Then suddenly it's cut to almost half. What could possibly cause that?'

Afnan shrugged, uninterested. 'Not enough money, the

177

new tax on each child,' she suggested. 'Why don't you ask Doctor Joseph? He will be in later on for the girls' inoculations. You could speak to him then.'

Marina closed her notebook, still perplexed. Something, somewhere, was teasing the edge of her mind, but as yet she was barely conscious of it. Perhaps a talk with Doctor Joseph . . .

Suddenly she heard a shout from outside, and the unmistakable sound of a gun recoil. The nurse shrank behind the desk, but Marina dived through the open doorway into the corridor, hugging the wall to avoid the windows. In the street outside she could hear shouts and screams, and the noise of running feet. Ahmed appeared in the passageway, and shouted for her to get down.

'What's happening?' she cried.

'The security forces came again to demolish the agitators' houses. They are doing it on purpose, to stir up trouble. Well, now they have it. We will be very busy soon. You'll have to stay, you cannot go out now.'

Marina crouched down below a window, peering cautiously through the grimy glass. Part of the broken pane was missing, and through the gap she could see the same scenes she had witnessed on the television before coming out here. She had seen it too often to be afraid, but Ahmed was right. The Casualty department would soon be very busy. There was no way she could leave now.

■ ROME, ITALY
11 June, 7.20 p.m.

David Cameron carefully fastened his bow tie in the mirror, trying to follow the workings of his fingers back to front. He was never sure which was more difficult: using the mirror or just feeling his way around the

178

material. Caryn was always trying to get him to use the selection of different coloured ready-made ties she had bought him, but stubbornly he stuck to his Gieves and Hawkes navy-blue silk.

As he finished the complicated manoeuvre he leant forward to peer at his reflection more closely, touching the purpling bruise on his cheek gingerly with one finger. He winced as he felt the swelling of the tender flesh. He had not seen that stone coming, and the blow had caught him by surprise. He had thought for a brief moment that he had been shot, then realised that if that was the case, he would not have been feeling the excruciating pain that now reverberated through his cheekbone. He would not have been feeling anything.

Carefully David worked his topaz cufflinks into the sleeves of his crisp silk shirt, automatically following an unwritten ritual with the same measured precision he brought to everything he did. First the shirt studs, then the bow tie, then the cufflinks. By eliminating chance, acting by rote, it was as if he could obliterate any thoughts that things might be done a different way, that he could live a different life. He was like a dictator to himself, denying his oppressed people the freedom to think, or the opportunity to be individual, so that rebellion would be unthinkable.

David sat down on the edge of the bed, and eased his foot into the stiff patent leather shoes he always wore with his evening dress. As he squinted down to tie the laces, he noticed with detachment that his left eye was already swelling shut, giving him a narrow field of vision like an old film that did not quite fit the television screen.

It was his own fault. He should not have got so close to the fighting, but as always, it had been the only way to capture the violence, the raw immediacy that pulled viewers into the screen and gave his stories the vivid edge

179

that those of lesser journalists lacked. It had almost cost him his life on more than one occasion. Twice he had been hit by stray bullets, and once he had been just a pace behind a WNS cameraman who stepped on a mine in the Falkland Islands.

And of course, there had been Seb.

David jumped as Caryn's voice shattered his contemplative silence, and quickly he bent down and finished tying his laces. Too many battles, he thought wryly, every noise was beginning to sound like a shot. God knows what he'd be like on Guy Fawkes Night.

Caryn appeared in the doorway wearing an exquisite Dolce & Gabbana crimson suit that showed off her slim figure to perfection.

'They'll be here in a minute,' she said tartly. 'It would be nice if you were actually there to greet our guests for once.'

David stood up and smoothed his trousers. 'You look nice,' he said peaceably.

Caryn smiled distantly and moved across the room to the mirrored wardrobe. She surveyed her reflection critically as she lifted her arms and teased her formation curls into a more precise alignment, then smoothed the front and back of her skirt with satisfied hands. The liposuction and intensive body massage seemed to have worked. She smiled and glanced back at David.

'You look a bloody mess,' she said coolly, meeting his eyes in the mirror as she saw his reflection behind her. 'Can't you clean yourself up a bit?'

For once David's patience snapped. 'I would have thought you'd like it,' he said angrily. 'You usually enjoy parading me around for your friends, the famous war correspondent. Well, now I've got the battle scars to prove it.'

Caryn spun round in shock. Before she had time to

reply, the downstairs doorbell pealed. Without another word, she left the bedroom, the heels of her David Shilton court shoes clicking across the marble floor as she made her way down the stairs. David heard her voice greeting the first guests brightly; her tinkling laugh rang out as she escorted her visitors to the outside patio. He groaned. He should not have said that to her. Damn.

'That's the best part about living in Frascati,' David heard her say as her voice came through the open window. 'I so love to entertain in the open, it makes it so much more casual, don't you think?'

David ran his hand despairingly through his hair. He understood Caryn's need to bury her loneliness and grief in a swirl of activity, but right now it was almost more than he could bear. The exhausting struggle in Gaza had left his soul battered by the brutal deaths he had witnessed. After days of foot-slogging backwards and forwards to the Palestinian territories to recount the daily toll of violence, death and maiming for the viewers back home, all he wanted when he finally returned to his home was a stiff drink and some peace and quiet.

Instead of the rest he had envisaged, he had been met with a guest list that topped fifty.

'Why the hell didn't you tell me you were having a party?' he had raged, as Caryn screamed at him to get into his evening dress before everyone arrived.

'You're never bloody here to tell!' she shouted back, angrily storming outside to check on the caterers.

He had gazed in disbelief at the rows and rows of gilt chairs and tables that lined the patio, at the four waiters busily engaged in setting the tables with sparkling cutlery and gleaming crystal glasses on the stiff Irish linen table-cloths. Monogrammed linen napkins were next to every place setting, and each guest had a tiny wrapped box in the centre of their sideplates. Miniature bottles of Chanel for the women, opal cufflinks for the men.

David buried his head in his hands in despair.

■ 11.20 p.m.

'It's just too annoying, everything completely shuts down on Friday . . .'

'Have you tried Sicily yet? Magnificent beaches . . .'

'Oh, but you *can* buy Marmite now, though it's terribly expensive . . .'

'Have you seen Pamela's new toyboy yet? *Awfully* dishy, I don't know how she does it . . .'

David let the vapid conversation flow around him as he mingled distractedly amongst the guests. He knew no one, although he recognised many of the faces from countless such parties. Diplomats and their wives, ex-patriots, UN advisors, Embassy staff. Caryn had made a career of her social gatherings since she had been living with him. David sighed. He could not complain. She saw him for less than two months of the year. She had to find something to fill the endless lonely hours, since the nanny, the maid and the gardener robbed her of all other purpose in her life. He wondered if it was enough for her.

Suddenly memories of Christie's soothing voice and the heat of her lips as she kissed him flooded his mind.

Almost without realising it, David found himself heading for the stairs which led down to his office in the basement. The underground room was his bunker, his sanctuary, the one place that Caryn never wanted to visit. She said it reminded her too much of Seb.

Quietly he let himself into the room, and sank into the chair behind his desk. He leaned his head back against the rest, and closed his eyes. His cheek was throbbing painfully, and he had not realised how stiff he was until he sat down and relaxed. It was the first moment he had had to himself for almost a week.

David opened his eyes again and let them roam around the room. Shelves ran down the two long walls of the 'L'-shaped office, filled with video cassettes, reference books and files. A plastic blackboard with important telephone numbers scrawled on it in felt-tip pen half-filled the wall opposite his desk, and beside it was a faded map of the Middle-East. His treasured model plane, the Nikko SkyAce that he had discussed with Christie, was balanced on its nose on the shelf above his video cassettes. He ran his finger along its daffodil-yellow side with a sad smile.

On the remaining wall, to the right of his desk, was the television, its greenish-grey screen silent, and beneath it was his trophy shelf. Slowly he eased himself out of the leather chair and walked across to it. A wooden model of a Scud missile with 'INN – Baghdad 1991' written on it. A black ceramic plate with the words 'Thank you sir always thanking' picked out in pink letters by the Palestinian refugee he had reunited with his family. A tank shell fragment from the '82 Israeli invasion of Lebanon. A 23mm anti-aircraft shell-case from the civil war in Chad a year later. The two bullets that had been cut out of him in Lebanon and Kurdistan. An Argentine bayonet and a scrap of rubble from Port Stanley that he had picked up in the last days of the Falklands War. He smiled as he remembered the ITN reporter who had tried to smuggle out an Argentine automatic assault rifle in tripod box, only to have it confiscated at Heathrow. Boys' things, all of them, souvenirs of his life. In the middle was a defused hand-grenade, and thoughtfully he picked it up, feeling the weight in his hand, the cold, hard surface. He had seen this in a military curio shop window in Islington, the morning he drove back after dropping Christie off at her flat.

Suddenly moving with a strength of purpose, David crossed swiftly to his desk, shoving aside the pile of expenses forms and memos that littered the surface, to reach for the telephone. Swiftly he dialled the number he knew by heart and waited, his heart pounding. The phone rang three times, then he heard a soft click as it was answered.

'Hi, this is Christie. I'm afraid I can't come to the phone right now, but if you'd like to leave your name and number, I'll get back to you as soon as I can.'

David slowly replaced the receiver without leaving a message, defeat swamping him and sapping his will. He found it difficult to believe how much he needed her, how hard the last weeks had been since he saw her, always longing to call her, but afraid of the implications if he did.

His guilt had not diminished. But slowly, a small part of him that he thought had died forever had begun to reawaken under Christie's touch. Twice he had given in to temptation and called her. Both times he had failed to find her.

His loneliness overwhelmed him. Still clutching the grenade in his left hand, he put his head on his desk and slept.

It could have been half an hour later, it could have been three hours, David had no way of knowing. When the telephone finally broke his exhausted sleep, he raised his head and reached towards it slowly, a futile hope glimmering. He picked it up, dreading the voice that might not be Christie's. As he heard Sam Hargrave's strong, deep tones he had to quell the miserable ache that flooded through his soul.

'David, you did bloody well with that last piece from Gaza,' the Foreign Editor said, genuine admiration tinging his voice. 'It made the Early Evening News, and we've been running a shortened version on the hourly

184

News Updates. You've had a sodding hard week, and you've given us some sterling stuff.'

David recognised a 'But' when he heard one.

'OK, Sam, give it to me,' he said wearily. He glanced at the clock above the door. Half-past midnight in London, which was an hour behind. Sam hadn't rung to exchange recipes.

'I hate to do this to you,' Sam began, inwardly cursing the logistics that made David the only man for the job, and him the one who had to tell him. He knew what it would do to David. 'Have you been listening to the World Service?'

Yeah, David thought disbelievingly, in between ducking stones and getting shot at, I had plenty of time. But all he said was a quiet, 'Not for a few hours.'

'Are you up to speed on Yugo?' Sam asked, flipping through the wires he had printed off in preparation for this phone call. He glanced around the empty newsroom, wondering where the hell everyone had got to. He had rung the Newsflash Standby team, the group of journalists assigned to cover emergency stories overnight, as soon as the story had broken, but so far he was on his own. Par for the course.

David flinched as he was catapulted back to his last visit to Yugoslavia. The story from which Seb had not returned. Jagged images filled his mind: the last time he had seen his best friend that terrible day, the bombed church, his own hands torn and bleeding as he scrabbled to find the cameraman, buried beneath the rubble. Oh God, if only Seb had received his warning to stay away that day . . . if only he had been able to reach him . . .

David shuddered. He had not been back there since, but he had known this moment would come. He forced himself to concentrate on the present, banishing the memories from his mind.

He had deliberately avoided the subject of Yugoslavia, but it was impossible to be in the news business without learning a little about a lot of things. Ever since the fighting broke out – God, it must be two years ago now – the whole Balkan region had been a bomb ready to explode. Every region was demanding autonomy from what it saw as its oppressors: the Serbs from Croatia, Armenians in Azerbaijan, the Albanians from Macedonia, the Croats, Serbs and Moslems from Bosnia Herzegovina.

'Not exactly across the story, but I get the gist,' he replied warily. His aches were forgotten as he pulled a pad of paper towards him and scrabbled in his desk drawer for a pen. Above him he could hear the thump of music as the stereo blasted out a distorted version of Tom Jones's 'Kiss'.

'It looks like Albania has just gone bang,' Sam said, unable to keep the newsman's excitement from his voice as he sank his teeth into a good story. 'It seems they've had enough. As of midnight, they've declared war on the Yugoslav province of Kosovo, which is three-quarters Albanian, and Macedonia, which is around a fifth Albs, or whatever you call them.'

David jotted the figures down absently. 'I thought Kosovo was under Serbian control,' he said. 'Why pick a fight with them?'

'Don't ask me,' Sam answered, shrugging his shoulders to the telephone. 'All I know is, the whole thing could go up like a tinderbox. The Government has already warned all correspondents and film crews, as well as the relief agencies, to get the hell out. I don't have to tell you that it's going to be bloody dangerous.'

'Sounds like a great place for a holiday,' David answered with grim humour. 'How am I getting there?'

'There's only one way in,' Sam said, poring over a map. 'Get yourself over here to London, and we'll meet you at

186

Heathrow with fifty thousand dollars and a flak jacket, plus Fabian Broak, who's your cameraman, and Steve Bower, your editor. You'll be on a plane to Athens, and then it's a long drive to the party, I'm afraid.'

David smiled. 'Bring a bottle,' he said.

'Only if it's a Molotov,' the other man grinned back down the phone.

Neither seemed to notice that there had been no question of whether David would agree to put his life in jeopardy for a few minutes of tape footage. It was the most dangerous war in television history, simply because there were no rules, no limits.

One American producer and a score of Yugoslavian journalists had already died in the bloody slaughterhouse the country had become. An ITN correspondent, David Chater, had almost lost his life when he caught a stray bullet as he sheltered in a church the previous year. As it was, he had one kidney and several feet of intestine removed by the high velocity bullet. A CNN camerawoman, Margaret Moth, had had half her face blown away by a sniper, and faced years of extensive plastic surgery. Red Cross workers had been blown up, UN helicopters shot down.

And Seb had died there.

For a moment David wondered why he kept on doing a job like this, when there were so many safer and more comfortable things he could be doing for double the money, like alligator wrestling or free-fall parachuting. He suppressed the thought that it might be because he had precious little left to live for.

'OK, I'll get going,' David said crisply. 'Can you get me a satellite phone, or I might as well give up and go home.'

'Yeah, already thought of that,' Sam replied. A satt phone was a lifeline in war-torn areas such as this where there were no telephone lines of any reliability. The size of a small suitcase, it could be assembled anywhere, relying on a signal from two satellites circling the earth miles above which was received by a metre wide collapsible dish. 'We can talk logistics at Heathrow – I'll be there to meet you. Alyssa has booked you on an 06.30 flight from Rome, that's five hours from now, so I'd better let you go.'

'It'll take me that long to get through the Italian security checks,' David said feelingly.

'Oh, just one more thing, nearly forgot,' Sam added. 'We think this is going to be a hell of a story, and you're going to have your hands pretty full. We're sending you someone else to act as a second reporter, or producer if it's necessary to run some tapes out.'

'You mean you've managed to find another mug crazy enough to risk getting his balls shot off?' David said, laughing.

'You wouldn't say that if you saw her,' Sam answered, unsuccessfully trying to hide his amusement. 'We're sending you with Christie Bradley.'

Chapter Seven

Ben Wordsworth slammed the newspaper down on his desk, catching the edge of his coffee cup in his anger. The fragile china fell against the glass surface, shattering and spilling the cold dregs of his cappuccino, which slowly oozed across the newsprint that had caused his rage. The front-page photograph of Paragon's tits as she emerged soaking and half-undressed from his pool filled his vision. Why the hell had the bloody paper waited until now to print the damned picture?

He knew the answer even before he finished framing the question in his mind. Because six weeks ago, when his ill-fated party had taken place, Paragon had been a nobody, in the minds of the viewing public at least. The snapper who had grabbed her picture had done so on the off-chance, and it had paid off. Now she was a star, co-anchoring the Early Evening News three times a week, and her tits were good copy. Damn!

Ben hoped the publicity would not upset any of the deals he was currently involved in. It was a delicate situation, not helped by having one of his top newscasters plastered across a rag like the *Daily Ethic*. He did not waste any time cursing the paper for taking advantage of a gift handed to them on a plate. In their place he

189

would have done exactly the same.

With a grin he recalled his first mentor's decision some years ago to go ahead with an 'Is-it-or-isn't-it?' picture of Princess Di's nipple when a long lens had captured her in a bikini on a beach somewhere – Barbados, was it? No, the Bahamas, an island with a girl's name . . . Eleuthera, that was it. She had been lying on her stomach with her bikini top undone, so that she wouldn't get a white stripe across her back, he supposed. A boat-load of photographers half a mile offshore were trying not to fall in the water as they focused their lenses on her in the hope of an exclusive. As she turned over, she wasn't quite quick enough with the bikini, and there was a tantalizing glimpse – or was it? – of Royal nipple. Ben's colleague had paid a cool fifty grand for the negatives one of the bunch of snappers had managed to collect, and lead his Evening News show with the picture. Just in case the slow-witted viewers hadn't seen the area of interest, he had got Graphics to draw a circle around the breast in question. Ben had been his biggest fan ever since.

Ben just hoped the Japs would not pull out now. He was beginning to feel like a medieval juggler, trying to keep a dozen balls in the air at once, and he was under no illusion that two of them were his. He was within an ace of pulling off the biggest coup in television history, and making every other news station look like provincial cat-up-a-tree locals. If he fucked it up now, that was it, end of story, pension and golf time.

There were three sets of people he had to keep happy, Ben ruminated morosely: the advertisers, the advertisers and the advertisers. He hated being beholden to anyone, but without the revenue from the commercials, INN would not be economically viable. It was largely private funding that had got INN up and running – thank you, Odile's Daddy – but it was the dollars that came rolling in from Baby Wipe-Aways and The New Abdominiser – Lose Four Inches in Two Weeks that kept the show on the road.

Idly Ben gazed at the six television monitors on the wall opposite his desk, each soundlessly churning out the usual drivel: BBC, CNN, ITN, Sky News, Channel Four and, in their centre in pride of place, INN. He possessed the valuable asset of being able to watch half a dozen television screens at once, and not a frame of picture was put out by INN that he did not see. What he did not watch live, he had Odile record on one of three videos at home. In this game, it paid to stay one jump ahead of the opposition – and that included his own staff.

Ben was in this game for one reason, and one reason alone: Power. Money was a pleasant bonus that inevitably went hand in hand with it. He intended to be the loudest voice on the planet, the one that everyone listened to, from presidents to peasants. Mentally he made a note of that line – he liked the alliteration, it sounded polished. Quantity, not quality, was what it was all about, and he knew exactly how to get it. Ben repeated his one and only rule of life softly to himself. You never lost money underestimating the taste of the viewer.

With these twin aims in mind – to give the viewer what he wants, even if he didn't yet know he wanted it, and to make the word 'television' synonymous with INN the world over – Ben was, piece by piece, creating a new phenomenon, one which had been oft-talked about but never really seen. Infotainment. News that entertained. Entertainment that informed. And he was doing it without shame, without embarrassment, with a lack of tact and complete absence of taste that made the *Daily Ethic* look like good convent reading. But the ratings were on the up and up. Now all he had to do was get the world addicted, and he would never look back. Get them hooked, then feed that craving like a Colombian drug dealer. To that end, he had lined up a series of deals across the globe; once they'd been signed and sealed, he'd have carte blanche to take television into a new era – his way.

Ben leant back in his sinister black leather chair, picking his manicured fingernails with a mother-of-pearl handled letter opener. It was a shame he had to run everything by the Board for approval, but he had little choice. When he had exhausted every avenue looking for a backer for INN, in the days before the company even existed, he had had no option but to relinquish some control in exchange for the start-up cash that had got INN up and running, and brought the advertisers rushing in. He could do without them now, but it was too late.

Fortunately, Board meetings tended to be an exercise in rubber-stamping. Ben owned a third of the company, which he had managed to pay for with Odile's dowry from her filthy-rich French father. He loathed having to keep his wife sweet while he waited for the rest of her inheritance. Once he had it, she'd be history, but until then, he was on the rack. How that miserable bugger's ancestors escaped the Revolution he'd love to know. If he'd been around then, his father-in-law would have been the first to get the chop.

Sadistically he kicked the stark white plastic pot containing a wilting aspidistra. He hated plants, and was always throwing the bloody things in the bin. With satisfaction he watched the aspidistra fall out of the pot, overdry brown earth spilling on to the cream shagpile.

It was just as well he also controlled a second third of the company, he mused, owned by a consortium of foreign television networks, of whom World News Service had the largest chunk. It never hurt to have an unfair advantage. The consortium had a limp-wristed representative, Eustace Pollen, who attended the quarterly Board meetings because they provided a water-tight excuse to his wife for him to visit London and rendezvous with his lover, an extremely nervous Bishop. He was well aware Ben knew of his close religious ties, and would have voted to ban red woolly socks if that was what Ben wanted.

The remaining third was split between the suave Minister for Energy, Dalmeny de Burgh, the hotel magnate Harry Foley, who unfortunately also happened to be Paragon's husband, and Sir Edward Penhaligon, who had demanded a fourteen per cent share of INN in exchange for the use of his face and prestige to launch the fledgling network. Up to now, there had been few differences of opinion – excepting over Princess Di's nipple, which had upset Penhaligon's finer feelings. Penhaligon was one of the last of those idealists who actually thought news had its own intrinsic value.

Ben ground the earth into the carpet with one polished black Charles Church shoe. The spilt coffee dregs dripped over the side of the desk, mingling with the earth in a sticky goo. He still had no worries about de Burgh's amenable compliance; the MP was happy to leave the running of INN to Ben, as long as he got plenty of airtime when he had a party political point to make. Thanks to Ben and INN, Dalmeny de Burgh was the most popular and certainly the highest-profiled MP in either party, including the self-effacing PM, and along the corridors of Westminster was already being tipped for the top.

Of Harry Foley, Ben was less sure, but Foley's business took him away from London – and fortunately from Paragon – for long periods of time. Ben thoughtfully tapped his gleaming shark's teeth with the letter opener.

The problem was Penhaligon.

The buzzer on his desk squawked impatiently, and Ben sat up straight, spinning his swivel chair around to face the intercom.

'Yes, Lisa?' he barked.

'Excuse me for interrupting, Mr Wordsworth, but you did say to call you . . .' Lisa said hesitantly, speaking into the intercom in the over-loud, slow, clear tones people usually reserved for addressing foreigners.

'What is it?' Ben asked impatiently.

'You did say – if Annie Charter came up – you did say to tell you right away,' Lisa said nervously. 'Only, she wants to see you, sir, and she said you'd know what it was about.'

'That's OK, Lisa, send her in,' Ben grunted, straightening his tie and tucking his striped shirt into the waistband of his trousers.

The door opened, and Lisa leant around it, contorting herself so as to keep one hand on the doorhandle whilst making sure her feet stayed outside Ben's inner sanctum. Absently Ben wondered why she looked more attractive than usual, then realised it must be because she was smiling. Christ, he'd never seen her smile before. Must be love. Idly he pitied the poor bastard on the receiving end.

Annie walked past Lisa's outstretched body, her stiletto heels making no noise on the carpet. She came to a halt three feet into the room, and pointedly turned her head and looked over her shoulder at Lisa, who was still clutching the doorknob.

'Thank you, Lisa,' Ben said dismissively, and with a start, Lisa eased herself back out of the room and shut the door.

Annie turned back and faced Ben, a knowing smile across her pink-lipsticked mouth. Slowly she licked her lips, then dropped her head to watch her hands trail slowly over her breasts.

Ben drew a breath. This lady wasn't backwards in coming forward. He thought he was good at getting what he wanted, but she made him look like an adolescent schoolboy. A flicker of desire swept through him as he took her measure. Few women dared to play him at his own game. Would she?

'You said you wanted me?' Annie asked, sure of herself. Ben admired her arrogant stance, the cool invitation in her voice, her sureness that it would be accepted. Despite himself, he was fascinated.

Ben let his eyes run over her body, knowing she could read his thoughts and not quite sure if he liked it. He eyed the filmy material of her plum-coloured dress. Through it he could almost see the dark outline of her nipples and the triangle at the top of her long, slim legs. Christ! She wasn't even wearing any underwear.

'I thought it was time we had a chat,' he said slowly, each syllable filled with innuendo as he eased his erection against the constraining fabric of his trousers beneath the desk. Annie crossed over to the chair opposite him, sinking into the leather sinuously and crossing one leg over the other. 'You've been with us now – how long?'

'Two years,' Annie replied, deliberately moving so that her dress rode up her taut thighs, revealing the lacy tops of her black stockings. She sensed Ben's uncertainty, and leant back in the chair, savouring his discomfort.

'Two years,' Ben repeated slowly, playing for time. 'I'm surprised I haven't got to know you before now.' Everyone else in the building had, he thought cynically, but it had taken her some time to reach as high as him.

Ben smiled. 'So, you're a PA now on the Early Evening News, isn't that right?' he said, dragging his gaze from her legs and up to her face. Hazel eyes met his, and he looked away first. Her control of the situation threw him off-balance, and he was not sure how to handle it.

Annie nodded. 'I think it's about time we found you something a little more suited to your abilities, don't you?' he asked suavely.

Annie smiled. Easy. He had swallowed the bait, and he

didn't even know it. She had been right. Her obvious come-on would drive him to try to reassert his control, and he would use the only way he knew how with a woman. Sex.

Slowly she stood up and unbuttoned the top of her dress, anticipating his every move. Ben stared mesmerised as she revealed an inch of peachy flesh. Confused, he told himself he liked a woman who was prepared to make a straightforward bargain; she wanted a job as a script-writer, and he wanted to fuck her brains out. Simple. He gazed lustfully at her round, full magnolia breasts which were suddenly revealed as the second button was undone.

Annie's eyes never left his. She had spent two years preparing for this, and there was no way she was going to get it wrong now. This man respected power, and she intended to prove just how much she had over him. Paragon was yesterday's news – or would be, in a few short minutes.

Annie Charter had had her eyes on the top job when she joined INN as a lowly secretary. Carefully she cultivated civilised relationships with helpful executives as she sought encouragement and advice for her successive pro-motions.

Her first boss had been almost too easy; married with two screaming kids, he'd been only too happy to give her a glowing testimonial once he'd sampled those magnifi-cent breasts and that willing body. He recommended her for a job as a General Assistant, which finally meant admission to the newsroom as a runner, copy-girl, and all-round gofer. Within a month she had been sleeping with her new boss – this time a woman, but who was she to care? – and soon found herself moving up to Produc-tion Assistant. Unfortunately, her next, male, boss was gay, and proof against Annie's charms, and so she decided to gamble and go straight to the top. Sudden death.

She'd almost worked her way through INN's entire bank of reporters by the time word of her talents reached Ben's ears. Shrewdly Annie waited until Paragon got her job as co-anchor on the Evening News slot, guessing that it would have taken a good deal of tantrums, tears and withholding of sex to get Paragon what she wanted, and that Ben would be growing a little weary of her and ready for a change.

With that in mind, Annie undid the last three remaining buttons. She stood before Ben's desk, clad in nothing but the black stockings and four-inch heels. Her large breasts rose and fell with her excitement, as she slowly moved around Ben's glass-topped desk. She stopped inches from his chair, the russet tangle of her bush at eye level as he leaned back, his eyes slits as he watched her with fascination. Deliberately she bent down, her breasts hanging soft and full against his chest, as she expertly unzipped his straining trousers and his cock sprang free.

Annie stepped back again, and languidly licked one slim finger. With her other hand, she encircled her breast and gently rubbed the finger she had licked over her engorged nipple, throwing her head back and widening her stance. As the nerves tingled she arched her back, seemingly oblivious to Ben's presence and obvious excitement. Her breath was coming in short gasps as, more urgently now, she played with both her nipples until the dusky pink tips stood out hard against her palms.

Suddenly Annie let her hands fall, and turned around, her back to Ben. Gracefully she bent over, her movements supple and fluid, and clasped the calves of her outstretched legs with her hands. Ben gazed entranced at the rust-coloured bush, softly framed with the creamy globes of her pert buttocks. He could see the entrance to her cunt, wet and slippery with her excitement. She looked over her shoulder, her tangled auburn hair flowing down her back.

197

With a sly smile, she reached down to her clitoris and began fingering it with expert strokes, wriggling her cunt on her palm with obvious pleasure.

Ben could stand it no more. Was the bitch going to bring herself off right in front of him and leave him sitting there? The fire of his anger and frustration and desire brought him to fever pitch, as she knew it would. There was nothing Ben wanted more than something he thought he couldn't have.

Abruptly he stood up, yanking down his trousers, his cock so hard he thought it was going to burst. He encircled Annie's waist with one arm, pushing her forward so that she had to put her arms out and grab at the cabinet on which the televisions were still flickering, in order to stop herself from falling. Fiercely Ben thrust his swollen cock into her from behind, stabbing hard into her, standing upright as his legs thrust against her.

Annie responded by clenching the muscles of her cunt tight against his cock, rippling them as the engorged mass pulsed hard inside her. Ben could not hide his start of surprise as he felt the strength of her grasp, her cunt working him as if she had hands inside her. He could not believe he could feel this aroused and not come, but it was as if her control of the situation and her accomplished, rhythmic contractions were holding his orgasm at bay, whilst simultaneously extending its depth and its peaks.

'For Christ's sake,' he grunted, gripping her buttocks with both hands, pumping her ass as if it would save his life. Over their sweating bodies the televisions mouthed their soundless words, flickering images of tanks, soldiers, a hospital bed, a cartoon, playing over the screens. It lent a whole new meaning to the phrase 'hard news'.

The telephone rang. 'Leave it!' Ben shouted, as Annie stretched out one languid hand to the desk to answer it.

His nerves were a screaming, tingling mass of electric shocks, and he could feel his orgasm building in every part of his body, pouring down to the cock buried deep inside her grasping, teasing cunt. Annie ignored him and answered it. 'It's a Mr Andretti,' she said evenly. She might have been his secretary.

Ben had no choice but to take the receiver. Mr Andretti was the Chief Executive of the largest Italian television station, poised to sign an agreement with Ben that would make INN the largest news network in Italy. To his amazement and dismay he found the idea of conducting business with his frantic cock thrust halfway inside this calculating bitch even more exciting. Christ, up to now he'd never even goosed his secretary in his office! Now he was screwing this cunt on the bookcase and handling one of the most important calls in his career at the same time. He felt a surge of adrenalin and desire unlike anything he'd ever experienced.

'Mr Andretti,' he said smoothly into the phone. 'How good to hear from you so soon. How are you?' Jesus, the bitch's cunt was working him even harder. If she didn't let up, he'd come right now.

One part of his mind heard Mr Andretti's rich voice congratulating him on INN's continued excellence. The rest was engaged with Annie's breasts, pliant and pillowing beneath his fingers. With a shock he felt her hand reach beneath them and caress his balls, sending new flames of desire sweeping through him.

'I'm glad you feel that way, Mr Andretti,' he murmured, pushing his cock so hard against Annie's cunt that her head crashed against the wooden shelving. 'The contract should be with you within the next forty-eight hours, for your approval.' Suddenly Annie moved away from him, forcing him out of her as he remained anchored to the telephone. What the hell was she playing at now?

199

'I'm sorry, Mr Andretti, it's a bad line,' he gasped. 'What was that?'

Carefully Annie eased her way around him again, nuzzling his cock with her buttocks. She hoped he wouldn't be too shocked to enjoy it.

'Of course, if you feel Italian subtitles are too expensive . . . no, no, I quite understand. We can talk about that when the contracts are signed.'

Annie arched her back, lifting her buttocks an extra inch. Holding on to the television cabinet with one hand, she reached behind her and grasped his distended cock with the other. Before Ben could realise what was happening, she shoved his prick deep into her ass, thrusting against the shelving as she did so. His cock was so wet with her juices he slid easily inside her, the almost painful tightness surrounding him like a second skin.

'Thank you, Mr Andretti. And to your wife. Goodbye, Mr Andretti,' Ben managed breathlessly. Desperately he punched the intercom. 'Hold all my calls, Lisa!' he gasped.

Every inch of his body was straining towards the sensations in his prick. He could not believe what he was doing, how much he was enjoying it, the power this woman was exerting. When he came with a strangled scream it was as if the world was exploding all around him, and he clung to Annie's arching body as if she were the only fragment of it left.

Outside his office, Paragon heard the muffled yell as she walked in. Suspiciously she turned to Lisa, who had a good idea what was going on.

'What the hell was that?'

'What the hell was that?'

Victoria Lawrence leaped off the bed, for once forget-ting about wrinkles as she frowned in surprise. The shrilling continued, and she picked up the alarm clock and shook it. She pressed every button, but the noise did not stop.

'It's my bleep,' Philip Cunningham said nervously. 'It's around here somewhere.' With a growing air of despera-tion, he groped around the floor, looking for his trousers, to which his message master had been clipped. 'Oh shit, Victoria, help me find it, it could be the Third World War, for God's sake.'

Victoria stood helplessly beside the bed, clasping the folds of a faded orange silk kimono about her. She might get away with candles in the dark, but there was no way she was going to risk broad daylight on her body. After all, she was forty-something. Surreptitiously she pulled the pale blue curtains closed and switched on the bedside lamp. She wished they were in her bedroom, the lighting was far more flattering, but that was out of the question.

'Don't you have a bleep?' Philip grunted, still scrab-bling. With relief he found his trousers, grimacing rue-fully at the crumpled Gianni Versace.

'Of course,' Victoria huffed, piqued. 'I am a news-caster, in case you'd forgotten. I just don't switch it on. It saves the batteries, you know.'

Philip did not stop to ponder the vagaries of Victoria's logic. 'Oh shit!' he exclaimed, his face looking even more worried than usual. 'A hijack! That's all I need on my first weekend off in a month. Oh God, why me?'

'I want to go,' Victoria pouted. 'I never get any foreign

stories, I'm totally unappreciated here. I had a very nice lunch with Chris Kramer of the BBC last week, and he said he was sure my talents weren't being explored to the full. It was a very nice lunch,' she added meaningfully.

Philip pulled on his jacket, scrubbing ineffectually at a stain on the right cuff. The pale green suit was a size and a half too big, but he hoped everyone would think it was fashionably baggy. They hadn't had his size in the sale. He was beginning to wish he had never started this with Victoria. There was no such thing as a free fuck. He hated this side of being INN's Executive Foreign Editor. Come to that, he hated most sides of being Executive Foreign Editor.

'Well, you can come if you want,' he said resignedly. 'But don't expect to travel very far. Some buggers have hijacked the HMS Belfast.'

By the time Philip and Victoria arrived at the INN building – in separate taxis, since Victoria's face was far too famous to take any risks – the buzz that came with a sudden breaking story was already in evidence. As Philip pushed open the wide revolving glass doors to the building, he saw two crew Volvos race out of the underground garage at breakneck speed. Other journalists called in to reinforce the skeleton weekend team were already arriving at the building, dressed in shorts and tee-shirts as they abandoned barbecues and mowing the lawn. One or two men winked at each other in relief.

As Philip reached the newsroom, a panting GA handed him the latest wire copy on the incident, the relevant phrases underlined. It seemed the hijackers were linked to some unknown Palestinian terrorist group, judging from their demands, and part of their number was holding some more hostages in Israel itself. Philip shuddered at the thought of the logistics he was going to have to handle to get crews and equipment into the relevant places.

Sam Hargrave was already sitting at the Foreign Desk, one telephone cradled between his chin and left ear, a second in his right hand and two more ringing on his desk.

'Allah be praised!' Sam said, getting into the mood. 'Now I can get on with a news story and forget about being an accountant.'

Philip ignored the remark, not sure if it was a compliment or an insult, and disappeared into his office at the edge of the newsroom to start balancing budgets. Shit, with the Albanian business, the last thing he needed was the extra cost of flying teams to Israel to cover the Palestinian end of things. That reminded him: David Cameron was halfway to Athens by now, which meant they were open and exposed in Israel. He'd have to find someone else to send. Quickly he dialled the Newsdesk extension.

'What?' Ollie snapped, grabbing the phone.

'Is there anyone you can spare to go to Israel?' Philip asked nervously.

'Are you kidding?' Ollie replied incredulously. 'It's a weekend, which means that all I've got are two freelancers and a trainee to run this whole ship. Just pray that Archie and Nick respond to their bleeps, and you might be in with a chance. Will someone turn that bloody row off?' he screamed, slamming down the receiver. A startled GA leaped on the radio blaring in the corner, and cut the music off abruptly, but not before Ollie recognised the track. Chris Rea's 'Road to Hell.' How appropriate.

Puffing from exertion, Janey arrived at his desk and slammed a wilting lettuce and cheese sandwich in front of him. 'Sorry I'm late,' she gasped, sinking into her chair opposite Ollie and logging into her computer. 'I was in the atrium with some of the lads from ENG Maint. –

Don's got this great new remote-controlled car, beats anything I've ever seen.'

Ollie glared balefully at her. Janey's fetish for model cars was well known throughout the building. On a normal weekend, he would not have minded the entire newsroom team bunking off to the atrium to play Brands-Hatch. Boxing Day was always a classic; everyone brought in the kids' Christmas presents and raced them around the vast open floor in the basement. Last year Archie had pinched his nephew's two model planes and piloted them up and down the twelve-floor atrium until one of them hit a terrified starling and crashed. But now was not the time for games.

Ben Wordsworth appeared at his elbow, his face flushed but his demeanour cool and efficient. Ollie wondered why he was here on a weekend before remembering the rumours he'd heard of trouble in the Wordsworth marriage.

'There's a meeting in my office now,' Ben snapped, Annie and her not-inconsiderable talents completely forgotten.

Ollie sighed. Just what he needed. Another executive meeting. For every member of management present, you could guarantee an extra package, and at least three story ideas, all totally unrealistic. In the meantime, nobody could get on with any work.

'Take care of the desk,' he said to Janey, giving up the unequal battle to get a crew down to HMS Belfast, establish links and get on air before the opposition. He prayed ITN and the BBC were as sluggish as INN on a Saturday afternoon.

Ollie followed Ben into his office, and shut the door. Brian Reynolds had already taken up his position as key groveller and yes-man on Ben's right. Perched on the uncomfortable wire chairs hurriedly assembled in a semicircle around the walls were Sam Hargrave, Philip Cunningham, Jerry Tallboy and two faceless accountants whom Ollie did not recognise. Shuffling in behind him came the Head of Bureaux, Robin something-or-other.

'OK, Ollie, why don't you brief us on the situation?' Ben asked unpleasantly.

Ollie sat down, determined not to let the Editor's bad mood get to him. 'Well, the news broke at 12.45 this afternoon,' he began, hoping Ben did not know the entire Newsdesk had been across the road having a quick one at Aristotle's at the time. Thank God Tommy had actually been in Assignments for once, albeit on the phone to his mistress. He was the only one in the office when Reuters flashed the story.

'Over an hour ago,' Ben reiterated with the air of a teacher explaining something to a small and rather stupid child.

Ollie carried on, riffling through the few wires that had come through on the story. 'A group calling itself the Warriors of Islam have taken over the HMS Belfast, which is permanently moored in the Thames. Simultaneously, a second group in Israel kidnapped three Israeli soldiers in the Gaza refugee camp of Khan Younis. It seems they grabbed them when they were out on patrol.'

'Three?' Brian interrupted. 'That doesn't seem very many.'

'You don't know the Israelis,' Sam answered him dourly. 'To them, three Jews might as well be three thousand. Can't say I blame them. They've got to make every one count.'

'Anyway,' Ollie said, hurriedly moving on before the exchange became too anti-semitic. 'They want an end to the peace negotiations, which they not unreasonably see as a farce, and the immediate withdrawal of Israel from the Occupied Territories, as per UN Resolutions 242 and 338.

They've threatened to kill a hostage every hour until their demands are met. That's it so far.'

'Any idea how many people are trapped on the ship?' Ben asked curtly.

'Well, there's no clear information yet, but it's a summer weekend. We know an American tour group was on board, which may be why they picked now to hijack the boat. I think you can assume up to a hundred tourists, plus the staff. Likewise, we don't know yet how many terrorists, but Scotland Yard thinks at least a dozen. It's a biggie.'

Jerry crossed one scrawny leg over the other, and leant forward, his hands pressed together on his clipboard.

'I take it the usual format's been ditched, and we're going into Newsflash mode,' he said hesitantly. He hated these meetings; he always got the dirtiest jobs if he did not go, and always got the dirtiest jobs if he did.

'A sixty-second Newsflash as of 14.30,' Ben said, giving Jerry a withering look. 'Then we go back on-air at 14.45, to give us time to get into position. We'll stay on air with it as long as we need to. Who've we got?'

Ollie sighed. He'd been dreading this one. 'Archie Michaels is on his way to HMS Belfast, with a full back-up team following. At the moment, all we've got actually on site is the trainee, Dom Ryan.'

'The biggest fucking story this year and we've got a wet-behind-the-ears trainee who doesn't know a story from a camel's arse!' Ben raged, standing up and thumping his fist on his desk in anger. For the second time that day, his coffee cup fell against his desk and broke, spilling its contents on to the glass. Brian Reynolds sprang forward obsequiously and started mopping it up with a tissue. Ben pushed him out of the way. 'Can somebody tell me why an international news network is being run by kindergarten kids?'

Brian flinched at the biting sarcasm in Ben's voice. 'It's the rosters,' he began nervously. 'The cost . . . the cutbacks . . .' His voice trailed off.

The accountants busied themselves importantly with their briefcases, opening and shutting them with a great display of industry.

'Don't tell me, we've got Peter bloody Pan in Israel,' Ben asked, throwing himself into his chair.

'We should be so lucky,' Sam retorted, refusing to be cowed. 'I did ask for a reporter to provide Middle-East cover, given that David is now on his way to Albania with Christie, which means we're two correspondents down. I was told there were no funds available. We're caught with our pants down.'

Brian prepared to lick Ben's shoes from a safe position under his desk. Robin, the Head of Bureaux, tried to fade into the wallpaper. It wasn't fair, he'd only just got over the Peter Princer row.

'In the meantime, I've got Nick Makepiece on the next flight to Dixie.' Sam used the journalists' name for Israel. Most experienced hacks referred to the Jewish state as 'Dixie' because of its southern location. The word 'Israel', uttered in Arab circles, could be highly dangerous. The wonder of it was that none of the Arabs seemed to have cottoned on to it yet.

Suddenly the door burst open and Jerry's number two, Rochelle Desker, the Chief Sub-Editor, dived in.

'Sorry to interrupt,' she panted, looking anything but. 'They've just hurled their first body overboard.'

'Jerry, I want you to take this one,' Ben said as he stood up, ignoring the look of indignation on Brian Reynolds' face. As the Producer of the Early Evening News slot, strictly speaking Brian was senior to Jerry, who was only in charge of the News Updates. Brian glowered, and Ben savoured his misery. It never paid to let them think they knew where they were. 'Brian, you stay here. I want a few words with you.'

Jerry gathered his team around the desk, as Sam and Ollie returned to their screaming telephones and the rest of the impromptu gathering filed out of Ben's office.

'Lynxie, I want a good graphic of the Thames and a few London landmarks,' he said to the Graphics girl. 'Make sure HMS Belfast is clearly a boat, I don't want some red X to mark the spot.' Lynxie's cropped white-bleached hair shook as she nodded. 'We'll need a map of Israel, and some good opening titles for when we take a break. This could be a long one, so make them interesting.'

He turned to the Production team, wishing Muriel was directing. Instead it was Basil Hemmingway, an effete man who considered his artistic talents were wasted on INN. Unfortunately, hefty alimony payments meant he could not afford to be choosy. 'Get some coffee in now, Basil, you'll be running this show,' Jerry said. 'We'll have Victoria in Studio One downstairs as our main anchor. I want Paragon in Studio Three up here in the newsroom to cut to with rapid updates. Rich, it'll be your job to feed her wire stories so she has something to say.'

Rich nodded, inwardly sighing. Trust him to have to babysit the bimbo.

'Basil, we'll also have live capability from HMS Belfast with Archie, and Ollie's getting the helicopter up for some aerials, again with live links back to the building. He's also trying to get the mini-chopper up, in case Scotland Yard slap a ban on over-flying. When Nick gets to Israel, we should get a satellite up there too. You'll be busy.'

Basil rolled his eyes heavenwards. 'I'm an artiste, not a juggler,' he pouted. 'I need an outlet for my creative talents. I should be making Madonna videos.'

'Funny, that's what we think,' Ginny put in swiftly.

The rest of the team giggled. Basil looked bootfaced.

'Has the Picasso special been cancelled?' asked Livvy. A producer who had been with INN only two weeks after four years on Channel Four, she still thought the 'Reader's Digest' was a news magazine.

'Unless he's drawing me the map, I think you can take it as read,' Jerry replied crushingly.

Livvy's bottom lip trembled. 'You lot are a bunch of philistines!' she said tearfully. 'Unless it's got sex and violence in it, it doesn't get airtime.'

'What you have to remember,' Rich said patiently, 'is that life at INN bears no relation to reality. It'll help, I promise.'

'There's a quick Newsflash at 14.30, then we're on air for the duration at 14.45. So get moving,' Jerry said briskly.

The meeting over, the team dispersed around the desk. Annie, the PA, wrote the On-Air times on a plastic board at the end of the newsroom. Ginny slid into her place and called up the Newsflash slot on the computer, where the scripts would be written.

'I think this lead-in is going to be a long one, Jerry,' she said, starting to write the opening words that Victoria would be reading in less than twenty minutes.

'Don't worry, write it as long as you like,' Jerry answered amiably. 'We'll soon cut it down to fifteen seconds.'

On Jerry's left, Rochelle was already hammering out a rough running-order. Even if it went by the board as soon as they got on air, it was reassuring to have some guidelines not to stick to.

'Hey, my chopper's working!' Ollie yelled from the Newsdesk. 'First time up and it's working!'

The activity in the newsroom ceased for a moment, as everyone present tried to make sense of Ollie's jubilation. There was collective hysterics as his unfortunate choice of words sank in.

Jerry tuned his monitor into the live signal coming back from the helicam. Essentially it was a highly sophisticated model helicopter, equipped with a camera, and at just under six feet in length, small enough not to be banned – yet – by the authorities, who were not sure if it counted as a toy.

The newsroom watched as the helicopter operator manoeuvred the machine within a few yards of HMS Belfast. It was their first close-up glimpse of the scene, the proper helicopter still grounded by Scotland Yard. A number of men in army fatigues were visible in positions up and down the deck, several of them with women as hostages. In the centre of the boat, below decks, the tourists had been gathered. As they watched, a lifeboat put out from the bank and headed towards what appeared to be a bundle of rags floating in the muddy water of the Thames. The helicam moved closer to the bundle, and suddenly it was possible to see that it was a body, a pale red stream pouring from the head.

The laughter in the newsroom ceased. That must be the man who had been shot in the head and dumped over-board. Few believed he would be the only victim.

INN went on air with a rough outline of the basic facts, Paragon reading the brief script whilst downstairs Victoria prepared for the main bulletin. On the bank of screens above the Newsdesk, Jerry could see the BBC, ITN and CNN do the same. INN's Newsflash ended after sixty seconds with the promise of continual coverage of the crisis from 14.45.

■ 2.40 p.m.

'On-Air in five minutes,' Annie called out.

Jerry and Rochelle sat tensely in the control room of Studio One. On one of the banks of monitors, they could see Victoria re-reading some scripts at her desk in the

210

studio. Her pale blue tailored suit set off her dark good looks to perfection. Jerry second-glanced Victoria's image.

'She looks different,' he whispered in Rochelle's ear. 'What's she done to herself?'

'She insisted the floor manager had the lighting man put in pink filters to make her look younger,' Rochelle hissed back. 'One of the tabloids said she was beginning to age next to Paragon Fairfax. She hasn't been out in daylight since.'

'Could I have some quiet?' Basil said petulantly from his position at the Director's desk. 'It's hard enough working for a Mickey Mouse outfit as it is.'

A harsh burst of static cut across the nervous silence as the Sound tech tested the link from HMS Belfast.

'Still getting nothing from them,' he said, with studied unconcern.

'Cut Story One!' Jerry bawled. 'Victoria, we'll be going straight to live pictures from the helicam. You'll have to ad-lib over it.'

In the studio, Victoria gave a thumbs up. Whatever she might be off-screen, on-screen she was every inch the cool professional. With the memory of Annie's Venus Fly-trap cunt still fresh in his mind – or rather his cock – Ben wondered exactly how necessary Paragon was. He couldn't get rid of her yet, it would make him look a fool. But give it time . . .

'One minute to On-Air,' Annie intoned.

The phone rang next to Jerry. He snatched it up, never taking his eyes from the bank of monitors in front of him.

'Yes?' he barked.

'Dom Ryan's got us the wife of the dead man,' Ollie said. 'She's at the links van down at HMS Belfast, and says she wants to talk to us, to plead with the kidnappers.'

'Is the line from there clear?' Jerry yelled, slamming down the phone and turning to the engineer at the end of the control gallery.

'Working on it!' the engineer yelled back.

'Thirty seconds . . .'

The live feed from the helicam was still visible on one of the monitors. Its output was being recorded in an edit booth in case anything happened that Jerry might want to show later in the bulletin. The phone rang again.

'Twenty to On-Air,' said Annie, clutching a stopwatch in her left hand as she watched the clock in front of her.

Jerry snatched up the phone. 'Scotland Yard says you've got to get the helicam away from the ship, in case it alarms the hijackers,' Ollie shouted frantically down the line, his voice audible to everyone in the gallery.

At the back of the control room, Ben stood up and lunged for the phone. 'Ollie, tell the fuckers to piss off!' he bellowed. 'I take full responsibility. Now let us get the fuck on-air!'

'Five . . . four . . . three . . .'

'The line from HMS Belfast is there!' the Engineer shouted, as a snowy screen suddenly shivered and gave way to a live-feed from the bank of the river. Archie's face loomed into view, the grey hull of the ship over his left shoulder. Behind him a middle-aged woman in a pink raincoat stood passively next to Dom Ryan, her eyes red-rimmed but dry.

'On-Air!'

Victoria looked up from the scripts in front of her, and assumed an expression of grim but reassuring authority. In clipped patrician tones she began reading Ginny's lead-in from the autocue.

'At least a dozen terrorists are holding more than a hundred hostages on board the HMS Belfast, in London's Thames River,' she began. A map of the capital

212

appeared on the screen as Victoria outlined the latest developments.

'Let Victoria give us a minute of ad-libbing over the live pictures from the helicam,' Jerry instructed. 'Then we'll take Archie for an update and an interview with the woman. Get Dom out of the picture before we cut to them. Do we know her name yet?'

Basil leant forward and flicked a switch to enable him to talk to Archie down by the river. 'Coming to you in one minute,' he said. 'Ask Dom to shift out of shot.' Archie gave him the thumbs up to indicate he could hear the studio, and Dom disappeared from view. 'Who is the lady with you?' Basil asked.

The live signal from the helicam as it circled the ship was now being beamed out. Over it Victoria described the scene in measured tones, making up the commentary to suit the pictures she and the viewers were now seeing. The lifeboat crew were clearly visible on the bank opposite the HMS Belfast, waiting in case they were needed again. One hijacker, clad in camouflage gear and wearing a black mask, dragged the woman he was clutching towards the edge of the deck. Orange police tape cordoning off the area fluttered in the stiff breeze.

'You've had forty-five seconds on this,' Annie said, glancing down at her stopwatch. 'Fifteen seconds to go.'

'Forget the timing, just let it roll,' Jerry answered. 'It's looking good so far. We don't want to cut to Archie and miss something.'

The helicam picked up muffled shouting from the figure on the deck, but it was impossible to make out what he was saying. The phone shrilled again, and Ben reached over Jerry's shoulder to grab the receiver. Without bothering to lift it to his ear, he set it down on the control desk, his eyes never leaving the screens in front of him.

'Keep it going, Victoria!' Jerry yelled.

'Archie, we'll come to you in a minute,' Basil told the waiting reporter, who nodded. 'The lady's name is Anna Greenway,' Archie said into his microphone. On Basil's left, Lynxie typed the words 'Anna Greenway – victim's wife' into a computer in front of her. When they took the interview, the subtitle would flash up to identify her.

'Let's have a "Live from HMS Belfast" subtitle,' Ben ordered. 'We're the only people with these pictures, let's bang our own drums a bit.'

Suddenly they saw three men rush out on to the deck, shouting and screaming at the terrorist holding the girl. All four men turned and faced the helicam, gesticulating wildly. It was clear they had access to a television inside the ship, and had seen INN's output. Ben cursed silently. He'd have enough trouble as it was keeping Scotland Yard off his back after going ahead with the pictures. If the girl got shot because of it, he didn't dare think about the consequences. Shit! If the papers knew he'd deliberately defied police instructions and put the hostages in jeopardy, there'd be hell to pay.

'Standby, Archie,' said Basil. 'We may need to come to you very quickly.'

They saw one of the men on the ship put a gun to his shoulder.

'AK 47,' Ben muttered. 'Very nice.'

Wildly the terrorist let fly a burst of shots, spraying the circling helicam, screaming as he fired into the sky. Suddenly the picture swung terrifyingly out of control. The helicam flipped nose-down, and the murky brown waters of the Thames rushed up to meet it.

'Shit, there goes twenty grand,' Ben muttered bitterly. 'Hope the fuckers are insured.'

'Cut to Victoria!' Jerry screamed, leaping up and throwing back his chair in his excitement. Ben howled as it hit him. 'Get the fuck out of my way!' Jerry snarled, without even turning round to see who he had hit.

Ben bit back a swift retort. The Producer ruled in the control gallery when they were on air, and right now Jerry was the Producer, and a bloody good one. Limping, he stepped back a couple of paces as Jerry swung into action.

'Apologise for losing the picture, and say our outside broadcast helicam has just been shot down!' Jerry instructed Victoria. The newscaster was already smoothly covering the gap, her precise voice giving no indication of the chaos she could hear in her earpiece. She was paid a hell of a lot of money for a few hours' work a week, but at times like this, she earned it.

'Then turn to Archie, and handover to him,' Jerry said crisply. Over his shoulder he shouted, 'Ginny! Get back upstairs, find the tape that recorded the helicam being shot down, and line it up. We'll play it again in ten minutes for everyone who missed it. Go!'

'Our reporter, Archie Michaels, is at the scene,' Victoria said into the camera. Gracefully she turned to the screen at her left, where Archie's face was visible. 'Archie, what's the latest?'

'Take Camera Three!' Basil roared, the affected tones vanishing from his voice as he got into his stride. The wide shot of the studio was replaced by Archie's face full in the screen.

'Well, Victoria, as you said, our helicam was shot down by one of the terrorists,' Archie replied. Behind him police helicopters whirred, and the lapping of the river water against the bank punctuated his remarks. 'It seems they were nervous when they saw the scene being played live on INN . . .'

'Good one,' murmured Ben from the back. It never hurt to rub the oppositions' noses in it.

Archie stood back to introduce the woman standing next to him. As he did so, the cameraman on location pulled back, widening the shot and showing the whole scene from the shore for the first time. 'What's going on?' Jerry said, suddenly noticing a throng of soldiers on the left of the shot. 'They weren't there two minutes ago.'

He thought rapidly as Archie carried on talking to the woman, who was tearfully explaining how boats made her seasick, which was why she was standing on the bank when the terrorists took over the ship with her husband on board.

The gallery door was flung open, and Ollie puffed through. 'You've got to cut the live link,' he shouted. 'Fucking Scotland Yard are planning something and they don't want us tipping the hijackers off.'

They could all see now that something was happening on the shore. The huddle of men edged out of the range of the camera. As they did so there was a terrified scream. The sharp crack of a single shot split the air, and was followed by the sinister sound of a large splash, and more screams from the hostages being held on the bridge and below decks.

'Archie, was that another hostage?' Victoria asked, with just the right amount of concern and dismay in her voice.

'Cut the fucking live link!' Ollie bellowed. 'Now!'

'Leave it!' Ben barked. 'I said it was my responsibility. Let it roll!'

'You could get those people killed!' Ollie roared back.

'Victoria, I'll be cutting to you in a moment, and when I do, I want you to recap what's happened,' Jerry shouted, as Victoria carried on calmly interviewing Archie. 'Basil, get the links cameraman to do a close-up of Archie's face, I don't want to be able to see anything but him.' Basil issued a swift instruction down the line, and the shot

216

narrowed, blocking out any view of the ship or the activity on it.

'Is the tape of the helicam being shot down rewound yet?' Jerry asked urgently, his voice cutting across the din behind him.

Basil leant forward and spoke into the intercom which connected him directly with the edit booth where Ginny was lining up the picture. 'Is it there, ES Four?' he demanded.

'Ready to roll,' Ginny replied, her voice sounding tinny in the intercom.

'OK, cut to Victoria!' Jerry instructed, standing like a conductor giving the performance of his life, both arms outstretched, discarded running orders clutched in his hands.

Ben strode forward and grabbed Jerry's shoulder, whirling him round with an unnecessary force. 'What the fuck do you think you're doing?' he snarled malevolently. 'I said stay with the live pictures!'

'You want me to produce, I do it my way!' Jerry shot back, his eyes glinting angrily. 'And that doesn't mean getting innocent people killed. Right?'

Ollie sighed in relief as Victoria smoothly recapped the situation for the viewers. An earlier recording of the signal from the helicam was replayed, and calmly she talked over it.

In the gallery, the journalists could still see the feed from Archie's camera position on one of the monitors, but the rest of the world – and the terrorists – could not. They watched in silence as dark figures moved into position around the ship, and noiselessly began slithering into the water. Most of those watching guessed nothing would happen until nightfall, but it was vital the terrorists were not alerted sooner than absolutely necessary.

The journalists heard another volley of shots ring out,

217

immediately followed by more screams and the frantic sound of running feet. Archie swung round in the direction of the ship. Everyone in the newsroom could see that the terrorists had opened fire on the hostages trapped on the bridge. Two men made a run for it along the deck. One was mown down before he had got ten feet. The other dived into the Thames, blindly making for the shore as the lifeboat rushed to pick him up. The black figures froze, but it was clear that the hijackers had no idea they were there.

'They must have panicked,' Rochelle whispered, a terrible pity in her voice. 'Thank God we're not transmitting this live, their families might see them murdered before their eyes. Oh God, how many have they killed now?'

Ben's voice broke the hushed silence. 'Just make sure this is being recorded,' he said icily. 'The minute we get the all-clear from fucking Scotland Yard, I want to show every bloody frame of picture around the world. We're sitting on an exclusive, and I want it milked.'

'Isn't it good to know he cares?' Archie said dryly from the link point.

■ REGENT'S PARK, LONDON
7.03 p.m.

Sir Edward Penhaligon turned down the sound thoughtfully with his remote control. He stood up and gazed out of the tall window of his study, the green landscape of Regent's Park a peaceful oasis in this urgent, grey city. The elegant curve of the porticoed houses on either side, the rare view, the glut of Mercedes and the odd sprinkling of Morgans and Lagondas; all bespoke the understated wealth of the privileged few for whom these properties were but a London *pied-à-terre*.

218

Sir Edward turned, and let his eye roam around the room, savouring its gracious style and well-proportioned dimensions as he always did. It was his favourite room, which was why he made it his study, where he spent so much of his time when he was in London. Its neutral tones and elegant furniture soothed his soul after the abrasive newsroom environment. His Sheraton desk bore the patina of age and years of loving polishing, the Savonnerie carpet lay infinitely lush beneath his feet. Several walnut tables of an earlier age bore favoured pieces of his extensive collection of European and Oriental porcelains, including a couple of fluted cloisonné vases. A Chagall adorned the only free wall behind his desk; the rest were filled with vast bookcases, containing the classics culled from English, French, Greek and German literature, all in the original languages, many of them first editions. The ancient philosophers rubbed shoulders with the latest modern psychologists; well-read tomes on botany and fishing were indications of his only outdoor pursuits.

The one jarring intrusion of the modern world flickered in the corner, its image silent now but thrustingly present. When not in use, even the television was banished behind walnut doors which disguised it as a cabinet.

It was already seven o'clock. INN had been on air for more than four hours, and Sir Edward had remained in his study, watching the crisis attentively but without undue concern. One eyebrow had risen in surprise when he caught a quick glimpse of a group of men gathered on the river bank, but the image was quickly replaced by a close-up of the reporter's face, and INN had then cut back to Victoria in the studio. Since then, the network had provided continuous coverage of the crisis without showing a revealing shot of the ship, no doubt due to pressure from Scotland Yard.

More than twenty people were already dead. Some had

been shot as hostages, one every hour, as the terrorists had threatened. Others had been killed when the hijackers panicked and turned their guns on those tourists who had been gathered on the bridge of the HMS Belfast, presumably the American tour group. An exclusive interview with the man who had swum to safety revealed that another eighty-four hostages were on board, of whom seventeen were children. INN had showed edited highlights of these events, which they had recorded and then vetted before transmitting. Sir Edward thought it was unlike Ben Wordsworth. Very unlike him.

It was obvious that the SAS were waiting for cover of darkness before making their move. Sir Edward wondered again about that glimpse of the huddle of soldiers he had spotted. If he had seen it on INN, the chances were that so had the terrorists. Obviously that was why INN was now recording the pictures and only showing them after they had been censored. But he was surprised Scotland Yard had permitted INN to keep up their live transmission as long as they had. He was even more surprised that the helicam had been allowed to get as close to the ship as it had done, until it was shot down.

Thoughtfully, Sir Edward picked up the nineteen-thirties Bakelite telephone that lay on the burnished surface of his desk, and dialled a Whitehall number. He asked three questions, and when he put down the receiver, a small smile curved his narrow lips.

So INN had *not* had permission for the helicam. They had defied a direct instruction to cease their live transmission, and Ben Wordsworth had taken personal responsibility for the decision. Interesting. If such details were made public, in the *Daily Ethic* perhaps, it would badly dent INN's image. The viewers would not be happy to know that the network had deliberately risked people's lives to get a good story. Ratings might fall. The shareholders might not be too happy. Wordsworth might have a difficult time with the Board members when they met next week.

Sir Edward intended to make life even more difficult for the INN Editor and Chairman. Having made his decision to wrest control of the network from Wordsworth, Sir Edward was moving his pieces into position with the dexterity and far-sighted strategy of an accomplished diplomat. Coolly he picked up the agenda for the Board meeting, and ran his eye down the closely type-written page.

If he was to force a vote of no confidence in Wordsworth, Sir Edward had to gain a majority share of the company, and seize control of the Board. His meeting with Denzil Calhoun, the media mogul desperate for a share in the burgeoning television news network, had provided the cash with which Sir Edward could buy the necessary shares to take control. The question was, who was going to sell?

Not Wordsworth, obviously. He owned just under thirty-three per cent of INN, and would never relinquish it willingly. Sir Edward himself had a little over fourteen percent. That left nearly fifty-four percent to play for, of which he needed at least thirty-six per cent to hold a majority position.

Sir Edward studied the list of shareholders, probing, testing for weakness, searching for a loophole. The television consortium looked sound for Wordsworth, but when the individual members were examined, there were possibilities. Distinct possibilities. Their mouthpiece, Eustace Pollen, was a figurehead, squarely behind Wordsworth, but with no intrinsic power of his own. He answered to the consortium.

Of the group of television networks which made up the consortium, the World News Service had the largest chunk, and Sir Edward knew its head, Patrick Courtenay, personally. He was confident that Courtenay would take little persuasion to desert Wordsworth, whom he loathed. The remainder – Japanese, Jordanian, French and Australian TV – only had a few per cent each, and they would be difficult to sway. They trusted Wordsworth to look after their interests, and would be reluctant to participate in a coup to oust him. Sir Edward knew he could expect nothing there.

But WNS alone would not be enough, assuming that Courtenay would indeed agree to side with him when it came to a showdown. He would still have little more than half the support he needed.

There were only two avenues left to him: Harry Foley, who had nearly thirteen percent, and the MP Dalmeny de Burgh, who had just under ten. With all their shares, and those of WNS, Sir Edward would control fifty point four per cent of the company altogether. Enough. Just. Just enough to hand him INN on a platinum platter.

And Sir Edward was sure that Foley and de Burgh would sell if they thought INN was disintegrating into cheap sensationalism at the expense of real newsmaking. Foley had too much integrity, and de Burgh too much political sense, to want INN to degenerate into the equivalent of a tabloid rag.

Still smiling, Sir Edward picked up the telephone again and dialled.

'Denzil,' he said pleasantly when the Editor of the *Daily Ethic* answered. 'This won't take up much of your time. But I thought there was something you should know.'

Chapter Eight

Christie was repainting her flat when the telephone rang.

She stood in her dungarees, one foot on the edge of the bath, the other wedged against the tiles around the wall, and stared at the unfinished ceiling of her bathroom. Her paintbrush was motionless in her hand as she debated whether or not to let the answer machine take the call. A spatter of paint fell across her face and strands of blonde hair that had escaped from the cotton rag with which she had tied it back. Christie sighed and threw her paintbrush down as she gave up the unequal struggle and dashed to answer the call. She knew her bathroom would remain a mixture of its original ivory and the newly-added peach until she had finished the story at the end of the telephone line. Perhaps she would leave it that way; its incomplete state reflected her life better than anything else, she thought with a wry smile.

Decorating was something Christie tended to do when she wanted to mark a watershed in her life. It was as if by completely changing the tenor of her surroundings, she could punctuate her life, dividing it into neat chapters, with a beginning, a middle and an end. Schooldays. Teenage traumas. The moment she fell in love. Whatever that meant.

The first time Christie had painted her room, she had been nearly eleven. She had just completed *The Mill on the Floss*, and in an agony of female ire at Maggie's capitulation to society's hypocrisy, had been determined to establish her identity as an individual. Abruptly she decided that her childhood had ended and that this fact needed to be publicly acknowledged. With this in mind, she had stolen a can of white paint from her father's garage and obliterated the kittens and puppies that adorned her bedroom walls. He had been furious at her clumsy attempts at decorating, but her mother had lead him away and subdued his dire threats of retribution, much to Christie's relief.

With the passing years, Christie's bedroom walls had passed through many changes. After the original sterile whiteness that had ousted the childhood kittens and puppies, Christie had leapt into pretty pink-and-white girlishness, followed by an angry statement against the pains of growing up that she believed to be unique. Her mother had winced as the pink was replaced with black walls and ceiling, cobweb grey curtains and silvery mirrors on every available surface. She had even maintained her silence when Christie took to burning incense and joss-sticks all around her room, silently praying that her seventeen-year-old daughter would come out of this phase before she drove her mother to distraction. The black vanished at the end of Christie's first term at Oxford, replaced with a Bohemian collection of postcards, photographs and trendy watercolour prints on pale yellow walls. When Christie left University and bought her own flat in Islington, she had furnished the graceful Georgian rooms with stark modern pieces that her mother found almost as jarring as the hippy phase had been. The matt black bookcases and desk, the abstract pictures, the total absence of colour, ill-suited the high moulded ceilings and tall, elegant windows. Her mother fervently hoped that the innate taste which had lead Christie to buy such a classic property would eventually surface and allow her to decorate it accordingly.

224

Abruptly, when she joined INN, Christie discarded the whole concept of an image and simply let each facet of her character be individually reflected in the way she lived. What could have become confused and rootless was instead original, a little of everything and all of nothing. For the first time in her life, she no longer felt an outcast, unsure of her identity or the way in which she wanted the world to perceive her. She allowed herself to be simply Christie Bradley, as easy to pin down and label as quicksilver.

All around the flat were quirky pieces Christie had picked up on her travels, the objects which had answered a need or satisfied a whimsical urge as she roamed markets and souks across the world. A pair of silver and burgundy Turkish slippers, a black and gold hookah from Pakistan, and a Syrian brass shoe-shining box were arranged together in one corner. An ancient Corona typewriter and a hundred-year-old camera graced two shelves of the bookcases. They had belonged to her grandmother, the tools of her trade; she had been a renowned Fleet Street theatre critic in her day. Half a dozen silver photograph frames were casually scattered around the flat. A grey African stone statue of a heavily-pregnant woman, kneeling with her arms around her distended stomach, stood on the exquisite marble fireplace. Christie's bedroom was more simply decorated. A burnished silver bowl containing faded petals gave the room a soft fragrance that mingled with the scent of Chanel No 5 and Cristalle that Christie habitually used. Each petal was from a bouquet of flowers that Christie had been given at some stage in her life: a bridesmaid's posy from her cousin's wedding, the first flowers ever given to her by a man, her grandmother's funeral wreath.

Christie's redecoration of her bathroom this time marked the departure of her last boyfriend and, with him, the compromise she had permitted to colour her personal life. David had ended all that. Painfully she accepted that there would probably never be a future for the two of them. David was too damaged, too afraid, to reach out to her. But her meeting with him had given her a glimpse of what she could feel, and even if she risked never finding that again, Christie was determined not to settle for what she knew to be second best.

Two days after she had last seen him, she had received a parcel, tightly wrapped in brown paper and tied with a black velvet ribbon. Opening it, a silver Syrian good-luck charm shaped like a tiny pencil, three hundred years old, its surface wrought with arabic writing, had tumbled into her palm. The hollow charm had at one time contained texts from the Koran, but was now empty except for a piece of paper bearing two words that Christie did not understand. *Amoud fiki.* She kept it hidden away at the back of her lingerie drawer. Its smooth cool surface reassured her fingertips every time she reached into the drawer to find it, slipped between the silky folds of her camisoles and teddies.

Now, Christie pushed all thoughts of David from her mind as she answered the telephone.

She did not even have time to wash off the paint that spattered her tanned arms before she was en route to Albania.

She travelled light and alone.

■ ALBANIA
14 June, 11.20 a.m.

Christie hunkered down in the bombed-out restaurant, and waited for the next burst of automatic gunfire. Cautiously she resettled herself on the rubble beneath her feet, her arms outstretched against the dust-coated walls on either side of her.

She had not yet thought how to handle the fact that David would soon be joining her. She could not risk being distracted in situations like the one that faced her now, as she considered how long the sniper would keep her pinned down. She wondered if David felt the same bittersweet mixture of delight and terror that suffused her when she thought of him, twisting her stomach into knots with more painful accuracy than any barrage of artillery.

Awkwardly she twisted on the stones, trying to ease the stiffness in her joints. Carefully she turned around, her back wedged into the corner of the wall, making sure she did not expose herself to a sniper by getting too close to the gaping hole wrought by a shell during some earlier battle. The hotel she was staying at was just across the street, damaged by shells and its walls pocked by automatic fire, but still standing. Christie had been returning from a foray to another part of the battered city when the sudden burst of fire had forced her to dive for cover into the nearest shelter. It was pitifully inadequate.

Anxiously she scanned the sky above her, the restaurant roof so much rubble on the floor. She could see no snipers in the buildings visible from her vantage point, but then you never could. Thank God she had bothered to put on her cumbersome flak jacket before venturing out; it would not stop a high-velocity bullet, but it was proof against shrapnel and the lethal slivers of glass a bomb might send flying.

A skitter of stones alerted her to the fact that she was no longer alone. Not daring to stand up, Christie pushed her hair wearily away from her face and scanned the room, half of which was in shadows.

'Hello, who's there?' she called, speaking with a

confidence she did not feel. 'I am a television journalist for INN. I am not armed.'

The movement ceased for a moment, then began again, more cautious this time. Christie's heart hammered in her chest. She doubted that any of the numerous militias would deliberately kill her, but every journalist dreaded the nervous soldier who might fire first and ask questions later.

'Do you speak English?' Christie tried again, deciding to risk moving away from the wall. Safe as she might be from snipers outside the building, she was right opposite the doorway into the room, and directly in the line of fire from anyone who might come in, guns blazing. Easing herself on to her stomach, she snaked her way carefully over the rubble towards the doorway, wincing as the stones bit into her palms. Once her back was against the wall, she resisted the temptation to stand, and continued the slow and painful progress of crawling to the end of the room, aiming for the shelter of what had once been the bar at the side of the restaurant. Abruptly she stopped. In front of her, two booted feet blocked her way. Reluctantly she looked up.

'I've been wanting you to swoon at my feet,' David said, his eyes glinting with humour.

■ 2.50 p.m.

Together with the cameraman, Fabian Broak, and the editor, Steve Bower, Christie and David loaded their equipment boxes into the dilapidated minibus that the three men had hired in Greece to carry their edit gear into Albania. The worst of the fighting was to the north of the country, along the border with Kosovo, the Serbian-controlled province which had once made up part of Yugoslavia. No news network had risked covering the

228

area up to now; the situation had simply become too dangerous. The outside world relied upon the intermittent reports of local journalists, whose English was negligible, and whose partisan status made every assessment of the situation questionable. The only other news now coming out of the country was that provided by UN press briefings, which had grown more terse and less informative as UN casualties rose. Initially a peace-*keeping* force, the UN troops had gradually taken on a peace-*making* role, distrusted by all sides. They had become subject to the kind of guerrilla tactics that the Americans had faced in Vietnam, and the cost – in money and lives – was high.

All four of David's team knew that no one's safety could be guaranteed in the area for which they were headed. But they also knew that that was where the story was.

'OK, who's in charge of this charabanc?' Christie asked, eyeing the rusty GMC warily. She opened a creaking door and felt the torn red plastic seat. 'Oh, great, an eighteen hour journey with no suspension. I wish I'd worn a cross-your-heart bra.'

Steve climbed into the driver's seat, easing himself around the accumulated debris on the floor of the van. Cautiously he wiggled the gear stick.

'Well, the chewing-gum is holding, but it's anybody's guess for how long,' he said cheerily. 'Never mind, let's just pray if the gear-stick goes, we're not stuck in reverse for four hundred miles.'

Christie groaned, and looked across at David as he climbed into the rear seat beside her. 'If this is your idea of a white horse, I can't wait to see your notion of a dream home,' she said, rolling her eyes heavenward.

'Pretty much like the one I found you in,' David retorted.

Christie blushed. He enjoyed catching her off-guard, she could see it in his eyes. She shuddered in embarrassment as she thought back to their reunion, the wicked amusement in his expression as he saw her lying on the floor at his feet, covered in grime and a white icing of brickdust and plaster. She laughed. Typical. She had spent a month planning their next meeting, what she would wear, how she would act. Forget the slinky black number and artfully tumbled hair. Christie shrugged her shoulders in good-humoured resignation.

'I guess not even Kim Basinger could look good in khaki fatigues and a flak jacket,' she laughed ruefully.

David looked at her and the smile in his eyes deepened. 'I don't know, you might start a trend,' he said casually, but Christie caught an undercurrent of intensity that belied the easy banter of his words. Unsure how to respond, she took refuge in silence.

'If you'd like to take your seats, ladies and gentlemen, the tour is about to begin,' Steve intoned, starting the minibus. 'On your left, you can see a perfect example of Albanian architecture, carefully reconstructed by the Serbs. The baroque addition of the shells is picked up in the thoughtfully interspersed bullet holes along the wall.'

Christie grinned, and tried to find a comfortable position against the hard back of the seat. Eighteen hours was going to be a long time. She was acutely aware of David's presence next to her, and sat rigidly avoiding his eyes. The easy companionship they had shared had suddenly altered, the unspoken words and feelings hanging in the air between them. Christie was disturbed by the emotions swirling within her, afraid and exhilarated by turns. A palpable sense of excitement filled the silence, as each played a delicate game of brinkmanship and waited for the other's next move. It never occurred to Christie that there might not be a next move. Neither of them could have drawn back now, even if they had wanted to. She remembered something her grandmother had once said: it is the things you don't do, the missed opportunities, that you later regret, rather than the mistakes you make.

But mingled with the promise she felt was a deep, nameless fear. The price she might have to pay for David was her hard-won independence, which she was beginning to realise would count for nothing beside the feelings she harboured for this man. Until now, her happiness had never depended on another person. Her vulnerability terrified her.

Christie felt David's eyes burning into the back of her neck as she gazed absently at the war-torn landscape around them. Bombed houses were visible along the side of the road, and here and there a burnt-out car stood out starkly against the barren fields. The few telephone lines still standing led nowhere, the wires trailing abruptly into nothing. Signposts pointed to desolation and tragedy. She knew from experience it would be far worse when they reached a town.

A sudden jolt of the GMC threw her against David and she put out her arms automatically to brace herself against the bucking vehicle. She was startled by the flash of heat she felt course through her veins as she touched him. Her eyes caught his, and his gaze seared her, and she felt curiously exposed. Unbidden, his hands reached out and curled around hers where she had grasped him. The electricity between them drew them together, although they barely touched. Softly he turned her hand over, and stroked the cuts on her palm that had been inflicted by the glass and rubble. Christie gave herself to the sensation, concentrating the whole of her being on the delicate movement of his fingers over her hand, longing to feel his touch all over her body, her face, her neck, her breasts, inside her.

David's signet ring grazed her fingers, and she smiled sadly at the reminder of the world outside them that it evoked. David was not hers to choose, she was not his to

231

be chosen. His past held him too closely. He was not free to love.

Her own thoughts brought her to herself abruptly. Who had said anything about love?

David looked down, and slowly moved his hand away, as if determined that his actions would be conscious, not born of chance or instinct. He sat immobile, staring at his hands unseeingly, as if some answer to his dilemma lay written in them. For so long he had battled with himself, determined to pay his debt for the mistake that had cost Seb his life. He had resigned himself to the fact that he would never share the love and happiness with a woman of which he had once dreamed. His job had always stood in the way, and now he had Caryn and Sandy to consider. He *owed* them.

Or was he just running away?

There was nothing more he dreaded than failure. With sudden awareness, David realised that he had never allowed himself to become involved with anyone else. He had used the demands of his job as an excuse to avoid intimacy. Instead, he had put all of himself into holding together the isolated life he had so carefully constructed. If he did not play the game, he could not fail. Did he now have the courage to gamble everything and risk himself?

Yes, he owed Caryn and Sandy. But he owed himself more. It was time he started living again.

The GMC shuddered, and in the distance a spatter of gunfire broke the silence. Steve swerved to avoid a deep rut in the road, carved by a past battle, and Fabian braced himself in the front seat as the minibus jounced across the verge and then back on to the road. The distant crumping of shells falling in the distance heralded the end of the latest precarious ceasefire.

Christie was aware only of the pounding in her own heart, and the heat of the man beside her. What if she had dared to acknowledge her own feelings to herself, only to lose him now? Without meeting her eyes, David carefully drew the gold ring off his little finger, almost to the end. He caught Christie's eyes, holding their gaze. Carefully he eased the ring off his finger. Christie felt the warm, hard metal in the palm of her hand as David closed her fingers around it. This was more than a good luck charm. It was a promise.

'It's over,' he whispered, so softly that Christie had to strain to hear him. 'It's over.'

The GMC jolted through the night, the sound of gunfire and sporadic shelling increasing as they grew nearer to the battle area. They took it in turns to drive, killing the headlights so as not to provide an obvious target, struggling over the pitted and rutted roads in the darkness. Always, at the back of their minds, was the threat of a landmine, ambush, a spray of machine-gun fire by a nervous soldier. So far they had not come across any checkpoints, but they had agreed that if they did, they would stop and try to talk their way out of trouble. Fabian clung on to his camera more tightly, and muttered darkly about the fate that would befall anyone foolish enough to attempt to separate him from it. Christie eyed the bulging muscles built by years of dedicated weight-training, and privately decided to stand well clear of him when the fun began.

Resolutely she pushed thoughts of David from her mind, and considered her two other companions with interest. So far she had not worked with either Fabian or Steve, although she knew them both by reputation. Fabian was in his late thirties, a faded, jaded cameraman who had seen everything and done even more. He had been in most of the major hotspots around the globe, and won a number of awards for his footage of some bitter and bloody battles. Two of the heavy, silver metal boxes in the back of the minibus contained not camera equipment but his training weights, which he insisted on taking with him on every assignment. Christie wondered how he managed to talk his way out of the astronomical excess baggage charges he racked up as he travelled around the world. In these days of accountants and cost-cutting, it was not unknown to have to weigh each piece of equipment before embarking on a story, to make sure budgets were adhered to. Christie herself had spent one night putting cameras and monitors on a pair of bathroom scales before her Somalia trip. She'd love to know Fabian's secret.

The editor, Steve, was a few years younger than Fabian; his speed and skill were legendary. An editor could make or break a story: no matter how good the cameraman or how expert the reporter, if the editor did not put it together correctly, all was lost. Steve was highly rated; working with him virtually guaranteed an out-of-the-ordinary piece. He had an instinct for finding the right shot, the precise piece of footage to illustrate the reporter's commentary perfectly, no matter how short they were for time. He was renowned for his ability to edit through anything – riots, bombs, shelling, even INN Christmas parties. He was also an accomplished cameraman, which meant they could split into two teams if necessary, David working with Fabian and herself with Steve. He was a good friend of Archie's, and the two of them were notorious lady-killers wreaking havoc and leaving a trail of broken hearts in their wake.

'Shit! There's a checkpoint ahead,' David muttered darkly at the wheel, interrupting Christie's thoughts.

Fabian and Steve sat up, blearily peering out into the darkness. Ahead of them, a twisted piece of metal piping had been dragged across the road, balanced on two piles of tyres. A gun barrel glinted in the moonlight, and the dark shapes of three or four figures were visible at the edges of the road.

'Keep driving! For fuck's sake, don't stop!' Steve shouted. Fabian ducked beneath the dashboard and peered over its top. 'Don't bloody stop, whatever you do!'

Christie sat up, all senses on alert as David slowed down. He was unwilling to run the gauntlet of who knew how many trigger-happy gunmen. A single shot rang out, setting their pulses racing.

'They're attacking! Keep going! If you stop you'll get us all killed!' Fabian shouted angrily.

'We said we'd talk our way out of it,' David argued, struggling to maintain an air of calm. 'They've no reason to shoot us, that was just a warning shot.'

Even as he spoke, they heard shouts as the soldiers let rip a volley of fire. David swerved, and put his foot down hard on the accelerator.

'If you go through that checkpoint, we've no way of knowing what's on the other side, and then they'll be ahead and behind us,' Christie stated coolly. 'We have to stop.'

David agreed with her, and slowed the GMC as they approached the checkpoint. Steve crossed himself.

'Tell Jilly, Katherine and Vicky that the last name I spoke was theirs,' he said gloomily. 'If you ever get out, that is.'

David pulled the minibus into the side of the road, where an upended coffin served duty as a sentry box, and wound down the window.

A soldier wearing mis-matching camouflage gear approached the vehicle warily. He gesticulated with the barrel of the gun for them to climb out, and silently they complied. Three more soldiers, looking weary and afraid, peered inside the minibus.

David produced his INN identity card, and handed it to

the soldier in front of him, who produced a torch and played its weak pencil beam on the laminated press pass.

'INN?' he said suspiciously. 'Television?'

David nodded. 'We're filming a report,' he said in precise tones, careful not to sound apprehensive.

'Which side are you on?' the man barked, swinging the gun against David's chest.

Inwardly Christie offered up a prayer. In these places, you did not even have a fifty-fifty chance of getting it right, since there were always more than two sides in any civil war. Get it wrong, and you could end up another statistic – a very dead one.

David did not hesitate. 'The side of freedom, of course,' he answered, as if surprised that the question could even be asked.

The soldier frowned, and privately David held his breath, joining his prayer to Christie's. He did not have a clue whether these gunmen were Albanian, Serbian or Martians, and there were so many splinter groups, they probably did not know each other either. Suddenly the barrel swung away from David, and the soldier broke out in smiles, revealing a gap-toothed grin.

'Friends! Welcome to our beautiful country,' he announced with a flourish. 'Most welcome, sir, than-kyou, yes, sir. Tea?'

David did not get the chance to refuse, as the soldier turned round and shouted something unintelligible to his companions. One of them reached into the upended coffin and extracted a battered thermos flask, which he handed to David, nodding expectantly, his eyes not leaving David's face. David unscrewed the cap, and toasted them before raising it to his lips, smiling as the soldiers surrounded him, nudging each other with their elbows conspiratorially, their guns cradled casually in their arms. He smelt the brackish liquid, and feigned a great gulp, then spluttered realistically. He had obviously gauged the strength of the brew accurately, for the soldiers' expectant expressions gave way to great roars of merriment, and they clapped him on the back. It was clear David was the only honoured guest, for the tea vanished without being offered to the others. Ringed by beaming gunmen, they were escorted back to the minibus, two of the ad-hoc soldiers letting off a volley of shots as the GMC resumed its journey. Christie crossed her fingers in the hope that the salute would not be the cause of another battle.

'I hate to dampen your diplomatic success,' Steve said, hiding his admiration at David's cool handling of the situation behind his usual dry banter. 'We seem to have run out of fuel.'

'Oh, don't worry about that,' Fabian said, grinning broadly, and pointing to a filthy drum at the back of the GMC. 'Whilst Giandominico Pico here was negotiating, I took the opportunity of liberating a little of their fuel. With any luck, we'll be long gone by the time they discover it, and they won't have the gas to chase us anyway.'

'And they wonder why the world is going to the dogs,' Christie said, burying her head in her hands.

■ PRIZREN, KOSOVO
   25 June, 3.10 p.m.

'I need the go-ahead direct from Ben,' David shouted into the crackling telephone line. 'And no, I can't hang on a minute. There's a fucking battle going on around me, and with this satellite phone sticking up like a beacon, I'm a sitting duck.'

He jumped as an incoming shell landed two blocks

away, and crouched down lower on the roof of the abandoned hotel where they had set up the satellite telephone. It was the only point where the signal was clear enough to transmit back to London, but the metre wide dish was clearly visible from a number of sniper positions in the deserted city around them. One shell was all it would take.

Christie appeared through the skylight which was their means of entry on to the roof, and mimed a thumbs up or thumbs down at him. David shrugged, and Christie rolled her eyes heavenwards before ducking back down inside. David listened to the buzz of the newsroom as he waited for Brian Reynolds to put Ben on to him, and a sudden vision of Christie, naked and in his arms, floated into his head. It was the first time he had allowed himself to think of her as he would like to see her, rather than as his colleague. Since he had handed her his ring on the journey to Kosovo – was it really ten days ago? – they had both submerged their personal feelings, adopting a professional relationship by common assent. David held on to an inner certainty that they had a future together. He did not allow himself to think of the barriers that had to be overcome, or where they were going. Subconsciously he, too, was relieved at the breathing space the story was forcing them to take. They had slept only a few hours a night in the past week, and between them had secured some unrivalled footage of the carnage taking place in the disputed Yugo-slavian province. There had literally not been time to think.

'Wordsworth here, David, what can I do for you?'

'Ben, I'll be brief because I don't know how long the line will hold out,' David said crisply into the receiver. 'We've got a chance to get into Dakovica, which has been beseiged for the last seven months. It's going to be dangerous and probably expensive, but if we get the

238

exclusive it'll be the hottest thing to hit the screen in a year.'

Half a world away in the newsroom, Ben listened carefully, biting his thumbnail as David spoke. He had no doubt that if David said it was a hot story, it would melt sets worldwide. He also knew that if the reporter said it was dangerous, he was not exaggerating; Ben had no wish to be pilloried as the Editor who put his staff's lives at risk to get a story – not after the beating he had taken in the wake of the HMS Belfast hijack. He still didn't know who had leaked the story to the *Daily Ethic*, but he was burning to find out. It had been splashed across the tabloids for days, and there had been renewed demands in the House of Commons that steps be taken to curb the freedom of the Press. The mother of a sixteen-year-old girl who had been gunned down by the terrorists had even started a campaign against him, saying if he had not given the game away by transmitting throughout the hijack, the SAS rescue might have cost fewer lives.

'I can't have you putting yourself, or anyone else, at risk, David, you know that,' Ben replied, the words hurting as he said them. Damn! He'd give blood – as long as it wasn't his – to get this story. The small town of Dakovica had been without food or medicine since before Christmas; the pictures would be devastating, the ratings would soar, and he could do with some good PR. It might keep the Board off his back for once.

'Come on, Ben, you and I both know simply being here is a risk.' David's voice crackled down the line, exasperated. 'We could get shot at just being on the bloody phone. But I need you behind me on this one.'

They can't say I didn't warn them, Ben thought. 'OK, if you want to go in, I leave it in your hands,' he said, after a brief pause. He knew he wasn't good at playing the reluctant virgin, and he knew David knew it, but what the

239

hell. 'But you're not taking the girl in,' he said, as an afterthought. A dead war correspondent, yes. But no attractive blonde women punched full of holes. The viewers would never forgive him that.

'Shit, Ben, I need more hands than that,' David replied angrily. 'How the hell do I watch my back? We're short staffed as it is.'

'I'll send you Karim from Beirut. He'll be with you in two days. You can take him and Fabian, and that's my final word.'

'I hope the bloody BBC or CNN don't beat us to it. They're arriving here later today,' David retorted.

'You can congratulate yourselves. They wouldn't be panicking to get there if you hadn't broadcast some bloody good pieces,' Ben said smoothly.

'I want an engineer out here,' David demanded. 'The local station is falling apart, and I want to feed this story. I'm not shipping it back by road like all the others, and having the competition scooping us.' Up to now, they had been sending their cut tapes back with a driver, and had lost two of their five shipments. Once the car had been ambushed, and the other time the driver had simply absconded with the money he had demanded up front, and had never been seen again. 'And if Karim isn't here in two days, I go without him.'

'You got it. But not with Christie, remember that.'

On the roof of the hotel in Prizren, David replaced the handset of the satellite telephone without replying. He'd got his own way, but he wished it was Ben, and not him, who had to tell Christie she was staying behind to babysit.

Ginny raced down the long corridor to INN's videotape library, relieved that she had worn soft trainers to work. She had had a feeling about today when she got up that morning, and it had been confirmed when she glanced at the calendar propped up on her bedroom windowsill. Friday 13th. Not that it was, but that was when she had last changed the date. She should have stayed in bed. It had been one of those days with no obvious news stories around, which meant Jerry had to flam up some kind of lead out of nothing. Days like this were always hard work and very unrewarding.

'Do you have any library pictures of Kosovo? Any last week's pictures? Any Yugoslavian TV pictures? Any other pictures?' she gasped breathlessly at the bemused man sitting calmly at his desk.

'God, you're worse than immigration,' he responded, punching a few keys on his computer.

Ginny leant against the side of the desk panting. She caught sight of herself in the polished glass that served as a wall between the library and the atrium. At head height were a row of circles which had been engraved on to the glass after three people had been hospitalised walking into it. Ben had decided the cost of making the glass walls visible was worth it. Ollie's suggestion that they simply not clean them had been frostily ignored.

Ginny turned her head slightly to get a better view of her new asymmetric hair-cut. Nick had loved her hair long, and privately she thought it made her seem softer, but there was no doubt that she looked more chic and elegant with it as it was now, tapering into the nape of her slender neck. Nick was over, finished, she thought firmly; like the parrot, he was no more. She was glad he had

241

found somebody else. After all, she had Charles now – some of the time, anyway. So why did she feel so lost and empty?

'Got some pictures of fighting from six weeks ago,' the videotape librarian replied. 'Might have a few shots of a bombed out town, if you give me a mo. I'll just check for you.'

Ginny nodded absently, and scribbled down some notes on her clipboard. Christie had just done a recorded telephone interview on the general situation in the troubled Yugoslavian province, but she had been unable to send any new pictures in time for the four o'clock News Update, so Jerry had decided to run some old library pictures – if they had any – over Christie's piece. David had gone further north, to Dakovica, so Christie was holding the fort for him until he returned.

'Yeah, we've got some footage of the aftermath of an attack on Pristina,' the librarian said. 'Trouble is, it's already out.'

'Who's got it?' Ginny asked, wrenching her mind back to the job.

'Try Rich, on the Early Evening News,' he replied, already turning back to his computer.

'Why is it I feel I am fighting the fifth column?' Ginny asked despairingly of no one in particular, and headed back towards the lift and the newsroom floor.

As Ginny turned the corner and entered the newsroom, she almost ran into Archie, who was sauntering out of the Editor's office looking very pleased with himself.

'OK, give me the gen.,' she said, looping her slim arms around his shoulders. 'Let me guess, they just made you Court Correspondent.'

'Close,' Archie said, his eyes glittering. 'Let's just say that Peter Princer isn't going to like me very much.'

'Archie! You got the Latin America bureau! Congratulations,' Ginny enthused, genuinely pleased for him. 'You
deserve it, you've done more cats up trees than Tom and
Jerry.'

Archie grinned. 'All I have to do now is make sure they
give me an on-line computer out there, so I can still hack
into the system,' he said, sliding into his desk. 'I still want
to know how come the only punishment Princer got was
to be demoted back to the desk here in London. If the
rumours are true, Wordsworth could have hung him out
to dry for what he did. And if they aren't, how come he
got hauled back at all? It doesn't add up.'

'Shame you weren't around when JFK was assassi-
nated,' Ginny said, laughing. 'You'd have had a field day
with the old conspiracy theory.'

They heard a familiar thud, and looked around to see
Mo, the ancient tea lady, pushing her dilapidated trolley
into the newsroom, her plump black face wreathed in
smiles. The two urns clinked against each other as the
trolley hit the bump in the floor caused by a group of
cables trailing under the carpet, and a couple of antiquated
cheese rolls tumbled off the shelf below the tea and coffee
urns. When INN had moved into their glittering new
HQ, the trolley had been abolished and replaced with
expensive automatic coffee machines, set in their own
pantries on each floor of the building. Petitions had been
signed, strikes threatened, resignations offered. Never had
so many done so much for a cup of tea. For once, the
disparate unions had been united in a common cause to
Bring Back The Trolley. Management threw up their
hands in submission before there was a general walk-out.
Mo's job and one of INN's most revered traditions had
been saved for future generations to enjoy. Twice a day, at
eleven and three-thirty, the trolley trundled around the
building. It was the only time Management met with

everybody else apart from to hire and fire them. The coffee pantries remained unfrequented by those seeking beverages, but alternative uses had been found for them. By Archie in particular.

'Troll-ee-ee-ee!' Mo yodelled thunderously. Across the newsroom work ceased as everyone stopped whatever they were doing and headed for the urns. It was a siren call that the whole building heeded. Wire-stories were dropped, telephone calls interrupted, conversations abandoned.

'You know you've had a good lunch when you get back, and the trolley's still in the newsroom,' said Sam Hargrave, leaning over to help himself to a Milky Way.

Ginny reached for a doughnut, and caught Archie's eye. 'Oh, don't make me feel guilty, I've got to have something!' she wailed. 'I haven't got the energy for sex, and alcohol gives me a hangover.'

Sam winked conspiratorially at her, and eased his way out of the cluster of people around the trolley. Ollie picked up another doughnut, and nodded at Ginny in agreement.

'Know what you mean,' he said gloomily. 'Even my hand complains of a headache these days.'

Dom picked up a plastic beaker filled with a muddy brown liquid, and stirred it thoughtfully with his pen. 'I used to go out with a girl who was slightly cross-eyed,' he said reflectively. 'When she had an orgasm, her eyes straightened out. It was bloody amazing – and it gave you something to aim for.'

Ginny shook her head at him in despair.

Bob Carpenter frowned slightly. Trainees these days. They even commandeered the trolley talk. It was different in his day. 'I bonked five times last night,' he said casually, pleased that he was cool enough to know the right word.

'How will you be able to type with that sore hand?' Ginny enquired sweetly.

244

Bob glowered as she headed back towards her desk.

'How you doing with the pictures?' Jerry asked as she sat down and took a sip of tea.

'Oh, we'll have enough to cover it,' she answered, leaning back against her chair and watching CNN on the newsroom monitor. 'Luckily no one else has got a satt phone up and running yet, so they don't have any live stuff. Can't wait to see what David brings back.'

'You and me both,' Jerry answered feelingly. 'It's a pretty thin show today. All we have so far is the Dutch motorway crash, and frankly we need a few deaths if it's going to be our lead story.'

'There's the missing baby,' Rochelle added hopefully. 'If we get another interview with the mother, it might stand up.'

Ollie paused as he passed by the News Update desk. 'Oh, sorry to disappoint you, but I'm afraid they found the baby. Left it in the car while they went to watch Wimbledon, and some woman rescued it.'

'Oh shit!' Jerry muttered, and turned round to call to the PA to alter the running order. 'Cut story 10! I'm pleased to say they found the sodding baby!' he yelled. 'There's no help for it. I'll lead on Christie's phono from Kosovo. I just wish we had some new pictures.'

He stood up, raking his hand through his curly dirt-blonde hair, and wandered in the direction of the gallery. They still had ten minutes to go until the headlines went on air; maybe something would happen. He grinned as he remembered Bob Carpenter's humiliating experience as an up-and-coming reporter, in the days before he retreated behind his OBE. Carpenter had been convinced he had found Lord Lucan, the missing peer, staking his reputation on a lead he had which traced the aristocratic fugitive to New Zealand. He had persuaded Ben to give him a crew and enough funds to spend three weeks wandering around the boondocks, before the hoax was exposed and he returned home to be ritually disembowelled by the tabloid press. It was not something of which he liked to be reminded.

'Jerry, there's been a pile-up on the M25,' Rochelle called out to the Producer as he reached the door of the control room. 'No details on casualties yet. I've ordered a map from Graphics.'

'OK, let's move that to story one,' Jerry instructed the director, Muriel. 'We won't need the Dutch car crash now. We've got our own one.'

Bob Carpenter stuck his head around the door into the Gallery. 'I've finished the piece on the new Education Bill,' he said pompously. 'It runs at one minute forty-five. Do you want to see it?'

'Yes, but only with a view to not using it,' Jerry said distractedly.

Rochelle grinned as Bob retreated crestfallen back into the newsroom. She jerked her head in Jerry's direction. 'Don't mind him. He's just been to a management course on motivation,' she said, gathering her clipboard and stopwatch and heading towards the Gallery.

Charles emerged from Make-Up, looking immaculate as usual. As he passed the glass window at the edge of the atrium he glanced at his reflection. The deep turquoise stripe in his charcoal-grey Savile Row suit definitely set off his eyes . . . and the Dior shirt was perfect. Just a glint of the gold cufflinks, not too much . . . he didn't want to distract the viewers from his face. He smiled as Ginny raced past him, clutching her stopwatch to her chest. No wonder that tantalising little piece found him irresistible. They all did.

He sat down at the anchor's desk, riffling expertly through the scripts in front of him. The floor manager inserted his moulded earpiece into Charles' ear, and immediately he heard the buzz of conversation taking place in the Control Gallery. Charles picked up the mirror from his tray beneath the desk, licked his fingers and swiftly smoothed down his eyebrows. In the monitor to his left he saw the shot of himself that Muriel had lined up. Only his head and shoulders were visible.

'Could you keep my hands in shot?' he asked, looking up and adjusting the sit of his jacket. 'The viewers think they're sexy.'

Jerry leaned forward in his seat, scanning the wires. It was a slow moving day, but he still felt the pulse of adrenalin surge through his veins as Annie started the three minute countdown. Reuters flashed a story slugged 'Motorway' as he watched, and Rochelle groaned. Jerry called up the story and sighed.

'Typical. No one's dead, and we're leading on it.'

'Could be worse,' Rochelle said, grimacing. 'At least we've got pictures of nobody dead and the BBC hasn't.'

As they went on air with the lacklustre bulletin, Jerry thanked God and all his angels for Christie's live phono from Kosovo. For once the satellite link did not go down forty-five seconds before they needed it, and Christie came on air, sounding tense but calm and in control. As she answered Charles' questions on the latest situation, Muriel played in the pictures Ginny had called up from the library.

'How much longer can the people there hold out?' Charles said, as the PA told him to wind up the interview.

'They've already lasted much longer than anyone believed possible,' Christie answered, her voice distorted by the crackling phone line. 'Seven months is a long time to be without any kind of outside aid. The problem is . . .'

Her voice was interrupted by a deafening thud, and everyone listening heard the roar of an explosion. There was a pause, and the newsroom held its breath, suddenly transfixed to the floor as they watched the monitors.

'It looks like our position is being shelled,' Christie said after what seemed like an endless moment. 'I'm afraid they're getting more accurate with practise . . .'

'Jesus, get her off the line!' Jerry breathed. 'She'll be hit if she keeps transmitting! Charles, wind the interview up *now*!'

Charles closed the interview, and started to read the lead-in for the final story of the bulletin. Ginny raced around to the Master Control Room, where the line was still up, and pressed the talkback button.

'Christie, you had us worried there!' she said, relief tinging her tone. 'Get off the bloody roof of the hotel, for God's sake!'

'If you lot would let me go, I would,' Christie replied. 'How are things your end?'

'Not the same without you,' Ginny answered loyally. 'By the way, Jenny Strand rang. Patrick's had the operation, and it seems to be going fine. His kidney hasn't rejected, and they think the drugs are keeping any infection at bay.'

'That's great news,' Christie answered. 'Send them my love, won't you? I'll call as soon as I get out of this picnic.'

'No worries. I thought I'd pop in on my way back home after this bulletin,' Ginny said. 'The only other message for you is from someone called Marina, in Israel. She says she rang before, and needs to speak to you. What do you want me to say?'

Christie frowned at the other end of the phone. She remembered that Muriel had tried to call before, but could not think what it could be about. A sudden burst of gunfire no more than a street away recalled her to her current position.

'It'll have to wait,' she said briskly, as another mortar landed nearby. 'I'm going to have to clear the line down in a moment.' She paused, then came to a decision. 'Ginny, I'm worried about David. I haven't heard from him for nearly forty-eight hours, and I should have had some message by now. I'm going to go in if there isn't any word from him soon.'

Ginny sucked in her breath in concern. 'Christie, are you sure? You could get into real trouble. The last thing he needs to worry about is you.'

'I know something is wrong,' Christie said urgently. 'I'll never get it past Ben if I tell him, but I need someone to know where I'm going. If anything happens . . .'

'It won't,' Ginny interrupted, worry making her more abrupt than she intended. 'Take care, Christie,' she added more gently.

'You too,' Christie replied. 'Just be careful, promise me?'

In the background Ginny could hear the battle intensifying. 'What do I have to be careful about?' she asked in surprise.

Christie just managed to answer before she was cut off.

'Charles,' she said simply.

■ CAMDEN, LONDON
6.20 p.m.

Christie's words echoed in Ginny's mind as she cycled home to her flat in Camden, enjoying the balmy feeling of the evening air. Even London's crowded, polluted streets seemed pleasant as she rode slowly down the back roads, a gentle breeze caressing her bare arms. It was warm, but not yet the sticky suffocating airlessness that often came later in the summer and made her long for the crisp onset of autumn. Outside the city pubs, benches and tables had been hauled out on to the pavement, and Londoners revelled in the unaccustomed warmth, propping up windowsills with tall glasses of beer clasped in their hands. For once she left her helmet in the wicker basket on the front of her bike, and let the wind lift her hair, cooling the nape of her neck.

Thoughtfully she turned into the narrow street where her flat was located, negotiating her way around the perennial roadworks that blocked one end of it. Christie's comment had breathed life into the nameless fear that lurked at the back of her mind, which she had resolutely denied existence up to now. As she locked her bike to the railings at the foot of her house, she forced herself to examine her feelings more closely than she had permitted herself to do before. She closed her eyes for a moment as Charles' face filled her mind. She could almost feel the sensation of his skin against hers as they made love in the vast silken bed of his Chelsea mews flat. As she opened her front door, she had a sudden desire to find Charles already there, sprawling on the array of multicoloured cushions on the floor of her sitting room, grinning up at her as she darted in to hug him.

Her feelings frightened her. What planet was she living on? As if Charles would sprawl on anyone's floor, least of all hers. He had not even promised to leave his wife, and she did not want to broach the subject, in case he thought she was going to turn into the whinging nag he said his wife, Ellie, was. Even thinking Ellie's name was painful. She wished she did not know it. Somehow it would be easier if Ellie had remained a nameless, faceless shadow in the background.

Ginny sighed. Who was she trying to kid? There was no such thing as easy where married men were concerned.

She poured herself a large glass of white wine and sat in the pale green canvas hammock that she had strung across the balcony that opened out from her bedroom. It was the main reason she had bought this flat. The rooms were small, but their high ceilings gave them an airy feel, and she had fallen in love with the tiny balcony the moment she stepped out on it. An artist friend of hers had helped her paint the entire flat, and once it was completed she felt as if she belonged here and nowhere else.

Ginny let her eye roam around the flat from her supine position. The sitting room was her favourite; it had taken four weeks to decorate. Layers of ruddy bronze, sea-green and dull orange had been painted onto the walls, then partially sanded down with a wire brush, leaving a swirling mix of colours that looked like a Caribbean sea-bed.

Her bedroom had been similarly decorated, this time in blues and silvers. The brass bed was canopied with faded aquamarine damask and loops of sky-blue muslin. Charles hated it, and had refused to sleep there on the one occasion she had invited him back. Perhaps he was right. Maybe she was too weird, too unconventional.

'How can you live with these cupboards?' he had exclaimed in horror when he saw her kitchen. Ginny had gazed regretfully at the purple stained wood and burnished orange handles. He had stormed out of the flat, holding his Burberry raincoat tightly against him as if afraid he would be contaminated by the outlandish decor.

The pealing of the doorbell interrupted her thoughts, and with a sigh Ginny eased herself out of the hammock and put her glass down. No rest for the wicked. She grinned ruefully to herself. Not that she got much chance to be wicked. It was Ellie's birthday this weekend, and Charles said she insisted on him being home for a family barbecue. A cosy night in with the vibrator. Again.

'Jack!' Ginny cried warmly as she opened the front door. 'I didn't expect to see you here!'

Her brother sidled through the narrow doorway, smiling shamefacedly.

'It was on my way . . .' he began lamely, unwilling to admit to actually wanting to see his sister. He felt a pang of guilt as he noticed her pale face and the hollows under her eyes.

Ginny gave him a quick hug, and followed him up the stairs to her apartment. 'It's an honour,' she teased, pouring him a glass of wine and curling up cross-legged on some cushions.

'How's things?' Jack asked, sipping his drink.

'Hey, you win some, you lose some,' Ginny answered with a shrug. 'Or in my case, you lose some. Full stop.'

'Still pining?' Jack said, dropping his eyes. It was tearing him in two, knowing he had stolen his own sister's lover, but the need in him was too strong to be denied, even for her. He prayed she would forgive him, if she ever found out, but he would not blame her if she never spoke to him again.

'Nick? He's history,' Ginny said firmly. 'You're welcome to him.'

Jack started, but Ginny did not notice. Don't be so paranoid, he told himself. She doesn't know.

'OK, out with it,' Jack said, thrusting his own thoughts aside with an effort. Guilt had driven him to see her, but now he was here he might as well act like a brother. Maybe talking to him would help. She deserved that at least.

'Oh, you know me,' Ginny smiled wryly. 'I always manage to find Mr Right. Trouble is, he's usually married to Mrs Wrong. But I know he'll leave her soon. I've just got to give him time.'

Jack winced. If she fell for some bastard on the rebound from Nick, it was his fault. Betrayed by her lover and her brother. Damn! He felt such a shit.

'Just be careful,' Jack said, unconsciously echoing Christie's words. 'I don't want you to get hurt again.'

'He's wonderful, really,' Ginny enthused, her voice sounding hollow even to her own ears. 'He's terribly thoughtful. And the sex is great!'

Jack could not suppress a smile. 'And you should know,' he teased.

Ginny lobbed a cushion in his direction, which Jack fended off laughing. 'You didn't come here to listen to my tale of woe,' she gasped, catching her breath. 'How's the great poison factory?'

'A little respect, please,' Jack admonished. 'You'll probably be wearing what you so rudely call my poison on your face next summer.'

'I didn't know you were into make-up there,' Ginny said, surprised. 'I thought ChemCo were more into drugs.'

'Well, I guess we are, most of the time, but often our research into drugs throws up a bonus, like that anti-cancer cream that turned out to delay the effects of aging. Someone just decided to make a bit of money out of it at the same time. It's not really my department, though. I just get to do tests on pregnant gerbils; or rather, trying to stop them reproducing themselves quicker than Catholics. They still haven't got the hang of the condoms, I'm afraid.'

Ginny laughed. 'I don't know why you can't go and work for Max Factor,' she scolded good-naturedly. 'I'm sure they'd find a good use for a research chemist. And think of all the perks you could give your loving sister . . .'

'And I thought you were looking out for my career,' Jack said, pulling a face. 'All the time, you were after my lipstick.'

His sister made to throw another cushion, and Jack

stood up, holding his hands palm outwards towards her to stave off the attack.

'All right, all right, I know when I'm not wanted!' he said, warding off imaginary missiles. 'Listen, I'll catch up with you next week, OK?'

Ginny walked with him to the door, and watched as he climbed into his battered Volkswagen Beetle. As she waved she heard the telephone ring, and Jack nodded at her to go and answer it. Still smiling, she bounded up the stairs and seized the purple telephone receiver.

'Darling,' Charles said smoothly, 'I was hoping I'd catch you in.'

As if I'd be anywhere else, Ginny thought ruefully.

Charles did not pause to wait for her reply. Of course she'd be in. Where else would she be if he wasn't free? 'Great news. Merili's just come down with measles, and Ellie's taken her and Raphael to her mother's for a week. She knows I mustn't catch it, with the AIDS special in ten days' time. So we can go away, just the two of us. Darling?'

Ginny drew a breath as Christie and Jack's words flitted through her mind. Now was the time to say no, while she still had her pride and – maybe – her heart. Firmly she blotted out the image of his wife, struggling to cope with a sick child on her own while her husband worried about his next television appearance.

Then she mentally shrugged her shoulders. What the hell. You were only young once, and she knew Charles really did love her. Why else would he be ringing?

'I'd love to, darling,' she said brightly into the phone. 'How soon do you want me ready?'

Chapter Nine

'I need to know, Caryn. I think it's about time we were straight with each other, don't you?'

Caryn Kelly swung her legs over the side of the bed and stood up, wandering lazily over towards the vast chrome and white dressing table that took up the far corner of her room. She sat down on the red furred stool and placed her elbows on the cluttered surface, sending a cascade of powder and half-used eyeshadows onto the floor. Ignoring them, she cupped her chin in her hands and gazed into the mirror.

'There's nothing you need to know,' she answered lightly. Dismissively she picked up a large brush and smoothed it briskly across her cheekbones and d own the length of her nose. She always liked the expression on her face after she had had a good fuck, Caryn thought consideringly. Something about the smudged mascara and smeared lipstick that she found exciting, erotic. A warm afterglow spread through her limbs, and she relaxed into the slightly light-headed sensation. She felt satiated, and a glimmer of satisfaction showed in her eyes, which shone with a deepened brightness. That was it, she decided suddenly. She looked softer, more contented. If she was a cat she would have purred. Unconsciously

255

Caryn arched her back at the thought, and wriggled her shoulders in pleasure. She wanted to enjoy the mellow sensation. What she had no taste for was an emotional scene.

'But that's just it. I do need to know,' the man in the bed persisted.

Caryn looked into the mirror at the reflection of her lover as he lay sprawled across the bright orange silk sheets. His dull brown hair fell into his eyes, and in a swift reflex gesture he pushed it back. He was a good deal slimmer than David, Caryn thought absently. Less full in the chest, and younger. But then that was why she had chosen him.

'Leave it, Kenny,' she said warningly, turning towards him for emphasis. Kenny held out his hand in a gesture of invitation, but Caryn swivelled back round to the mirror and expertly began reapplying a rich plum-coloured eye-shadow.

Kenny hauled himself up in the bed, and sat back against the peach satin headboard, the tangerine pillows billowing out on either side of his pale body. Thought-fully he raised his arms and leaned his head back on his hands, regarding her through narrowed eyes. Caryn stopped what she was doing and reached for her Caligri lighter. His silent gaze unsettled her, and nervously she lit a John Player and took a deep drag. Perhaps she had made a mistake wandering down this particular memory lane. It was beginning to be altogether too much trouble.

'I've left it nearly two years,' Kenny replied softly. 'It wasn't me who started this again, if you remember. I was happy to leave it the way it was. Shit, I've got a wife now, a wife I thought I loved very much. I don't know what the fuck I'm doing here, but now I am, I want some answers. I think you owe it to me, at least.'

'The hell I do!' Caryn blazed. 'What makes you think a

quick screw every two years gives you the right to charge into my life and start making demands?'

Kenny lowered his hands and sat up straighter, his face contorting. Caryn stood up and strode to the window, heedless of her nakedness as she stared into the garden and drew deeply on her cigarette.

'You called me, Caryn. You said you thought we should get together for old time's sake. Just what were those old times, Caryn? I'd love to know, really I would.'

Caryn turned and faced him, all traces of post-coital softness erased from her expression. 'You tell me, Kenny,' she replied bitingly. 'I thought we had a few good fucks, and parted friends. Forgive me if there was something I missed.'

'Jesus, you can be a real hard bitch,' Kenny said disbelievingly, more to himself than to her. 'I was in love with you, stupid as that may seem to you now. I thought you loved me; at least, that's what you told me. I believed you. I really believed you. I thought you were just too loyal and too scared to leave Seb. Did I get it so wrong, then?'

Caryn heard the note of wistful sadness that lay beneath his anger, and drew a silent breath of relief. This she could handle. Slowly she crossed over to the bed and sat down next to Kenny.

'Kenny, you know I could never have left Sebastian,' she said carefully. 'He would have killed me. You never really knew him. He could be jealous, and paranoid, and unforgiving. If he had found out about us, he'd have killed you, and then he'd have come after me. I cared too much about you to risk it.' The strange thing was, as she spoke, she almost believed it herself.

'But it's different now,' Kenny said pleadingly.

Caryn shook her head, allowing tears to fill her eyes. 'I

can't. It would be wrong, after what happened to Seb. I feel it was my fault. I betrayed him.'

'Seb's dead. You have to accept that,' Kenny urged. 'It wasn't your fault. You can't bring him back. You have your own life to live now.'

Caryn turned away as if too moved to reply. She hoped he would not see the mingled exasperation and anger in her face. Did he seriously imagine she would give up the chance of being Mrs David Cameron, now, when she was so close to winning him? She already shared David's home and life: the cars, the parties, the servants, the money. Sooner or later, she would also share his name. And finally, perhaps, his love.

She had never cared for Kenny, any more than she had cared for any of the other men in her life. They had been substitutes for David. The one man she wanted more than any other: the one man she could never have. Until now.

'I can't do that, Kenny,' she said, imbuing her words with just the right amount of sadness and regret. 'It would hurt too many people, ruin too many lives. Think of your wife. You've only been married eighteen months. Think what it would do to her.'

'I only married her to try to forget you, Caryn darling, you must know that. I thought when I left you to go back home I would never see you again. I never dreamed I'd be sent back here – that you would call me . . .'

Caryn fervently wished she had never contacted Kenny again. If David had not been away being a hero, she would never have bothered telephoning him. Foolishly she had thought they could rekindle their casual love affair where they had left it. It seemed she had seriously misread the depths of his feelings.

'I'm so sorry, Kenny,' Caryn said, standing up and returning to her dressing table. She picked up her hairbrush and began running it through her hair.

'Is it David?' Kenny asked suddenly. 'Is he the reason you won't come with me?'

Caryn froze, shocked at the unexpected accuracy of his words.

'It is David, isn't it?' Kenny pressed. 'My God, I should have guessed. You share his house, his life, everything. How could I be so stupid? How long has this been going on, Caryn? Before me? Before Seb died –?'

'No!' Caryn shouted, whirling around to face him. 'There's nothing between us! I was married to his best friend, that's all. That's all there's ever been!'

'But you love him, don't you?' he breathed. 'That's why you won't leave. That's what this is all about. Damn you, Caryn. Damn you and your lies.'

Caryn stared silently down at her hands, unable to find an answer. Suddenly Kenny leaped out of the bed and strode across the room with a long, lithe movement. He grasped her shoulders and twisted her around on the stool so hard that she gasped in pain. Angrily he bent down and held his face inches away from hers, the mingled scent of Shalimar and sex assailing his nostrils. His brown eyes glittered with pain and rage as he faced her.

'I don't give a damn about you,' Kenny hissed, the very quietness of his voice more terrifying than his earlier rage had been. 'But I care about my child. I'm giving you a choice. Either you tell me whether Sandy is mine too, or I tell David about us. We'll see just how long you last when he finds out you were cheating on his best friend.' His expression was bitter as he turned from her. 'It's up to you.'

As Caryn wandered through the house after Kenny had flung himself out in rage and misery, she wondered with a shiver of alarm if he would really carry out his threat. He had just as much to lose as she did, but there was no way of knowing how deeply his anger and hurt might twist him. She had no intention of confiding the truth about her son to him. If she was honest with herself, she had to admit that even she was not sure what the truth was anyway.

Fidelity had never been Caryn's strongest suit, even before she met David. She had always believed in safety in numbers. After all, she had learned it the hard way.

With a blend of contempt and suffocatingly cloying affection, Caryn's mother Maud taught her that love was always inextricably entwined with betrayal and hurt. And most of all, it could never be trusted.

A resentful and difficult woman, Maud had looked around at her two-roomed council house, the cheap, DIY furniture, the threadbare carpet, the Woolworth china, and the failure of her life overwhelmed her. Deserted by her husband when she was pregnant with Caryn, she had watched her body sag within the shapeless chainstore garments, and decided that marriage and children had ruined her life. Caryn was blamed for her father's desertion, her sister's desperate flight from home at the age of sixteen. Maud's feelings for her remaining child became obsessive and conditional, a mixture of love and blame.

As Caryn grew older, every boy she brought home would be dismissed as not good enough for Maud's eldest daughter, insulted over the chintz tea-table and made to feel so uncomfortable that he never returned. Maud would hug her daughter, telling her how lucky she was to have a mother who loved her so much, whatever those boys thought. But when each failed to ring, and Caryn sat waiting forlornly by the telephone, Maud would mock her daughter's misery.

'You didn't really expect him to call, did you?' she would crow, laughing in derision. 'What would he want you for?'

Caryn never experienced affection without the accompanying pinches, emotional and physical. It seemed to her that approval was inescapeably linked to material status; the more you were loved, the bigger the present, the more expensive the dresses, the larger the car. No matter who Caryn brought home to meet her mother, dreading the confrontation but desperate for Maud's approval, he was never rich or important enough. When a man told her she was beautiful, she waited for the put-down. Each time she was kissed, she wondered if he was secretly laughing at her. And if, as had happened once or twice, he told her he loved her, she could never believe him. Instead, unsure and unhappy, she immediately sought confirmation in another man's arms that she was indeed lovable, desirable, wanted. She began taking men to her bed quicker than the government did U-turns.

With Sebastian Kelly, Caryn had hoped that at last it would be different. Surely even her mother would approve of his position and status as one of INN's top cameramen, and finally she believed she had found someone who would love her. She had even thought she loved him: until she met David Cameron.

For the first time in her life, Caryn had not been able to take the man she wanted. And then Seb had died, and she had realised that this was the only chance she would ever have.

But it had not taken her long to realise that whilst David gave her every material comfort she could desire, and as much of himself as he was able, there was a secret corner of his mind and heart that she was unable to penetrate, no matter how hard she tried. She had everything but the man himself.

Every time she saw him, she loved him more. And every time they spoke, David withdrew a little further from her. Angry and resentful, she used his guilt as a

261

weapon against him. Every time he received a telephone call sending him on a story, she would erupt in rage and tears, accusing him of neglect. When he returned exhausted and disturbed from a brutal war or a cruel famine, she would not even let him speak about it. Instead he had to escort her to an endless round of parties as if his other life simply did not exist.

As they each became more isolated, and Caryn took consolation in affairs which she dared not reveal to him, her possessiveness deepened to an obsessive jealousy. Every woman David spoke to was a rival to be obliterated. She was consumed with the need to own him, body and soul, desperate to dig out the part of him she could not reach, and terrified he would leave her, sooner or later.

It was whilst Seb was away in Lebanon covering the release of the Beirut hostage Jackie Mann in the September of 1991 that Sandy was conceived. Caryn was not sure which of her several lovers was the father of her child – Kenny amongst them – but the one thing of which she was certain was that Sebastian was not. Her initial terror that she was about to lose everything she had worked for was replaced by a clear-headed determination to use the situation to her advantage.

The minute Seb returned the following month, Caryn ensured that he would have no doubts about the paternity of the baby. Fatigued and battle-weary, Seb succumbed to her demands, and duly made love to his wife in a parody of the conquering hero returning home that held as much love and desire as masturbating into a test-tube.

Three weeks later, Caryn announced that she was pregnant, and in the following May she had given birth to her son. Few queries were raised over Sandy's four-week premature arrival into the world, least of all by Seb, who was delighted with his child and spent hours exclaiming over his perfect features, and comparing his son's resemblance to him.

Caryn hated him. She could not forgive him for not being David's child.

Until now, she had not thought what might happen if David discovered that she had cheated on Sebastian. Suddenly the spectre of revelation haunted her, and she realised how much she depended on David for her position and her social survival. If the truth came out, she would be an outcast, humiliated and publicly discredited. Firmly she suppressed the shudder of nausea that passed through her at the thought. She had always seen Seb as a stepping-stone, her key to the world of the rich and famous. Sooner or later she would dump him and take the quantum leap to the super-rich world of shipping magnates, arms dealers and bankers. Then she had met David, and her need for him became her driving force.

But she was allowing her emotions to cloud her mind. She could not afford to let her love for David come between her and her instinct for survival. She had no guarantees he would marry her. And if he didn't, she needed to find someone else. Just in case.

It would not prevent her from taking David, sooner or later.

Caryn picked up the telephone and began to dial. 'Giovanni?' she asked as soon as the number answered. 'I need a flight to London Heathrow on Monday. First Class. You can put it on David Cameron's account.'

■ WIMBLEDON, LONDON
12.21 p.m.

Sir Edward Penhaligon proffered his Press pass courteously, but the Wimbledon usher waved him past with a polite nod of recognition. As Sir Edward made his way to the centre court, he barely noticed the usual whispers around him as passers-by searched their memories, trying to remember where they had seen his face. It was not uncommon for someone to come up to him and greet him warmly, certain that he was a friend of theirs since his face seemed so familiar. Fortunately Wimbledon always contained a smattering of celebrities, so that the crowds were less startled by the appearance of a famous face than when he wandered through Harrods' Food Hall.

Like the Queen, Sir Edward never allowed the weather to dictate his attire. Despite the sultry July sunshine, he was still clad in his usual elegant Savile Row suit, his ivory-and-charcoal shirt neatly pressed, a discreet burgundy silk tie at his neck. His hand-made leather shoes made little sound as he wove his way through the baseball-cap-and-shorts brigade who thronged the narrow aisles between the courts. Still walking briskly he reached the covered entrance to the Centre Court, and entered the cooling shadows with relief. As he did so, the shambling figure of Sir Joseph Bower appeared, and the two friends greeted one another with dignified pleasure. Few men reached the levels of achievement that the two distinguished broadcasters had attained, and each recognised and respected the intelligence and success of the other. Along with a select group of men such as Sir Alastair Burnet and Sir Robin Day, they represented the gentlemanly pursuit of journalism, as rapier-sharp as the lesser breed who followed them, but with an edge of distinction and courtesy the new self-styled 'investigative reporters' lacked. In their hands reposed the power of the industry, and they knew how to use it. Outsiders were politely but firmly shunned. These men knew their own.

'Not your usual day, Edward. Thought you avoided the Birthday?' Sir Joseph said, a droll smile curving his lips as he tilted his head forward, his eyes magnified by his thick spectacles.

Sir Edward nodded his acknowledgement. His friend and rival knew him too well; it was not Sir Edward's usual habit to visit Wimbledon on the Princess of Wales' birthday, since the crowds were even heavier in anticipation of a quick glimpse of their favourite Royal.

'There's always the exception, dear chap. Can't become an old stick-in-the-mud, you know. Anyway, it keeps you guessing,' Sir Edward responded smoothly, a smile in his voice.

Sir Joseph shook his head laconically. 'You always do, dear fellow. Never know what you're thinking. Just as well, I have a suspicion. But let me know what you're up to. Might be able to help, you never know.' He eyed Sir Edward shrewdly. 'Whatever it is you're plotting.'

Sir Edward arched one eyebrow in assumed surprise. 'My dear Joseph, just here for the tennis, you know. What could be more pleasant on such a delightful afternoon?' Inwardly he wondered how much the veteran television broadcaster knew of his approaches to the various networks who owned a slice of INN.

'What else indeed?' Sir Joseph replied. He had not missed the glimmer of acknowledgement in Sir Edward's eyes, and in the unspoken language of such men, the indication was enough. The suggestion of support had been made and accepted. When the time came, Sir Edward would know where his allies lay.

With a smile the two men parted, and Sir Edward

265

continued down the narrow concrete corridor that lead to INN's Centre Court box. The tiny room had been bought for a seven-figure sum the previous year, when the news company who owned it had decided that it could no longer afford to sit on a valuable piece of real estate in the midst of the worst financial crises in the company's history. The BBC had been hungry to buy it for decades, confined as they were to a minute box positioned at an angle at the opposite end of the court, but their bid had failed. Into the cramped space were crushed all the BBC correspondents filing reports, as well as those providing the live commentary to their coverage.

Sir Edward mounted the narrow staircase into the INN box, his shoulders brushing both walls. The cameraman on duty that day, Mickey Beaumann, was already in position, his lens protruding out of the letter-box slit that did service as a window. If one leant out and craned back at a dangerous one-hundred-and-eighty degree angle, it was just possible to see into the Royal box above them. On a raised wooden platform in front of Mickey a number of tabloid photographers were shuffling into place, the click of their cameras audible as they dashed off a few shots of the crowds who were filing into their seats. To his right, half a dozen collapsible chairs were crammed in front of an ice-box containing cans of beer, pepsi and pineapple crush. Ginny Templeton sat perched on one chair, leaning out of the window and chatting conversationally to a *Daily Express* snapper crammed on to the wooden platform.

'What's the order of play?' Mickey asked as he bent his head to the eyepiece and zoomed in on a particularly scantily-clad seventeen-year-old in the crowd.

'Slobodan Zivojinovic and some unknown are playing first,' Ginny answered, interrupting a fascinating discussion on the varied sexual preferences of the Royal Family with the *Express* photographer, and effortlessly getting the thirty-year-old Yugoslavian player's name right. 'Then it's Agassi against Jeremy Bates, which will really get the crowd going.'

'So how much do we want of each?' Mickey queried.

Ginny wrinkled her nose in a frown. 'We're only doing a three-minute piece for the Early Evening News,' she said thoughtfully. 'I think we'll just go for the Agassi/Bates match. That's the one everyone will want to see – the crowd favourite against the Best of British.'

Mickey straightened up and locked off his camera, and Sir Edward eased his way past him to one of the vacant seats. 'I might as well have a beer,' Mickey grinned. Ginny reached towards the ice-box and tossed him a can.

'Do you think you could do me a favour?' she asked mischievously. 'My mother's got a thing about Zivojinovic's legs. Give me ten minutes of close-ups and I'll buy you lunch.'

'Never mind the lunch. Anyone who can pronounce his name deserves to get a freebie.'

A cheer from the crowds drew their attention, and looking out of the window they saw the two players walk on to the court. The grass was already well-worn from the previous week's play, and the unseasonal heat had burnt what remained to a dull brown. The players bowed towards the Royal Box, and the snappers spun round to take pictures of the Princess, the whirring of their cameras sounding like a drove of angry bees. Sir Edward glanced at his watch. Although he enjoyed watching a close-fought game of tennis, it was not his primary purpose in being here today. He wondered how long he would have to wait.

At the other end of the box, Mickey filmed a quick ten minutes of the Yugoslav's rippling thighs and firm buttocks. Ginny giggled as Mickey ejected the tape from the

267

camera and replaced it with a fresh one.

'My mother'll love it,' she laughed as she slid the tape into her canvas shoulder bag. 'Better take this now – don't want to risk a mix up. We'll be known as the Early Evening Screws forever afterwards.'

'It'd almost be worth it to see Brian's face,' Mickey said regretfully.

'Nice to see someone's working,' Jimmy Maxwell, INN's other Wimbledon cameraman, grumbled as he climbed the stairs into the crowded box. 'Nothing much doing on Court One. How come I never get the nubile fifteen-year-olds?'

Mickey grinned smugly. 'You were the one who wanted Centre Court yesterday,' he reminded his colleague. 'Was it my fault if I got Jennifer Capriati? Gorgeous legs,' he added in reminiscence.

'You sod, you knew the Navratilova match hadn't finished here, and I'd get lumbered with it,' Jimmy retorted. 'Then I had the dubious pleasure of Boris Becker. Meanwhile you get the frilly knickers and bouncing tits. It's a conspiracy.'

'What are you doing here anyway?' Ginny remonstrated. 'You should be perched fifty feet high on the other court, not making sexist remarks over here. Bugger off.'

'Give a poor man a beer, before you banish him back to the dizzy heights,' Jimmy pleaded. Ginny relented and threw him an ice-cool can. The television vantage point on Court One was an eagle's eyrie, high in the roof, and required climbing up a number of stomach-churning ladders to get to it. When it rained, the roof leaked, and when it was warm, it was suffocatingly stuffy. Accordingly, the crews took it in turns to rotate between the Centre Court box and Court One.

As Jimmy made his way back down the narrow stairs,

he almost collided with a good-looking man in his early forties, who stood politely aside for him before mounting.

'Sir Edward! Not late, am I?'

'Dalmeny, glad you could make it. Little difficult to find, if you don't know the way,' Sir Edward responded.

The dark-haired MP smiled engagingly. 'Got shown the way, or I'd never have got here. Rather hidden away.'

Dalmeny de Burgh came further into the small room, ducking his head to accommodate his six-foot-two height. 'Marvellous view you get from here. It's a good deal closer to the court than I expected.'

Ginny turned towards Dalmeny and grinned. 'Don't miss a trick from here,' she said conspiratorially. 'You should hear what they really say about each other in between the grunts.' She extended one hand. 'Ginny Templeton. I'm the producer on this one.'

Dalmeny returned the handshake. 'You obviously know the right people,' he said approvingly. 'I wouldn't mind a few days watching Wimbledon for a living.'

Sir Edward stood up and made his way along the box towards Dalmeny. 'Oh, you don't do so badly,' he said drily. 'Long summer holidays, half-days, Friday afternoons off. I think most people could stand a few stints in the House.'

He motioned towards the staircase, and reluctantly Dalmeny dragged his eyes from Ginny's slim figure and dancing eyes. The two men left the INN box, and headed towards the Debentures' Bar, of which both were members. Sir Edward ordered his usual Scotch, and Dalmeny nodded for one of the same.

'Quite a while since I've been here,' Dalmeny offered. 'My wife, Morgan, usually has me in a half nelson and boarding a plane to Necker or some such place to soak up the sun.'

'I usually make time for a few games every year,' Sir

Edward replied, picking up his drink as an immaculate waiter delivered their drinks to the table.

Dalmeny swirled the Scotch reflectively in the glass. 'It's always a pleasure to see you, Sir Edward, but I have a feeling that you didn't ask me here to discuss the relative merits of Steffi Graf's backhand,' he said, glancing across at the older man as he took a sip of his drink. 'And I suspect that, fascinating as my work as Minister of Energy may be, you're not that interested in updating the National Grid.'

Sir Edward smiled slightly. 'As you say, fascinating but not really my line.' He paused, and eyed the other man shrewdly. 'Tell me, Dalmeny, what's your feeling on the way INN seems to be going? I mean you personally, not the Party.'

Dalmeny looked somewhat surprised, and leant back in his chair, crossing one slim leg over the other. 'To be honest, I don't really follow the ins and outs all that closely,' he said, with an apologetic shrug of the shoulders. 'As long as they're nice to me whenever I'm on, I pretty much leave it at that.'

Sir Edward eyed him with renewed respect. Little disturbed the calm waters the forty-four year old MP presented to the world. Charming and debonair, there were few who remained unaffected for long by his air of amiable hedonism. If he was confused by Sir Edward's tack, it did not show. His air of mild surprise and vague disinterest was exactly right. But much as Dalmeny might give the impression of a playboy with little but women and pleasure on his mind, Sir Edward knew that beneath it all he was very perceptive. No Cabinet minister got where Dalmeny was without a streak of ruthlessness and well-developed sense of self-interest. He tilted his head in a gesture of acknowledgement and smiled.

'It would be a pity if, owning a tenth of the company,

270

you still didn't get the airtime you wanted,' Sir Edward said lightly. 'But one has to make sure it's the right kind of press.'

Dalmeny stiffened almost imperceptibly, and raked his fingers through his curly brown hair in a way that melted female resistance across the country. 'As Oscar Wilde would say, there's only one thing worse than being talked about, and that's not being talked about.' He grinned boyishly.

'Quite. But a flattering editorial in the *Sunday Times* is worth far more than a rave review in the *News of the World*, I think you'll agree.'

'I don't know about that,' Dalmeny smiled. 'A lot more people read the *News of the World* than care to admit it.'

'Exactly,' Sir Edward said. 'Popular it may be, but credible it is not. I don't know many men in your position who greatly benefit from an appearance in the gutter press as far as the respect of their colleagues is concerned. In fact, I think a few too many cuttings from the *Ethic* and their like would do more harm than good, Oscar Wilde notwithstanding.'

Dalmeny frowned. 'I don't quite see where this is all leading,' he said edgily.

Sir Edward paused as Tim Taylor passed by their table with his mother-in-law, the Duchess of Kent, who smiled at the newscaster in friendly recognition. The slim young man was laughing at something she said, and teasingly the Duchess shook her head in mock dismay. As the crowded bar made room for them, Sir Edward turned back to Dalmeny.

'I shan't bore you with the facts and figures, but a glance at INN's output recently should convince you of what I am about to say,' he said briskly. 'Ben Wordsworth is getting carried away with his own success, and sooner rather than later, you will get as much credibility from appearing on the network as a double-page spread in the *Sunday People*.'

Dalmeny hid his annoyance. He had no wish to offend the influential journalist, and there was no doubt that Sir Edward migh have a fair point. But it was a gloriously sunny afternoon, there was a delicious redhead giving him sidelong glances from the bar, and the last thing he wanted was an in-depth discussion on INN policy.

'I don't really see what this has to do with me,' Dalmeny said. 'I'm just a shareholder. I have no say in editorial decisions. I leave that up to you. After all, you get paid for it.' He smiled to take the sting out of his words. 'I'm sure you do the job far better than I ever could.'

'I need more support than I can command at the moment,' Sir Edward said. 'Frankly, if I'm to turn the network around and make it the political heavyweight you and I both want it to be, I have to be able to out-vote Ben Wordsworth.'

'Exactly what is it you want me to do?' Dalmeny said abstractedly, half his mind on removing the slinky emerald-green dress the redhead was almost wearing.

'I want you to sell your shares. To me,' Sir Edward said.

Dalmeny started, and deserted the redhead just as he was mentally toying with her nipples. 'You want me to do what?' he asked in disbelief.

'I am prepared to pay you fifteen per cent over the market value for your block of shares in the company,' Sir Edward said. 'I have access to the necessary funds, and the transaction could be completed with the minimum of fuss. You would still have the personal support you need, but from a network with considerably more influence and respect. And financially you would more than benefit.'

'I would have to think about it,' Dalmeny said carefully.

'Of course. I wouldn't expect you to rush your decision. But I will need to know within the next six weeks. Longer than that, and it could be too late to undo the damage Wordsworth is doing.'

Dalmeny stood and held out his hand. 'I'll let you know as soon as I make up my mind,' he said. 'Thank you for the drink. It's been most interesting.'

Sir Edward half rose from his seat and shook the younger man's hand firmly. Dalmeny walked briskly away, and Sir Edward considered their conversation. If Dalmeny agreed to sell his shares – and Sir Edward saw no reason why he should not do so – he had only to persuade Harry Foley to follow suit and INN would be his.

As he had suspected, the consortium of television networks, with the exception of WNS, had nervously declined to get involved in any boardroom battles. All were sticking firmly by Ben. The head of WNS, Patrick Courtenay, had readily agreed to sell his company's shares in INN in return for a guarantee that WNS would have unlimited rights to INN broadcast material.

Sir Edward raised a hand, and a white-jacketed waiter threaded his way through the crowded tables towards him. He ordered another Scotch, and glanced at his watch. Three-fifteen. He was due to present the Early Evening News in a little under three hours, which still gave him a couple of hours before he had to appear at the studio. If things continued to fall into place as smoothly as they had done so far, it was a studio that would soon be his.

It almost seemed too easy.

Ginny stood poised at the top of the narrow staircase in the INN box, waiting for the final ball, one arm outstretched to receive the tape the minute Mickey Beaumann had captured the moment on film. It was six-thirteen. The Wimbledon story was due to roll into the Early Evening News at six twenty-six. That gave her precisely thirteen minutes to get the tape back to the feed-point, where Peter Princer was waiting for the last vital shots to finish the package he had already cut for the show and fed back to INN.

A thirteen minute margin might have been considered generous. But Ginny knew that the moment the final shot was played and the winner leaped over the net to embrace his sporting opponent, the crowds would surge from the Centre Court, blocking up the entrances and clogging the narrow pathways between the outside courts. Ginny sighed. The INN box was in the heart of Centre Court. Great for getting superb close-ups and unequalled footage of the match. A nightmare when it came to a quick sprint back to the editing van.

Ginny might have thirteen – make that twelve – minutes left. But the truck from which the final shot would be replayed to the studio was ten minutes away. And the match was not over yet.

'Can't they just call it quits?' she asked in an agony of impatience.

'If it's bad for you, think of their mothers,' Mickey said.

'If the Brit's going to lose, I think he could at least do it in time for the Early Evening News. Selfish bastard,' Jimmy said, aggrieved. He had long since abandoned the uninspiring match on Court One to come and watch the drama on the Centre Court.

Any other time, and Ginny would have revelled in the enthralling battle taking place on the grass in front of her. The match had already gone to five sets, to the amazement of the crowd and the exasperation of the INN team, who had all expected Jeremy Bates to put up a brave but futile

274

fight against the champion, Andre Agassi, and lose in straight sets. In the event, Bates had taken the first two sets 6–4, 6–2, sending the crowd wild with excitement, with the exception of Agassi's faithful band of groupies. Back at INN, where the newsroom was watching the BBC output on their monitors, Jerry had even moved the story up to the top of the running order in anticipation of the first British player to make a Wimbledon semi-final in more than a decade.

But Bates was nothing if not fair. With the spirit of Empire he handed the American the next two sets, taking only three games. As the crowds groaned their disappointment, Ginny anxiously watched the minutes tick away. If Bates fought back for each game, there was no way they would make the six o'clock bulletin.

The British player did more than that. In a comeback that had the commentators recalling the epic games of Borg and McEnroe, Bates romped through the next five games, and was 40–0 up in the sixth. Three match points away from victory, and it was still only quarter to six.

To Ginny's lasting resentment, the American showed a selfish disregard for INN's scheduling difficulties. As Bates threw away his advantage, Agassi clawed his way through the fifth set to equalise. Each game was punctuated by Jerry's frantic voice demanding how much longer it would take, as he watched the match played out at INN. Finally Ginny lost her patience.

'Jerry, you can see as much as I can!' she stormed. 'I left my crystal ball back at the coven, so I'm as much in the dark as you are. Now for God's sake stop ringing or you'll get us thrown off the court!'

Tradition dictated that there was no tie-breaker in the fifth set; instead, one player had to gain a two-game lead to win the set, and thus the match. The score was currently standing at 16–15 to Bates, and still both players held their serves. The crowd held its breath, willing Bates towards victory. Ginny held her patience, fervently praying for a result, any result.

'Game Agassi. Sixteen games all in the final set. Quiet please,' said the umpire.

Ginny shrugged hopelessly. 'I shouldn't complain. We'll have a great exclusive for tomorrow. Twenty-four hours late, but who's counting?'

'I hope you're good at the four-minute mile,' Mickey commented. 'You're going to have to fucking fly to get this back in time.'

'Just imagine Caryn Kelly behind you. That should help,' Jimmy added.

'Love-forty.'

'Damn! Agassi's about to break serve. Typical.' Mickey groaned. 'There are only three things the British are good at: queuing, strikes and coming second.'

'Remember the War,' Jimmy said.

'Don't talk about the War!' Mickey whispered. 'Steffi might not like it.'

'Game Agassi. Agassi leads by seventeen games to sixteen in the final set.'

'This must be killing Jerry,' Ginny said.

'So there is a point to this after all,' Jimmy replied.

'It's twenty past six. I'll never do it. Peter's got to edit it into his piece yet, and that's assuming I make it past the adoring crowds to the edit van. Our only chance will be to play it out live from here.'

A sudden roar focused their attention on the court just in time to see Agassi fall to his knees and throw his racquet in the air in jubilation. Ginny almost felt like ripping her shirt off and throwing it to the crowds along with him as she grabbed the tape from Mickey and pelted down the stairs.

The corridors were already heaving with people leaving

the court, discussing the match in tones of incredulity. Deciding that aggression was the better part of valour, Ginny dispensed with any attempt at politeness, and elbowed her way through them to the exit. She took a moment to orientate herself as she reached the sunshine, glancing at her watch. Six twenty-three. She had exactly three minutes.

Not for the first time Ginny cursed the Wimbledon organisers who insisted on putting the television crews' editing trucks in the furthest possible field from the courts. The vast mobile trailers of the American networks were interspersed with the smaller trucks of their European counterparts and the monolithic BBC structure. Together they formed a maze of cables, edit vans, live camera positions and canteens, all linked by a network of metal duckboards, designed with British weather in mind for when the field became a sea of mud.

Expertly Ginny pushed her way through to the TV village, and ran along the duckboards towards the INN van, puffing with excrtion. As she passed one trailer, its occupant carelessly flung open the door. It thudded into Ginny's back, throwing her full length on the ground, the tape spinning across the grass under the trailer. A searing pain flamed across her knee. Gritting her teeth, Ginny dived under the mobile van and grabbed the tape. Peter was already standing with his arm outstretched in the doorway of the INN edit van, waiting for the final shot for his piece. Half-standing, half-falling, she thrust the cassette into his hand. As Peter shoved the tape into an edit machine, she glanced down at the deep gash the metal duckboard had made in her leg. Blood was pouring through the thin white canvas of her jeans.

'Oh great,' she said in disbelief. 'Christie goes to Albania and nothing happens to her, and I go to Wimbledon and get sliced in two. No one will ever believe it.'

Ginny wound a grimy handkerchief around her leg as she watched the unfinished package play out live from INN on the monitor in the corner of the editing booth. She checked her watch. It was six-twenty-six. Fervently she prayed nothing would go wrong. INN were taking a risk in playing out the incomplete story, which would end abruptly and go to black three-quarters of the way through the tape. Split seconds before it did, the editor at the Wimbledon feed-point would play in the pictures from Ginny's tape. Peter was already standing by on the audio line to pick up his commentary live as the new pictures played.

As the piece reached the point at which it was due to go to black, Ginny sucked in her breath. Swiftly the editor played in the new pictures as Peter started describing the last few points of the match down the line. With relief Ginny saw the footage switch from the pre-recorded incomplete piece to the shotgun marriage of new pictures and live commentary. All the viewers saw was one seamless package. Ginny hoped Jerry had no idea how close it had been.

'Thirty seconds to the titles,' Annie, the PA, said clearly, as Jerry stood at the back of the Gallery and watched Penhaligon do a swift recap of the main stories of the day. If he had not seen the newscaster drink two-thirds of a bottle of Scotch during the hour-long broadcast, he would never have noticed the slight elision of his words, the infinitesimal pause between paragraphs as he read from the autocue in his usual precise, measured tones.

Penhaligon had never completed a show on less than half a bottle, but although it might be an open secret in the newsroom, there had never been a whisper in the Press. Penhaligon had never made a mistake on air, and his habit of having a tumbler of Glenfiddich at his elbow as he read, in lieu of the usual glass of water, had become part of his own inimitable style, an essential part of the man himself. In fact, Charles Silversmith had lately started to emulate the distinguished anchor in the belief that a glass of Scotch was simply another status symbol the successful and famous adopted, rather like hand-made shoes.

'Ten to Off-Air . . . nine . . . eight . . .' Annie chanted. Behind her, the various producers on the show shuffled their papers and stood up, zeroing stopwatches as they made their way to the Gallery door. Jerry stood alertly watching the bulletin to the final frame. Only when the credits rolled did he move.

'Thanks, everybody, that was a smooth show. We'll have a quick debrief at 7.15, and then we'll call it a day,' Jerry said over his shoulder as he strode back into the newsroom.

Ollie and Sam left their respective Home and Foreign Desks to join him as he made his way towards Ben's office for the evening meeting, which was always held immediately after the Early Evening News at 7 p.m. The idea was that the various editors and programme producers would pool resources and discuss the way various stories had developed during the day, with the aim of freshening up their approach to them for the Late News, the hour long bulletin that ran from 10p.m. to 11p.m. It also meant Ben could make sure his network was run according to his rules. Initiative was out.

In reality, unless a story had genuinely developed during the evening, the changes were purely cosmetic, and resulted in intense rivalry between the two programme producers, each desperate to make their show look fresh and different. If the Late News team came up with a new angle or interview before the Early Evening News had come off-air, it was not unknown for them to hold it back so that they had an exclusive to kick off their bulletin. Similarly, if Jerry was developing a line of thought on a story, he made sure Brian did not know about it until it was too late for him to do anything but grit his teeth. In these days of cutbacks and job losses, the main danger came from the enemy within.

'Nice piece on the Kenyan refugees,' Ben said as the three men entered his office and sat down. Robin Fernly was already sitting in a corner biting his fingernails, and beside him a faceless accountant was busily punching figures into a calculator. Brian hurriedly ran in and nodded apologetically in Ben's direction.

'Do we have any more fresh pictures for the Late News?' Ben added, ignoring Brian and scanning through a page of notes he had made whilst watching the Early Evening News.

'A few we haven't used before, but I think Bob used most of the best stuff already,' Sam replied, consulting his list and glancing up again. 'I can get him to re-jig some shots, and there's a new piece to camera, but that's about it.'

'OK, we'll go with that,' Ben answered. 'Before I forget, can someone explain to me why the death toll in Italy has gone down a bit more in each broadcast since our lunchtime show? This has to be the first volcano I've ever seen that kills fewer people the more it erupts.'

Ollie looked suitably regretful that he could not help, since it was a Foreign story and therefore out of his domain. Brian frowned in outrage, exuding an air of it-wouldn't-happen-on-my-programme. Robin tried to adopt the expression of one concerned only with Bureaux and the smooth running thereof, whilst Jerry shrugged and looked at Sam.

'I can see I might as well talk to a wall,' Ben sighed, exasperated. 'If we could try and sort out a realistic figure and stick to it?' He glanced around the room. 'Now is there anything else on that story?'

'We've got an interview with the Italian finance minister,' Sam answered, relieved that he could offer something concrete to the proceedings. 'He's good, he says there may be a billion dollars worth of damage, and up to one hundred thousand people homeless.'

'Excellent!' Ben said, dismissing the fate of thousands with relish. 'Let's get him live on the Late News.' Brian busily wrote something down on the pristine pad of white paper he always brought in with him. Ben turned towards him with a vulpine smile.

'Now, moving on. How are we getting on with this Chinese Resistance story?' he asked innocently, well aware nothing had been done about it since he suggested it at the morning meeting.

'We're still efforting that one,' Brian replied with false heartiness. Ollie suppressed a smile. If Brian didn't know that was the oldest euphemism in the book for 'Oh Christ, you weren't serious about that idea?' he had no doubt that Ben did.

'Have you had any response at all?' Ben asked, arching one eyebrow incredulously.

'They're calling me back on it,' Brian said nervously, hoping Ben had no idea he hadn't even made the call.

Ben had. 'Who is, exactly?'

Brian started sweating. 'Let me come back to you on that one,' he said, playing for time. He wished he had the nerve to tell Ben to bugger off, but he turned hot and cold just thinking about it.

Ben tired of the game and swung back to the rest of the room, who had been enjoying seeing Brian squirm. Robin looked sympathetically towards Brian, who realised things must be bad if that miserable little toe-rag thought they were in the same boat. Suddenly Robin caught Ben's glare of disapproval and dropped his eyes, as he started to reshuffle his notes earnestly. Three pieces of paper slid from his grasp and wafted towards Ben's desk, caught in the blast of air-conditioning.

'It may not concern you, but we've been slipping,' Ben said. 'Our ratings fell behind the BBC's for the first time last month, and CNN are so far ahead of us they aren't even in sight. If they ever have a real crack at us, we're in serious trouble. And let me tell you, if it doesn't concern you, it fucking well should, because it concerns me,' he added. 'There are going to have to be some cuts around here. Think of yourselves as cruise missiles. Reliable, flexible, and easily fired. You want to hope I don't.'

Ollie noticed Robin's fixed stare, and followed his gaze. He caught sight of a scrap of red silk behind the potted plant that was riveting Robin's attention, and suppressed a guffaw of laughter. He wondered whose they were. Evens on Paragon and Annie Charter.

'I want some exclusives. I want some decent investigative reporting. I want to be top in the ratings. And I want it to cost me less money, not more.'

Sam met Ben's gaze without flinching. 'You can't have it both ways, Ben,' he said coolly. 'Stories – especially exclusives – mean satellites. Satellites cost money. So do airplanes, hotels, bribes. You get what you pay for.'

'I'm not afraid of spending money where we have to,' Ben said, holding up one hand to stem the Foreign Editor's ire. 'But I want it to be on the right stories. Don't worry, our mission hasn't changed. INN will remain the pre-eminent global television news service. We will serve different regions of the world and different marketplaces with different services. We will do it better, faster, and more efficiently, than anyone else. But this is a tough, demanding, competitive business, and that means we must each come up with more creative ways to deal with our work force.'

'Considering how that's gone in the past, do you have a Plan B?' Ollie asked.

Ben silenced him with a glacial stare. 'And I'm not just talking about what we cover, but how we cover it. I want our writing to be fresh, new. I don't want to hear that anything "remains to be seen", I'm fed up with "floral tributes", and if our correspondents can't guess how a mother who's just lost her three children in a fire feels, they should be exiled to the Political Unit. It's yellow journalism, and I don't want it.'

Robin saw a chance to redeem himself, and took it, dragging his gaze from the direction of the potted plant. 'Shall I send round a memo?' he asked eagerly.

Ben smiled magnanimously in his direction, and Robin blushed with pleasure. 'Do that,' Ben said, 'And whilst you're at it, I'll send round a few suggestions for our on-the-road reporters, starting with stopping their dry-cleaning. I've had enough of those buggers taking their wives' ballgowns to the Amman Intercontinental because it's cheaper than Sketchley's.'

'We need to talk about the direction our coverage of the situation in Kosovo is going,' Sam said quickly, before they lost double time on Bank Holidays. 'One of the American networks in northern Albania lost a cameraman last week, and French TV have had two of their crew injured in the last three days. I think we should consider pulling David and Christie out, before we get into another Sarajevo situation.'

Sebastian Kelly's name hung unspoken in the air. Ben thought rapidly. Sarajevo had claimed more media lives than any other war in the history of journalism, mainly because the news crews had actually become targets. All war correspondents and cameramen were used to being in danger from accidental fire or shelling when they covered battle zones, but this was the first time journalists had been deliberately shot and killed. Three of the main sniper nests in the city had been right outside the ramp to the hotel where most of the journalists stayed, putting them at risk every time they moved. Eventually, most of the networks had pulled out of the beleaguered town because the risks had become too great.

If Sam was worried enough to suggest doing the same thing now, it was not without good reason. Ben was unconcerned about the danger his staff might be in; it was part of their jobs, and he paid them well for it. But his public image was important, now more than ever. He could not afford to be seen to send his crews deliberately to their deaths, particularly since they had already lost Kelly; not with the ratings slipping and half the contracts he had spent two years setting up on the point of signing. Much as he hated to do it, he would have to pull out of Kosovo.

'If we do pull out, Sam –'

Suddenly the door burst open, and Janey ran in without knocking, her eyes wide with alarm.

'Sorry to interrupt,' she panted, looking wildly around the room, and reaching for Ollie's hand as he leaped up and extended his arm to steady her. 'We just had a call from CNN's correspondent, who reached Kosovo yesterday. He and the BBC man have spent twenty-four hours trying to make contact with Christie. He's very worried. She's vanished.'

'What the fuck do you mean, vanished?' Ben exploded. 'She can't have disappeared into thin air!'

Janey clutched Ollie's hand tighter. 'It seems that when David didn't come back from Dakovica after three days, as agreed, she followed him there to see what was going on. That was forty-eight hours ago. There's been no sign of either of them, nor of Karim and Steve since.'

'They're probably having difficulties getting back across the lines,' Sam said, concern etching deep scores across his face. 'Dakovica's been under siege for more than seven months, don't forget. These operations don't always run to time.'

'They'd have got some message through, somehow,' Janey said, biting her lip. 'No. They must be in trouble. Serious trouble.'

Chapter Ten

David had not underestimated Christie's fury when she heard Ben's instruction that she remain behind whilst he went into Dakovica with Karim and Fabian, but he had been impressed by the fact that she had quickly recognised the futility of her anger and got on with her job. CNN and the BBC were hard on their heels, once they realised that someone had dared to enter the dangerous northern region of Albania and Kosovo, and David knew Christie would be needed to file day-to-day packages on the developing situation whilst he tried to get the Dakovica story.

'Send in search parties if I'm not back by Christmas,' he had teased as he said goodbye, but the laughter did not reach his eyes. Six months ago, he would have welcomed the danger he was facing in going into the besieged city. But not now. Now he had something to live for.

'Just come back to me,' Christie whispered. Risks she would dismissively have taken herself – had done, on many occasions – suddenly seemed reckless, foolish, for him to take.

'Promise me, if anything happens, try not to be too angry. And whatever you do, don't come after me. Do you promise?'

'Don't talk like that!' Christie said angrily, pulling away from him. 'If you think it's so dangerous, don't go. You don't have to, you know.'

'Promise me you won't follow me?' David persisted. 'I need to know I don't have to worry about you.'

Suddenly Christie slumped against him as if in surrender. He felt rather than heard the softness of her reply as she buried her face in his shoulder.

'If that's what you want,' she whispered.

■ DAKOVICA, KOSOVO
2 JULY, 03.45 a.m.

The journey to Dakovica had been as fast and silent as possible under cover of darkness. Karim had driven across the rough terrain without headlights, anxious not to advertise their position to the snipers who haunted all the roads in the area. Every so often the air sang as bullets rang past them, hitting the road ahead and behind them. They had no idea how close. In the distance they heard the dull crump of shells landing. As they swerved and bounced on the tarmac churned by tanks and pitted by explosions, all three men prayed mines had not been sown along the road. They were not consoled by the thought that if they hit one, they would know precious little about it.

As dawn broke they reached the outskirts of the town, and Karim left them at a deserted farm to travel the rest of the way alone on foot and recce the territory. He had spent almost a year in the sundered provinces of Yugoslavia when the civil war first tore the land apart in 1991, and had survived for five months inside Sarajevo the following year. He had also spent several weeks in this area of Kosovo and knew the terrain well. David hoped he knew it well enough.

David and Fabian concealed the jeep amongst a cluster of deserted farm buildings, and took refuge inside an ancient woollen mill and tower that David chose for its height and the fact that it had only one door. As they entered the cool stone building, David wondered fleetingly what had happened to its owners.

At the northern end of the mill area was a fragile ladder, which David guessed must lead to the tower that he had noted from the outside. Cautiously he climbed it and pushed open a warped trapdoor to find himself inside the circular tower, which had once been used as some sort of storeroom for the cloths the mill produced. A staircase adjoined the wall, spiralling up the tower towards the crenellations. A few stumps were all that remained of the wooden banister that had once escorted the staircase. David imagined a body falling down the stone steps, breaking the flimsy balustrade, crashing spread-eagled on to the trapdoor. At the top, he could see the various approaches to the tower, the sprawl of the city away to his right. The landscape was grey and sodden, belying the calendar which proclaimed that it was summer. Here, the miasma of death and decay created its own weather.

Most of the dying city lay in ruins, shelled into rubble. Silent and ghostly, it was disturbed only by the occasional scatter of gunfire as snipers aimed at fluttering leaves, windswept rubbish, scavenging rats. The Serbian troops attacking Dakovica had slowly but inexorably forced the trapped citizens into the Old City at its centre, until finally they were surrounded. And then they had simply sat down and waited.

David and Fabian settled themselves in the lower floor of the tower, the stone staircase rising up above them, the trapdoor at their feet. Karim would wait until darkness fell before returning, whistling the INN theme tune to alert them to his presence. David had the uneasy feeling that Roger Moore would appear at any minute.

Fabian eased his camera down beside him, cradling it loosely with his left arm, and leaned against the cool stone of the tower. David opened his rucksack and extracted two heavy flak jackets, their navy webbing padded with layers of kevlar.

'You'd better take this,' David said, thrusting the heavy jacket across the wood of the trapdoor towards the cameraman. 'Next to Marks & Spencers knickers, they're the most solid underwear I've ever seen. Should've had them on before, really, but they're so sodding uncomfortable. We're going to need them for the next bit. Won't stop a bullet but they might make us feel better.'

'I'm not wearing a bloody straitjacket,' Fabian said, kicking the edge of the navy webbing with his foot. 'Damn big girls' blouses. Only poofters wear them. You won't catch me in one of the sodding things.'

'Don't give me a hard time,' David said wearily. 'It'll be me who has to haul you out if you take a hit, and you weigh a fucking ton. Just put one on – I won't tell if you don't. But try not to get shot, they're bloody expensive.'

'Forget it,' Fabian growled.

David did not push it. He left the discarded flak jacket where it was, and eased his aching muscles into his own, leaving the zip half-undone in a futile attempt at comfort. He'd never beg a woman to wear a basque again. David grinned at the thought, and closed his eyes to let images of Christie dance across his mind. They had not kissed since that pre-dawn morning after Ben's party, but thoughts of her filled his heart and soul. He longed to feel her touch on his face, her lips on his, her hands in the small of his back as she held him close to her, her breasts crushed beneath his chest. He could taste the freshness of her skin, smell the heady fragrance of her hair, feel the firm silken length of her thighs against him. He had had no idea of what was missing in his life until he suddenly realised that he had found it.

The soft scrape of shoes on pebbles and stone brought David awake with a start, and in the same moment he became aware of the rhythmic stutter of gunfire in the distance. Above them the doorway leading on to the ramparts of the tower showed that it was night. Fabian awoke simultaneously, and grasped the handle of his camera as he stiffened in his place.

'Karim?' Fabian whispered softly.

'I sure as hell hope so,' David muttered back. Cautiously he bent his head to a narrow chink in the trapdoor, and peered through the slit. Below him he could see the silhouette of a man standing in the entrance to the woollen mill. A second figure appeared.

'We've got company,' he whispered to Fabian, not moving his eye from the chink.

'Do they know we're here?'

'Impossible to say.'

David watched as the second figure drew back outside the entrance. His companion scanned the lower reaches of the mill as if searching for something, before following the other figure out of David's eyeline.

'What are they doing here?' Fabian asked edgily.

'Well I can't see a red book, so chances are it's not *This is Your Life*,' David replied. 'When did you last pay your Poll Tax?'

'I think I'd rather it was the Serbian Fourth Army,' Fabian said feelingly. 'Have they seen us, do you reckon?'

'They may have found the jeep, but they're not sure if we're still here,' David said. 'Keep an eye on what's happening below. I'll check on things from the top of the tower.'

Fabian nodded silently, and David climbed the stone staircase as silently as he was able, thankful for the dim moonlight which streamed through the half-choked door-way. His fingers felt the lip of the steps in front of him, and when he grasped nothing, he realised that he was at the top. Cautiously he slithered over the pile of brick and stone to the edge of the rampart, careful not to break cover. Below him he could see the two figures conferring in the shadow of the tower.

Suddenly he gave a low laugh. As one of the figures turned and gestured towards the concealed jeep, his jacket swung open. Glinting in the moonlight was the silvery-green badge bearing the world-famous logo. INN.

During his childhood David had wanted to be a soldier, a burglar, James Bond, and a Hollywood movie star. Hey, join INN and you get to be all your boyhood dreams, he thought with an inward smile.

He whistled the INN theme tune, and clattered down the staircase, calling softly to Fabian. The two men eased back the trapdoor and descended the ladder, Fabian sling-ing the camera across his back as he climbed down. Karim met them at the bottom with a sigh of relief.

'Thought I'd lost you,' he said, his white teeth shining in the dark. He indicated the second man who was with him. 'This is Becirovic. He's part of the Serbian Fourth, who're manning the southern checkpoint into the Old City. He'll get us inside for ten thousand dollars, and out again in three days.'

'It's nice to know that in this unstable world, money still talks,' David said with satisfaction.

Fabian glowered at the man suspiciously. 'How do we know we can trust him?'

'We don't pay him until we're home and dry. Apart from that, you just have to hope I'm a good judge of human character and the BBC aren't paying him more than we are,' Karim responded with a grim smile.

'Let's go. We've wasted enough time already,' David

said briskly. He extended his hand to the Serbian, and shook hands. 'Thank you for your help, Becirovic. I take it we'll travel with you?'

The Serbian nodded, and spoke rapidly to Karim in a language David did not understand. 'We'll go past two checkpoints, then before we get to the third, we leap out of the truck,' Karim translated. 'Becirovic will carry on driving, whilst we get across the sandbanks, beneath the barbed wire and through the gate.'

'Reminds me of the time I interviewed Madonna,' David said, reaching for his rucksack.

Karim grinned. 'Becirovic will make sure no one is watching the gate when we go in. After that, it's anybody's guess.'

'Sounds like a picnic,' David said. 'OK, let's go.'

'I haven't heard any details yet about how we get out,' Fabian said warily. 'I'm not that happy with what I hear about going in, come to that.'

'If you want to change your mind, now's the time,' David said tersely, wondering what was eating the other man. Fabian shook his head and walked past the others towards Becirovic's truck. David had the disquieting sense that he was taking an unguided missile with him, and prayed that whatever was unsettling his cameraman so much would work itself out without jeopardising the story, or their lives.

■ 4 JULY, 6.20 p.m.

Fabian did not crack until the second day inside the besieged Old City.

They had entered Dakovica undetected. As they passed the second of the checkpoints Becirovic had indicated, they had thrown open the doors on the blind side of the truck,

292

and tumbled towards the shelter of the sandbanks the Serbians had erected around the Old City. Scrambling into a low crawl, they had slithered under the curls of barbed wire, holding it for each other in turn, and made the relative safety of the City walls without a shot being fired.

Inside the city was worse than anything David had imagined. When he had gathered the military position of the town, he could not understand why the Serbs had not simply shelled the Old City to rubble as they had the rest of Dakovica, and driven the trapped Albanians out of the beleaguered city completely. Instead they had sat outside the walls for seven months, allowing nothing in or out.

Then he understood. The Serbs were slowly and quite deliberately starving the people to death. They wanted to take the oldest and most beautiful part of the city intact; and most of all, they wanted to set an example to the rest of the country. There would be no quarter, no mercy, no surrender accepted, no easy death permitted. Every man, woman and child who had once inhabited Dakovica was now condemned to starve to death inside its oldest walls.

Like the rest of Dakovica, the Old City had been gutted by scavengers, human and animal. Before the siege had even begun, the pavements had been split open so that the copper from the underground cables could be extracted and sold. Wooden casements and doors had been burnt for warmth and cooking. Every home had been looted for blankets, clothes, utensils, the everyday necessities of survival. Every building was pock-marked with bullet holes, slates and bricks and glass littering the streets. Makeshift shelters had been constructed from pieces of wood, plastic sheeting, corrugated iron, bound together with scraps of string and rope to form curved beehives in which whole families crouched.

Rubbish was piled high in the streets, mingling with the fetid excrement of humans and stinking carcasses of the

293

few cats and dogs that had escaped being eaten. The rich soil of rotting refuse had produced a glory of flowers, the riot of colour and heady fragrance underscoring the abject misery around them. Animals and children sifted the decaying mounds desperately searching for something, anything, to eat.

Dakovica had tried to bury its dead, but the corpses soon outnumbered the living, and they had nowhere to take them. Along the sides of the road, the dirt verges were filled with shallow graves, many of them washed half-open by the rains. David watched one woman bury her last child by the roadside, weighing the fragile body down with rocks and a broken piece of plastic sheeting, in a futile attempt to prevent the corpse being washed away. The woman did not weep. She had long since cried all the tears she had inside her. Without a flicker of emotion she pointed out the four graves where her other children and her husband were buried.

Silently Fabian gathered the pictures as David strove to come to terms with the full human tragedy of what he was seeing. The pain of it clenched around his heart like a vice. 'It may not be the end of the world, but you can see it from here,' he muttered grimly, more to himself than to his companions.

On their second night in the Old City, the Serbian tactics changed. Without warning, the sky was illuminated with bullet tracers, and David recognised the whistle of shells as they soared over the city walls to land with the familiar crump on the homes beneath. The air was filled with screams as walls caved in, crushing the occupants. Snipers on the tall buildings around the Old City shot at the terrified people who poured out onto the streets.

In the flimsy shelter of a derelict church, David rapidly went through their options with the other two men.

'They've obviously decided not to wait any longer,'

294

David said in between shells. 'This must be it. I don't think the city can hold out more than a couple of days.'

'Just as well, with the BBC right behind us,' Fabian said.

'I reckon they've heard Kate Adie's on the way, and they're getting out whilst the going's still good,' David replied, hunching down below the level of the narrow windows whose stained glass had long since been blown away. 'We are in the middle of this story, and I want to finish it. But it's highly likely our contact car will be nowhere in sight come tomorrow evening. We're on our own.'

'I'm with you, whatever your decision,' Karim said swiftly, scanning the night sky with sharp eyes. 'But for what it's worth, I think we have to stay until the end comes. Otherwise we lose the story. What good is what we've done if we leave before the end?'

David nodded, but turned towards Fabian. 'We're a team, and it's your pictures we'll be needing,' he said.

'I say no, it's too dangerous,' Fabian muttered. A shell landed just the other side of the wall, and the ground shook. All three men leaped up and dashed towards the altar, away from the teetering church wall that had been their only shelter just minutes before. A volley of shots hit the ground where they had been crouching.

Fabian's breath was coming in short gasps. 'I told you! It's too fucking dangerous! We'll never get out of here if we stay any longer, you bastard!'

'Karim?' David asked.

'Well, they won't be stopping to ask us for our fucking press passes,' the other man responded. 'But you're paying me by the day, so I'll risk it.'

Karim and David exchanged glances. Fabian had seen one too many wars, and his nerve had broken. He must have known right from the start that he was close to the edge, but for all his posturing as a fearless war cameraman he did not have the courage to acknowledge his own fear.

'We stay together. That means we have to leave. We'd better make it soon,' David said expressionlessly.

'How! How the fuck do we get out? It's impossible, you'll kill us all!' Fabian screamed, his voice shrill with fear.

With an effort David controlled the simmering rage inside him.

'We swim,' he said simply. 'That is, if you can manage without armbands. The irrigation channel on the other side of the fields behind this church leads straight to the farm where we left the jeep. We swim.'

'Are you mad?' Fabian shouted. 'They'll pick us off one by one!'

'They'll be too busy elsewhere,' Karim interjected coolly, contempt written across his face. 'I'll take the camera above the water. We will be fine.'

Before Fabian had a chance to object further, David stood up and half-running, half-crouching, led the way across the fields towards the water. Karim had been right. The assault was so fierce that their passage went unnoticed. None of the men noticed the putrid reek that emanated from the stagnant water as they slid into it, pushing their way around floating animal carcasses, not daring to ask themselves what squelched beneath their feet as they made their way along the irrigation channel.

Unknown to him, on any other night the route David had chosen would have been fatal. Aware that the trapped people inside the city could well use it to escape under cover of darkness, it had been strictly monitored by the encircling army. Not all the corpses floating in the rank water were animal. But the final assault had drawn the soldiers away from such perimeters to the main arena of battle, and the three men were able to slip unnoticed through the net.

The journey seemed to David to be one of the longest of his life. As he waded through the water, he expected to feel the impact of a bullet at any moment. He felt as if he had a giant target sign tacked to his back. He was also uneasily aware of the danger of leaving the channel too early in the dark, before they reached the relative safety of the deserted farm.

As the dawn pinked the sky, David suddenly saw the unmistakeable silhouette of the crenellated tower appear above a sparse group of trees. With relief, the three men clambered up the bank and hugged the shadows of the outhouses until they reached the sanctuary of the woollen mill. David did not even remember climbing the ladder to the first floor of the tower before he fell into a deep, dreamless sleep.

'Sleeping on the job, huh? That's the last time I trust you to get anything done.'

David blinked his eyes rapidly, staring at the slim figure framed against the cool stone walls. As he tried to pull the jagged edges of memory together to form a complete and comprehensible whole, Christie climbed the last few steps of the ladder and came through the trapdoor.

'Well that's a fine welcome, after I've come all this way to bring you your good morning cup of tea.'

Christie unscrewed the thermos flask in her hand and poured some steaming liquid into the plastic cup. David took it gratefully, and threw back a scalding gulp before even attempting to ask her what the hell she was doing there.

'I just hope you keep this up after we're married,' he said, easing himself on to one elbow as Christie rocked back on her heels and raised an eyebrow at his remark. David glanced around the tower and found it empty. Christie intercepted the look.

'Fabian went out to do some end shots, and Karim is off looking for Becirovic. So it's just you and me,' she said, gazing directly into his eyes.

'About time,' David grinned.

Steve stuck his head through the trapdoor. 'Hi, David,' he said. 'I hope you're pleased to see us after the trouble we went to getting here.'

David sighed.

When Fabian and Karim came back from their various errands, Steve and Christie produced three packs of bacon and two fresh loaves of bread from their rucksacks with delighted and smug expressions.

'If you think this is supposed to excuse you for following us here . . .' David threatened.

'It does,' Karim finished. 'Completely and absolutely absolved, my child.'

'Hey, I thought pork was the one thing you and the Jews agreed about?' David exclaimed, winking at Christie. 'That and hating the Americans.'

Karim did not pause in unwrapping the bacon. 'Allah's not watching. These are heathen lands.'

'In that case, you might as well have one of these,' Christie said, tossing the Lebanese a can of lager.

'What, not chilled?' David queried.

'Damn, I knew there was something I'd missed,' Christie frowned, snapping her fingers in the air. 'Steve, you should've reminded me. How could we forget the ice?'

Fabian sat in a corner of the farmhouse they were using as their bivouac, glaring into the distance with an expression that forbad conversation. After they had cooked the makeshift breakfast on a fire Karim fashioned in the hearth, Christie took David aside and asked him what the problem was. Concealing his anger, David explained briefly and succinctly.

298

'You still want to finish the story?' she asked, when David had finished speaking. 'You want to go back in there?'

David hunkered down on his heels in the corner, and Christie slid down the wall beside him. For a few moments David said nothing, tracing a pattern in the dirt floor with his fingers and Christie saw the faint white band on his little finger where his signet ring had been.

Finally David raised his head, the dark curls clinging to his brow. 'Fabian is out,' he said grimly. 'Karim can manage sound, but he's just not up to shooting pictures. I'm prepared to risk going back, but it's a bloody high risk. I'm not sure I should ask Steve to take it. I don't want him to feel he has to say yes.'

Christie rolled back the sleeve of her pale pink denim shirt where it had fallen down her left arm. Slowly she pushed her hair back from her forehead. 'I think Steve has the guts to say no, if that's what he feels,' she said at last. 'The question is, how far do you want to go for a story?'

'I think the world has the right – the *need* – to know what's happening here,' David argued, remembered pain clouding his eyes. 'You cannot possibly understand how brutal it is, until you see it. I have to *show* people. It has to stop.'

Christie did not argue any further. She felt a flicker of fear clutch at her heart, and made no move to quell it, knowing she would feel this stomach-churning anxiety until David was back safely.

David outlined the situation to Steve, explaining the risks involved, without detailing exactly why Fabian was out of the picture on this story. Steve did not ask. They agreed that this time it was safer – and cheaper – not to use Becirovic, and decided that Karim, David and Steve would enter the Old City after dark through the irrigation channel. Christie would remain behind to watch their rear for twenty-four hours. After that she would have to assume they were in trouble. What she would do then David did not ask.

It was night before they realised that Fabian had gone. With him he had taken the jeep.

■ 6 JULY, 5.20 p.m.

Regardless of the defection of the cameraman, they still had a job to do. Unable to alert INN to what had happened, David decided to take a chance and go back into the city with just Steve and Karim. It was a risk, but then so was this whole crazy escapade. What was one more?

The three men had managed to get safely in, and had gathered some horrifying pictures of the wholesale slaughter taking place. It was on the way out that the Serbians launched a barrage of Rocket Propelled Grenades into the town. Steve had paused in their flight towards the irrigation channel to take a shot. Behind the three journalists were half a dozen Albanians who had realised that the Westerners had a way in – and therefore a way out – and had followed them. As Steve lined up his camera, focusing the nightscope on the hail of bullet tracers lighting up the sky, an RPG landed feet from him. Two of the Albanians disappeared immediately. David and Karim lost sight of Steve in the cloud of dust.

'Steve! *Steve!* Are you OK?' David shouted, rushing from the channel back towards the crater the RPG had gouged out of the ground.

A hail of bullets rang out, hitting two more of the fleeing Albanians. The remainder turned round and ran back towards the city, not daring to risk trying to reach the irrigation channel.

300

'Steve! For God's sake, *answer me!*' David yelled into the choking dust, dirt caking his eyes and nostrils as he tried to see through the gloom. Terrifying images of Seb's broken body filled his mind. *Not again. Dear God, not again.*

'He's here!' Karim called. David ran over towards the cameraman, who was lying twisted on the ground.

'I'm OK,' Steve muttered, trying to summon a grin. 'Just don't give me a drink. I've got a belly full of holes.'

David knelt next to Steve in the leeway of a wall that had once been part of someone's home, and tried to staunch the flow of the editor's blood with the makeshift dressing he had fashioned from the sleeve of his shirt. He felt the blood trickle down between his fingers, and wondered how much longer they had left. They had to get Steve to a hospital soon, or it would be too late.

'Wait here,' he whispered to Karim. 'I've got to check out the road. We have to get away from here somehow, or that wound will prove fatal.'

Karim nodded, and took over from David, pressing the heel of his hand into the gaping hole left by the high-velocity bullet, listening to Steve's shallow breathing with concern. The blood flow was slowing, but had not stopped. He had seen enough such injuries in his native Lebanon to know how little time remained.

Cautiously David edged his way along the rough verge that ran down their side of the wall, and deliberately skittered a stone into the road a few feet from him, where the teetering rubble ended. A spray of shots followed the stone, and David heard the unmistakable zing of a bullet splicing the air around him. Those who were new to gunfire always thought the louder the sound, the nearer the shots, the greater the danger. Experience had taught him to dread rather the zither-like hiss of the lethal bullets, which meant they were just inches away.

301

There was no way they could make the road. The snipers had them completely pinned down. They could not go over the wall and across the field behind them for the same reason. The only way out was back the way he had come. At the edge of the house beneath which they were now sheltering was a shattered sewage pipe, which had run the length of the village. The piping was large enough to crawl along, and led beneath the main street to a jumble of buildings that were still standing a few hundred yards away. If they could reach that, they had a chance – a slim chance – of getting away. But there was no way they could all make it. Not with a wounded colleague. David would never have countenanced leaving any team member bleeding to death, even if he jeopardised his own life by staying.

He half-crouched as he ran back towards Karim, still sheltering with Steve in the lee of the wall. The cameraman was deathly pale, and sweat was beading his brow. David knew at a glance that he would not survive much longer without medical help.

'We're going to have to risk the sewage pipes,' he said, meeting Karim's eyes over the wounded man's face. Steve's breathing was hoarse and shallow, and he was shivering despite the heavy coat David had put over him. His lips and fingernails were blue.

'If we move him, we could start the bleeding again,' Karim replied anxiously.

'We've got no choice. If we stay here, he'll die anyway.'

'What do we do when we get to the other side? The jeep's gone, remember?'

David cursed and thought rapidly. 'The buildings will give us cover from the snipers for as long as it takes them to realise we've moved. Maybe an hour. I'll try to get across the fields and double back towards the farmhouse. We may be able to get some transport from there.'

'Like what? Start up a tractor?'

'For Christ's sake, Karim, do you have any better ideas?' David's anxiety made him sharper than he intended. He reached out and clasped his colleague's shoulder. 'I'm sorry, my friend. But we are running out of options.'

'Poor bastard. We were so nearly clear,' Karim said softly.

It always happened like that, David thought, a knot of anger at the futility of it building inside him. Just when you thought you were safe. Sod's law.

As Karim and David carried the injured man towards the sewage pipe entrance, he was barely conscious. David noticed the wound start to bleed again as they moved crablike along the concrete tube, and wondered with foreboding if he was haemorrhaging inside. By the time they reached daylight at the other end, twenty feet away, Steve was groaning in pain.

David clambered out of the entrance, warning Karim to stay back until he had ascertained that it was safe enough to carry Steve into shelter. Somehow he was not surprised to see Christie standing beside a jeep, its engine idling.

'Remind me never to let you promise not to follow me again,' he gasped as he hugged her.

■ ALBANIA
8 JULY, 11.15 p.m.

David followed Christie into the room, shrugging off his flak jacket as he did so. He let his gaze trawl around the walls, noting the heavy faded blue velvet curtains, the warmth of the wooden panelling, the midnight blue carpet that felt soft beneath his feet despite its worn patches. A single lamp with a pale peach shade gave a dusky light to the corner of the room beneath the window, casting tall shadows on the ceiling. In the centre of the room was a low four-poster bed, its velvet hangings matching the curtains and trailing on to the carpet. Facing the end of the bed, a log fire flickered and glowed, casting its warmth into the room.

David smiled, and moved towards Christie, who was standing in front of the fire, gazing into its flames as if she would find all the answers there. He put his hands on her shoulders, and turned her gently towards him. The firelight flickered across her face, gilding her brow and cheekbones with amber highlights. Her hair glittered copper and russet in the glow.

'I don't know how you managed it – any of it – but thank you,' he whispered softly, drawing her towards him. He felt her tremble beneath him, and pulled a little way away to gaze into her eyes, which in this dim light were the fathomless green-black of the deepest seas.

'Think of it as an unbirthday present,' she smiled back at him, touching the side of his cheek.

'You saved Steve's life, you know that, don't you?' David said. 'Not to mention mine and Karim's. If you hadn't been there with the jeep, we'd never have got him back in time . . .'

'Sssh,' Christie said, laying a finger across his lips. 'As long as he's safe now, that's what matters. And meanwhile, you and I are here, together, alone, alive.'

David closed his eyes at the memory of their frantic drive south from Dakovica, racing for the Kosovo/ Albanian border, Christie cradling Steve's head in her lap and praying he would survive. For once, luck had been on their side, and they had passed the various roadblocks without coming under fire. They had reached the relative safety of southern Albania without mishap, Steve unconscious but still alive. A UN team had performed an emergency road operation as soon as they reached the field hospital, and managed to stabilise the cameraman long enough for him to be flown to a hospital in Athens.

'I called the desk,' David added, as Christie moved across the room to a deep brocaded sofa. 'They were very relieved to hear from us. Apparently they thought it was you who had been shot. Ben was doing his Chinese pieces.'

'I bet he was,' Christie said drily. 'Robin probably gave him the medivac bill. I take it they're happy for us to stay here to edit and feed the Dakovica piece?'

'They wanted me to send you straight home, but gave in when I pointed out that it would delay the piece by several days,' David said. 'But they want us both out and en route to London as soon as we've finished.'

'No sign of Fabian yet, I suppose?'

'No sign, no,' David confirmed. 'CNN and the BBC have had to pull back from Kosovo along with us, because it seems the whole Serbian Army is on the march. They didn't see him. Looks like we got out just in time.'

'It's nice to be in a room that doesn't rattle to the sound of gunfire,' Christie said, hugging her knees to her chest at the memory. 'The night before I left to follow you, I could see the discs of green lights from sniper guns trailing around the walls of my room like spotlights. If I'd stood up, they would have had me in their sights.'

'I'm glad you don't sleepwalk,' David said, crossing the room and bending over the back of the sofa. 'I couldn't bear to lose you now.'

'Me too. That's why I had to follow you.'

'I know. Thank God you did.'

'So I'm forgiven?' Christie asked, twisting round to look into David's face.

David held her tighter. 'I would forgive anything except losing you,' he murmured. 'I've lost too much

305

already. You are my reason for being. How could I not forgive you for saving my life in every way?'

Christie smiled, not trusting her voice to speak. She had no doubts any longer. David had committed himself to her, body and soul, when he gave her his ring. She had given herself to him when she accepted it. There was no other way but this.

David straightened up, and looked down at her. 'Next to seeing you, my dream over the last five days has been a shower,' he grinned. 'I'll leave you to sort out the champagne, seeing as you've managed everything else so well without me.'

David entered the bathroom, as warm and welcoming as the bedroom he had just left. His feet sank into the thick cobalt carpet, the tiny window curtained against the night. David leaned over the bath and turned the shower on, expecting a jet of ice-cold spray. To his surprise, warm water gushed from the showerhead, steam rising to fog the mirror over the sink. David drew off his clothes, which were stiff with mud and filth from the past few days, and climbed into the shower, feeling the grime sluice from his body as the hot needles played over his skin. With a deep sigh of contentment, he turned his face upwards into the spray, standing motionless with fatigue and relief.

When David opened the bathroom door again, clean and freshshaven, a large fluffy white towel wrapped around his waist, he saw Christie sitting where he had left her, swathed only in a pale green outsize silk shirt, her hair half-tumbling from a casual chignon. She held out a tulip-shaped glass to him with a smile.

'I could only find Moët, but I hope it will do,' she laughed.

David scooped her in his arms, and placed the glass of champagne on the table.

'The champagne can wait,' he murmured hungrily in her ear. 'This won't.'

With a deep sigh, Christie melted softly against his chest as he carried her over to the bed, laying her gently on the white linen sheets and straightening up to gaze at her.

'You're so beautiful,' he whispered, as he bent over her and kissed her lips so lightly she almost wondered if he had touched her. She smelt the musky male scent of him as he bent his head lower, his fingers moving quickly across the pale green silk of her shirt, unbuttoning and opening lightly, imperceptibly. He held her to him, slipping the shirt off her shoulders, so that she was naked in the firelight before him. He drew his breath, marvelling at the slim contours of her body, the high, firm rounded breasts, the pale gold triangle at the top of her thighs.

He bent his head again, and traced the features of her face with his lips, his breath sweet and soft against her skin. Christie tasted the sweetness of his tongue as his mouth met hers. Her hands reached out to him, and he moved so that his body lay full length against her, his towel falling away. Christie felt his hardness swell against her thighs, firm and insistent.

David pulled back, cupping her breasts in his hands. 'Not yet, not yet, my darling, my love,' he murmured, taking one erect nipple between his teeth and teasing the rosy bud with his tongue. He flicked it across the surface of her nipple, quick, teasing darts, which sent silver arrows coursing through her veins, tugging cords connected directly to the core of her body. Christie groaned with longing, and wrapped her arms around his shoulders, her nails trailing along his skin and searing him with fire. David's tongue grew firmer, rougher, and he took the whole of her nipple in his mouth, feeling it harden

307

against his lips, and her body stiffen in response beneath his.

She tangled her hands in his hair, pressing his mouth firmly against her breast, writhing beneath him as she felt his hardness rearing against the soft flesh of her inner thigh. She was aware of the wet warmth of her arousal flooding through her, every muscle straining towards David as he kissed and caressed her breasts with languorous strokes. He paused and lifted his head, his eyes on hers.

'I love you, Christie,' he said, his gaze steady and unwavering. 'I've loved you from the moment I met you.'

Christie met his look, her eyes searching his face as if the truth would lie there. She yearned to give herself to David, to surrender herself to him completely and have him know her absolutely. Deep inside she had always known it, from the moment she had seen him. Her face flooded with desire and happiness and wanting.

'My David, my David, I love you, oh how I love you,' she cried, burying her face in his shoulder, tasting the saltiness of his skin.

Suddenly it was David's turn to gasp with pleasure, as Christie moved and crouched over him like a cat. She slithered down the length of his body, her finger tracing the whorls of dark hair that travelled from his chest to his navel, and down to mingle with the hairs that curled around his hardness. Slowly she bent to his nipples and sucked gently, then firmly, her own breasts hanging heavy and succulent against his chest as her tongue darted fire. The heavy curtain of her hair hid her face, and David closed his eyes to everything but the exquisite sensation of this woman loving him.

He reached for her, but she slid out of his grasp, the softness of her body caressing his like satin as she moved lower. David experienced a sensation like dreaming, as he

308

felt the skin he had so long and so often imagined. Christie dipped her head, and he quivered as she took him in her mouth, cradling him in her hand, her tongue and teeth and lips nibbling and sucking him, slow, fast, slow. David moaned with desire, feeling himself harden still further in response to the teasing motions of her mouth and kisses, the featherlike brushes of her fingers along the inside of his thighs, around his maleness, creeping up towards his navel and then darting back down to hold him in her hands. Her back curved along the length of the bed, the downy white globes of her buttocks glistening as the shadows rippled across the room. Every inch of his body smouldered with the passion she raised in him.

He tasted himself on her lips, and tasted too her own desire. Her own cries of pleasure whetted his already heightened appetite and his body burned. Suddenly he was filled with a yearning to possess her, to be inside her and lose himself in her. With a swift motion of his hips, he swivelled so that he was above her, and gazed down in her face, her eyes wide and her lips soft and blurred with desire.

'David, please, my darling, now,' she gasped, pulling him towards her and opening her legs to receive him.

And then he was inside her, filling her with his length, driving into her. Christie moaned and clung to him, burying her face in his shoulder, muffling her cries as he moved rhythmically within her. Every part of her body seemed to fit perfectly with his; her shoulders against his chest, his stomach against hers, her legs wrapping around his and embracing him again and again. She had the feeling that she was dancing an ancient, long-forgotten pattern that somehow she had always known, but never before remembered. She gave herself up to the long, wing-like beats of passion, her body claiming its

309

own fluidity and pleasure and speed.

Waves of pleasure ebbed and flowed within her, lapping along her veins and surging through the muscles in her arms and legs, around and along and about her stomach. Every part of her stiffened, then relaxed as the pulses of desire flowed through her. She tensed and shivered and relaxed and tensed and shivered, always aware of the building within her, gathering its forces.

David paused momentarily and reached for one of the soft pillows above Christie's head, slipping it beneath her hips in an easy movement. She gasped as the new angle gave him added depth, feeling as if he were burying not into but through her. And suddenly she lost all conscious thought and was aware only of the relentless surging inside her, the pressure reaching an intense trembling peak. There was nothing but David thrusting into her body, nothing but the endless pleasure surging through her, nothing but the two of them as they became one as they poured themselves into one another, coming together until both were spent.

For a long time neither of them moved. The shadows flickered and fell as the fire died, and Christie remained in the hollow of David's arm. She was aware of having experienced an intensity of love she had never even imagined. Her absolute surrender to David had given her a freedom and independence she could never have attained alone. She felt complete on every level with him. His strength, his determination, his vulnerability, his love, matched hers.

She smiled. My grandmother's generation was permitted no existence without a man, she thought, and my mother's fought so hard to stand alone, independent. Perhaps mine will discover that the ultimate freedom is being allowed to make the choice to be together. She

310

turned towards David, who was looking at her, his eyes glistening with love.

'I never dreamed,' she murmured.

'I've always known,' he said.

Chapter Eleven

■ INN, LONDON
13 JULY, 10.56 a.m.

'Not again. This is ridiculous!' Victoria Lawrence spat angrily.

Jerry hastened to soothe his affronted newscaster's ruffled feathers. 'I'm sure she didn't do it on purpose,' he said placatingly.

'Even I worked that one out,' Victoria snapped. 'Unless she sat at home outside my house it would be pretty difficult for her to know what I was going to wear.'

Not really, Jerry thought to himself. Victoria always wore the red jacket on alternate Tuesdays.

Paragon stood up, dragging her dove-grey Judith Leiber clutch bag across the desk. 'I'm quite happy to go home and change,' she said obligingly. 'I know what it's like once you get into a routine. You hate to change it.'

Victoria bridled at the suggestion. 'I'm quite happy to change myself,' she sniffed. 'I'm sure I have far more suitable things to choose from than Paragon. I know she won't want to wear the blue and cream jacket *again*.'

'One of you will have to change, and that's for sure,' Jerry said quickly, before Paragon could take offence at Victoria's emphasis on the word 'again'. 'You can't both wear scarlet jackets. You'll look like Butlins' redcoats.'

'I was so sure you'd worn the red already this week,'

Paragon said sweetly. 'Maybe you forgot. But the viewers wouldn't have noticed.'

'Well I'm sure they would,' Victoria retorted, her voice laced with venom. 'That's why I always make a point of returning my clothes to the end of my on-camera clothes rail.' She paused to allow the implication to sink in that she had other, more exclusive, off-camera clothes on other, longer, rails. 'I only take from the front. That way I don't repeat myself too often.'

'Pity you can't do that with your scripts,' Ollie interjected, as he passed the embattled Early Evening News desk.

Victoria glared at the News Editor. 'Isn't there something you should be doing?' she said frostily.

'If only you'd let me,' Ollie returned with a leer.

Victoria glowered. 'I'm going to report that man,' she said after him as he walked away. 'He's always sending me obscene messages on the computer. I wouldn't mind if it wasn't for the fact that he comes from Manchester.'

She stood up and spun on her Manolo Blahnik heels. 'I'm going back to Hampstead,' she announced with as much dignity as she could muster. 'I'll wear the emerald Lagerfeld. I had my doubts about the red Versace anyway. It's such an obvious colour, and just a little bit dated this year.'

Paragon had the uneasy feeling she had been outmanoeuvred as Victoria swept out of the newsroom on a wave of Ma Griffe. Jerry grinned reassuringly at her across the desk. 'She doesn't like the competition,' he said. 'As long as she's being a bitch, you're OK. The time you really want to worry is when she suddenly starts being nice.'

He turned back towards the desk, and picked up his clipboard. The rest of the production team gathered around him, loitering with intent against the desk and trying to watch the end of the Test Match on their monitors whilst appearing to attend the meeting. Ollie wandered back to join them and fill Jerry in on the stories available for his bulletin.

'How come you're producing the Early show again?' he asked, as he settled his large bulk into a chair next to Jerry with a wince.

'Simon's back at the drying-out clinic, so Brian's doing the Late show and I'm standing in for him on the Early again,' Jerry said. 'Rochelle's doing the News Updates. This place gets more and more like the Magic Round-about every day.'

'Time For Bed, said Ben,' Ollie put in, with a pointed look at Paragon, who blushed and studied her David Morris gold bracelet with intense fascination.

'It's one way of getting promoted,' Dom Ryan said feelingly. He was getting just a little tired of doing the football results.

'You want to wait until you've been here yet another year,' Ollie answered. 'Christ, I've been passed over more times than Heathrow Airport.'

Jerry looked peeved. 'Can we discuss our personal grievances later?' he said testily. 'I am *trying* to hold a meeting.'

Suki, the twenty-one-year-old weathergirl, suddenly appeared at the desk, her grass-green velour tracksuit freshly pressed, a pair of spotless pink aerobic trainers on her feet. 'I didn't have time to change,' she said distractedly as she sat down and put a green plastic Marks & Spencer bag beneath the desk. She gazed at Jerry with wide-eyed concern. 'Muffi had to be rushed to the vet.'

Jerry looked alarmed, and the rest of the team stifled giggles. Jerry and Suki's devotion to their ginger-and-white cat was legendary.

314

'Is it serious?' he said, running his hand through his curly blonde hair. 'I'm owed some compassionate leave.'

'Girl trouble,' Suki whispered. 'Not in front of everybody.'

Jerry was suddenly aware of the intense interest of the rest of the newsroom, and swivelled back towards his desk in a belated attempt at authority. 'We're still leading on the UN response to the crisis in Dakovica,' he said, as Ollie disappeared to the News Desk to take an urgent call. 'We're doing a pull-together in Washington on the latest there, and we've got David Cameron's last piece in his Dakovica series. I haven't seen the picture yet, but I'm told it's pretty horrific.'

He turned towards the producer. 'Now Rich, I want to go really big on this one. We've got an interview with the little Dakovica girl who's just found her father in Berlin, and I want to really effort the graphics. I want chapter headings for each of the three VTRs, maps, straps, the works.'

Lynxie, the graphics girl, scribbled on her art pad. 'We thought we'd start each of the VTR packages with a freeze-frame of the airlift,' she said.

'We should get the verdict on the Bournemouth Ripper trial sometime this afternoon,' Ollie said, coming back to the desk. 'Peter Princer's got a backgrounder together, and Nick Makepiece is at the High Court, so you could go to him live if it happens in our time.'

'I don't normally go in for backgrounders, but as this one's got sex and violence in it, I don't mind,' Jerry said, adding it to his list of stories with his silver propeller pencil, last year's Christmas present from Muffi. 'Ginny, could you take care of it? We'll need the Court artist to do us some drawings of inside the courtroom.'

'You've got two trials today, actually,' Ollie amended. 'The haemophiliac who got AIDS from screened blood is

315

taking the hospital to Court today.'

'How the hell do you spell haemophiliac?' Rich asked, noticing it was his story.

'Just talk about blood,' Jerry said. 'This is the Early Evening News, not Channel Four.'

Ginny wondered despairingly if anything was sacred any more.

Victoria deliberately made sure she was late for Fiona in Make-Up to wind Jerry up. There was nothing he hated more than not having his newscasters in the studio at least fifteen minutes before the bulletin.

'The usual?' Fiona asked, selecting Victoria's favoured foundation and picking up a large brush.

Victoria nodded, and the make-up girl swiftly applied a layer of the pancake make-up, dusting powder over the surface to take away any shine. Expertly she outlined Victoria's glacial blue eyes with a kohl pencil, skimming her cheeks with a soft brush of apricot blusher, and filling in her lids with honey-coloured hues of eye-shadow. Television studio lights were demanding and unforgiving, and what looked heavy and artificial in the newsroom merely made Victoria's skin look flawless – and more importantly as far as Victoria was concerned, ageless – in front of the cameras. Finally she sprayed the newscaster's dark shoulder-length hair with Elnett so that it stood crisp and brittle around Victoria's cheeks. If she fell over it might crack, but on the screen she would present her usual unruffled groomed perfection.

Calmly Victoria strolled into the studio, taking care to avoid the heavy cables snaking across the floor. The Floor Manager hurtled to her side, and Victoria could hear the angry squawk of Jerry's voice from his earphones as he escorted her towards the news set.

Victoria froze.

'What is she doing in my seat?' she inquired icily, turning towards the gallery where she knew Jerry could see her.

Inwardly Jerry quailed. He knew Ben's decision was going to cause trouble, and had a strong feeling that that was why the Editor had made it. The Early Evening News was a prestige programme; the newscaster who read the headlines, introduced the show and said the goodnights was always the most senior on duty, depending upon the pairing. Sir Edward was Number One when he was presenting, but in his absence an unwritten code gave Victoria precedence. It was only a matter of time before the UN would be called in to mediate.

'Ben thought it would be a good idea if you took turns to lead the show,' he explained over the intercom. He did not hold out much hope that Victoria would be having any of it.

She wasn't. 'I hardly think he can have meant a *beginner* to try to hold his prestige newscast together,' she said bitingly. 'You have obviously made a mistake.'

Jerry wondered what the hell he should do now. If he let Victoria take the chief anchor position, Ben would murder him. If he insisted Paragon took precedence, they might not have a show. Fervently he wished he could change places with the BBC or ITN producers, who had only one newscaster to humour for their main evening broadcasts.

'I think Ben felt Paragon needed the experience,' he said diplomatically. 'After all, with your *expertise* . . .' Jerry allowed his voice to trail suggestively.

Victoria thawed slightly, and Jerry drew a sigh of relief.

'Five minutes to On-Air,' Annie, the PA, said cheerfully.

'I realise that,' Victoria said, as if humouring a child. 'But I'm afraid that I have a duty to my public. I can't let

317

them down. I'm sorry, I shall have to talk to Ben about it. Now.'

Coolly she wandered back towards the studio exit, her designer heels tapping briskly as she skirted the cameras and unused sets. Desperately the Floor Manager threw himself across the door as Victoria bore down on him, her pink Dolce & Gabbana organza jacket whispering as she moved. Paragon scowled; she realised Victoria had deliberately selected it in favour of the emerald Lagerfeld to clash with her own outfit. Jerry buried his head in his hands.

'Three minutes,' Annie intoned.

Paragon stood up with the air of one gracefully giving in to unreasonable demands to save the peace. 'If it means so much to Victoria, I'm very happy to switch places. I'm sure I can learn a lot from someone so much *older*,' she said patronisingly. 'And we can talk to Ben later about tomorrow.'

Victoria threw her a poisonous glare, and returned to her seat, her pink jacket making Paragon's crimson Prada look cheap and obvious as she had known it would. Frantically the Floor Manager hooked up Victoria's mike to the translucent material as she inserted her earpiece, and Fiona materialised to give both newscasters a fresh dusting of powder. As the titles rolled and Victoria read the headlines, Jerry wondered what on earth was left to go wrong.

As the first story started rolling, Victoria leant back in her chair and sipped from the glass of water next to her scripts. Suddenly she caught sight of her screen image in the monitor to her right.

'What the hell is going on?' she hissed to Tony, the Floor Manager.

Paragon leant across the double desk, and glanced at the screen. She smiled smugly as she saw every flaw in

318

Victoria's face revealed by the harsh tungsten glare of the lights. 'Oh, of course, they would have taken the pink filter out when they thought it was for me,' she said sweetly. 'They didn't think I needed it.'

Before Victoria could reply, Muriel was counting her into her next story from the Director's desk in the Gallery. Crisply Victoria began reading the intro to the Washington piece, aware of an uncomfortable tingling in her cheeks. In the control room, Jerry turned to Ginny and Rich, who were sitting at the back of the Gallery to oversee their stories.

'What's up with Victoria?' he asked with a puzzled frown.

Victoria was asking the same question. As soon as the Washington story started rolling, she reached under her desk and pulled out a mirror. She gazed at her reflection with alarm. There was no doubt about it: a strange pink rash was spreading over her skin. Horrified, she looked frantically around for Fiona, who rushed to her side and patted a fresh layer of powder on her cheeks and forehead. The rash disappeared beneath it, but Victoria could still feel her skin tingling.

'The man known as the Bournemouth Ripper has been found guilty of murdering and raping eleven women . . .' Paragon read smoothly. Her glossy blonde hair rippled in the studio lights as she moved, her lips curving around the words with the same expertise they had shown on Ben's cock two hours before.

Halfway through the show Victoria realised that there was something seriously wrong. Jerry had already taken two calls from Ollie upstairs on the Newsdesk, who was being besieged by anxious viewers demanding to know what was wrong with Victoria Lawrence this evening. In between every script the unhappy newscaster read, Fiona was repairing the damage as best she could, but there was

319

no doubt that the rash was worsening. As they went into the commercial break, Victoria grasped the make-up girl's wrist in desperation.

'I need something more concealing than this,' she said anxiously, spinning the tub of powder in the girl's hand. Suddenly she stiffened. Reaching for the compact again, she turned it and raised it carefully, examining the shimmering surface of the powder in the studio lights.

'Victoria, we're going to have to get Charles to replace you,' Jerry said urgently over the intercom. 'We're just getting too many calls.'

'Don't worry, Jerry,' Victoria said, her eyes glittering with anger. 'I know exactly what's wrong. And I know exactly how to put it right.'

She glanced at the studio clock. She had four minutes until they went back on air. Swiftly she stood up and left the studio without a backward glance, heading for the Make-Up room next door. She aimed straight for the bench beneath the mirror where Fiona kept the various foundations and powders for the news station's anchors. As she picked up the pale green powder compact at the edge of the table, she drew in her breath in triumph. So she was right. Someone had switched her usual hypo-allergenic powder for the translucent shimmer she had noticed Fiona using in the studio. The tubs were the same colour; only the lids were different. Someone was playing games. And Victoria had a good idea who.

Without pausing for thought, she removed the powder she was wearing with a ball of cotton wool, reapplying a fresh layer from her own compact in her clasp bag. As she re-entered the studio, she was relieved to feel the tingling already starting to subside. No one noticed her flip an insignificant grey switch as she manoeuvred her way back across the tangle of cables towards the desk.

320

Jerry watched the second half of the show go on air with a deep sense of relief.

It was short-lived.

'Now what the hell is going on?' he moaned, throwing his scripts up in the air as Paragon stumbled haltingly through the next lead-in. 'Who do these two think they are? French and Saunders?'

'More like Bonnie and Clyde,' Rich muttered with a smile.

In the studio Paragon was struggling hard to make sense of the autocue, which should have been controlled from the peddle beneath her desk, but tonight seemed to have a life of its own. The faster she spoke, the faster the words rolled. In desperation she groped for the scripts in front of her, reasoning that reading from them would be simpler than trying to beat the manic autocue. With despair she realised she could have delivered a flawless performance of Victoria's scripts, but had not one word of her own. When they had changed desks, they had not exchanged the vital paper back-up every newscaster needed in case the autocue crashed. Mentally she groaned and glanced across at Victoria. One all.

Victoria read her remaining stories calmly and with authority. You might be screwing the Editor, Paragon, she thought venomously, but you bloody well won't screw me.

Charles Silversmith watched the uneven progress of the Early Evening News with the satisfaction of a man who has been proved right in the face of vehement opposition. That's what happened when you let women do a man's job. Put two of them together and there was bound to be trouble. He was a fair-minded man. He had no objections to having women in the work-place, as long as they were attractive. Brightened things up, there was no doubt

321

about it. And there were some jobs you simply couldn't ask a man to do. He had no quarrel with secretaries and PAs; he wasn't one of those old-fashioned men who believed a woman's place was in the kitchen, although he had a suspicion that all most of these hardbitten bitches needed was a good seeing-to. That little Templeton girl hadn't complained. And he wouldn't mind giving that blonde Christie Bradley a bit of attention. But it was no use giving them responsibilities they simply weren't designed to handle. Charles turned back to the lengthy form he was filling in for a profile one of the women's magazines was doing on him. Favourite things. Easy. Cufflinks he had worn to interview Reagan and Thatcher. Now there was a damn fine looking woman . . . Most unforgettable moments . . .?

'Aren't you going to put me down in there somewhere?' Ginny asked, slipping her arms around his shoulders and breathing softly into his ear.

Charles dragged her hands away from him in alarm. 'Not in here,' he hissed, glancing around the newsroom to see if anyone had noticed.

Ginny stepped back, stung. 'Where would you prefer?' she asked coolly. 'Your wife's bedroom?'

Charles realised he had gone too far, and hastily spun round in his chair. 'Darling, you know we have to be careful,' he said, imbuing his eyes with regret and desire. 'I can't let Ellie find out until the time is right, you know that.'

Ginny smiled. When he looked at her like that, her resolve melted and she forgave him everything. 'I'm sorry, darling, it's just so hard, when I want to be near you every minute of the day,' she whispered, perching on the edge of his desk. 'Last night was so wonderful. I can't wait to be with you again.'

Unforgettable moments, Charles thought. If his wife

ever found out, there'd be a few more of those.

'Later, we can talk later,' Charles said hastily as he saw the rest of the Early Evening News team straggle back into the newsroom from the studio. 'I have to go to Ben's meeting. He's decided he wants the newsanchors to have more input into the show.'

'Aristotle's? After the Late show?' Ginny asked, anxious to pin him down. They had to talk about where their relationship was going. Especially now.

'Yes, yes,' Charles agreed, pushing his chair back from his desk and standing up. 'Later then, angel,' he murmured as he slipped past her. Ginny caught the fragrance of his aftershave, Yves St Laurent's Jazz.

Ginny watched Charles walk towards Ben's office, a streak of desire darting through her as she studied the taut planes of his muscles rippling beneath his Italian-tailored jacket. She felt an answering tug between her legs and the warmth as the moisture flooded her. Her doubts about him faded. Damn it, if only she did not find him so devastatingly attractive perhaps she might be in with a chance.

Fleetingly she wished Christie was here to talk to, but she and David were both away on leave after the incredible story they had brought back out of Dakovica. They were together, Ginny was sure, although Christie had not said anything about David. She had not needed to. Ginny had heard the laughter in her voice when she spoke to her on the telephone, and sensed the new tranquillity that filled Christie's words. Deep inside her, Ginny felt an unidentifiable sense of loss.

Whatever Christie and David had together, she hoped it was worth it. She wondered how much time they would steal for themselves before the storm broke.

Ginny felt a clutch of pity for David. Most of the newsroom knew a little of the inner torment he had suffered since Seb's death, although few understood the terrible guilt that had driven him to take responsibility for Seb's widow and child. His concern for her was clearly unreciprocated. Caryn had arrived unannounced in England a week ago, and Ginny had been stunned when she did not even bother to ascertain David's whereabouts after the risks he had taken. She had obviously assumed David had gone trailing home to Rome, where he would find an empty house.

Slowly Ginny walked across the newsroom, waving at Rich and Dom to indicate that she would join them in the wine bar later. She pushed open the double doors at the side of the lifts and paused for a moment at the edge of the atrium. Two floors below her she could see the surge of people moving around the News Mall, a group of tourists having their picture taken with the cardboard statue of Ben Wordsworth. Water from the fountain murmured quietly into the pool beneath it. The sculpture of coloured pipes swayed gently in the atrium, slivers of sunlight piercing the glass roof twelve floors up and glancing off the structure. People moved in and out of the restaurants and souvenir shops, hugging monogrammed mugs and autographed photographs, or queued outside the cinema to watch the history of INN. One version of it anyway.

'If you're going to jump, can I watch?'

Ginny turned and smiled at Lucy Wordsworth, who leaned nonchalantly against the wall, her rubber catsuit gleaming.

'I'm flattered anyone would be that interested,' Ginny said, gesturing ruefully down towards the News Mall. 'I'm not sure that lot down there would notice.'

Ginny eyed the voluptuous curves encased in shining PVC, the newly bleached tresses and provocative pose, and secretly sympathised with Lucy's long-suffering mother. This one had more than her fair share of her father in her, and exuded a heady scent of hidden promise and secret pleasures that would crumble a man's resistance in seconds.

Lucy winked at Ginny and sashayed off down the corridor towards the newsroom, leaving a trail of erections in her wake. Ginny pushed open the double doors to the bathrooms and slipped quickly inside a cubicle before she could be drawn into the conversation of lipsticks and Lean Cuisines around the mirror.

She leant her head against the cool white tiles of the wall, and drew a deep breath. She knew before she looked that the pale blue lace of her panties would be spotless, a silent reproach. Fervently, she called back the many times she had cursed the pain and inconvenience. Oh, for a drop of crimson blood, a single drop, a sign, a release, I promise I won't ever complain again, you can double me up with cramp for a week, please, just one drop.

She wondered how Charles would take the news that she was now two-and-a-half months pregnant.

Paragon was determined. Archie was available.

It was an unbeatable combination.

Quietly they slipped into the empty studio, closing the heavy soundproofed door behind them. In the grey half-light, the cavernous room seemed alien and surprisingly erotic, Paragon thought with a shiver of desire. She glanced around at the deserted sets, an image of the studio as it looked when she broadcast the Early Evening News superimposing itself over the furled backdrops and desks shunted against the walls. In a few hours, this room would be alive again with lights, the sets neatly in place against the taped crosses marked on the white floor, the autocue rolling as Muriel barked instructions across the intercom. Now it had the peculiar sense of neglect and desolation that only a stage or studio could possess when empty.

'You really are the most alluring woman I have ever met,' Archie said softly, leaning against the desk to survey the figure in front of him.

Paragon smiled provocatively and shrugged off the tailored scarlet Prada jacket she was wearing. 'I'm luring you,' she replied deliberately, turning from him and slowly walking over towards the studio camera that usually recorded every expression on her flawless face. Casually she draped her jacket over the lens, blinding it. She swung round, leaning with calculated poise against the camera.

She watched as Archie let his gaze travel slowly over her body. Beneath the jacket she was wearing a translucent white chiffon blouse that almost, but not quite, revealed her opulent breasts as she moved, her chocolate nipples darkly visible against the flimsy material. A clinging crimson skirt that matched her jacket sheathed the voluptuous contours of her body, stopping a delicious two inches above her knees, her legs encased in sheer black stockings. As always, she wore spiky three-inch black high heels. Whatever the feminists might say, she was well aware that few things excited a man more than a woman wearing nothing but black stockings and high heels.

Archie moved slowly and consideringly towards her, drinking in the sensuous creature teasingly draped over the camera in front of him. His tall frame towered over her as he stopped twelve inches away from her, so that Paragon had to tilt her head backwards to gaze up into his face. She revelled in the naked desire she saw in his dark eyes.

Archie smiled, his dark hair falling over his forehead as he leant towards her, brushing her ear with his lips. 'So who's luring who?' he murmured, reaching behind her to unfasten the buttons that secured her skirt with swift, practised movements.

Paragon slid her arms around his back, feeling the firmness of his muscles, toned by many hours of squash and swimming, the strong width of his shoulders, the young, taut buttocks beneath his slim waist. She deliberately banished the comparison between his vibrancy and youth and her husband's sagging, flaccid flesh from her mind, but with a smile she thought of Ben's faded, jaded body. She trailed her fingers around to Archie's cock, which strained against his trousers.

Paragon's fifteen-hundred-dollar skirt slid to the floor in a silken crimson heap, and Archie gasped despite himself as he realised that she was wearing nothing but a scarlet lace suspender belt beneath it. Paragon felt the answering surge of desire as she unzipped his trousers and unbuttoned his grey silk boxer shorts to let his splendid cock spring free. Archie groaned as she skilfully manipulated him to the very edge of passion, using her other hand to reach beneath his balls and gently massage that erogenous but forbidden region.

He dragged his mind back from wherever Paragon's hands had sent it, and looked into her eyes, which glistened with naked lust. Firmly he grasped both her arms in one hand, and raised them above her head, pressing her against the camera so that her back was hard against its cold surface, the metal biting deep into her bare buttocks. The jacket she had draped over it slid to the floor. With his other hand he undid the buttons of her chiffon blouse, cupping one magnolia breast as the diaphanous material fell away. Paragon groaned as he bent his head and took her erect nipple in his mouth, his tongue teasing across its surface as his hand caressed the soft flesh of her breast. Slow and then fast, his lips and tongue and

327

hands moved across her nipple, silken cords of lust tugging at her cunt as she felt the moisture flood through her, dampening her thighs.

'So this is why they call you Paragon,' Archie whispered, releasing her arms as he let one hand trail down towards her mound whilst the other continued to caress the firm lushness of her breasts. Paragon parted her legs so that one heel rested against the grey metal casing that housed the camera wheels, the other on the floor.

Archie's cock filled the space between her thighs as he pressed her back so that she felt the rim of the camera turning-wheel against the small of her back. His fingers played maddeningly with the dark whorls of hair on her mound, before sliding into the moist space beneath, finding her clitoris and gently rubbing it with his fingers, wet with her own juices. His mouth nuzzled her breast, his lips sucking the engorged cinnamon-tipped nipple, as Paragon writhed against his body, her soft skin slick with sweat and excitement.

'Now, baby, take me now,' she murmured huskily, her fingers massaging the demanding cock that pressed insistently at her cunt.

Suddenly she gasped in surprise and dismay as Archie drew away from her, and stood gazing at her, her head thrown back against the camera in abandon, her legs parted to reveal the damp hairs of her mound, glistening in the dim light, framed by the scarlet lace of her suspender belt. His turgid cock strained impatiently at the sight of her creamy thighs encircled by the sheer black stockings, the long, long legs and wicked spiky heels. Her expensive white chiffon blouse covered only one shoulder, and he found her partial undress far more exciting than her nakedness would have been, with its suggestion of the forbidden, and the danger of their discovery aroused him more than he would have thought possible.

With a swift movement, he embraced Paragon's body again, and lifting her upwards, placed her so that she rested on top of the camera lens, her head against the playback monitor that surmounted it. He ducked down and loosened the wing screws that fastened the long, curving handles that were used to manoeuvre the heavy camera around the studio.

Paragon leant backwards across the camera, her cloud of blonde hair trailing down along the autocue monitor, her heels resting on the camera turning-wheel, a distant part of her mind wondering what Archie would do next. It was a long time since she had had such a young lover, and even whilst she knew the liaison was one of many – for them both – she appreciated his excitement, his freshness, his inventiveness.

Rapidly Archie shed the remainder of his clothes and moved towards her. 'I always knew the camera loved you,' he murmured, his lips soft against her ear. 'I think it's time you showed it your appreciation, don't you?'

Paragon did not even have time to tense before Archie swivelled the curving camera handle around and buried it deep inside her cunt. He kissed her breasts with mounting fervour as his hands stroked the hard bud of her clitoris, and suddenly Paragon found herself embracing the cold metal that had invaded her with growing excitement as she clenched her inner muscles against it.

'Is that enough for you, Paragon?' Archie whispered, his hands still playing her body with expertise that amounted to virtuosity.

Paragon writhed against the metal, all conscious thought obliterated from her mind as she felt the sensations in her breasts, her cunt, along every surface of her body. She bucked against the top of the camera, her legs rising to wrap themselves around the camera handle as if forbidding it ever to leave her body. As the handle impaled her she willingly embraced it, her hands forcing it deeper into her body as she came, her screams echoing around the empty studio.

Archie reached for her again. Caressingly he lifted her from the camera and took her across to the double desk that was used for the Early Evening News.

'I think it's time you gave me a few headlines,' he said with a grin.

Paragon looked up at him with a dazed expression as he laid her on her back and slid into her. 'The main news tonight . . .' she murmured as she felt his warm, rippling cock replace the cold, impersonal metal of the camera handle.

The tired muscles of her cunt shuddered around his cock as the dying waves of her orgasm slid into the first ripples of renewed desire. Her fingers slid around Archie's back, pulling his firm body hard against hers as he rammed home into her cunt, the delayed excitement of watching her come adding to his own pent-up arousal. She dug her nails into his back, as he bit hard on her still swollen nipples; her breasts and cunt and mind were wracked with fresh pulses of lust, deeper this time but even more intense.

Archie plunged inside her, his hand gripping her arms as he held her down on the desk, half lying, half standing against it himself. Suddenly he stiffened, and came hard and fast and furious into her, thrashing against her body as he shouted her name.

Paragon hoped Ben could see and hear every word. After all, that was the whole point of this.

In the control room, Ben gazed transfixed as Archie pinned Paragon to the Early Evening News desk in the studio. His own body was damp with sweat and desire, and he could feel the uncomfortable bulge of his frustrated excitement straining hard against his trousers. He groaned, and threw his body back against the seat, glad of the concealing darkness in the deserted Gallery as he grasped his turgid cock in his hand.

Ben was quite well aware of what Paragon was telling him, and despite himself, he felt a grudging respect for her. The message she had left with his secretary for him to meet her here had been deliberately intriguing, and now he knew why. Up until now, he had treated her any way – and to anyone – he chose, and now she was giving him some of his own. He shrugged philosophically. Annie Charter had played her hand, and Paragon had retaliated with interest. Oh yes, plenty of interest, he thought ruefully, as he watched Paragon slide to her knees and take Archie's cock in her mouth.

Suddenly she excited him again, and he felt a burning desire he had not experienced since the first time he had fucked her. He had found seeing her with another woman exciting, but he had never expected to be so fully aroused watching a man take her, and witnessing her own obvious enjoyment as he did so. Ben could never resist a challenge; Paragon knew it, and he knew she knew it, and she knew he knew she knew it.

He would get his secretary to inform Annie that she would be promoted to a scriptwriter at one of INN's many regional bureaux. Edinburgh, probably.

Two-one to Paragon, Ben thought admiringly, as he watched Archie tie Paragon to the floor with a length of cable and start all over again.

Sir Edward Penhaligon was unimpressed by the fumblings of the Early Evening News; at the same time he recognised that he needed to do little to damage INN himself whilst it was busy destroying itself. His slim fingers beat a tattoo on his oak desk as he glanced through

331

the memorandum for the next Board meeting. He could sense a new fear at some hitherto-unidentified threat in Ben's latest aggressive, self-laudatory memo. Sir Edward smiled grimly. Ben's main problem was that, whilst he was now aware that there was an enemy without, he had as yet no idea that the real enemy was the one within.

Sir Edward picked up a slim manila envelope lying on his desk, and extracted its contents once again. The report in it was unsigned, but he knew exactly who had written it. Quickly he scanned the closely typed pages, skimming past the detailed profit analysis of his contribution, pleasing though it was. He reached the section that had concerned him earlier, and read it carefully again, his mind sifting both the facts presented in the concise report and – more importantly – the details it omitted. His finely honed intellect detected an unanswered question that the author of the document had not even asked.

'Distribution in the control area of Dar el-Baran has been more successful than we had hoped. Accordingly the operation has been extended to a number of other areas, with administration reaching ninety-five per cent of the target population. Production of Loc33 has been increased more than seven-fold, with corresponding profit margins for yourself. We estimate this to reach in excess of $40 million by the end of the current year. Interest in the developing situation has been minimal, although agencies such as WRAPR seem to be favourably receptive. Their representative in this area has expressed cautious approval of the latest statistics . . .'*

Sir Edward reread the final sentence. There was nothing obvious in the report to alert him, and yet he felt uneasy. It would seem that he had no reason to do so; indeed, he was making a very healthy personal profit, the situation seemed to be developing in accordance with all their hopes, and no questions were being asked. And yet . . .

and yet . . . All his journalistic instincts were telling him that something was badly wrong.

The buzzer on Sir Edward's desk squawked, and with a slight air of irritation he pressed the talkback.

'Mr Foley on the line for you, Sir Edward,' his secretary said, her voice rendered tinny by the intercom.

'Ah. Thank you.' Sir Edward's impatience vanished. 'You may put him through.' He replaced the document in the manila envelope, and slid it into his grey calfskin briefcase. It would join its predecessors in the security of his safe at his Regent's Park flat.

'Sir Edward, Harry Foley here,' the voice at the other end of the line said briskly.

'Good evening, Harry, good to hear from you,' Sir Edward replied. His secretary opened the door and entered his office, placing a cup of coffee on the occasional table next to his desk. Sir Edward ignored her.

'I'll come straight to the point,' Foley said. 'I've been considering your proposal to sell my shares seriously, very seriously indeed. But there are one or two questions I should like to put to you before I give you my final answer.'

'Please, go ahead,' Sir Edward responded warmly. He desperately needed the hotel magnate's support if he was to oust Ben Wordsworth from the Board of INN; all the more so since Dalmeny de Burgh was still stalling and playing for time. Sir Edward had the feeling that de Burgh's wife was behind his vacillation. At least he had nothing to fear from Foley's. Paragon Fairfax was not likely to start asking difficult questions.

'What is it exactly that you are so sure you can give INN that Ben Wordsworth can't?' Foley asked.

'Before I answer that, Harry, let me assure you that my criticisms are not of INN itself. I believe we have a very strong team of correspondents and crews in all our bureaux, and all the pieces are in place to make us the single most important voice in global television.' Sir Edward paused for a moment. 'But we do have two major problems: credibility and distribution. Both of those could be solved if we altered the focus of our news programmes, but that is something Ben simply is not prepared to do.'

At the other end of the line, Harry Foley leant back in his wine-red leather chair. He agreed with many of the points Sir Edward had raised when he had first discussed the issue with him, and quite apart from his professional respect for the broadcaster, he had a personal liking for the man. He sympathised with Sir Edward's desire to keep INN prominent as a hard news organisation. He too had fought many battles against those who would sacrifice quality to quantity and dollars.

Harry Foliwiczski had been twelve years old when he fled Poland in 1943 to escape the purging armies of Nazi Germany. He had witnessed the shooting of his father, the rape of his mother. Together with his sister Anna, he had walked the thousands of miles through Czechoslovakia and Austria, assisted by those who risked their lives to save the Jewish race, witnessing the full horrors of geno-cide along the route. Anna had never uttered a word, withdrawing into her own world, her eyes empty and lifeless as she trudged beside her elder brother. When Harry finally reached the security of Switzerland, it was alone. Exhaustion, malnutrition, shock; all had taken their toll, and as Harry buried the last surviving member of his family, he had vowed never to be poor, never to be vulnerable, never to be hunted, again.

By the age of thirty-five Harry Foley was a multi-millionaire; ten years later he had an hotel in every major city in the world. The Presidential suites were invariably full; the high society of Paris, Milan, New York and

London chose to stay at Foley's as they moved around the globe. Harry concentrated on making every guest feel that their stay at one of his hotels was a luxurious necessity they could not do without. Each was presented with a velvety white bathrobe, embroidered with the hotel's monogram, at the end of their stay. The toiletries ranged on the bathrooms' marble shelves were Chanel, Gucci, Yves St Laurent; the brushes on the antique French dressing-tables were silver backed and replaced after every stay. Freshly cut flowers – orchids, lilies, gold roses (never red) – filled porcelain vases on every surface. Harry knew the value of quality, and would never cut costs. Sir Edward Penhaligon was of the same breed.

'Sir Edward, I understand the arguments behind your proposal, and to a large extent I agree with them,' Harry said at length. 'I would be only to happy to see an end to the downmarket sprigs of INN that seem to be sprouting everywhere I turn, from the Airport Channel to the new service I understand Ben is planning for Kentucky Fried Chicken. It's not quite what I had in mind when I invested my money in Benjamin Wordsworth.'

'INN's strength is the strength of the Western world, particularly Britain and America,' Sir Edward replied forcefully. 'It's a window for the world on the more powerful and influential countries of the planet. I do not intend to change that.' He paused, and sipped his coffee, closing his eyes in order to assemble his thoughts more clearly. 'However, we are facing rivals, such as CNN, whose strengths are the range and depth of its coverage and its international tradition. If we are to survive, we must become more than just an open door on an unfolding event. We must learn to analyse it and unravel the implications.'

'Meaning?'

'Meaning that we have to move ahead. We have to

show more than just the ability to be on the spot: we have to look at our programming and try to create new angles within the structure of what we already have.'

'I understand that. But it will mean some changes in your management structure,' Harry said thoughtfully. 'INN's strength is in the field, from what I understand. Its weakness is in those who make many of the decisions.'

'Expensive decisions, and expensive mistakes. It's time for a change.'

Harry nodded quietly to himself on the other end of the phone, and glanced up at the antique mirror in front of him. Behind him he saw reflected the portrait of his first wife, Philippa, her soft smile a reproach to the many mistakes he had made since he lost her guidance two years ago. He grimaced. He had to live with those errors – and Paragon – whatever his regrets.

'There is just one question I have left. Tell me, Sir Edward, in all of this, your plans for an upmarket, credible future; tell me, what place is there for my wife?'

Sir Edward drew a breath. It was the one question he had hoped Harry Foley would never ask. Paragon Fairfax, with her voluptuous curves and vacant mind, would be the first change he would make after ditching Ben Wordsworth.

'I do not fear the truth,' Harry said sadly into the silence. 'I realise what my wife is, but you have to understand, my first loyalty must be to her. I would ask you to respect me enough to answer me truthfully.'

Sir Edward sighed. He knew now he would not gain Harry's support, and with it, the chance to salvage INN, but he could not in honour lie to the man. 'She would be one of my changes, yes,' he said eventually.

'Thank you, Sir Edward. I appreciate your honesty. But I am afraid I have to refuse your offer. No, I will not sell.'

'I am genuinely sorry,' Sir Edward said. 'I very much wish it could be different. But thank you for giving me so much of your time. If you change your mind . . .'

'I think that will be unlikely to happen. But if it did, I would turn to you. Goodbye, Sir Edward.'

Sir Edward replaced the telephone slowly in its cradle. Without Harry Foley's thirteen per cent, he could not hope to force Ben from the Editor's chair, unless he could turn around the consortium of other television investors. It would be almost impossible to persuade the Japanese, Jordanian, French and Australian networks to sell; but it might be done.

If he had Dalmeny de Burgh's ten per cent.

Sir Edward rose and moved towards the oak drinks cabinet in one corner of his office. Absently he poured himself a double measure of Scotch into a Waterford tumbler, and took a sip. He swirled the amber liquid around the glass. Dalmeny had an Achilles' heel . . . or rather, not so much an Achilles' *heel*, exactly . . .

If Dalmeny did not yet have a reason to sell, Sir Edward would have to provide him with one.

Quickly Sir Edward drained his glass, and took his Burberry from the cupboard he had had installed for the purpose. He picked up his briefcase and left the office briskly, pausing only to nod to his secretary before taking the lift to the ground floor. As he emerged into the warmth of a late summer evening, his chauffeur opened the door of the waiting limousine. Sir Edward shook his head.

'Thank you, Denver, but I feel in need of a drink and a little conversation this evening. If you could come across to Aristotle's in – say – half an hour?'

As always at this time of day, Aristotle's was filled with staff from the INN building, drowning the stresses of the day in numerous bottles of house white, many of them on

337

company credit cards. The excuses that were invented to explain the receipts away were possibly the most creative work that took place within the INN building.

At a table near the end of the bar, Sir Edward could see Charles Silversmith deep in conversation with a slim brunette whom he recognised as one of the producers. From his vantage point, Sir Edward could see Charles's back was rigid with tension, and the girl's face was white and anxious. Even as Sir Edward watched, Charles detached himself from the small table and approached the bar to order another drink. His lips were compressed tightly, his face drawn with suppressed anger. Sir Edward did not waste his pity on the girl. He reserved that for Charles's wife.

Sir Edward ordered a glass of Scotch and leant his back against the bar, watching more people drifting across the road from the gleaming INN building, and settling at the tables scattered along the pavement outside the wine bar. Jerry and his young wife, the weathergirl Suki, scurried along the road towards the bus-stop, Marks & Spencer plastic carrier bags swinging between their clasped hands. An extraordinary looking teenager, clad from head to toe in sculpted rubber, swayed across the road. Bob Carpenter followed slowly behind her, his eyes devouring her as she shimmied into the wine bar.

'Excuse me. Is this stool taken?'

Sir Edward turned towards the attractive, slim woman now standing beside him.

'Please,' he said graciously, inclining his head in a gesture of invitation.

The woman slipped gracefully onto the stool, the elegant wool of her Nicole Farhi wraparound skirt parting for a moment to reveal an alluring glimpse of thigh. Sir Edward caught the scent of her perfume as she opened her handbag and extracted a packet of cigarettes, glancing swiftly around the wine bar as she felt for her lighter with one hand. She sighed and smiled, closing her bag.

'Excuse me, Sir Edward, do you have a light? I seem to have forgotten mine.'

'I'm afraid not,' Sir Edward replied. 'Perhaps behind the bar?'

The woman swivelled on her stool and waved towards the barman, and the young man hurried towards her, proffering a book of the wine bar's matches. She took it and lit her cigarette, inhaling deeply before turning towards Sir Edward. She smiled. 'I know I should give up, but I just can't seem to.'

Sir Edward drained his drink and glanced at his watch, knowing it was time for him to leave, but drawn despite himself towards the woman beside him. She seemed somehow familiar, although he could not place her immediately. He eyed her with growing interest. Her make-up was skilful, but it was not enough to hide the fact that although she appeared at first glance to be in her early thirties, she was probably nearer forty. Her clothes were expensive and discreet, her auburn hair precisely arranged on her shoulders, her figure almost painfully thin. Her blue gaze when she met his eyes was direct. Sir Edward had the impression of a woman who knew what she wanted, and exactly how to get it.

The woman smiled. 'Of course, you probably don't recognise me,' she said engagingly and extended one hand. 'It *has* been quite a while. I'm so sorry, Sir Edward, I don't make a habit of picking up strange men in bars, however famous and charming. I must introduce myself. I'm Caryn Kelly. We met through David Cameron?'

The pieces slotted into place. 'Of course. How impolite of me. I do remember you. The opening of INN, wasn't it?'

'How good of you to remember.'

339

'You're not someone who is easy to forget.'

Their eyes locked, and both smiled. Both knew this meeting had not been by chance. Sir Edward beckoned for the barman to replace their drinks.

Suddenly he knew exactly how he would make Dalmeny sell.

Chapter Twelve

Christie moulded her body to the warm rockface, the fingertips of her left hand seeking a crevice above her head. The rough stone seemed to be almost part of her as she found the hold she was searching for and pushed upwards on her right leg. With a controlled movement she extended her left foot, the tip of her shaped rubber boot gaining purchase on the slight outcrop that had been her handhold moments before.

Immediately above her head was an oblong steel clip, securely fastened to a strengthened bolt embedded in the rock. With her free right hand, Christie reached around to the back of her waist and took a similar clip from her belt, which she passed through the rope around her harness and secured to the clip in the rock. In climbs such as this, with dizzying falls of up to a thousand feet, the clips were placed at roughly ten foot intervals along the ascent. If she slipped, the distance she could fall before the rope halted her descent was at most twenty feet, although she could still break a limb if she hit the side of the rock awkwardly. Of course, it all depended on the person at the other end of the rope.

The strong sun beat down on her back. Christie wriggled her bare shoulders in the form-fitting lycra bodysuit, and dipped first one hand, then the other, into the chalk bag hanging from her harness. She squinted her eyes as she gazed up at the thirty feet of sheer rockface she had yet to climb. The tricky bit would be negotiating around the overhang that jutted out from the main body of the cliff. It would mean going against gravity, putting all the strain on her arms to haul her body around the rock.

Christie looked down, resting her face against the rock, her hair plastered damply across her forehead. Several hundred feet below her, David covered his eyes against the sun with one hand as he peered up at the slim figure hugging the rock. Christie could just see the glint of his teeth as he smiled. She drew a breath and let her hands seek out the next hold, the chalk on her fingers absorbing the sweat of her palms and increasing her grip. As she moved up the rock in sure, confident movements, David paid out the rope that anchored her to him.

Scattered along the rockface were other climbers, the bright neon colours of their bodysuits shimmering in the sunshine like butterflies against the grey stone. Christie could hear the gentle clink of the steel clips against each other, the whisper of the ropes against the rock, and the occasional low calls as the climbers alerted each other to their descents when they reached the end of the route they were following. For the first few feet of her climb, she had been able to hear the buzz of bees flitting across the bright yellow gorse that grew around the base of the rock, the susurration of the wind in the pines, and the faint roar of the river at the bottom of the gorge. But here, hundreds of feet up, the silence was deafening. She could almost hear the rushing of her blood as it coursed through her veins.

As she reached the top of the route she was following, the wind whipped around her shoulders, teasing her hair from the neat French pleat she had used in an attempt to tame it. Christie paused a moment to savour the view. As

342

far as she could see, the rich, verdant green of the Provence countryside was spread out beneath her, a promise of infinite warmth, peace and fertility. The air was crisp and clear, the late afternoon sunshine burnishing the rock with gold and bronze light. Far below her, she could see the silver ribbon of the river twist its way along the Gorge du Verdon. Despite the two-hour climb, she felt refreshed and invigorated. This country filled her soul, washing away the many horrors she had witnessed, imbuing her with energy and life.

Christie shook the rope around her waist three times to signal to David that she was about to descend, since the overhang obscured her from his view. She leant backwards, using her harness as a sling, so that she was sitting down, her feet perpendicular against the rock.

She called out to alert any climbers who might be beneath her, listening a moment for a reply. Hearing nothing, she began paying out the rope as she bounced gracefully down the rockface, her feet dancing against the surface. As she passed the clips she had placed during her climb, she collected them and slipped them back on to the waist of her harness. Within minutes she was at the bottom, where David was coiling the pink-and-green ribbon of her rope.

He smiled as she unhooked herself and hurled herself into his embrace. 'I wondered if I was ever going to see you again,' he said, hugging her.

'I'm just relieved you didn't wander off for a coffee,' Christie teased.

David laughed. 'And leave you? No, that will never happen, I promise.'

Christie smiled into his tawny eyes, not needing words to understand his love or express her own. The breathtaking closeness they had shared the first time they made love had not dissipated. If anything, their rapport had deepened.

Christie was almost afraid of the intimacy that had developed between them. She felt that she was climbing free, without a rope to secure her.

She sat down on a rock, unlaced her moulded, high-tension rubber boots and undid her harness. David finished coiling the rope and gathered his own equipment, which was scattered around the base of the cliff.

'Are you sure you don't want to climb?' she asked, watching David packing their gear in his rucksack.

'The last one we did, next to the waterfall, was more than enough for me,' David replied, smiling. 'I need to save a little energy . . .' He caught her up in his arms, so that she could feel his hardness against her waist, and Christie gasped despite herself. 'Satisfied?'

'Not yet . . . but I think I will be,' she grinned. Her nipples hardened beneath the flimsy lycra of her bodysuit, and she felt a delicious tingling flickering like fire along her limbs.

'I think I'd better take you home,' David whispered, drawing back from her so that he could drink in the radiant creature in front of him.

Christie laughed, trailing one finger along his cheekbone towards the soft fullness of his lips. The more they had of each other, the more they seemed to want. Since they had arrived in Provence ten days ago, they had not spent a minute apart, wrapped together in an embrace of love and friendship and sunshine.

Kosovo seemed a lifetime away.

They walked slowly back along the narrow path that meandered along the bottom of the gorge beside the river, their hands clasped together. Lizards skittered around their feet and glittering dragonflies swooped around their shoulders, as gradually they left the ravine behind them, plunging into a deeply shadowed crevasse that led to the main road. They reached the open-top sports car Christie

344

had borrowed from her French godmother, and David slid behind the wheel. Expertly he manoeuvred the low-slung car around the lethal curves of the mountain road, waiting for the breathtaking view that would herald their approach to La Palud where they were staying. No matter how many times he saw it, he never failed to marvel at the frightening splendour of the mountains, the stone homes embedded in the hills, the layers of grape trellises and the misty blue darkness of the graceful pine forests.

David parked the car outside the bakery in the centre of the tiny village, and Christie darted out, still clad in her lycra bodysuit. The villagers were used to the many climbers who made this hidden eyrie their base, and smiled indulgently at her as she emerged back into the late sunshine, a long French loaf and wheel of Camembert in one hand, two bottles of red wine in the other. It had been their staple diet since they arrived, but neither of them tired of it, or of the life they had lead together.

Each day they had walked through the wooded mountains, ignoring the main tracks to roam off piste, bathing in the chill mountain streams, lazily scything through the long grass, gently making love in the hollows of the forests, revelling in the fact that they saw no one but each other. Some days they climbed one of the many routes along the Gorge du Verdon; on others, they swam through the underground caverns honeycombed in the cliffs around the river, descending deeper into the earth than they climbed above it. In ten days they had grown tanned and fit, Christie's hair streaked white and gold, David's grown burnished and coppery in the sun. Slowly they relaxed with and into each other, the shadows blown from beneath their eyes by the fresh winds, the lines in their faces washed away by the clear waters.

And every night, in the flickering shadows of the

scented pine log fire, they poured their love into each other.

Christie nestled against David's shoulder, feeling the warmth of his body through the thin cotton of his shirt. As he swung the car on to a rough track pitted with stones and tenacious weeds, she felt a sensation of peace and homecoming that she had never experienced before. Her godmother's ancient stone chalet, carved deep into the mountainside, glowed warmly as the last dying rays of the sun lit up its mellow walls, the trees that cradled the house glinting with the first colours of the approaching autumn. It was their last night alone together. Chantal and her family joined them from their home in Marseille for a weekend of climbing, walking, laughter and sleep the next day, and whilst she looked forward to seeing her godmother again, Christie felt a tinge of regret at the intrusion into their private paradise.

'It's our last night alone together for three days,' David whispered as he climbed the couple of stone steps to the front door. 'I thought I should make it a night to remember.'

'Every night with you is a night to remember,' Christie murmured as he laid her down on the soft vastness of their bed.

Christie awoke at first light, and looked across at David with an expression of delight and wonderment as she recalled their love-making of the night before. Every time seemed to take them to new peaks of pleasure, plumb new depths of feeling. Gently she stroked his face and trailed her fingertips across his back, his skin butter-coloured from the sunshine. Slowly David opened his eyes and smiled as he saw Christie.

'Good morning, my golden princess,' he smiled.

Christie's answer was another kiss as David drew her

down into the bed with him. She laughed, and reluctantly disentangled herself from him.

'If only I could spend the rest of my life in bed with you . . .' she groaned regretfully. David kissed her again, and Christie felt her resolve weaken as fingers of desire danced along her back. David held her in his embrace until he felt her body mould itself to his, dropping kisses across her face and neck, as she closed her eyes and buried her fingers in his hair.

David laughed, low and teasing. 'Are you sure you want to visit the waterfall before breakfast?'

Christie slithered from his arms, leaping resolutely out of bed in one swift movement. 'It's our last morning together before Chantal arrives, so stop driving me wild,' she said, moving to the window and opening the shutters. A stream of early morning sunshine danced across her, gilding her skin. The woody scent of the pine trees mingled with lavender and dew on newly-turned earth, the cool freshness of the first hour after dawn lingering in the air, with the promise of sunshine and warmth yet to come. Christie opened her arms wide to the gentle caress of the breeze on her naked skin, throwing her head back and closing her eyes in an unconscious gesture of sensuality. She felt intoxicated by David's nearness, by the ripe abandon of nature; her nipples hardened with a sudden pulse of desire.

David leaned back against the pillows, his hands beneath his head, as he regarded her through half-shut eyes. 'One more kiss?'

Christie turned. 'You know if I kiss you, we won't be doing anything else for a long time,' she smiled.

She slipped into a turquoise bathing costume and pulled on a pair of jeans. Expertly she caught her hair up and fastened it with a black velvet headband. As David dressed, his eyes never leaving her, she added some of the

347

French bread and Camembert to the rucksack with which they usually walked, which already held a rug, a compass, two Guernsey jumpers and a sheathed hunting knife. She paused a moment, then slid in a couple of apples and a chilled bottle of still water. By the time she had finished, David was standing beside her in faded blue denims, a white T-shirt highlighting the strong planes of his broad chest, his skin glowing with vibrancy and happiness. Christie almost took him straight back to bed.

They left the house, threading their way through the apple-orchard which would lead them into the mountains, their feet leaving pale imprints against the dewy grass where the sun had not yet reached it. Christie breathed in the heady freshness of the air, her senses suffused with the life and lushness of the forest. The first slivers of the sun as it rose above the mountains glanced across her forehead, and she paused as its brightness hurt her eyes. She reached for her sunglasses, and realised that they were still on the table inside the house where she had left them.

Leaving David leaning against a beech tree she ran swiftly back the way they had come, stopping only to gather a few wild mushrooms as she passed. As she entered the cool shadows of the chalet, she was just in time to hear the click of the answering machine as it received a call. Christie put down the mushrooms and paused to listen; very few people had their number, so it must be important.

'Hi, David, this is Sam Hargrave on the Foreign Desk,' the voice said into the stillness. 'I hope you get this message before lunchtime. I'm sorry to interrupt your holiday, old friend, but we need you to go to Beirut; two French Aid workers have been missing for two days and are now believed to have been kidnapped. We've booked you on a plane out of Marseille in six hours, which you should just be able to make. If I don't hear from you by the end of the day, I'll have to find someone else, but it is you we need, since you know that part of the world so well. Talk soon.'

Christie shivered in dismay as she heard the click of the receiver being replaced, and the answering machine spooling back to the beginning of its message. Through the open doorway she could see David relaxing in the sunshine. This call would propel him back into the middle of one of the most dangerous places in the world, where his every movement would be shadowed by fear and the threat of kidnap, if the abduction of Westerners had indeed become a weapon once more in the war of the Islamic fundamentalists. Whatever peace of mind and body he had achieved would be wiped out in an instant.

'Is there a problem?' David called, seeing Christie framed in the doorway.

Christie wrestled with her journalistic loyalty, and the fear for David that the summons awoke within her. This would plunge them both into the whirlwind of a breaking story; and she also knew that Caryn would swoop down on them the moment they emerged from their retreat, reawakening the demon of guilt that still tormented David. Firmly she told herself that if she had not returned for her damned sunglasses, David would not have been recalled. INN would have had to send somebody else, and the two of them would have savoured the last days of their holiday together.

'Nothing, darling. Just coming. Be with you in a moment,' she called back.

She made her decision. Swiftly crossing the room, she rewound the answering machine tape to the beginning. With her finger on the erase button, she played it back. Moments later, there was no trace that there had ever been a message.

'I want a full metal jacket on this.'

Sam Hargrave looked at Jerry in disbelief. 'A full metal what?'

'The works. I really want to go to town on this one, I want a today piece, a backgrounder, live links, graphics . . .'

Sam shook his head dazedly. 'I'll see what I can do, Jerry, but so far you don't even have an International Affairs correspondent.'

'Why the hell not?' Brian Reynolds interrupted, approaching the desk with a sheaf of ominous looking papers.

'He's too busy having an affair somewhere international,' Sam responded laconically. 'And if you don't stop shoving pieces of paper in front of me, you won't have a sodding frame of picture to put on your show.'

Brian looked nervous but stood his ground defiantly. 'It's a memo from the Editor,' he said with reflected importance. 'Details of the new rationalisation system we're introducing on assignments. This is Daniel from Accounts. He's just completed a Manager Orientation Seminar and will be assessing your productivity ratio.'

Jerry and Sam eyed the pale-faced man who was sheltering behind Brian with a stricken expression. Brian smirked and vanished, leaving Daniel to the decidedly untender mercies of his colleagues.

Sam leant across his desk, ignoring the four flashing lights that immediately lit up his telephone system. 'Tell me,' he said, 'How do you get to be an executive these days anyway?'

Daniel's mouth opened but no words emerged. Jerry spoke for him. 'You have to appear on five consecutive

350

breakfast TV shows, none of them your own,' he said, wandering back to the Early Evening News desk in disgust.

Daniel's Adam's apple bobbed nervously as he perched on the edge of the chair next to Sam. He pushed his wire-rimmed glasses further up his nose. 'Is it always like this?' he asked fearfully.

'I tell you, working in this place is a bit like having John Major as Prime Minister,' Sam said, grabbing a phone. 'You know it's happened, but you can't quite believe it.'

Rochelle looked up from her desk as Jerry approached, looking dejected. 'We've got an interview with Pierre Guillot's mother in Paris,' she said, referring to one of the missing French Aid workers. 'Any luck finding David yet?'

'No reply. Probably not even the right bloody number anyway,' Jerry said, logging into his computer. 'Damn, it's been years since we had a Beirut kidnap. I'm trying to remember how we did it last time.'

'Badly, probably,' Victoria Lawrence said cuttingly.

'I think I love you,' Ollie said. Victoria looked deeply offended.

Jerry turned to the television monitor on his desk just in time to see the credits roll for the end of the News Update.

'Bugger these bloody Updates,' he said feelingly. 'They're like a fucking Scottish summer. By the time you get there, it's over.'

'Better than the Early Evening News,' Ollie grinned. 'That's more like an arctic winter – goes on forever, and when it does finish you're still in the dark.'

'OK, quit enjoying yourselves, we've got a news bulletin to produce,' Jerry said, handing out rough running orders to the team as they assembled. 'The Beirut

351

kidnappings are the only story we seem to have so far. Any suggestions, anyone?'

'How about getting Terry Waite or John McCarthy to tell us what's probably happening to the French guys,' Ginny volunteered. 'What are their names again?'

'Pierre Guillot and Jean-Paul Canard,' Rochelle said.

'Perhaps we could get Terry or John to come into the studio, talk about the first few days of imprisonment, how they survived, and so on,' Ginny said. 'I think Terry has his book to promote, so he should be happy to talk to us.'

'Yes, I like it, you don't have to sell me on it anymore,' Jerry said delightedly, scribbling on his clipboard. 'We've got the mother, we've got the Aid charity they worked for, we've got a Middle East expert to tell us what it all means. All we need now is a fucking correspondent.'

Rapidly Jerry ran through the remainder of the news bulletins on the agenda, assigning them to the various producers working on the Early Evening News show. He glanced at Ginny with concern. She was looking pale and drawn, deep shadows under her eyes marring her usually vibrant expression. He noticed Charles glare at her as she sat down at her desk next to Victoria, and wondered what had irritated the immaculate newscaster so much. Run out of his favourite hairspray, probably.

Victoria straightened her saffron Armani jacket and tapped a perfect French-manicured nail on to her keyboard. 'I see the Pope's come out against abortion,' she said to Jerry, by way of demonstrating her news judgement and willingness to communicate with even the lowliest of hacks.

'The Pope comes out. Now there's a story,' Rich commented.

'The Pope comes. That's an even better one,' Jerry said.

Victoria flicked back a stray stalactite of chestnut hair and ignored the sarcasm. 'What we need is some more inspiration,' she said helpfully.

Jerry jumped as Sam appeared from nowhere. 'If you haven't got at least two exclusive interviews for me, don't bother,' he said crossly.

'A thought has crossed my mind – admittedly it hasn't had far to travel,' Sam said, pre-emptively. 'We may not have a correspondent in Beirut, but Karim is there with his camera, recuperating from the Kosovo trip. I could get him to shoot some fresh pix of the area where the two French workers disappeared, satellite it over from Damascus, and Bob can put a voice on it here.'

'It's not as good as having someone there, but I suppose it's better than radio,' Jerry said. 'OK, thanks. What time can we expect it?'

'Four or five hours, earliest,' Sam said. 'I've a feeling it's the same place John McCarthy was snatched. Anybody in contact with Waite?'

Jerry nodded in Ginny's direction, and Sam strolled over and perched on her desk, waiting for her to finish her telephone call. Ginny signalled that she would be with him in a moment, and scribbled furiously on her notepad. As soon as she had replaced the cradle, she turned to Sam with a smile.

'You the producer on this story?' Sam asked.

'For my sins, which are many, yes,' Ginny said with a wry grin.

'Fancy a chat about it over a coffee?'

'I'd love one. These days if I manage to get as far as the canteen I feel as if I've been on a foreign trip.'

She stood up and slipped her notebook into her shoulder bag, following Sam towards the lift. As they waited for it to arrive, she leaned back against the wall and closed her eyes for a brief moment. Sam put one arm around her in a reassuring hug of friendship. He felt Ginny lean into him, and tightened his hold.

'Is everything OK?' he said, concern etching lines into his face. His clear blue eyes met hers, and something in them sapped Ginny's resolution to keep silent. Suddenly she needed a friend more than anything in the world. Tears glistened on her lashes, and she buried her face in the soft blue cotton of Sam's shirt.

'Oh, Sam,' she said in muffled tones. 'I've got myself in such a mess.'

Sam stroked her soft hair awkwardly, unsure how the situation had quite come about, but enjoying the feel of Ginny's body held against his. Before he could reply, the lift door opened and he half-led, half-carried Ginny into it. With an embarrassed smile, she withdrew from his supportive embrace. Reassured by his undemanding presence, she surreptitiously glanced across at him as he studiously avoided her eyes to give her time to hide her tears. He had always offered her unthreatening friendship and unswerving loyalty, and impulsively she decided to trust him.

Ginny stirred her strong black coffee and explained what had happened with a self-deprecating humour and a genuine lack of rancour that gained Sam's lasting respect. To his intense surprise, he felt a burning rage gathering within him as Ginny sketched out the details of her relationship with Charles, with an honesty which she admitted had been lacking in her relationship with the newscaster. Slowly the gentle warmth left Sam's face as he listened to her detached description of Charles' callous abdication from his responsibility, and he felt the urge to dangle the bloody man over the atrium until his teeth rattled.

'But you don't still love him, do you?' he asked, as Ginny paused and took a gulp of lukewarm coffee.

354

'Yes . . . no . . . I don't know,' Ginny sniffled, renewed tears sliding down her cheeks. 'I don't know anything anymore. I suppose I ought to love him, after all the trouble I've been to over him . . . but somehow, I feel a bit – well – empty.'

Sam wondered what it was about a beautiful woman crying that reduced him to a soft heap. Or maybe it was this beautiful woman in particular.

'Do you want to keep it?'

Ginny looked at him in surprise. 'Oh, yes,' she said. 'It's funny, until I spoke to you I wasn't sure, but I am now.' Absently she broke a plastic spoon in two, then busied her fingers dismembering the polystyrene coffee cup. 'I thought I loved Nick, and maybe I did, once, but it wasn't a very adult kind of love. It was too much based on my idea of what I thought he was, rather than what he actually is, and Nick couldn't live up to my image of him. I don't seem to have any trouble with anything else in my life, but I more than make up for it when it comes to men.' She laughed, and looked up from the remains of the coffee cup. 'I guess with Charles I was on the rebound; he couldn't have been more different from Nick.'

'You can say that again,' Sam muttered darkly.

'Once I'd got into this thing with Charles, it snowballed rather,' Ginny said thoughtfully. 'He can be charming when he wants to be, and it was as if, having gone through so much trouble to be together, I had to love him to make it worthwhile. If I left him, it would be like admitting I'd been wrong all along.'

'How long before . . .?' Sam said, an embarrassed flush stealing across his rugged face.

'The middle of February. I've got a little longer to sort things out before it becomes obvious,' Ginny said, pushing back her chair. Sam leaped up to help her, and she laughed. 'You don't have to treat me like an invalid just

355

yet!' she teased, touched by his solicitude. She turned, and looked up into his face, her dark eyes serious again. 'You've been a wonderful friend to me, Sam. I can't tell you how much that means to me right now.'

Swiftly Ginny leaned across and kissed his cheek. Sam was startled at the flow of electricity that seemed to emanate from her touch, and looked at her, baffled. Ginny smiled, warmed by his friendship, and walked towards the lift, her arm casually linked in his. The sensation of her fingers against his arm seemed to burn through the cotton of his shirt, and suddenly he felt an overwhelming desire to kiss her like she had never been kissed before. He wondered how he could have been so oblivious to his own feelings for so long.

'Karim, are you damned sure about this?' Sam asked.

'I promise you, boss, it's the word on the street. I spoke to the same people I talked to when Terry came here. They weren't wrong then.'

Next to Sam, Daniel scribbled, 'This call is costing ten dollars a minute. Are you sure it's necessary?' and pushed the piece of paper towards the Foreign Editor. Sam read it and cowed the miserable accountant with a glare.

'Run it by me again,' Sam said, picking up a pen. 'I want to get it down word for word before I go to Ben with this.'

Over the satellite telephone the Lebanese fixer's voice crackled with static. 'You need to know a little of the on-the-ground feeling here now,' Karim said. 'After the Hezbollah did so well in the parliamentary elections last year, they're very keen to stay in the legitimate mainstream of Arab and World politics. That means no more kidnapping.'

Karim paused for a moment. 'Now, obviously there are a lot of factions who don't want to rule by the ballot box.

They feel they're not getting anywhere. In particular, there are a number of extremist elements in Iran who don't like the Hezbollah.'

'With you so far,' Sam said, ignoring Daniel who was by now waving his arms in agitation.

'OK. So they're paying various splinter groups on the fringes of the Hezbollah to resume kidnapping and thereby upset the applecart,' Karim said briskly.

'What's your in on this?' Sam asked.

'A friend in the Hezbollah. They don't want to be held responsible for the two French workers, or any other kidnaps.'

'And this friend is saying what, exactly?'

'The Frenchmen are being held by the Sword of Jihad, one of these fringe groups. They are determined to take as many people as possible, particularly British and American civilians. At the moment, there is no one here they want . . .'

'Except the journalists,' Sam finished for him.

'Except the journalists,' Karim confirmed. 'I tell you, Sam, if you send anyone, they will be kidnapped. I am certain of that. Don't come now. It is too dangerous. You must use Lebanese people, they will be safe. If you put any of your people in here, they won't last twenty-four hours.'

'Thanks, Karim. Keep in touch.' Sam turned towards the terrified accountant, Daniel. 'And before you ask, yes it was bloody necessary.'

Ben leaned back in his chair and fixed Robin Fernly with the steely-eyed gaze that reduced him to a gibbering wreck.

'OK, Robin, sit down and run the figures by me,' he said.

'I'm afraid we've still got a bit of realigning to do,'

357

Robin began warily, seating himself on the sofa which was deliberately well below Ben's eye-level. He squirmed on the squashy leather. 'Washington's doing all right since you banned dry-cleaning and newspapers on the road, but Rome is well over budget. Mrs Kelly's expenses . . .'

Robin paused, uncertain where Ben's loyalties in that direction lay, rumour having it that they had lain on occasion with the cameraman's widow. Noting Ben's studied air of innocence, he wisely moved into safer areas.

'Forget it, it's history,' Ben said with careful nonchalance. 'But I'm not a bloody charity. You can tell Kelly's widow to cut down on the monogrammed caviar.'

'We've got to do more than that if you want to come in under budget this month,' Robin said fearfully. 'The way things are going so far, we can't afford to spend anything until October. Not even a bus ticket.'

'A little tricky, wouldn't you say, given that we have somehow got to cover international news for the next four weeks? Unless we can persuade it to all happen right here in our own building, of course,' Ben replied scathingly.

'We *have* managed to fully equip and staff all the Bureaux now,' Robin replied with enthusiasm. It was short-lived. 'They just can't travel.'

'If only our efficiency wasn't marred by stories getting in the way,' Ben said drily. 'In that case, we shall have to scale down. We travel only on the huge stories and those of compelling interest. We don't need to have an INN team everywhere, all the time, especially if we're obtaining good, reliable coverage from outside sources,' he continued, getting into his stride. 'I want us to spend wisely, leanly and meanly. And we have to make the most of our affiliates, learn to use them, take advantage of their local talent.'

Outside Ben's office, Sam frowned as he overheard

358

Ben's words. The last thing he needed was some accountant telling him where he could and could not send a crew, and ending up being knocked into touch by the BBC or CNN. It was all very well for the Men in Suits to tell them to tighten their belts for a month, but if INN missed a major story, it would take them a year to claw back their reputation, if they ever could. Still frowning, he knocked and entered before Ben's secretary had a chance to announce his presence.

'Need to talk, Ben,' Sam said, without preamble.

Ben looked up, casually throwing a few pages of closely typewritten notes across his desk. 'Robin was just leaving,' he said curtly, nodding at the Bureaux chief who scuttled out of Ben's office with heartfelt thanks at Sam's interruption.

'Shoot,' Ben said coolly.

Sam wished the Editor didn't watch so many American movies. 'We have a problem with Beirut,' he said, watching for Ben's reaction.

Ben let his gaze flicker over to the bank of television screens. 'What problem?'

'Firstly, we haven't located David Cameron,' Sam said, concealing his irritation at Ben's channel-hopping. 'He is on leave, but I've tried all the numbers he left and there's no joy from any of them. I even spoke to Caryn Kelly, who seems to monitor his every move, but unfortunately she thought he was still away working. I've a feeling I won't be David's favourite person when he gets back.'

Ben shrugged and Sam continued. 'But more importantly, I've spoken to Karim, and he says Beirut's simply a no-go area. David is the only person I'd chance sending in right now, and even then only if he was happy with the situation.'

Ben swivelled his chair around and gave Sam the benefit of his full attention. 'What the hell do you mean?' he asked angrily. 'Of course we send! This is a major fucking story, and I'm not just dipping a toe in to see if the water's cold.'

Sam held his fury in check. 'I'm telling you, I've had a direct warning from a very reliable source that it's too risky to go in,' he said, his voice dangerously quiet. 'John McCarthy spent five years in a hellhole because someone sold him out. I'm not about to do the same to one of my colleagues.'

'If it's the responsibility you can't handle, don't worry. I'll send, and I'll carry the can. Happy?'

Sam tried again. 'Listen Ben, I'm telling you not now, not right this minute,' he said reasonably. 'I'm not saying not forever. Hell, in a week, things could be different. I'll send someone to Damascus, and Karim can ship the pictures to Syria to be voiced there until things cool down.'

'In a week, the story will have gone cold,' Ben retorted.

'In a week, so could your correspondent,' Sam flared, his anger rising despite himself.

'I'm not prepared to have CNN and ITN and Christ knows who else stealing exclusives because we're too scared to cover a news story,' Ben said. 'Fuck it, in '87 Brent Sadler got in and out of a Palestinian refugee camp in Beirut when everyone said it couldn't be done, and won an RTS for his trouble. You have to take a few risks in this business. As your Editor, I'm overruling you on this one, Sam.'

Sam stood up in fury, and leant over Ben's desk, his clear blue eyes as cold as the depths of winter. 'Not with me as your Foreign Editor, you don't,' he said ominously.

'So you'd rather I put someone inexperienced on the Desk as well as in the field, is that it?' Ben inquired.

Sam stiffened, his eyes narrowing with disgust. He realised that if any correspondent was to have even a slim chance in Beirut, they would need all his experience to back them up at home. 'You ruthless bastard,' he whispered disbelievingly. 'You really think of everything, don't you?'

'I find it pays,' Ben said calmly.

'Let's hope it's only in dollars, not blood,' Sam spat, spinning on his heel and slamming Ben's office door so hard the glass panel cracked.

■ BEIRUT, LEBANON
24 JULY, 2.05 p.m.

Nick Makepiece pushed his dull blonde hair out of his eyes and sat back on the hard wooden chair, massaging his neck muscles with one hand as he replaced the telephone receiver with the other. Wearily he turned around and addressed the slim Lebanese man behind him.

'Could you get the operator to dial up London again, Karim?' he asked resignedly. 'We got cut off midsentence.'

Karim nodded and spoke rapid Arabic to the man presiding over the hotel's bank of telephones behind a high wooden counter.

'He says it may take a while, the lines are very bad tonight,' Karim translated. 'Too many power cuts, too many wires down. Why don't you try telexing Syria? They may be quicker passing the information on to London.'

INN's Syrian bureau was based in a corner room of the Sheraton Hotel in Damascus. Ginny had flown there as soon as news of the kidnappings had broken, to act as Nick's Producer and back-up. Any material Nick shot in Lebanon had to be sent to Damascus and transmitted from the Syrian television station, since there were no such facilities in Beirut.

Swiftly Nick punched the number of the telex and waited for Ginny to respond. He glanced at his watch. Quarter past two. He had been travelling for more than twenty-four sleepless hours, ever since Sam had asked him to go to Beirut in David Cameron's stead. Nick frowned at the recollection. Sam had been very unhappy about sending him, that much was clear; he hoped the Foreign Editor did not doubt his ability to cover the story successfully.

At the beep of the telex machine Nick looked up to find Ginny's response glowing in flickering green letters from the screen. He smiled. They seemed to be managing to create a viable working relationship from the debris of their personal lives, and Nick felt reassured to have Ginny in this with him. It only made it harder to think of his double betrayal.

His fingers moved expertly across the keys. 'Talked to Aid workers who were with the Frenchmen when they were kidnapped. Have detailed interviews. They were given message from Sword of Jihad to pass on to outside world. Ben should love it.'

Ginny's reply played out swiftly across the screen. 'Well done. Have you shipped the tapes?'

'Quentin has sent four tapes the usual way,' Nick replied, referring to the French Lebanese who orchestrated all the networks' cars from Beirut to Damascus.

Nick waited for Ginny to telex her response, stretching his long legs beneath the desk. Deep in the relatively civilised heart of the Summerland Hotel it was difficult to imagine the anarchic regime that operated outside in the Lebanese capital. Here one saw only the inviting Olympic swimming pool, the sultry elegance of the women's shimmering gold chains and diamond rings, the unceasing flow of vintage champagne. But Beirut was also a vast oubliette, where men could lie forgotten for years just the thickness of a wall away from those diplomats and politicians who argued so desperately for their release.

Ginny confirmed the satellite booking Nick had suggested, and wished him luck. Nick grinned wryly as he typed his reply. 'I'll need an exclusive with the kidnappers, never mind luck, to keep Ben happy,' he telexed. 'Should be meeting the French Ambassador at the airport this afternoon. Will be in touch then.'

Standing up, Nick logged out of the telex computer. On his way out of the underground telecommunications office he did not even check if the lift was working; it never had in living memory, and Nick did not feel it was likely to have changed its habits to accommodate him now. Slowly he climbed the stairs from the hotel lobby to his own room, dreams of a shower and shave dancing in his mind as he unlocked the door. He glanced at the messages that had been left on his desk; Quentin confirmed that the tapes were already en route to Damascus, and informed him that a car would be waiting for him in two hours as requested to take him to the airport to meet the French Ambassador.

It did not even occur to Nick to wonder how the Lebanese driver already knew of the rendezvous.

When Nick emerged into the late afternoon sunshine outside the hotel, he felt renewed and invigorated by the hour's sleep he had managed to snatch. He stood at the entrance of the hotel waiting for his car, surveying the complicated dance that was the Lebanese traffic system; each vehicle seemed certain to collide with another but somehow eluded disaster at the last moment. Across the street destroyed buildings lurched drunkenly towards the road, their floors caved inwards by shells, their walls pock-marked with the neat stucco pattern of gunfire. Dust swirled as the ancient cars bounced across the black-and-yellow striped kerbstones to out-manoeuvre each other, their bonnets and boots rising and clashing down again as they did so. Nick was caught up in the vitality and exotic strangeness of the scene he had seen so many times on tape, but never before in reality. It was the first time he had been assigned to the Middle East, and he relished the danger and passion and fanaticism that was Lebanon.

A battered pale-green Mercedes drew up close beside him, interrupting his thoughts. The driver leant out of the window, spitting a gob of saliva into the dusty street. 'INN?' he asked laconically.

Nick nodded and glanced around for Karim. He had asked the Lebanese fixer to meet him at the hotel gates, but there was no sign of him. Edgily he glanced at his watch. If he did not leave now, there was every chance he would miss the French Ambassador at the airport, and he was unlikely to be able to steal an interview once the diplomat disappeared into the shady political world of Beirut. He noticed a slight figure already sitting in the back seat of the car, and gestured towards him in inquiry.

'*Akhu* – my brother,' the driver said with an explanatory shrug. '*Mataar*?' He stretched his arms in an expansive gesture to suggest a plane.

Nick felt a disquieting uneasiness. Where was Karim? The Lebanese fixer had left him a message suggesting that they leave the hotel half-an-hour earlier than they had originally planned because of the heavy traffic on the airport road, and Nick was puzzled that Karim was now delaying. Nick checked his watch again with irritation. He had not ventured into the heart of Beirut without his fixer before, but he could wait no longer. With a final glance around, Nick climbed into the back of the Mercedes.

Nick was unfamiliar with the streets of Beirut, but he knew enough to realise that the narrow alleys through which the driver was speeding were not part of the route he had travelled on his way from the airport to the hotel. With a shiver of fear Nick realised that he was entering the heart of the southern suburbs, where Terry Waite and John McCarthy and Jackie Mann had languished in chains; where, even now, two French Aid workers were somewhere concealed.

Abruptly a cream BMW pulled across the street, five men diving out of it and yanking open the front doors of the Mercedes as it slew to a halt. Nick did not wait to be dragged from the car. With an instinctive movement he flung himself against the door on his right, rolling as soon as he hit the ground towards the shelter of the building nearest to him. Unaware for a moment of what had happened, the men circled around the Mercedes, AK 47 rifles aimed towards the car. The driver leaped from his seat, slamming his fist against the windscreen and letting fly a volley of Arabic as he gestured towards Nick, now fleeing along the narrow alley.

Nick felt the blood pounding in his veins as he hugged the shadows, crouching low to present less of a target, expecting at any moment to feel the thud of a bullet tear into him, a hand grab his shoulder and whirl him around. Pain knifed his ankle as he ran, and a distant part of his mind registered that he must have twisted it as he dived from the car. Desperately he ducked into one narrow street and then another, hearing the cries of his pursuers, gazed at with indifference by the throng of people milling around him.

His muscles screamed their defiance as he pushed them to their limit, weaving in and out of the buildings, heedless of the direction he was going. Nick paused for a moment in the shadowed doorway of a burnt-out apartment block, wiping away the sweat dripping into his eyes. His breath came in gasping, heaving gulps, his heart beat

365

frantically against his chest. The first flush of adrenalin was fading, leaving in its place a cold knot of fear. He was in the middle of the most dangerous part of Beirut, alone, vulnerable, lamentably conspicuous.

He glanced around the friendless streets, sensing the hidden eyes. Whatever he did, the longer he remained here, the more danger he was in.

Warily Nick left the shadows of the derelict house where he had taken shelter, and doubled back down the nearest alleyway, checking over his shoulder every so often for any sign of his pursuers. The streets were once more undisturbed, as if a stone had been thrown into the midst of a lake, the ripples ebbing slowly, until finally stillness returned, leaving no sign. The shuffling black figures paid him no heed as he searched desperately for a landmark he could recognise. At last he felt a sensation of familiarity, and prayed that somehow he had returned towards the centre of the city.

It was not until he emerged into a square and saw the cream BMW that Nick realised he had run straight back to his kidnappers.

And he did not know he had been shot until the ground tilted crazily around him and his mind exploded into pain and his thoughts disintegrated into black and red and then nothing.

Chapter Thirteen

■ MARSEILLE–LONDON
26 JULY, 9.20 a.m.

Christie's guilt and grief were total.

During the flight back from Marseille to London, she sat trapped in her own private world of misery, unable to share her crushing agony with David, incapable of communicating even while she longed for his reassurance. Silent and unseeing, she gazed ahead, desperate to reach out for him but unable to break through the impenetrable shield which the defences of her mind had erected around her. David could feel the warmth of her body next to him, smell the heady scent of her perfume, but the shadowed creature beside him was a pale shell, the woman he loved hidden deep within some secret recess of her mind, locked behind a door to which he could not find the key.

She was unable to forgive herself for the price she had sentenced Nick to pay by daring to seek just a few more hours of happiness with David. Ruthlessly, mercilessly, she tried, convicted and condemned herself for Nick's abduction – maybe even his death – with a severity no court in the land would have wielded. If she had not erased the message summoning David back to London . . . if Nick had not been sent, inexperienced and unknowing, into the maelstrom of Beirut . . . if she had

not let her own personal feelings colour her judgement . . .

Yet at the same time, a part of her could not help but
think: thank God it wasn't David.

David reached across and drew her head down on to his
shoulder, feeling her tense and unresponsive against him.
He glanced down at her face, pale and drawn beneath her
tan, his heart clenching as he saw the tears slowly seep
down her cheeks.

'It wasn't your fault,' he whispered, trailing his fingers
along her cheekbone and brushing her lips so softly she
barely felt the caress. 'You couldn't know.'

He could see the pulse of her heart beating in the base of
her throat, her collar bones prominent beneath the skin.
Impulsively David hugged her to him, desperate to
infuse some warmth and life into her. Where was the
vital, radiant woman who had laughed and loved and held
him such a few short hours ago? Inwardly he was
bleeding for her, knowing the private torment she was
enduring, knowing too that there was little he could do
but be there for her. He knew, better than anyone,
how guilt could control and warp your life. The terrible
irony was that just as he had finally managed to overcome
his own destructive feelings and dare to live and love
again, Christie's guilt threatened to come between
them.

'*Amoud fiki*,' he breathed softly into the gold of her
hair.

'I can't let myself destroy you too,' Christie said,
shaking her head blindly, careless of the tears that slid
beneath her closed lids and ran down her cheeks. 'I love
you so much, I have to let you go.'

David drew back. 'Christie, Christie, you could never
destroy me, except by leaving me,' he said. 'Don't you
understand? You have given me hope, given me the

chance of another life. I would be nothing without your love.'

Christie shook her head. Only one thought penetrated the shock and guilt she felt at Nick's capture. It beat like a hammer within her brain, obliterating everything but the depth of her love for David. And now she had to cut herself off from that, in order to save the man she loved more than life itself.

Overwhelmed with grief, she could see only that she had wrought destruction on someone she cared for, by putting her own feelings and needs first. She had never realised that her love for David could be wrong, could cause so much distress. If she had made such a harrowing error of judgement once, she could do so again.

'I'm so sorry,' she whispered. 'I can't do it. It's over for us, David. It's over.'

David gazed at her numbly, knowing that she was lost to him. He could not reach her. He had to love her enough to let her go. If she was his, she would come back to him in her own time, when she had worked out her own answers. If she did not come back, it would be because she had never truly loved him. It was the hardest thing he had ever had to do in his life.

His own fears rose within him, and he struggled to contain his anger and pain. He had trusted her enough to love her as he had never loved a woman before, despite everything. Could she do the same?

A terrible inner silence filled his soul, and he knew that without her it would always be a part of him. Despairingly he held her against him as if for the last time. With every fibre of his being he prayed that it was not.

'So, you're not going to change your mind?'

'Why should I do that?'

Lucy leant against the door nonchalantly, one leg tucked up behind her so that the spiky heel bored a hole into the discreet oak panels. Defiantly she tossed her blaze of hair and challengingly blew a large pink bubble of gum.

Bob Carpenter stopped unbuckling his leather belt and crossed the soft-carpeted room to stand immediately before her. He raised one finger and popped the translucent bubble.

'That's been done before,' she complained petulantly, plucking the bubble-gum from her face. 'Can't you think of anything more original?'

She pushed herself away from the wall, a sulky expression on her face. With a sly smile, she sashayed provocatively towards the bed, deliberately swaying her hips, conscious of Bob's devouring gaze. Slowly she draped herself across the embroidered coverlet, one knee bent towards the ceiling, the black latex rubber of her cat-suit gleaming in the shadowy lighting. Tantalisingly she reached one hand towards the zipper catch and teasingly drew it down a few inches, revealing an inviting glimpse of high, firm young breasts. Her dark eyes never leaving his, she licked one finger with deliberate sensuality and trailed it across her full mouth, along her chin, then down the soft triangle of skin at the base of her throat towards her nipples.

Bob gazed at Lucy in helpless fascination as she lolled across the silk bedspread. She possessed that rare combination of childlike naivety and inborn eroticism, a breathtaking mixture that exuded from every pore of her young, supple body. Her limbs had barely emerged from the rounded chubbiness of childhood, but her liquid eyes with their fringe of glossy dark lashes seemed to glow with knowledge centuries old.

Lucy masked her uncertainty as Bob slid off his blazer and loosened the paisley silk tie at his throat. His narrow grey eyes were bright with desire, glinting with an almost feral quality as he surveyed her hungrily. Abruptly he turned from her and opened his briefcase, extracting a package wrapped in deep violet tissue paper. He tossed the parcel across to her, shooting his cuffs and unclasping his monogrammed cufflinks as he watched her reaction.

Lucy sat up in excitement, her nebulous fears banished, dropping her studied air of boredom in her pleasure. 'For me? What is it?'

Bob shucked off his shirt and double-checked the door to the bedroom to make sure it was locked. The last thing he needed was room service interrupting him and this jailbait sex siren. 'Open it and see.'

With unselfconscious eagerness Lucy tore into the flimsy tissue paper, violet shreds scattering across the roseblush carpet. A heavy navy wool tunic fell into her lap, along with a pair of thick black lisle stockings and a plain white cotton shirt. She looked up at him in dismay. 'What the hell is this?' she asked, a knot of anger building inside her. 'I haven't worn this kind of thing since I was twelve.'

Bob felt himself harden at the thought, and with one hand he reached to ease the bulge of his straining cock against his trousers. 'Put them on,' he said smoothly, turning from her to unzip his flies. His cock sprang free, and Bob massaged it gently as he thought of plunging it into her tight, hungry little cunt.

Lucy leaped up from the bed, throwing the package on the floor, and furiously pummelled him on the back. Her dark eyes were bright with anger, and Bob felt another surge of desire as he contemplated the spirit he was determined to control. 'I fucking *won't*!' she raged at him as he whirled to meet her.

'Oh yes, you *will*,' Bob said with ominous quiet. The light menace in his voice was unmistakeable. 'Or are you too much Daddy's little girl to dare go through with this? A prick-tease, is that it? Scared when it's time to actually do the deed? And I thought you were ready to do your own thing. Seems like I was wrong.'

Lucy bridled at the suggestion. 'I'm not too scared, and I'm jolly well not Daddy's little girl,' she retorted defiantly, her voice trembling slightly. Deliberately she yanked the zipper of her cat-suit down towards her navel, slithering out of the top before she could change her mind. Her pink-tipped nipples pointed invitingly upwards towards his chest, the ripeness of her small breasts at odds with the lurking child evident in the pout of her lips, the awkwardness of her limbs.

Bob licked his lips and shrugged with apparent indifference. 'If you're so grown-up, you'd better get used to playing grown-up games,' he said mockingly. He picked up the tunic and stockings, and threw them at her so that she stumbled backwards to catch them. 'Now put them on.'

Lucy struggled out of the sheathlike cat-suit, her veneer of worldliness peeling away from her as the folds of rubber gathered in a glossy sheen at her feet. She stood hesitantly on the soft pink carpet, her bare feet burrowing deep into the soft pile. Unconsciously she clasped her arms across her budding breasts, the gesture of vulnerability alluringly at odds with the crazy defiance of her long bleached tresses and sophisticated makeup. Christ, how old *was* she? Bob bent, hooking his fingers into the coffee-coloured lace of her panties, and drew them down

372

over her plump thighs, revealing a tangle of fine, downy dark hair nestling between them.

'That's better,' he breathed throatily, his eyes glittering with desire. 'Now put your present on.'

Bob sat back on the bed, his stiff cock rearing under his hands as he watched Lucy slip into the white cotton shirt and stockings through narrowed eyes. She glanced across the room for approval as she picked up the navy tunic. Her deliberately provocative air of tantalising seductiveness had shattered, replaced by an uncertainty that Bob found far more erotic and arousing. Her body glowed ripely in the light from the lamps recessed into the walls, its lushness emphasised by the childish clothes she had put on. Lucy stood awkwardly beside the bed, unwilling to let her eyes stray downwards towards the angry member pulsating under his hands. Desperately she dredged her mind for the bright spark of anger against her parents' protectiveness that had propelled her to this hotel bedroom with a man ten years older than her father, but the surge of rebellion had gone, replaced by fear and uncertainty.

Bob was aware of Lucy's reluctance, and relished it. Every time he sucked on one of those pert little nipples and plunged into that succulent cunt he would be fucking Ben Wordsworth, not his daughter. He smiled in grim anticipation. He had no doubt that she was a virgin. In his experience, the ones who acted like they knew it all had rarely even been kissed. It was a state of affairs he intended to rectify.

Impatiently he pulled Lucy down on the bed beside him, grasping her hand in his and dragging it down to hold his engorged cock. Inexpertly Lucy mimicked his movements, keen to conceal her inexperience, her pride already flayed by his humiliating words of disdain. Bob groaned his approval, pausing only to correct her rhythm.

373

His hand reached around for her, pushing the rough woollen tunic up to her waist, his fingers plunging into the tangle of hair framed by her thighs, searching for the tiny bud that would open this child-woman to him and destroy her innocence forever.

Lucy gasped as his hand found her clitoris and sudden darts of distilled pleasure shot through her, her adolescent breasts tingling. She closed her eyes as Bob reached upwards and pinioned her arms above her head on the pillows, half-aroused, half-repelled, his hot breath whispering against her skin as he moved his lips across her face. His hand brushed the heavy cloth of the tunic, and suddenly he grasped the yoke and ripped it away from her, stifling her cries as he bit down hard against her lips. Lucy felt his mouth against her breast through the soft fabric of the shirt, and tensed; her nipples were erect despite herself. Buttons scattered as he tore the shirt away from her, groaning as he buried his face against the creamy buds, his free hand pinching their pink tips with calculated cruelty.

'Tell me how much you want it,' he panted, inserting his knee between her soft thighs and forcing her legs apart.

Lucy writhed beneath him, reeling with a mixture of desire and anger. Dismay mingled with excitement as the danger whetted her arousal.

'I said, tell me you want it,' Bob breathed, his hand reaching down towards her cunt and teasing her lips apart. 'You're desperate for it, aren't you? You're all the same, you little cock-teases.'

He inserted a finger into her slippery moistness, groaning with lust as he felt its tightness. Ruthlessly he pushed two fingers inside her, his erection pulsing so hard that he thought it must burst as she stiffened in pain against him. His knee shoved her legs far apart, and he let go of her

374

wrists to push himself up on his arms, hovering over her. Lucy's eyes widened with fear, her small hands fluttering against the buttress of his chest, the torn shards of her clothes giving her an appearance of both wantonness and vulnerability.

'Tell me,' Bob gasped as he poised to enter her, his hand running across her breasts and down to her moistness. 'I said, tell me.'

'I want it! I want it! Oh please, please, I want it!' Lucy cried, her body bucking beneath him. 'Now! Oh God, *now*!'

With a deep thrust, Bob penetrated her, and she screamed as he met the barrier and drove through it. Almost immediately the burning agony gave way to a surge of pleasure, and Lucy's tears dried on her cheeks as she reached around his back and clasped him closer to her, forcing him ever deeper into her. She rocked her hips against his, picking up the rhythm and adapting it to her own, her erect nipples rubbing silkily against the greying hair of his chest, her thighs gripping his legs as desire caught her in its thrall.

Bob grinned appreciatively as the muscles of her cunt worked against his cock, rippling around him with unconscious sensuality. 'You learn fast,' he rasped into the hollow of her throat. 'You're all the same. You all know you want it.'

Lucy's breathing was shallow and uncontrolled as she felt silver hooks of pleasure trailing across her mind and body. Her awareness had narrowed to the sensations of his cock thrusting deep inside her, the buds of her breasts grazing against him. The whirlpool of arousal sucked her down, and desire bit deeply into her. She screamed her pleasure at this exquisite pain as she came. Bob held her hard, his body bucking as she orgasmed beneath him, the sight of this child–woman sending him over the edge. He poured into her with a savage cry.

Lucy sat up, pushing his body away from her, and smiled secretively, triumphantly. Intuitively she sensed that she had wrested control of her own pleasure from him, that now he was bound to her by his own desire. Forty years her senior, he was as a child to her own instinctive, inborn knowledge; a knowledge which he had just released. For he knew only how to take pleasure, but she now knew how to give it; he was hooked.

Lazily she turned towards him, raising herself up on her hands to straddle him. 'You told me to tell you when I wanted it,' she whispered, her eyes glittering, every inch her father's daughter. 'I'm telling you. I want it now.'

■ INN, LONDON
27 JULY, 3.10 p.m.

Ben stormed through the newsroom, his face white with suppressed anger. His stride did not falter as he passed the Home and Foreign Desks, barking a terse 'My office. Three-thirty,' at them without pausing.

Sam took no pleasure in the fact that he had been proved right. Furiously he berated himself for ever capitulating to Ben in the first place, and the fact that he had been given no choice was little consolation.

There was no doubt that Nick had been abducted, although as yet no message had been received from any group claiming to be holding him. Karim had already contacted his many sources in Beirut. Apparently, Nick had responded to a message from Karim himself, suggesting that they leave half-an-hour earlier than they had planned. Karim had left no such message.

As the farther reaches of his underground network of ears and eyes reported back, Karim learned that Nick had been picked up in a pale-green Mercedes, which had later been found abandoned in al-Hamra, the main shopping area of the city. To all intents and purposes, the young INN reporter had disappeared without trace. The waves of Beirut had closed over his head, leaving barely a ripple.

On the Home Desk Janey motioned wildly with her arm to attract Sam's attention. 'Bernie Turner from the *Ethic* on the phone,' she called, covering the mouthpiece with her hand. 'Wants to talk to you. What's your extension?'

Sam cursed volubly. 'I refuse to tell you,' he said, unplugging himself from the bank of telephones flashing impatiently at him.

The last thing he needed was the tabloid jackals camping outside the doors of INN, waiting for a glimpse of Nick's unhappy friends and colleagues. Freedom of the press was indeed a double-edged sword.

'There's a lot to be said for modern journalism,' Ollie mused. 'By giving us the opinions of the uneducated, it keeps us in touch with the ignorance of the community. Oscar Wilde, 1891.'

Sam and Janey exchanged looks and grinned. 'Tell him I'm in a meeting,' Sam called, relenting. 'I'll get back to him when I've something to say. Not that he'll be able to print it,' he muttered under his breath.

Jerry wandered over to the Foreign Editor, his clipboard clutched in one hand, the other distractedly twiddling a strand of his curly blonde hair. 'What can you give me for the Early Evening News?'

Sam looked up in surprise. 'You still producing that?' he asked, raising one eyebrow and biting into a Mars Bar.

'Simon's finished drying out, and is now having a nervous breakdown,' Jerry said enviously.

Sam stood up and walked back with him to the Early Evening News desk, ripping off the latest wire stories from Reuters and AP as he passed the printer. Jerry sat down, logging into the computer absently as Sam perched on the edge of the desk next to him. 'I'm waiting to see how Ben wants to handle the Nick story,' Sam said, munching, handing Jerry his list of future stories. 'I can fill you in on a few details in the meantime, if that'll help.'

Jerry shrugged mournfully. 'It's not ideal, but it'll do.'

Ollie grinned as he joined them. 'Isn't that your motto?'

'Listen, we've got the highest ratings of any INN show so far, so you're not doing all this for nothing,' Jerry retorted. He paused thoughtfully in the act of calling up his running order in the computer. 'Well, actually, nothing is exactly what you *are* doing it for, but at least somebody's watching it.'

Dominic debated asking Jerry to explain that to his bank manager, who considered journalists the second-lowest form of life after people with portable telephones, but decided against it.

'Are the other networks covering Beirut?' he asked instead, as the remainder of the team gathered around the desk.

Sam riffled the pages of his notebook. 'CNN are staying there for the moment, but they're only travelling with armed protection. It seems a sensible precaution to take, given what's happening there. I wish all networks cared as much about their staff. Apart from them, no-one else is there.'

'I take it we'll be sending David in when he gets back with the flyaway,' Jerry said immediately. 'It's not a story we can leave uncovered.'

Sam frowned, wondering why Ben had prohibited any action until after his meeting. 'Ginny has already got the dish established in Beirut,' he answered evasively. 'As soon as Karim telexed her with what had happened, she drove overland from Damascus with the flyaway and a satellite telephone, thank God. As a woman, she should be safe enough – none of these fanatics have figured out a way to deal with PMT so far. I don't intend to let her stay for long, whatever happens.'

Sam had been furious when he heard the risk Ginny had taken, but he felt a grudging respect for her courage and unbreakable independence. She might be three months pregnant and hopeless when it came to personal relationships, but there was no one to beat her in the field.

'Fine. When can I expect a piece out of there?' Jerry asked.

'Ginny will do you a phono within the next hour, and she'll be sending some uncut pictures of the area where Nick was last seen, the abandoned Mercedes, and an interview with the hotel guard who seems to be the last person actually to have spoken to him,' Sam said, as Janey rushed puffing to join them. 'You'll have to cut the track and rushes when they come in, and drop in some library pictures of the French Aid workers.'

'I'm sorry to interrupt, but Ginny is on the line from Beirut,' Janey said breathlessly, her ample breasts heaving beneath her denim dungarees. 'Do you want to talk to her?'

Sam stood up. 'I need to discuss feed times,' he said, heading towards the bank of telephones. 'If CNN are staying, we may be able to share the cost of a bird with them.'

'Brothel economy. I like it,' Ollie said with a lascivious leer.

Lynxie giggled. 'The trouble with you is that you're just a life support system for your cock.'

'It's not my fault,' Ollie complained. 'It's got to the stage where I've got so few friends, I'm going to group therapy by myself.'

'You just don't understand women,' Lynxie said, with a

379

shake of her cropped blonde head.

'Are you surprised? My wife never let me meet any,' Ollie said dismally.

For once Jerry smiled at the banter around the Desk, glad of a break in the tension. All of them had been shocked and horrified at the news of Nick's abduction, their dismay worsened by the fact that they had to carry on and deal with it as if it were just another story. Each of them silently prayed that Nick would survive his ordeal, and that they would not have to mark anniversary after anniversary of his kidnap as John McCarthy's colleagues had, year after year.

'OK, let's wait until after Ben's meeting to finalise the details,' he said briskly. He scanned his list, assigning the remainder of the day's stories to the producers, ruefully noting that apart from Beirut, there was very little around. Silently he cursed Ben Wordsworth. It was all very well for the Editor to declare an economy drive, but it was the Programme Producers who had to fill the gaping holes in their running orders. Contrary to public opinion, the world's news did not happen in convenient half-hour packages. There were days when they were hard-pressed to come up with three minutes' worth of news, which was precisely when they needed to do a little old-fashioned investigative reporting and actually break a story that hadn't yet hit the headlines. But that was invariably expensive.

Jerry glowered towards the Foreign Desk at the hapless accountant Daniel, who was perched uncomfortably on the edge of his chair. Daniel paled. He was not looking forward to telling Jerry he could only have one satellite booking a day until the end of the mouth, and fervently prayed that nothing newsworthy would take place anywhere further away than W1 for the next ten days.

'OK, that's it, apart from the oil slick off the edge of

France,' Jerry said finally. 'If we could have a map, Lynxie, and let's make it a bit interesting, throw in a few drums.'

'If I'd realised you wanted music, I'd have given it to you before,' the Graphics girl retaliated swiftly.

Suddenly the team turned as one towards the atrium. A siren lure had sounded, and not one of them could resist.

'Trolle-ee-ee!' Mo yodelled.

Jerry gave up. There were some things with which he could compete, but the tea trolley was not one of them. He drew his thermos flask from beneath the desk, wondering fleetingly whether he should defy Suki for once and go for the canteen's homebrew and an obscenely sticky jam doughnut. With the sigh of a man who has turned his back upon the Promised Land, he poured some camomile tea into his plastic cup and tried to feel excited about his homemade nut crunch.

'Jerry! Take a look at Reuters,' Sam called from the Foreign Desk, one telephone in each hand and a third under his chin. 'A Greek tourist ship has gone down off the coast of Spain. No idea of any casualties yet.'

Jerry summoned up the relevant wire-story on his computer. 'Rich, can you handle this one for me?' he said over his shoulder, as the producer returned to his desk with a cup of brackish liquid. Jerry tried not to look jealous. 'Coastguards, travel company, the usual.' He turned towards the PA. 'I'll need an extra slot in the running order, but keep it t.b.a. until I decide where to put it.'

'Surely you'll lead on it?' Livvy asked, shocked.

'Depends how many dead and what nationality,' Jerry said curtly, sifting through the wires as further details flashed on Reuters and AP.

Rich grinned. 'It's the Wordsworth Sliding Scale of Death,' he explained laconically, leaning back in his chair and sipping his tea. '100,000 starving Africans equals 10,000 persecuted Kurds, equals 5,000 drowned Bangladeshis, equals 1,000 massacred Bosnians or 300 Romanians, but only if they're babies. Then you start creeping up the running order: 100 Spaniards killed in a train crash equals thirty Americans murdered in a riot, equals ten dead Scots, equals one Londoner who's lost his luggage.'

'It's got to be at least 2,500 dead in China before it makes the Early Evening News,' Ollie put in as Livvy decided to apply to Panorama and mentally started composing her CV.

Victoria wafted up to the desk on a cloud of Ma Griffe, a Hermès scarf draped casually across the peach tints of her Rifat Ozbek suit. Jerry made an attempt to speak her language.

'Is that another new outfit?' he asked with an expression of acute interest on his face that would have earned him his Equity card.

Victoria laughed patronisingly. 'Darling, no. I've had it at least a month.' She sat down gracefully, fluttering one expensively-manicured hand through the running order on her desk. 'Ah yes, poor Nick,' she said. 'Far too young for an assignment in Beirut.'

'I thought you liked them that way,' Ollie grinned slyly.

Victoria winced. Did he know about her *petit liaison* with the somewhat youthful Foreign Editor, Philip Cunningham, or was she being paranoid? She shuddered. It was just as well she had already decided to end that unproductive dalliance; despite his fervent promises, the only foreign story to which Philip had so far assigned her was the Edinburgh Festival, and she had had enough of lentils and ripped jeans to last her a lifetime. In future she would stay well within the bounds of civilisation. London, one or two of the Home Counties, and perhaps the

382

Seychelles. Anyway, Philip's cunnilingus left a lot to be desired.

'What about this shipwreck?' Victoria asked, shrewdly changing the subject.

Jerry looked up from his desk. 'Don't worry, there are only thirty-five dead, and they're all Greek,' he said, glancing at Livvy with a wicked grin. 'That's why it's not in Part One.'

In his office, Ben waited for silence, a tiny muscle in his jaw working as he attempted to contain his inner anger. Sam met his eyes steadily, and Ben read the disdain there. He shrugged. He didn't give a damn what his Foreign Editor thought, as long as he didn't actually resign.

'I want us to plan for two contingencies,' Ben said without preamble. 'Firstly, we have to deal with the current situation; and secondly, we have to plan for Nick's release, which we all hope will be as soon as possible.' But not before we get our team in place, he added to himself.

'We have to assume that any hostage release will follow the same pattern as those in the past – they will be taken initially to Syria, and then directly to either Cyprus or the UK after a tightly controlled appearance,' said Sam. 'We know that the Syrians have a highly developed approach to publicity and its money making potential; in the past, the first pictures of the released hostages have come from Syrian TV, although we have an assurance from the Minister that on this one INN will have exclusive access to their pictures.'

Sam paused for a moment. 'Chances are we will be allowed inside the Syrian Foreign Ministry for the thank-you and handover, and possibly a short presser by Nick. We can't take any links gear, but there will be live Syrian coverage to which we can have access at the feedpoint.' He glanced across at Daniel, who had been summoned with his calculator. 'We can hire an OB for $12,000 a day, up to a maximum of three days.'

Robin Fernly thanked God for the accountant, who was nervously pressing buttons and paling at the results.

'Do we have any guarantee the link from the Outside Broadcast site to Syrian TV actually works?' Ben asked dryly.

'Not unless you count numerous reassurances that it is in the Hands of Allah, no. We can test it, but that will cost another $12,000.'

Daniel shuddered.

'I'll think about it,' Ben growled.

'All other material will be pooled, so no exclusives,' Sam said. 'I'm working on getting David accredited to travel on the release plane with Nick back to the UK.'

'That covers his release, but what about the story now?' Brian Reynolds asked.

'I want Christie Bradley in Beirut,' Ben stated flatly before Sam had a chance to answer. 'She's a woman, and she will be safer there than a man. She knows the area well, she's reported out of the Middle East a number of times, and I'm impressed with her work. She's also a close friend of Nick's, which could be useful.'

'What about David?' Sam asked. 'I've dragged him halfway across the world to go to Lebanon.'

'He's too high profile,' Ben argued. 'I've lost one correspondent, I'm not prepared to risk another.' And certainly not with all the attendant publicity. He saw the expression on Sam's face and resolutely bit the bullet. 'I made a mistake once. I don't intend to repeat it. David has been into Beirut too many times, he's too well known. I want him in Israel instead. There has to be a deal going down there, and if anyone can find out what it is, David can.'

Sam gave an eloquent shrug of exasperation. 'So who

do you want? We need at least two reporters to cover Beirut and Damascus. Christie will have to have more backup than Ginny can provide alone.'

Ben smiled grimly. 'I'm sending Bob Carpenter,' he said coolly.

Brian looked up in surprise. 'Bob? He hasn't covered the Middle East for some time. Why him?'

'Why not?' Ben said, tapping his fingers impatiently against the glass surface of his desk. He had no intention of telling them that he had just discovered that the fifty-five-year-old reporter was screwing his daughter.

■ BEIRUT, LEBANON
1 AUGUST, 11.30 a.m.

'Fuck. Not another checkpoint,' Bob Carpenter groaned, closing his eyes in annoyance. 'OK, might as well get it over with.'

As the INN car drew to a halt, Bob climbed out of the veteran Coronet Dodge and strolled casually towards the dilapidated wooden hut that had been erected in the middle of a traffic island. A uniformed Lebanese Army soldier lounged against the barrier obstructing the road, a M16 American-made assault rifle cradled in his arms.

'*Sabaahel-kheer*,' Bob said politely.

The soldier grinned, his white teeth glinting in the sunlight. 'Good morning,' he replied in impeccable English.

Bob looked slightly nonplussed, but swiftly recovered his colonial poise. From the back of the Dodge, Christie watched in amusement. She found the constant lacing of checkpoints manned by a shifting pattern of Syrian and Lebanese gunmen as irritating as the older correspondent did, but she was experienced enough in the ways of the

385

Middle East to know that the only way to deal with them was to smile. Any expression of arrogance or annoyance only exacerbated the situation.

Bob attempted to conceal his discomfiture as the soldier swung his weapon from one arm to the other, caressing the trigger lovingly, and glanced back towards the car for inspiration. Christie deliberately avoided his gaze, leaving him to it. With the embarrassed air of a host attempting to entertain a particularly uncommunicative guest, Bob nodded towards the soldier's rifle.

'Great weapon,' he said, speaking in the slow, overloud tones reserved for foreigners. 'Can I have a look? *Khallinee ashoof?*'

The soldier turned around to look at three of his companions, who had emerged from the hut and were regarding the situation with open fascination. One of them shrugged and sat down on the black-and-yellow striped kerbstone, spitting carelessly in the dust. A volley of rapid Arabic elicited knowing smiles from his colleagues.

'You want to fire it?' the soldier asked casually, grinning back widely in the direction of his audience. This time the American twang to his speech was clearly discernible.

'Oh God,' Christie groaned, covering her eyes with both hands. In the front of the car, Jimmy grinned and slid his camera beneath the seat. 'Someone had better hold his hand,' he said resignedly, climbing out of the car.

Karim leant his head against the steering wheel in despair. 'I thought we were supposed to be avoiding attracting attention to ourselves?'

Christie watched the soldier escort the two journalists fifty metres towards a bombed-out building leaning crazily towards the road. Bob turned back towards the car and smiled encouragingly. Christie shook her head in

386

disbelief. Bob Carpenter's obsession with weapons and artillery – as long as he was safely away from the front line – was legendary. It was said he could recognise a gunshot with ninety per cent accuracy, provided it was on tape. His more cynical colleagues observed that such expertise was essential for him to know which way to run.

Bob took the M16 rifle from the grinning soldier, who reached into his pocket and extracted a cigarette, lighting it and inhaling deeply. With exaggerated caution, the correspondent took aim against a china ornament still resting elegantly on an inner windowsill of the derelict building. Behind it the sky shimmered blue; a bed hung drunkenly from the floor above, see-sawing gently in the breeze. A vine curled itself around a once-graceful French writing table, half-a-dozen books piled carefully to one side.

The silent unreality was shattered as the shot reverberated around the street, echoing in the empty buildings as dust and plaster filled the air. The windowsill disintegrated, leaving a clean, jagged edge of mortar that seemed incongruous against the faded neglect of the building's facade. Bob staggered backwards with the force of the recoil and handed the M16 to the soldier with an absurdly proud air of achievement.

Jimmy took the proffered rifle from the gunman, with an apologetic shrug in Christie's direction, and let off several shots at the same wall. Seconds later automatic tracer fire exploded around them as machine-guns raked their position.

'Hit the deck!' Jimmy screamed as bullets slammed into the dust inches away from them. The two men dived towards the shelter of the building, skimming forward on their stomachs in the direction of the Dodge. Karim revved the engine and drove the car hard against the high kerbstones, bumping onto the pavement and steering wildly around the checkpoint.

'What the hell is going on?' Christie cried, throwing herself on to the floor of the car as Karim careered towards the two journalists.

'I'll tell you what's happening!' Karim roared back. 'They've started a damn battle!'

As the ancient car reached the two men, Christie threw open the doors, which slammed against the brickwork of the building, providing the two figures with a measure of cover. The four Lebanese Army soldiers had already taken up positions behind their barricades and in a doorway across the road from the Dodge, returning fire with equal measures of enthusiasm and inaccuracy.

Christie guessed that the journalists' gunshots had provoked one of the trigger-happy bands of factional gunmen who still haunted areas of the city, despite the new atmosphere of democracy and co-operation that their leaders officially embraced. She did not pause to ponder the point.

Karim screamed as a bullet hit the car, penetrating the metal and slicing through his shoulder. A second burst of gunfire raked the side of the car which bucked under the impact as the two offside tyres exploded. Before they could react, a jeep bounced across the pitted tarmac, shielding the Dodge as five Lebanese soldiers leaped out and opened fire on the snipers.

Christie did not wait for instructions. Yanking open the door against which Karim was lolling, clutching his shoulder, she pulled the injured man out of the car, thrusting him into the jeep as the Lebanese soldiers yelled at them to hurry. Bob slithered towards the vehicle on his stomach, half-crawling, half-climbing into the jeep, which was already moving out of the line of fire.

'Wait!' Christie screamed frantically. '*Laa taruh*! Jimmy isn't on board yet!'

388

Bob turned to her, his face twisted in anger and shock. 'We can't wait!' he spat furiously. 'We'll all be killed. He'll have to take his chances.'

Christie stared at him for a moment in disbelief. Then, with a contemptuous glare, she threw open the door of the accelerating jeep, hanging out of the vehicle as Jimmy dived out of the shelter of the Dodge. Clutching his camera to his chest like a rugby player aiming for touchdown, he hurtled across the exposed street between the abandoned car and the moving jeep, throwing himself towards Christie's outstretched hands.

Christie felt his fingers, but she was dragged out of his reach before she had the chance to haul the cameraman into the vehicle. Desperate, operating on pure instinct, she seized the gun cradled in the arms of the soldier next to her, swinging it around and burying the cold steel of the muzzle in the shoulder of the driver.

'I said *wait!*' she said coolly, the authority in her voice backed up by the grim command of the M16.

The driver did not debate the issue. He slammed on the brakes, sending the jeep swerving to the side, the ground around them dancing as bullets hit the dust. Jimmy flung himself through the open door as the vehicle spun around and headed rapidly away from the gunfire.

Christie smiled disarmingly at the soldier from whom she had hijacked the rifle as she handed it back. '*Shukran jezilan,*' she said graciously.

'You're welcome,' the dazed soldier replied automatically.

Jimmy grinned. 'I'm bloody glad you're on my side,' he said, leaning back against the seat in relief.

The militiaman turned to them. 'Me too,' he said feelingly.

Bob stood at the entrance to the Summerland Hotel,

squinting slightly as the afternoon sun caught his eyes. 'Make sure you're tight in on me,' he said brusquely. 'I want to see the buildings behind me, but nothing else.'

Jimmy straightened up behind the camera. 'Can you hold up your notebook? I need to do a white balance.'

Bob opened his notebook and held a clean page before the camera so that Jimmy could set the light balance using the whiteness as a reference point. Without this simple check, the final picture might end up tinged yellow or whitened into blueness. The cameraman rolled for thirty seconds, then extended his thumb towards Bob to indicate that he was ready to film.

Bob pressed the play button of a tiny cassette recorder in the pocket of his safari jacket. He had already taped his pre-written piece to camera, and as he started the cassette, his own words sounded in his concealed earpiece. Bob repeated them as he heard them, staring straight into the camera lens, giving the appearance of ad-libbing from memory as he spoke the words. Before he had a chance to finish, a gaggle of teenage Arab youths strutted past him in the background and paused as they saw the camera. Jimmy waved at them to move on, but they stood grouped around the correspondent, some staring silently, others jeering in Arabic. One made a victory sign over the top of Bob's head, hooting with laughter, the eldest amongst them spitting in the dirt at the reporter's feet to signify his contempt of all things Western.

'*Ruh min henaa*!' Bob yelled angrily. 'Go away!'

Jimmy sighed as the youths crowded around the camera, peering into the lens, jostling the two journalists, laughing mockingly as Bob swore at them. One circled his groin in the correspondent's direction, rubbing his crotch with a leer, whilst another made a pistol of his fingers and held it against the older man's head. Two taxis, obstructed by the boys as they lounged across the

390

road, sat on their horns, cursing loudly, and the youths, tiring of the sport, ran off, their lithe figures weaving expertly through the chaotic traffic system.

With a final expletive, Bob extracted a mirror and comb from his travel bag, running it through his cropped greying hair and settling the result with a thorough application of Alberto Mega Hold. He wiped the sweat and dust from his face with a towel, and checked his appearance in the mirror. Carefully he readjusted the tiny microphone clipped to his shirt, rewound the slim cassette recorder and struck a suitable stance.

Jimmy held two fingers before the lens to signify that this was the second take, and repeated the thumbs-up signal. Bob glanced at the ground to compose himself, and then looked up swiftly, an expression of concern and rugged seriousness on his face.

'In modern-day Beirut, a violent jungle still struggling for democracy, the only absolute law is that of the gun. Somewhere concealed behind me are three new Western hostages, the latest a journalist attempting to report on an increasingly dangerous situation . . .' The correspondent broke off as something startled him, ducking instinctively towards the ground and the extreme edge of the shot. To Jimmy's surprise, instead of starting again, he quickly recovered his rhythm, resuming his piece to camera with barely a pause. 'In the midst of this beleaguered city, these men are languishing, perhaps only feet away. Meanwhile, their governments work desperately for their release, but whilst their policy remains one of non-negotiation with hostage-takers, it could be a long time coming. Bob Carpenter, INN, Beirut.'

Bob paused a few moments, spooling back the radio cassette in his pocket as the cameraman eyed the clouding sky suspiciously. 'Sorry about the break,' Bob apologised, straightening his collar. 'Bit jumpy after this morning.

I'm happy with it otherwise. Let's go for a final take.'

Karim rewound the half-edited tape, wincing as pain burned through his damaged shoulder. He eased himself carefully against the chair, glancing out of the hotel window at the glinting blue waters of the swimming pool. Thank God it had only been a minor flesh wound. Another inch or so and it could have been a different story.

'OK, give me fifteen seconds of GV's around the Green Line, and then it's straight into the piece to camera,' Bob said, scribbling his script down into the notebook spread across his lap.

Karim inserted into the Edit deck the tape that Jimmy had shot around the wasteland which had divided the Muslim West half of the city from the Christian East. Much of the past twenty years of fighting had taken place within a hundred yards of the Green Line. Now, in theory, it no longer existed, but to the Lebanese people, it would always be there. The desecrated wasteland had the appearance of a stage-set, waiting for the cast to appear to bring it to life. The shelled buildings leaned haphazardly against each other, furniture and possessions strewn where their owners had left them decades ago, their facades sliced away to expose their interiors like dolls' houses. Heaps of rubble blocked the cratered roads, tangled cables coiled from shattered telegraph poles, burnt-out cars littered the pavements. An orange tree grew through what had once been a Chesterfield sofa; frangipani ran riot across a silk-covered wall. Until the recent ceasefire at the end of the civil war, anyone venturing across the Green Line had risked their lives to a sniper's bullet; now, it was possible to witness the utter destruction the battles had wrought. But what chilled the soul was the absolute silence.

Karim spooled through the tape, selecting fifteen seconds' worth: poignant, dramatic images of remnants of the bitter civil war. He laid the pictures down on the half-edited package Bob was constructing, waiting to hear the line of script the correspondent had written to accompany the images and check that the two meshed.

'What time is the satellite?' Karim asked as he laid down the last shot of the Green Line and ejected the tape.

'20.00. We've got half-an-hour,' Bob said curtly.

Karim slipped in the tape containing the piece to camera Jimmy had shot outside the hotel. He sped the tape through the first two takes, and began lining up the shot for the third, when Bob laid a hand on his arm.

'I want the second take,' he said coolly.

Karim looked surprised. 'That was the take where something spooked you,' he said. 'You ducked down out of shot. We'll have to go with the third.'

'No. I said I wanted the second take. Are you going to put it down or do I have to edit it myself?'

Karim shrugged and laid down the take Bob had demanded, certain that the correspondent had made a mistake and would want to rectify it once he saw the edited shot.

'I can't hear that gunfire properly,' Bob said casually. 'Can you whack up the audio on that bit?'

'What gunfire?' Karim asked, astonished.

'Why do you think I was ducking?' Bob demanded, looking up from his script in irritation.

Karim played back the piece to camera in silence, the audio channel turned to maximum. All he could hear was the squeal of tyres in the street behind Bob, the distant sound of horns blaring and youths shouting.

'There is no gunfire on this tape,' he said firmly.

'In that case, you'll have to dub some across from old library pictures,' Bob said, as if talking to a child.

393

Karim looked at the correspondent steadily. He knew Bob was attempting to fake the tape and appear as if he had come under fire whilst reporting; knew, too, that the reporter had deliberately ducked with this precise scheme in mind. Nothing had startled him, and there had been no gunfire. He was also quite certain that Bob knew he knew, and did not care. The viewers at home would think Bob Carpenter was a hero, prepared to put his life on the line for a story; they would cry out for more, which INN would have no choice but to provide, whether they liked it or not.

Bob picked up the library tape that David had shot six months previously. 'I think this is the one you're looking for,' he said, tossing the tape into Karim's lap.

Chapter Fourteen

Marina Mehdi threaded her way unsteadily through the maze of tables littering the pavement, and sat down at one farthest from the throng of people spilling out of the café. She glanced across the shimmering blue waters of the Mediterranean, watching the waves purl around the heaps of rocks that formed breakwaters along the Israeli coast. With a sigh she pushed her sunglasses back across her forehead into her thick, dark hair, turning her face so that the soft late afternoon sunshine washed over her, the wind whipping her scarf around her shoulders, bringing with it the sharp tang of salt. A scattering of solitary windsurfers skimmed across the waves far out to sea, the deep, low orange sun casting lengthening shadows across the silvery stretches of sand, while the steady pulse of the waves pounded rhythmically against the rocks. Here, her half-formed fears seemed just foolish nightmares, dredged up from the depths of her imagination, fuelled by the ancient unreasoning hatred that consumed all her people.

The manila envelope on the chair beside her caught her eye, and Marina shivered.

A slim-hipped Israeli boy approached her, weaving towards her with unconscious grace, his dark eyes flickering disinterestedly across the other tables as he straightened his white linen apron.

'*Shalom*,' he said with distant politeness, handing her a cardboard menu.

Marina smiled and waved it away. '*Shalom*. Just a black coffee, please,' she said, watching him with a curious detachment as he scribbled her order down in his note-book and dived attentively towards a gesticulating customer three tables away. He was fifteen, maybe sixteen years old; little more than a child, a stranger to her, but if her terrible fears were not nightmares but the unconscionable truth, they were deadly enemies, poised on opposite sides of a widening gulf that could destroy them utterly.

The Palestinian situation was one which the world could not hope to solve. It was not a question of which side was wrong; the problem was that both sides were right. Each could lay valid claim to the land through history, tradition and possession; both believed that for their race to survive, the other had to be destroyed.

The sun sank slowly into the sea, seeping crimson across the darkening sky and turning the aquamarine water a deep blood-red. Marina sipped slowly at her coffee, a dull pain throbbing behind her eyes, an inexpressible sadness flooding through her as she gazed across the water. Palestine. Was there ever such an unholy Holy Land, had any other country been falsely Promised to so many? It was a land so filled with hope and pain, beauty and terror, hatred and riches and treachery; it had been fought for and died for and desired by so many. Conquered by Assyria, Persia and Rome, vanquished by Byzantines, Crusaders and Turks, parcelled out by the British and finally bequeathed by the world to the Jews in guilty atonement for the Holocaust. It was a country where Islam, Christianity and Judaism came together yet never touched.

In the midst of the turmoil and chaos, caught in the

middle as boundaries were redrawn, were her people, the Palestinians, a disenfranchised nation seemingly without land or rights or political voices, a diaspora scattered throughout the Arab world. They had turned to terrorism, and gained nothing. Eventually they realised that they would never have the world's sympathy until they renounced violence, and from this realisation, the Intifada was born. Again and again the Palestinian campaign of stones and curses against tear-gas and rubber bullets backed the Israeli Government into a corner, forcing them to take the iniative and thus make the Palestinians the victims in the eyes of the world. The expulsion of four hundred Palestinians into the no-man's-land between Israel and Lebanon in December of 1992 had even lead to a new UN resolution against Israel. Gradually, sympathy for the Palestinians grew.

But while the Intifada was a PR success, redefining the image of the Palestinian people who had, until then, been synonymous with the PLO in the minds of the world, the status quo had not changed. Bitterly, the Palestinians realised that there was one weapon that the Israelis feared more than any other. They did not hesitate to use it. What they could not take by force, they would seize by sheer weight of numbers. Every child born a Palestinian was ammunition in their deadly fight for survival.

Marina slipped the folder out of the manila envelope, and gazed at its neatly typewritten pages. She could understand the Israelis' fear of her people. The Jews had been driven from every country in the world, all but destroyed by the Nazis, and Israel was their refuge, their sanctuary. Marina knew without a doubt that if the Israelis showed the least sign of weakness, their Arab neighbours would destroy them utterly. Their friends were few. The UN resolutions were a constant threat, a lever forcing the Israelis to return again and again to a negotiating table at which they dared not compromise if they wished to survive.

But the real danger to the Israeli peace of mind was the enemy within their own borders, and the Palestinians had time on their side. Already they numbered more than two million, and despite the immigration of Soviet Jews, the Israeli population could not hope to match their growth. The Palestinians were a demographic time-bomb the Israelis were desperate to defuse.

But to destroy an entire race?

The figures danced across the page as the last of the evening light diminished and faded, and Marina stared at them unseeingly as the wind unfurled her dark curls, whipping them across her cheeks, and ruffled the pages of the folder. Marina picked it up with a deep sigh. Dar el-Baran, just one of the many over-populated villages cramming the Occupied Gaza Strip, becoming ever more crowded at the rate of two thousand children a year. And then suddenly there were no more babies.

Marina's acute legal mind had been alerted. Her instinct told her something was very wrong. Perplexed, curious, but not yet alarmed, she had studied the figures that Afnan, the WRAPR Health Clinic nurse, had given her when she last visited Dar el-Baran, searching anew for possible reasons for the discrepancy she had discovered. The dramatic, inexplicable fall in the birth-rate of the district in 1991 could have been dismissed as a fluke, one of the cyclical dips that occurred over a long period of time. But the following year the figures were even lower, and although the final numbers for 1993 were as yet incomplete, there was an undeniable trend downwards.

As the figures for other parts of the Occupied Territories were gathered by refugee officials and filtered back to the WRAPR offices, Marina searched them in growing consternation. Elsewhere in the West Bank and Gaza

398

Strip, the Palestinian population had continued its rapid expansion. Complaints and appeals for more room, more funding, flooded into their offices. Until Marina turned to the incomplete statistics for 1993. She felt an icy trickle of fear run along her spine. Silently, unobtrusively, like lights switched off across a shimmering city, the birth of children was stopping all over the Palestinian lands.

There was no explanation for it. In her search for the truth, Marina returned to Dar el-Baran, the centre of it all, questioning her colleagues, tramping for hours through the cramped, dusty streets, talking and listening to the people of the village. They seemed unaware of any change. The feelings of the Palestinians had not altered; they still rejected birth-control. Large families were still their best weapon in the fight against those they saw as their oppressors, their hatred still burned bright. They showed Marina to their children, who were healthier, happier than ever; the new doctor gave them all vitamins and inoculations, the infant mortality rate was decreasing.

Finishing her coffee, Marina left six shekels on the table and stood up, slipping the folder back into the manila envelope. She made her way along the beachfront promenade, watching the lights on the coast curve around the bay that edged Tel Aviv. A young couple strolled past her, their arms entwined around each other as they gazed out over the blackened ocean. Marina paused by a postbox and slid in her envelope, then descended a flight of steps to the beach. Impulsively she kicked off her sandals and bent to pick them up, relishing the feel of the cool sand between her toes. She strolled to the edge of the sea, letting the warm wavelets swish over her feet.

She felt inexpressibly weary, and the surges of dizziness that occasionally overwhelmed her seemed to be becoming more frequent. Perhaps Doctor Joseph had been right: she was overwrought and overtired. When she had visited him in his tiny, battered clinic in the centre of Dar el-Baran last week, he had been more concerned about the shadows beneath her eyes, the lines etched into her face, than the questions she asked about the dwindling numbers of babies.

'My concern is with the living, not those who have yet to be born,' Doctor Joseph had smiled, the deep grey eyes behind his glasses warm with compassion. 'I try to make sure that those children we have now survive to adulthood; that is my priority.'

'But you have so few new babies – doesn't that alarm you?' Marina had asked, gesturing towards the empty pre-natal clinic.

Doctor Joseph had smiled. 'Maybe if the children they have are living, they do not need to have so many.'

'But that their attitude should change so quickly . . . doesn't that surprise you?' Marina pressed. 'What reason do they have to suddenly believe that things will change? You have no more space, precious few medical facilities, constant outbreaks of dysentery, gastroenteritis . . .'

The doctor rose from his chair, crossing to the shining new cabinet at the end of his office. He unlocked the padlock and swung open the doors, revealing shelves packed with boxes of drugs. He selected one, and closed the doors, securing the padlock. 'This is the reason,' he said, opening the box and handing the slim packet of pills to Marina. 'Concentrated vitamin supplements. They give the children resistance and make up for the lack of nutrients in their food. We have also found them very helpful in teenage girls, particularly at the onset of puberty. When they begin menstruating, the girls lose iron and can become anaemic; these help alleviate those symptoms.'

Marina turned the packet in her hand. She recognised the manufacturer – a reputable Western firm known for their innovative and ground-breaking work. 'You give these to all the children you see?' she asked with interest.

'Only those we feel are in need of the extra vitamins,' Doctor Joseph said, leaning forward earnestly. 'We cannot hope to reach all of those in need, but in the last three years, we have had very good results. In fact, we have begun to extend our programme to adults, using monthly injections instead of daily pills for convenience.'

Marina made to give the packet back to him, but he waved his hand with a smile. 'Please, keep them,' he said, handing her the remaining packets in the box. 'Six months' supply. Perhaps when you next come to see me, those shadows will have gone.' He touched her cheek with his forefinger kindly. 'More sleep; less worry, that is what I prescribe for you.'

He had seen no reason to question the breathing space that the falling birth-rate gave to his overstretched resources; from his point of view, such a situation could bring with it nothing but good. His explanation was plausible at first glance, suggested, she suspected, more to pacify her than because he had ever really considered the puzzle, and there was seemingly no reason for him to look further. But to be credible, it required a change of attitude in the Palestinian people that Marina knew simply did not exist. There had to be some other reason . . . some other explanation . . . apart from that which she already suspected . . .

She started back along the beach to the flight of steps that would bring her back to the pavement. Wearily she climbed them. The vitamins had not helped her exhaustion; in fact, if anything, they had exacerbated it. She was finding it difficult to sleep, she had lost so much weight that her mother was convinced she was pining after some man; even her periods were becoming increasingly erratic. Perhaps, now that she had at last decided to confide her terrible misgivings to Christie Bradley, the burden of worry would be eased a little.

She extracted her car keys from her handbag, and drew her scarf closer about her shoulders, the cool air from the sea chilling her slightly. She opened the door of her Volkswagen, sliding into the seat and leaning her head back against the rest. A vision of a steaming bath filled with patchouli oil and fragrant bubbles made her smile in weary anticipation. For once she longed to return home, to be soothed by her mother's everyday cares and worries, fussed over and cosseted. Marina massaged her neck with one hand, already feeling the warm water enveloping her and her anxieties evaporating.

She leant forward and turned the key in the ignition.

The explosion as the bomb detonated destroyed not only her car, but half-a-dozen all around her, sending a fireball sweeping down the street, shattering windows and burying the Volkswagen in a pile of masonry.

■ DAMASCUS, SYRIA
25 AUGUST, 4.30 p.m.

The heat in the un-airconditioned car was suffocating.

Christie's hair clung damply to her forehead, her cotton shirt lying wet against her skin. She longed to roll up her sleeves, but knew that even her naked forearms would be considered offensive in these Arab circles. She sighed. Ben was probably right: it was safer for a woman to be in Beirut at the moment, which was why she had been sent there. But it was a great deal more difficult to operate as a journalist when even the wearing of sunglasses by a woman was considered decadent. Wearily she plucked her damp shirt away from her breasts as trickles of perspiration ran down between them. Even though Sam's telephone call had catapulted her into Lebanon more than three weeks ago, she had still not acclimatised to the cloying summer heat of the Middle East.

She turned towards Jimmy, who was kneeling up on the passenger seat, training his camera on the newly-released French hostage, who was sitting in the back of the car. Jimmy sat back on his heels, bracing himself against the dashboard, checking the shot once more in his eye-piece before giving Christie the thumbs up to indicate that he was ready to roll. The Syrian driver stared stolidly ahead of him as they entered the outskirts of Damascus, seemingly unaware of the activities of the camera crew as he had been throughout the three-hour drive from Leba-non.

'Monsieur Guillot, *pourriez-vous répéter, s'il vous plaît? En anglais?*' Christie asked, leaning back so that Jimmy could get a clear shot of the exhausted man.

Pierre Guillot's gaze flickered over the Syrian official squeezed into the back of the Mercedes with Christie and himself. He shrugged wearily. '*Que desirez-vous?*'

Christie smiled. 'I know this must be very tiring for you, but I hope you understand that it is important that we do not make a mistake, for the sake of the other hostages.'

'*Oui, je comprends.* Please, ask me, and I will try to help you,' Guillot responded in heavily accented English.

Christie glanced across at the Syrian, who nodded approval. 'Monsieur Guillot, can you tell me why you were released?' she began, meeting his gaze steadily.

The Frenchman nodded. 'I have been told, by the man who released me, that they were paid many dollars ransom.'

'Did he tell you by whom?'

'Yes. He said the money came from the UN.'

Jimmy tightened the shot, closing in on Guillot's face.

The ordeal of the past few weeks was written in the shadows under his eyes, the fading bruises across his cheeks, the unnatural pallor of his skin. His jaw was cut in several places where he had been forced to shave with a blunt razor in preparation for his release, and his clothes hung loosely on his shrunken frame. It was clear that he had been chosen for release before his compatriot, Jean-Paul Canard, because of his ill-health. To the kidnappers, a dead hostage would be worse than none at all.

Christie felt the pulse of excitement that always flooded through her when she knew she was on the edge of breaking a major news story. 'You are quite sure he said the ransom was paid by the UN?'

Guillot's eyes were fathomless. '*Oui*, this is what he said.'

'Do you believe him?'

'Yes. I saw the suitcase full of money. They were counting it, very excited, talking about the Americans. It was American money, thousands of dollars.' Guillot passed his hand over his head, and stared out into the darkness. 'They were saying that this is the easy way to get money to buy guns. They say they can do the same thing many times. Americans are fools, they say.'

Christie was neither surprised nor shocked by the Frenchman's story. It had long been rumoured that the speed with which many Western hostages had been released in 1991 had more to do with hard currency than soft diplomacy, but so far it had never been substantiated. Guillot might not be able to offer tangible proof, but his testimony could well detonate the most damaging scandal since Irangate.

'When was this?' Christie asked compassionately.

'This morning, they collect the money, they count it the way I have said. Then they unchain me, they make me wash and shave, then they put me in – *comment appelez-vous cela en anglais?* – the boot? – in the boot of the car,' Guillot continued as Christie nodded. 'We drive for fifteen, twenty minutes, then they take me out of the car, and put me into the back of another one. We drive again, this time only ten minutes, and suddenly we stop. The door opens, and a man shakes my hand, says he is from the UN.'

'Did he say anything else to you? Or to your kidnappers?'

'Yes, that is why I know the story of the money is true. The man driving my car, the chief of the kidnappers, he speaks Arabic to the UN official, but of course I understand, I have lived here for several years,' Guillot replied. 'He says that they must pay the same again for my friend.'

'You are quite sure of this?' Christie asked, stunned by the foolishness of the UN diplomats, not only in dealing with kidnappers in this fashion, but in being overheard doing so.

'Of course. Two million dollars. He was quite clear,' Guillot said.

'And then?' Christie prompted, praying that she would capture this on tape before they arrived at the Syrian Foreign Ministry and the UN managed to annex Guillot and effectively silence him. That she had achieved this extraordinary interview at all was thanks only to the fact that she knew the Syrian officials who orchestrated these hostage releases; the UN themselves would never have sanctioned it. Nor, for that matter, would Bob Carpenter, had he known she was about to break an exclusive that would rock the political world to the very top.

'I was taken to the hotel – the Beau Rivage – although I did not recognise the route, because this part of Beirut was unfamiliar. Waiting for me are the Syrians, and of course, you.' Guillot smiled, the first time he had done so since

Christie had met him in the hotel foyer. 'The rest you know.'

'Pierre, I know you are tired, and I thank you for talking to me, for telling me the truth,' Christie said, as Jimmy stopped filming and quickly ejected the tape, slipping it into Christie's shoulder bag and inserting a fresh one into the camera.

She pushed her hair out of her eyes and leant back in her seat as the car drew up outside the back door of the Syrian Foreign Ministry. It was already besieged by hundreds of journalists who circled the front gates like starving predators, held back only by armed guards. Arc-lights pierced the darkness, cables snaking across the pavements towards half-a-dozen OB vans, whilst correspondents from all over the world jostled one another for position. The light glinted off a hundred camera lenses poised for the first photograph of the released hostage. In the streets around the ministry, cars kerb-crawled backwards and forwards, youths crammed into the back seats and leaning out of open windows to wave banners and chant their support for the Syrian President, horns blaring. As the buzz of their arrival blazed through the throng, the journalists surged *en masse* towards them.

Christie smiled grimly. 'I think you can be sure that the world will listen now,' she said.

'We took a hit! Re-rack, Atlanta!' the American producer screamed into the telephone as CNN's satellite transmission went down. The engineer sweating over the feed-point rewound the tape ready to send it again. 'OK, we're up to speed! Go ahead, Atlanta, we're up to speed, let's go!' She howled as the satellite cut out again. 'OK, OK, we're down, we lost the bird. Re-rack!'

Christie sped into the feedroom at Syrian television, negotiating her way around the frantic journalists thronging the narrow passageways, each desperate to send their tapes of the newly-released French Aid worker to their respective television stations. As she reached the bank of monitors where Ginny was standing, arguing with a *Daily Mail* reporter anxious to use INN's telephone, she collided with the square back of James Braithwaite, the Middle East correspondent of one of the new ITV franchise winners, Andromeda TV.

'Miss Bradley, how charming,' James said tightly as he turned and recognised her. 'What a cosy little gathering this is becoming.'

Christie flinched and attempted to conceal her dislike. James Braithwaite had had a chequered career with a number of networks before joining Andromeda, earning himself a reputation as breathtakingly mediocre in achievement but unequalled in duplicity. He had been observed many times standing on the scales at an airport check-in to increase his excess baggage – and the consequent profit he made by changing money on the black market but claiming for it from his company at the official rate. Thus a receipt for 100 local dinars would cost him perhaps five dollars on the black market, but earn him a thousand when he put in his expenses. Christie's distaste, however, was more fundamental: the last time she and James had clashed was when she watched him deliberately send his cameraman into the field of fire in Mozambique, against all advice to the contrary, for just one shot, remaining safely at his hotel himself. The cameraman had never returned.

Before Christie could frame a reply, Ginny broke off her conversation with the *Daily Mail* reporter to drag her into a corner. 'I've told the desk to expect something pretty sensational,' Ginny whispered, her dark eyes glittering with satisfaction. 'You'll be leading the Early Evening News, then after your piece, they'll come to you live for a two-way. Charles will be doing the interview with you, and then you'll throw to Victoria, who'll interview the Foreign Minister down at the Westminster studio.'

'How long do they want from me?' Christie asked.

'The piece you're sending is – what? Ten minutes long?'

'Eleven minutes twenty-five all up. We used nearly all of the Guillot interview, it's powerful stuff.'

'OK, they'll want about three minutes with you,' Ginny said after a quick calculation. 'I'll confirm it with Sam when I send the piece.'

'I take it Guillot didn't say any of this at the press conference he gave at the Syrian Foreign Ministry after we arrived?' Christie asked, as she opened her portable computer and began writing some notes for her two-way with Charles.

'Not a word. I logged it all as it was relayed back here while you were editing your piece,' Ginny replied, glancing through her notes. 'It was just the usual thing: glad to be free, can't wait to see my family, and a plea for Canard and Nick. I doubt the UN have any idea of the content of your interview, or they'd be raising hell by now.'

Christie thanked God for a decent Producer. It made all the difference, when you were up against a deadline and racing to put a story together, to have an efficient Producer who liaised between frantic correspondent and impatient Desk, co-ordinated the feed times, kept an eye on what was happening elsewhere whilst you were busy, commandeered telephones and generally saved your life with coffee.

'What time is the bird?' Christie asked, glancing at her watch. The Early Evening News was in half-an-hour.

'We're sharing a bi-lateral with Andromeda,' Ginny said, grinning wryly. Christie groaned. She loathed having to rely on someone else's satellite booking and share

408

their feed; it meant they got to send first, always an advantage in the unpredictable world of television satellite transmissions.

James sauntered up to the feedpoint with his Editor, who slid Andromeda's tape into the machine and lined it up. They started transmitting, the older correspondent standing smugly watching his piece as it played out, unaware of the ill-concealed smiles from the other journalists listening to the torpid, clichéd script. A good reporter could not do much with a tired story; but a bad correspondent could render the most exciting footage as dull as a party political broadcast.

As James's Editor ejected his transmitted tape, Ginny dialled London and was put through to the Master Control Room, where Christie's piece would be taken in to the INN building and recorded. Sam was already in MCR, waiting for the story to come in. Ginny slid Christie's tape into the machine, and as soon as Sam confirmed that he was seeing the countdown, pressed the play button.

The countdown gave way to a picture of Pierre Guillot's tired thumbs-up as he walked into the Beau Rivage hotel in Beirut, and Christie's commentary began.

James started forward in surprise. 'What the hell is this? I haven't seen these pictures,' he shouted angrily.

Ginny smiled. 'It's what is known as an old-fashioned scoop,' she said sweetly.

The *Daily Mail* reporter laughed. 'Damn you, Christie, you didn't let on a whisper,' he said, giving her a rueful smile of congratulation. 'I guess we'll just have to tail you wherever you go next time.'

The other journalists in the feedroom paused a moment to watch the piece, which they all immediately realised rendered their own efforts obsolete. As what Guillot was saying became clear, they reached for their telephones, frantically dialling their Foreign Desks to alert them to the breaking story that they had all missed.

Abruptly James strode forward and ejected Christie's tape, his hand shaking with barely controlled rage. 'Sorry, Ginny, London say we have a technical problem with our feed. Got to send the piece again.'

Ginny looked at her watch, aware that James was playing for time, but unwilling to jeopardise the delicate picture access agreement between INN and Andromeda by causing trouble until it was absolutely necessary. There was nothing he could do to update his piece at this stage, anyway.

Christie met her Producer's eyes significantly. 'We've got nineteen minutes left until the bird goes down, and since this is a bi-lateral, fifteen minutes of that time is INN's,' Christie said quietly. 'We'll have to let him have his four minutes. But only four. We've only got one shot at our piece as it is, so we'll have to pray we don't take a hit.'

Ginny told Sam what was happening as James started retransmitting his story, and the Foreign Editor groaned down the telephone line. 'Watch him, he's a bastard,' he said grimly. 'Your piece is more than eleven minutes long, and we only managed to get the first three minutes in just now before you cut the connection. If you don't make the first pass, we lose it. It's going to be a tight turnaround to lead the bulletin as it is.'

Christie watched as James's package played out, sighing with relief as it ended with his lengthy piece to camera. Fourteen minutes to go. That should give Sam just over two minutes to get the tape rewound and ready to play at the top of the hour into the Early Evening News.

'I'm sorry, Miss Bradley, but London say I still have some kind of technical glitch with my piece,' James said smoothly. 'We seem to have a problem with the sub-

410

carrier. I'm afraid we'll have to use the rest of the bird ourselves.'

Christie stood up and moved towards the Andromeda correspondent, her green eyes glinting fire. 'This is a bi-lateral, James. You don't have a choice. You've already used two minutes of INN time.'

James barred her way, his arms folded across his chest. 'I'm sorry, my dear, but Andromeda booked the satellite, and Andromeda will need to use it. *All* of it. In other circumstances . . . if we didn't have any problems . . .'

'You made an agreement with INN to go bi-lateral,' Christie said, dangerously quiet. 'You cannot renege on that now.'

'I'm sorry, girls, but I don't remember signing anything. We won't be charging you for half of the satellite cost, if that's the problem. Now if you'll excuse me . . .'

James turned back towards the feedpoint, watching as his editor rewound the tape and started another pass. Christie glanced at her watch. Eleven minutes left. They could just do it; she would have to transmit the last eight-and-a-half minutes of her piece, and let London lace it together with the three minutes she had already managed to send. Ginny put the telephone receiver on the table in the hallway and strode over to Andromeda's Editor.

'I've spoken to Sam at INN, and he says he's seen your piece as it was routed to Andromeda,' Ginny said firmly. 'It's as clear as a bell, no problems. Give me a break and let's get on with this like professionals.'

James grinned malevolently. 'Sorry, darling, no can do.'

Christie suddenly dived towards the machine and pressed the emerald green eject button. The Andromeda tape slid quietly out of the machine before their Editor realised what she had done.

411

'Put that back right now, you bitch!' James raged, springing across the feedroom and grasping Christie's hand.

Ginny slid under James's arm and replaced the Andromeda tape with Christie's piece, hitting the replay button as soon as the tape slid home. The livid correspondent threw Christie against the wall, screaming at his Editor.

'Get that fucking harpy away from that machine!' he yelled, oblivious to the incredulous stares from the other journalists.

The Editor backed away from the feedpoint, shrugging his shoulders diffidently. 'It's not my battle,' he said nervously, aware that this incident would have grim repercussions and unwilling to share the blame with the correspondent.

'Hey, Andromeda, you're out of order,' the CNN producer commented laconically from the other side of the room.

'He's out of order so often people think he's a public telephone box,' Ginny said, guarding the machine as the tape continued playing.

James suddenly advanced towards the diminutive Producer, wrenching her roughly away from the feedpoint before anyone could stop him. His hand rose to eject the INN tape. In one fluid movement, Christie crossed the room, slid between the correspondent and the machine, and drove her knee hard against his groin. With a stifled curse, James fell backwards towards the wall, his hands clasped against the injured area.

'I'll have you for that,' James gasped, his face florid with rage and pain. 'I'll sue you for assault . . . you'll never work again . . .'

Christie grinned as the last frames of her exclusive piece

412

rolled to an end. 'Please, do your worst,' she said, a gleam in her eye.

Ginny laughed. 'I don't know what she does to the enemy, but she sure as hell terrifies me.'

■ MUSWELL HILL, LONDON
25 AUGUST, 6.05 p.m.

'But if she *is* pregnant . . .' Brian Reynolds continued pettishly.

His wife rolled her eyes heavenwards. 'What is so wrong with that?' she asked, not unreasonably. 'It may have escaped your notice, but Tarquin and Ashley didn't appear from under the clematis one morning.'

'He's married. To another woman,' Brian said in shocked tones.

'So you said,' Anne sighed. 'It's hardly unusual, if somewhat unfortunate. Marriage doesn't destroy your hormones, just your opportunities.'

Brian sat up against the pink velour headboard, firmly fastening the top button of his striped pyjama jacket which had inadvertently come undone. 'Charles Silversmith is one of our most respected members of staff,' he began pompously.

Anne eyed the self-righteous expression of her husband with annoyance. 'Certainly one of the most respected members, not to mention most widely sampled,' she observed, not inaccurately.

Brian frowned at the *double entendre*, then opted to ignore it. 'Well, I'm sorry, but I cannot have these kinds of goings on in my office,' he said, pushing his spectacles further up the bridge of his nose. 'It's bad for team spirit, not to mention bringing the company into disrepute if the Press get to hear about it. You'd think these sorts of women would take more care about such things. She has been utterly irresponsible. No, the Templeton girl will simply have to go. I can't put Charles into the undignified position of facing her across the tea-trolley every morning, her condition brazenly displayed for all to see. It wouldn't be fair to him.'

Anne's gaze wandered towards the flickering television screen in the corner of the bedroom, where the muted voice of INN linked the viewers of Ben Wordsworth's global village. 'It's reassuring that you're so thoughtful about your staff's welfare.'

'I like to think we're just one big family, when it comes down to it,' Brian said, without a trace of humour. 'I see my job as more than just the Head of the Department. I want my team to feel they can come to me if they have any problems, large or small. Of course, I won't be giving her any maternity pay. That would only encourage her.'

'Encourage her to do what?' Anne asked in surprise. 'How much more pregnant can she get?'

'It's the principle of it that's at stake here,' Brian replied. 'Not to mention the slur it casts on my Department. I can't have people taking advantage. You'd be surprised what some of them think they can get away with. Steve Bower, the editor who was shot in Kosovo, actually put in an expenses claim to replace the leather jacket he was wearing when he got hit. Of course, I couldn't allow that. They'll all be wearing Armani jackets next and expecting me to give them new ones on the Company when they're ruined.'

'I suppose he could have had the bullet holes repaired,' Anne commented dryly. 'Bloodstains might have been a bit more tricky.'

'There are some wonderful cleaning agents on the market now,' Brian said seriously. 'But these journalists seem to think I'm an open chequebook. We all have to

414

economise these days, you know.'

'I had noticed your company Mercedes hadn't been cleaned this week,' Anne said, straightfaced.

'I have to lead from the front, set an example,' Brian said, straightening the orange candlewick bedspread carefully. 'It's a hardship, I know, but we have to tighten our belts. It'll be once a fortnight from now on.'

Anne decided that her husband had been quite assertive enough for one evening. 'Brian, I think it is time we made love now,' she said firmly. 'Please turn out the light, and lower the television volume.'

'Yes, dear,' Brian said dutifully.

'I'd like a bit of cunnilingus first,' Anne said decisively, lifting the hem of her yellow Vyella nightgown.

Brian moved down the bed, his bald head gleaming in the neon light from the streetlamp outside.

'And Brian?'

'Yes dear?'

'I'd like to hear your appreciation, in the usual way,' Anne said.

Brian lifted the orange candlewick, wincing as he grazed his shin against the four-day-old stubble on his wife's legs.

'This is a great opportunity,' he said, his voice muffled. 'It is a chance to move forward, to enter the next phase with the slate wiped clean. But if we are going to succeed, we must be fully prepared.' He twisted his wife's nipples as if he were once more lowering the television volume. 'Inevitably there will have to be some sacrifices, but if we grasp our opportunities as they come, the situation can only improve.'

'Very nice,' Anne said, lying back against the pillows, still watching INN.

'Take a wide-shot, camera two,' Muriel called out.

Charles's head and shoulders gave way to a wide view of him sitting at the anchor desk next to a large monitor, in which Christie could be seen, the lights of Damascus clearly visible behind her.

'How seriously can we take this accusation against the UN?' Charles asked.

'Close up on camera three,' the Director barked.

Christie's face filled the screen. 'So far, we have had no official denial,' she said into the camera. 'I have spoken to one member of the UN team, but he declined to comment. Normally one would expect some sort of rebuttal, as in the past, but their silence over this accusation has been deafening.'

'Take "Live from Damascus" again,' Jerry called, as the caption appeared on the preview monitor. 'I know we're probably being over-optimistic in assuming our viewers can read, but it'll make Ben happy.'

The Producer sat back in his seat, as Christie continued her two-way with Charles. 'How long do we have on this?'

The PA glanced at her stopwatch. 'Another fifty seconds.'

Muriel leant forward and picked up the telephone on her right. 'Damascus, are you there?'

At the other end of the open line, Ginny heard the Director's voice crackling through the static. 'Hearing you,' she confirmed.

'Tell Christie to wind it up after this answer,' Muriel instructed. 'Then she has to throw to Victoria who'll do the interview with the Foreign Minister at Westminster; she knows that, does she?'

'She knows,' Ginny said, circling her arm widely so that Christie could see the signal, which told her she had thirty seconds left to complete her answer and handback to London.

'Westminster, are you ready?' Muriel asked through the intercom to the INN studio, which, like most of the British television networks, was based in the QE2 building adjacent to the House of Commons.

The Foreign Minister looked suitably blank, saying nothing.

'Dammit, the line's gone down to Westminster,' Jerry shouted, spinning his chair backwards and leaping to his feet. 'How come I can get a fucking live two-way from bloody Damascus, and we lose the line to a studio down the fucking road?'

■ MUSWELL HILL, LONDON

In their neat bedroom, the whip froze in Anne's hand as she gazed in fascinated astonishment towards the television screen. It had to be the most interesting statement the station had broadcast all year. Brian's head turned in horrified disbelief as Jerry's words reverberated around the world, relayed to the millions of viewers watching INN. He buried his face in his free hand as the furious Foreign Minister leaped to his feet, angrily storming out of the studio. His face eloquently bespoke the Governmental wrath which would fall upon the broadcasting fraternity quicker than you could say White Paper. Brian whimpered.

Whatever cruel sleight of hand had caused the gallery microphone to be open when Jerry had lost his temper, he knew that Ben would be after blood: and it would probably be his.

'Unrestricted access? What are they after?' Bob Carpenter asked, his voice distorted by the line from Beirut.

Ben Wordsworth leaned back in his leather chair, one hand idly yanking off the pink flowers on the plant struggling to survive next to him. 'We have a deal the Israelis want to cut,' he said easily. 'We give them pictures of Yorum Ben-Haim. In return, they give us this exclusive.'

'How the hell do we know Ben-Haim is even alive?' Bob asked. 'It's almost four years since he was kidnapped from southern Lebanon. We've no proof he hasn't just been executed; there's not been a single photograph of him since '89.'

'Which is why the Israelis are so keen to see something positive,' Ben replied. 'Our local Lebanese fixer, Hadawi, says he has seen a video of Ben-Haim holding a newspaper dated 17 July this year. He promises on his mother's grave that he can get a list of questions to those holding Ben-Haim, and that they will video Ben-Haim answering them. That piece of footage alone will make a world exclusive.'

'And the other half of the deal?'

'You'll be given unrestricted access by the Israelis to the El-Khiam prison in southern Lebanon. It's right in the middle of Israel's self-declared security zone; they've never even allowed the Red Cross to see inside it, let alone a television crew. You'll get full interviews with the Palestinians held there, uncensored filming, the works,' Ben said. 'The only proviso is that we hold the story until we have the Ben-Haim video in our sticky little hands, and the Israelis have seen it privately to make sure it is the right man.'

'So what do those holding Ben-Haim have to get out of

this?' Bob queried, shouting to make himself heard above the static.

'They get to see the issue of the Palestinian prisoners brought to the forefront of the world's attention – for all the good it will do them,' Ben said cynically. 'They're pissed off that everyone is creating such a song and dance about the Western hostages, and ignoring them, as usual. This way, they get a few headlines.'

'So we broker a deal, whereby the Israelis get to see Ben-Haim is alive, the Arabs get a bit of publicity for the Palestinians, and we get two thumping exclusives?'

'You got it.'

Bob gave a low whistle. 'You're stepping way beyond the mark on this one, you do know that, don't you?' he said carefully. 'It's not exactly uninvolved reporting.'

The Editor shrugged, raking his eyes across the bank of televisions at the end of his office. 'It gets ratings,' he answered curtly.

'It also puts INN right in the firing line,' Bob said edgily. 'We're setting up this whole deal. If it backfires, it could look very much like we're taking sides, which will put all your correspondents in danger.'

Ben grinned. That was the whole point. This aging roué was the man who had screwed his daughter. 'So be a little more careful,' he said calmly. 'If we pull this one off, it puts INN right back on the world centre stage. Including the reporter who breaks the story.'

The satellite telephone crackled with static. 'Oh yes, I meant to ask you,' Bob said with studied casualness. 'When are the RTS nominations?'

Easy. Hook, line and sinker. 'When we recommend our correspondents' stories to the RTS Board, you won't be forgotten,' Ben said smoothly. Idly he flicked the volume on the remote control as Christie appeared on the screen.

Jerry's unfortunate tirade of abuse echoed around the office.

Ben leaped out of his seat, thundering through his outer office where his secretary had taken refuge beneath her desk. He erupted into the newsroom. Jerry left his chief sub, Rochelle, to bring the Early Evening News to a subdued close, and bravely stuck his head above the parapet.

'My office! *Now!*' Ben roared, spinning on his heel and demolishing the scenic plants artfully arranged along the edge of the atrium with a malicious kick.

As the programme ended, Victoria unclipped her microphone and straightened her Jasper Conran suit.

'Poor Jerry. Shot down by friendly fire,' she commented as she left the studio to join the remainder of the team as they trooped up to the newsroom.

'There was nothing friendly about Ben just now,' Rochelle returned, wincing at the memory. 'More of a cluster bomb. Exploding in all directions, causing damage over a wide area, and regularly used to render all communication useless.'

Philip Cunningham was waiting in the newsroom as they emerged.

'This has to be the Stealth Editor,' Dom muttered. 'The nation's leading aircraft, coming out of its hangar only rarely and then to enormous public acclaim. Over recent weeks it has been covered with a special "Party Conference Organiser" coating, which has enabled it to evade newsroom radar.'

'I wanted to talk about the rosters for the Conservative Conference,' Philip began hesitantly, trailing after the journalists as they wandered back towards their desks.

Brian Reynolds hurried into the newsroom, his face scarlet with exertion. Fifteen minutes from Muswell Hill to Euston, door to door. The journalists melted away as

420

he dragged the bemused Foreign E[...]
pantry for an emergency discussion on [...]

'There go two men completely u[...]
Rich observed.

Rochelle sighed as she sat down at h[...]
the computer to see if Jerry's remarks we[...]
wires. They were. 'Oh great. The tabl[...]
field day with this one, particularly the [....] Calhoun's
been out to get INN for months now, God knows why.'

Charles paused by the desk long enough to appropriate
the newsroom copy of the *Daily Express*. 'I'm not surprised it was a disaster – from a Production point of view,
of course. Trying to do too much at once.'

'It shouldn't have been a problem,' Rochelle retorted in
Jerry's defence. 'Damn it, if we can manage Damascus we
should bloody well be able to get an interview from
Westminster.'

'The trouble with all this input is it's like having sex
without a contraceptive,' Rich mused. 'The newsdesk gets
it all in, but they take no responsibility for what happens
next.'

Victoria gave an exclamation, and held up an exquisite
carton containing a flask of Chanel No 5. 'I've been sent
some perfume by a lunatic with really good taste,' she
said.

'All I ever get are obscene letters demanding money
with menaces,' Ollie said mournfully. 'And that's just
from my wife's solicitors.'

Victoria dabbed a little of the Chanel on to her wrists,
and leant forward earnestly. 'I get some *unmentionable*
letters sometimes,' she said confidingly. '*Utterly* disgust-
ing.'

'You're not the only one,' Dom said. 'Only in my case,
it's my contract of employment.'

'It's too bloody easy for you women,' Ollie said

421

you have to do is look attractive, slap on ... ck, grope the Editor and there you are.'

... asy for you. You'll never be mistaken for just a ... ty face,' Victoria said indignantly. 'It's so difficult to be ...ken seriously. And it takes a lot longer for a man to reach his sell-by date than a woman. Not that I'm anywhere near mine,' she added hastily. 'But a man can go on air with bags under his eyes, grey hair and two double chins and everyone just says he looks distinguished. You don't know how lucky you are, being a man.'

'You don't know what I had to do to get this job,' Ollie retorted.

Victoria was not to be deflected. 'And who is it who has to go through the agonies of having children? My child-birth was so terrible, I wouldn't have cared if three rugby teams were present.'

'I suppose it would make sense for the birth to be the same as the conception,' Ollie said, running for cover.

Sam sidestepped neatly around the fleeing News Editor and leaned casually against the side of the Early Evening News desk.

'Jerry still being spit-roasted?' he inquired.

Rochelle grimaced. 'How bad is it?' she asked.

'There's only one thing worse than being talked about – and that's not being talked about,' Sam grinned. 'The papers will be full of it tomorrow, which is a tad troublesome as there's a Board meeting next week. Ben's going to have a hard time.'

The assembled journalists did not look too dismal at the prospect. Rochelle ran her eyes down the Foreign futures list as Sam handed them around the desk. 'Christie's managed to get on the plane back to Paris with Guillot?' she said in surprise.

'I'm amazed they've let her on the flight, after that piece she just transmitted.'

422

'Guillot insisted she travel with him, apparently,' Sam shrugged. 'She'll bring anything she shoots straight back to London to edit. Should have it for the evening slot tomorrow.'

'Is it wise, keeping Bob in Lebanon so long?' Rich asked. 'He's not my favourite person, admittedly, but it seems a little risky, given the threats there have already been.'

'Ben's decision. Our's is not to reason why.'

'Surely David would be a better choice?' Rochelle asked. 'He does know the streets better, and he's far more likely to score an exclusive than anyone else.'

'He's back in Rome, working on a half-hour documentary Ben wants to run on the new face of Eastern Europe,' Sam answered, turning as Janey approached them, a large brown envelope clutched in her hands.

'When did you say Christie was back?' Janey asked, tossing her long chestnut hair out of her eyes, and regarding Sam solemnly through her – unnecessary – owlish glasses, adopted to counteract the effect of her voluptuous figure.

'Should be back tomorrow sometime. Why?'

'Well, it's this letter,' Janey said, waving the envelope. 'It's marked extremely urgent, and it's been sitting on my desk for days. I was a bit concerned in case it's important.'

'Where's it from?' Sam asked.

'Post-marked Israel. Doesn't say who sent it.'

'I'll give it to her when I see her,' Sam said, taking the envelope and slipping it beneath his clipboard. 'I wouldn't worry about it. I'm sure it's nothing important.'

Chapter Fifteen

■ ROME, ITALY
14 SEPTEMBER, 5.20 p.m.

David drew a deep breath as he unlocked the front door, pushing it open with his left shoulder as he hauled his suitcase into the hall with him and shut the door with a deft kick. The marble floor echoed his footsteps as he wandered past the sweeping staircase into the empty reception room beyond it, pausing once or twice to caress a favoured object. Mellow evening sunshine flooded through the tall unshuttered reception windows to his left, motes of dust dancing in the warm light, enhancing the rich blue and crimson tones of the Persian carpets which were scattered throughout the villa. David crossed through into the darkened sitting room and unlatched the French windows which looked out across the valley, standing back as they swung inwards. He stepped forward and threw open the creaking ivy-green shutters, breathing deeply as the mingled scent of mint and bougainvillaea rose on the cool breeze. In the distance he could see the spent vines that rippled across the Italian hills, and the dusty ribbons of cart tracks winding lazily through the groves. The air carried the fresh tang of approaching autumn, the trees already beginning to turn gold and russet and ochre.

David watched the last rays of sunshine dipping behind

the hills as the dusk deepened. He almost fell as his foot tangled with something concealed in the shadows, and cursing, he dropped to his knee and picked it up. His frown became a smile as he turned Sandy Kelly's wooden tricycle over in his hand. Sandy could barely walk, but still insisted on careering around the vast rooms of the villa on his tricycle, often abandoning it where he tumbled. David gazed at the gaudy red and yellow toy, a sudden image of the child filling his mind, and the colours blurred as tears filled his eyes. His heart clenched at the thought of losing the boy when Caryn eventually resumed her own life, and angrily he shoved the tricycle away from him towards the wall, where it crashed and fell on its side.

Abruptly, the emptiness of the villa seemed oppressive, and suddenly David longed for Sandy's laughter to fill the rooms and bring them to life, to give his own arid existence some measure of meaning once again. A fresh wave of anger passed over him. Caryn had left a brusque message with the Foreign Desk informing him that she was spending a month with her parents in England, and had taken Sandy with her; she hadn't even bothered to telephone him personally and advise him of her plans. He was deeply relieved that he did not have to face her just yet; but he ached to hold Sandy, to feel the wriggling impatient little body hard against his chest, see the unquestioning love in the child's eyes. He could not have loved Sandy more if the boy had been his own son. Guilt flooded through him as he thought of the pain he would bring to the child's life by walking out of it. He sank down on to the sofa and buried his head in his hands. Sandy had already lost one father, thanks to him. Now he was about to lose another.

In the days and weeks that had followed Christie's anguished decision to leave him, David had spent hours beyond count agonising over his decision to separate his life from that of Caryn and her son. In the end, it had been the memory of Sandy's misery when he confronted his mother and David during one of their endless rows which had finally decided him that, with or without Christie, he had to build a new life alone. He had lived in the past long enough.

But now that it came to it, he did not know if he had the strength.

Slowly, David rose and wandered through the desolate villa which had always seemed to him to be more of a mausoleum than a home. He sighed despairingly. He had believed that he owed Caryn a life, and for a time he had given her his. But it had not been enough. He had tried to fulfil her every material need, striven to live with his mistake and to replace what he knew in his heart was irreplaceable; all had been futile. The guilt of his failure was overpowering. He did not know if he could live with himself after what he was about to do; he knew only that he could not live with his life the way it was, whatever the cost.

His bedroom was shuttered and dark, and David switched on the light, dragging his suitcase on to the vast expanse of his double bed and twisting the combination lock to open it. Thank God he had a month's leave. He would need it to sort out his life. He flung back the lid and began to unfold his clothes, crossing the soft carpet to open the door of his walk-in wardrobe. He paused as he replaced his flak jacket at the back of the cupboard, remembering Seb. How many times had he thought: if only his message to the cameraman had reached him in time; if only Seb had not followed him to the burnt-out church in Sarajevo. *Oh God, if only he could turn back the clock.*

He returned to the sitting room and selected a Bob

Dylan CD from his collection, inserting it into the sophisticated sound system and turning up the volume. The melancholy sounds of 'Lay Lady Lay' filled the echoing rooms as he walked distractedly into the dining room, opening the walnut drinks cabinet that had once belonged to his father. He poured himself a gin and tonic, then sank into the cream canvas hammock that he had slung between two of the cypresses that grew near the veranda. As he lay back and gazed at the moon, already hanging heavily in the darkening sky, the air was filled with the citrus fragrance of the lemon tree and the pungent scent of the bougainvillaea. Around him the sound of cicadas and grasshoppers competed with the evocative Dylan lyrics and thoughts of Christie filled his mind. Dylan was one of her favourite musicians; perhaps that was the unconscious reason behind his choice of music. David could almost feel and taste and touch her, her image was so strong. His body ached to hold her, to bury itself in her until everything else was forgotten.

He took a deep swallow of the gin and tonic, enjoying its bitter taste. He could see the silhouette of the villa to his right, its solidity an uncompromising reminder of the realities of his life. The enormity of what he was about to do engulfed him, and suddenly he was uncertain. He would be tearing apart not only his own life, but those of the child who had come to depend on him and the woman he had promised to protect for as long as she needed him.

David swirled the drink in his glass, gazing at it unseeingly. A year. That was all it had taken to come to this. Twelve short, interminably long months.

He knew that Christie was not the cause of his dissatisfaction with his life. Loving her had made him appreciate how pointless and empty his existence had been before he met her, but it did not explain why his life had become so futile. He thought back to the time before Seb's death. He had had girlfriends: attractive, intelligent women who had made every effort to understand both him and his job, women who were attentive and companionable. Yet he had always withheld the deepest part of himself from them, drawn back from any real commitment, moved on when the relationship became too important to him.

It had taken a year of living with Caryn Kelly to teach him the real meaning of loneliness. He had shared his life and his home with her yet they had never communicated on any level. There was something deeply buried at the root of their relationship, something that went beyond Sebastian's death. He had given up trying to understand what it was.

And then he had met Christie, and everything had changed.

A chill breeze scudded over the vineyards and raised the blond hairs on David's bare arms. He shivered and drained his drink, easing himself out of the hammock with unsteady legs. He felt a sudden longing to touch base with reality again, and making his way back into the villa, he glanced around for a picture of Sandy. Maybe it would give him the courage he needed to break free from the past. He would take it with him when he left the house. Caryn could stay here until she was ready to leave, of course. He owed her that much.

A rapid search of the bookcase revealed that Caryn had taken the photograph albums with her, presumably to show to her parents. He frowned in concentration; there were other pictures elsewhere, surely? He was certain there was one in a silver frame somewhere, taken on Sandy's first birthday a few months ago, a sleepy smile on his crumb-covered face as he regarded the camera with the confidence of a child who knows it is well-loved. David remembered that the maid had broken the glass in the frame when she was dusting Caryn's bedroom; he had a vague feeling that Caryn had thrust it in the bottom drawer of her chest-of-drawers. But the picture itself had been undamaged.

Still a little unsteady, David headed towards the staircase, flicking switches as he made his way towards her bedroom so that the marble floors and brilliant white walls reflected light around him. He gained the first floor and entered her room, crossing the carpet soundlessly and yanking open the bottom drawer of Caryn's bureau. His fingers slithered through the layers of black, red, cream, cherry camisoles and suspender belts. The tips of his fingers felt something cool and hard, and triumphantly he withdrew the silver frame, gazing at the happy face of the child for several moments.

If he left now, he would lose Sebastian's son, the only person he loved. And for what? He had failed to make *any* woman happy so far, and he did not know if he could change. What chance did he have of finding happiness? Perhaps he should stop looking for it. He should stay with Caryn and Sandy. At least with them he was needed.

As he turned to shut the drawer, David noticed a heap of envelopes that had been caught at the bottom with the photograph frame, and dragged to the lacy surface of the silky garments. He made to replace them, glancing with detached curiosity at the writing as he picked them up. He paused. All were addressed to Caryn, although not all in the same hand, and postmarked from as far apart as Kenya and New Zealand. He opened one that had no address on it, and stared in disbelief at the hundred-dollar bills that were heaped inside. There must be fifteen . . . maybe twenty thousand dollars. *Why?*

His hands shaking and his heart thudding in his chest, David opened another large, unmarked envelope. He stared at the contents in confusion. Seb's last effects. His keys, his goodluck charm, the silver identity bracelet he always wore.

And a crumpled note that bore David's own handwriting.

His world fell apart, as understanding dawned and suddenly everything made sense.

But it could never ease the pain.

■ ROME, ITALY
   9.10 p.m.

Caryn patted the skirt of her new three-thousand-dollar Yves St Laurent black cross-back dress with satisfaction. She enjoyed the sensuous feel of the clinging material against her skin, and for once she wore more than Shalimar beneath it. She shivered as she thought of the crimson silk panties and suspender belt she was wearing, and the memory of Edward's hands smoothing the soft silk on to her body. She sank back against the leather seat of the Mercedes which had collected her from the airport, savouring the recollections of the past ten days. She had never felt so sated, so utterly fulfilled. He played her body with an expertise approaching virtuosity, and she had responded like an innocent discovering the pleasures of the flesh for the first time. She respected and delighted in his skill all the more knowing how much it took to stimulate her jaded sexual palate. The attraction of his power and prestige which had initially caught her attention was fast being replaced by a far more personal desire. No, more than a desire. It had become a need.

Caryn reached for her Louis Vuitton clasp bag, and extracted her gold powder compact, peering critically at her face in the mirror. Her skin now possessed a unique glowing radiance that betrayed her satisfaction, and unusually Caryn forsook the heavy foundation she generally favoured, contenting herself with a swift brush of powder across her cheeks and forehead. The ice of her eyes had melted; instead, they glowed a brilliant, pale cerulean blue. The smudged grey shadows beneath them had faded, her tinted lashes curling back thickly against her eyes, and Caryn smiled at her reflection as she pencilled around her mouth, before applying her lipstick. Edward did not really like so much make-up, but she was sure they would come to some compromise . . . if their relationship was to continue . . .

With one hand, she teased her auburn hair into shape, twisting a stray lock into the formation curls under her chin. Absently she fiddled with the gold Chanel earrings he had given her only yesterday. Being the mistress of the distinguished and respected broadcaster Sir Edward Penhaligon definitely had its advantages, but Caryn possessed too much savvy not to know that all good things must come to an end. She would be very foolish to expect the arrangement to become anything permanent. At least, not without a good deal of Machiavellian planning. But then that was her field of expertise.

'*Per piacere?*' the driver asked impatiently as they reached a crossroads.

Caryn glanced through the window, wondering once again why the Italians seemed incapable of illuminating their streets.

'*Un attimo, per favore,*' she said, trying to orient herself. It was ridiculous: after all this time, she could not even find her own way home. In the front of the Mercedes, clasped in the arms of Isabella, Sandy murmured in his sleep, and Caryn favoured them both with a glare of annoyance. '*Vada sempre diritto,*' she said eventually, and the driver gunned the car across the junction. Caryn smiled ruefully. Her Italian might be limited, but at least she knew enough to get where she wanted. She had always known how to do that. After all, she had had enough practice.

As the Mercedes made its way along the twisting mountain roads that led to their villa nestled deep in the hills, Caryn felt a renewed surge of the fierce anger that had consumed her when she learned of David's love affair with Christie. Resolutely she forced it down, refusing to let her fury cloud her mind, a terrible desire for revenge burning deep into her soul. Her hand trembled on the arm rest, her nails embedding themselves in the beige leather, leaving half-moon imprints on the soft surface, as she fought to contain herself. Mingled with her passionate fury was an aching sense of loss, a searing jealousy that another woman had managed to gain David's love, which she knew he had never even thought to give *her*. It was not the fact that he had slept with someone else that caused her incandescent rage to become something deeper and colder and altogether more deadly – she knew, better than David could ever imagine, how irrelevant a good fuck was in the scheme of things – but what ate into her very soul was that he had given his *love* to another woman.

Angrily she thumped her fist against the seat. *Damn* him, she needed him still. She could not afford to let him walk out on her, whatever it took.

As the Mercedes approached the villa, Caryn was surprised to see the lights blazing in every room. So David had already returned. Alone. He had not gone to *her*. Now, she would be able to heap guilt upon him, lash and destroy him with her tongue knowing that he would not be able to retaliate. And when she had ensured that his – liaison – was utterly shredded, that he had nothing left to live for but Sebastian's son, she would take Sandy away from him too. He would pay for what he had done to her . . . how he would pay.

Caryn tapped the driver on the shoulder as they drew into the wide circle at the front of the villa. '*Per favore si fermi qui,*' she instructed curtly, opening the door the moment the Mercedes drew to a halt. She indicated the four Vuitton suitcases crushed into the boot. '*Puo aiutarmi a portare le mie borse?*'

The driver shrugged and hauled the suitcases out of the boot, as Caryn walked towards the porticoed front door, her feet crunching on the gravel. Behind her Isabella climbed slowly out of the car, careful to ensure that the child was not disturbed in her arms as she manoeuvred her way around the luggage. The driver shut the boot with a thud, and turned expectantly towards Isabella.

'*Quanto?*'

The driver held up four grubby fingers, and Isabella extracted the requisite lire notes from her handbag, cradling Sandy in her free arm. Over her shoulder, Caryn nodded at the nanny to take the child straight upstairs to bed, and twisted the front doorknob. The door opened, and Caryn froze.

David stood in the hall, watching her with eyes devoid of expression. His arms were stiff by his sides, his body motionless. Caryn felt a whisper of fear stalk along her spine, as for the first time she realised how much wrath was waiting to be brought down upon her head.

'Aren't you going to ask me how my flight was?' she asked flippantly, disguising her fear.

'How was your flight?' David replied woodenly.

'Wonderful. Just wonderful.'

Unnoticed, Isabella scuttled in behind her and darted up the stairs with Sandy still in her arms. Caryn took a couple of steps into the hall, and made to put her Vuitton clasp bag on to an octagonal occasional table just inside the doorway.

'No.'

She looked up, startled by the venom and anger in the single syllable David had uttered. Slowly she straightened up, but did not move forward.

'No?' she asked, query mingled with apprehension.

Suddenly David covered the distance between them so fast that Caryn was unaware that he had even stirred until she felt his hand around her neck, his body propelling her backwards until the cold wall pressed against her back.

'David! You're hurting me!' she gurgled, her voice choked by his hand against her throat.

David stopped abruptly and let her go. He stepped backwards, gazing with repugnance at his hands. 'My God. I could kill you.'

Caryn rubbed her bruised throat with her hands, staring at him. 'David! What's going on?'

'Don't pretend you don't know,' David said coldly. 'Don't lie to me any more.'

Caryn looked dazed. 'I don't know what you mean. David . . .'

'It seems there's a lot I didn't know about you, Caryn,' he said. 'All this time I thought you were grieving for Seb, but you were playing games with me, weren't you? Like you played games with Seb.'

'I don't understand . . .' Caryn whispered, backing away from him.

'Oh, I think you do,' David said sharply. 'Did Seb know how many times you betrayed him? I hope not. I hope he never realised that Sandy wasn't even his child.'

'Why are you saying all this? What are you talking about?'

David ignored her. His arm drew an arc in the hall behind him. 'You liked all this, didn't you? You didn't want to lose it, and you saw me as your ticket for life. I was your blank cheque. I killed Seb, and so I owed it to you. Isn't that right?'

434

'No . . . you've got it all wrong . . .'

'Oh yes, I got it all wrong, but that was the whole idea, wasn't it? I thought I was responsible for Seb's death, and that was the way you wanted it.' He stepped closer to her. 'But it *wasn't* my fault. And you knew. You knew, all along, that Seb *did* get my message telling him not to come, and came to that church anyway. It was *his* choice, his fault. Not mine. You knew, and you didn't tell me.'

'No! I promise! I swear to you, I don't know what you're talking about! Please, David, you've got to believe me. I swear on Sandy's life . . .'

David stared at her, the loathing in his gaze almost tangible. Caryn flinched and turned away from him. He stood quietly as she started to sob, his eyes blank, his expression stony.

'Don't ever say that again,' he said quietly. 'Don't ever use that child's life to hide what you have done. How could you do this to me, Caryn? And why? Just tell me *why*.'

'I know why you're saying these crazy things,' she said desperately. 'It's your own guilt that's making you do this . . . it's nothing to do with me . . .'

'No, Caryn, that's where you're wrong. My guilt has everything to do with you. It's why I looked after you, why I stayed with you.' I did everything I could to make it up to you David said softly. 'But you didn't give a damn about Seb. Why did you do this to me, Caryn?'

'Because I loved you!' Caryn cried out, moving towards him. 'I've always loved you. But you never loved me back. You've given me everything except what I really wanted. *You*. Seb had more of you than I ever did.'

David stared at her in disbelief, then strode across the room, anxious to put some distance between them. He leant his head against the cool stone of the wall, listening to Sandy's distant cries as Isabella bathed him and put him to bed.

'How can you say you love me, after what you've put me through?' he said at length. 'You had the note that I sent Seb, the message that would have saved his life, if he'd listened to it. You knew I wasn't responsible for his death. And yet you let me think I was.'

'Can't you understand?' Caryn cried. 'I loved you! You would never have even given me a second thought if it wasn't for Seb's death. I had to do it! There was no other way!'

David whirled around. 'For Christ's sake, can't you stop lying for once?' he shouted. 'Can't you tell me the truth, now, when it's finally over? Or don't you know how to?'

'Over?' Caryn whispered, whitening. Until now, she had never really faced the thought that David might leave her to fend for herself. Suddenly she was terribly afraid.

'Don't tell me you really think all this can be forgiven and forgotten?' David laughed harshly. 'You do, don't you? You really think you can lie your way out of this one. No, it's over. This lie, this life, it's over.'

'But I haven't done anything!' Caryn cried, rushing to him and dragging on his arm.

'Haven't done anything?' David said incredulously, shaking her away from him. 'You cheated on Seb from the moment you married him; all those love letters hidden upstairs prove that. And who is Sandy's father? Kenny? Or don't you know?'

'They meant nothing!' Caryn screamed desperately. '*Nothing!* It was because I couldn't have you . . . because I loved you!'

'And then you let me believe that I had killed my best friend. How could you be so cruel? You let me believe that the fault was mine, you made my life a hell. I put up with it because I thought I deserved it. You call that nothing?'

Caryn sank to the floor, tears streaming down her cheeks, as David turned from her. 'I love you . . . I've always loved you,' she whispered brokenly. 'I thought you might love me, if I just waited long enough. If I was there, with you. Please . . .'

'Don't worry, I'll make sure you're well provided for,' David said, as if she had never spoken. 'You'll have money. That's all you've ever wanted anyway, isn't it? I'll even pay for your son.' He met her eyes steadily, not knowing and not caring if the misery he saw there was because she was losing him, or because she was afraid of living without his protection and position. 'I love him, and I won't see him suffer, whoever his father is.' He took a step up the stairs. 'I'd like you to leave. As soon as you can.'

'But where will I go?' Caryn pleaded. 'What will I do?'

David gestured to the heap of envelopes at the foot of the stairs. 'There's nearly twenty thousand dollars there,' he said, shrugging. 'I don't care where you go, just tell me where to send you a cheque for Sandy.'

Caryn silently retrieved the money, unable to stop herself from glancing inside the envelope to make sure it was all there.

'I suppose you're going to that woman,' she spat, her anger reasserting itself now that she knew there was no point fighting for him any longer.

'Yes, I will go to her,' David whispered, more to himself than to her. 'I just hope she'll have me.'

20 September, 3.30 p.m.

Christie leant back in the soft armchair, kicking off her shoes so that she could curl her legs up. Through the half-open window behind her she could hear the rough crashing of the waves on the Tel-Aviv beach. Awkwardly she held the telephone receiver beneath her chin so that she could riffle the pages of the document in her lap.

'She hasn't been wrong once so far, Ginny,' Christie said into the phone, pulling one closely-typed page from the others and holding it up before her. 'It all checks out. Everything.'

Ginny's voice was edged with concern. 'If Marina *is* right, what you're dealing with is too much for you to handle alone . . .'

'I know exactly what you're going to say,' Christie interrupted, with an exasperated smile. 'But there's no way I'm having you coming out to Israel to join me in your condition, so don't even ask. That child is going to be born with its passport in its hand as it is!'

'You're hopeless, I can't trust you an inch,' Ginny groaned in protest. 'You just dashed off the minute you opened that parcel without a word to anyone. Someone needs to be there with you, if only to talk some sense into you!'

Christie laughed ruefully. 'You're doing that fine from where you are!' Thoughtfully she scanned the lines of the document in her hand as she spoke. 'I'm sorry I didn't give you much warning, but I had to move quickly; this letter had been waiting days for me, and I didn't want the trail to go cold. And anyway, you'll be far more use to me on the Desk than dashing around the Occupied Territories out here with me.'

Christie sensed Ginny's momentary hesitation, and

438

pushed her advantage, astutely selecting the one argument that she knew would carry weight with her friend. 'And if you're right – if it is dangerous – I need to be able to react accordingly, not to be tied down worrying about you.'

On the other end of the line, Ginny smiled wryly in defeat. She knew exactly what Christie was doing, but unfortunately, ultimately she was right. Softly she reached down to cradle her stomach with her left hand, tenderly stroking the bump that was her child. She had already taken enough of a risk travelling halfway around the world to Damascus when Nick had been abducted; she could not chance her baby's life again.

There was an alternative. Ginny braced herself to say the words she knew Christie did not want to hear.

'Why don't you ask David?'

Ginny sensed the pain in her answer when she spoke. 'I can't.'

'Christie, whatever happened between you, you must see that this is too important to let it cloud your judgement,' Ginny urged. 'David knows that part of the world so well, he has the contacts, he has the experience. He's on leave in Rome for a month now, but I know he would want to help. Can't you let him?'

In her hotel room, Christie's eyes filled with tears, and angrily she brushed them away with one hand, letting the manila folder slip onto the floor. How many sleepless nights would she have to spend curled up in her empty bed, her arms wrapped around herself, crying his name aloud into the darkness before she could hear it spoken aloud without this agonizing pain knifing through her? How long would it take before she could even think of him without feeling that terrible aching yearning to have him hold her in his arms, crush her against his chest and banish her desperate loneliness forever? Was any principle

439

worth this much agony, this much misery?

Oh God, had she been right to leave him?

She could not – dared not – risk seeing him again, not when she was so consumed with doubts and racked with overwhelming need and longing for him. If he walked back into her life, she would run to him and never let him go.

Her whisper was barely audible through the static. 'No.'

Ginny sighed. Whatever inner battle Christie was fighting, she had to do it alone. 'Can't you at least let me tell the Desk where you are, what you're trying to do?'

Christie dragged her mind away from her own private hell by sheer strength of will, and forced herself to concentrate on the unfolding story she was beginning to piece together. 'Not just yet, Ginny. Give me a few more days. Hold them off with something, anything. I just need to get some more evidence, or at least a clearer idea of what we're dealing with, before I tell Ben. He's not going to like it as it is. If all of this is even half true – and I pray that it isn't – it will make Watergate look like a domestic tiff.' She sighed. 'Just reporting it will antagonise a lot of people: obviously the Israelis themselves, but particularly their supporters in the States. Ben gets a lot of his money and backing from them, and I will have to nail his foot to the floor with proof before he runs with the story.'

'Do you think he'll go with it?'

'In the end, if I give him enough evidence, yes, he'll have to. But it's not going to be easy.'

'What exactly do you think we've got here?' Ginny asked, her mind filled with foreboding.

'There's no doubt that Marina's right,' Christie said. 'The Palestinian birth-rate has collapsed, and there's no apparent political reason behind it. The Palestinians are still determined to win back their lands by sheer force of numbers. They intend to overwhelm the Israelis without ever needing to fire a shot; all they have to do is wait long enough. From what I can see, their resolve hasn't wavered. In fact, my feeling is that it's growing ever stronger.'

Ginny frowned. 'So in other words, whatever is causing this fall – financial persuasion, propaganda, coercion, whatever – has to be coming from outside the Palestinian community?'

'That seems logical.'

'The Israelis?'

Christie's voice was infinitely weary. 'It's possible, but I have an instinct that the Israeli authorities don't even know about the situation, far less what is causing it, or they would be much more unhappy about the questions I'm asking than they have been so far.'

'What do you think is causing it?'

'I wish I knew. I'm sure Marina had an idea, but she was too unsure to say anything. But I think . . .' Christie paused for a moment, and drew a deep breath. 'It must be physiological, something that's causing women – mainly young girls – not to conceive.'

'Christie . . . are you sure?'

'Oh God, no I'm not, not yet. There's a piece of the jigsaw missing, and I need to find it, and I just hope it proves I'm wrong. But Ginny, if I'm right, if that's what is happening . . . on this scale, it has to be deliberate.'

Ginny gasped. 'Deliberate?'

'Yes.' Christie's voice shook with suppressed anger. 'What we may be witnessing could ultimately destroy the Palestinian people.'

Ginny closed her eyes and groaned. 'Christie . . . that can't be . . .'

'I'm running out of options,' Christie replied despairingly. 'I keep trying not to see it, but I'm forced back every time. Ginny, I think that's why Marina was killed. She came too close to the truth, and she was eliminated before she could reveal it. What her murderers didn't count on was her sending me this file before she died.'

'But *how*? Who can be doing it, and without anybody knowing, not even the Palestinians themselves?'

'That's what I have to find out before I can go to Ben. And if he won't listen, I shall go beyond him, appeal to the Board if necessary.'

'Christie, I'm not happy about you staying there alone,' Ginny demurred. 'If you're right, and whoever is behind this *has* already murdered Marina, they aren't going to welcome you asking questions.'

'I've already thought of that, but I don't think they can afford to eliminate an INN correspondent so publicly,' Christie reasoned. 'They don't know who else is aware of all this. I think they're far more likely to try to cover their tracks, which is why I have to move fast.'

'How long do you intend to stay there?' Ginny asked.

'As long as it takes,' Christie said tiredly. 'I have a meeting with one of Marina's friends, a WRAPR official, in about half an hour; I have a hunch the trail is going to take me back out of here. When it does, I'll be with it.'

Christie's voice was heavy with sadness, and Ginny's heart reached out to her. 'It could be the work of a few fanatics, I suppose, but it could be more sinister than that. Oh, Ginny, the horror of it all.'

Ginny had never heard Christie sound so defeated, so hopeless. For the first time, she wondered if Christie had the strength to fight so many other people's battles when she was being sucked down by her own misery.

'Keep in touch, Christie, promise? Every day?'

'I promise. And Ginny?'

'Yes?'

'Thanks.'

442

Christie slowly replaced the receiver, standing up to ease her stiffness, and drew back the heavy pale-blue brocade curtains behind her to open the French windows that led on to her hotel balcony. As she stepped out, she drew a deep breath and leant wearily on the rail, breathing in the tang of the salt on the wind that whipped her strawberry hair free from the neat chignon on the nape of her neck. The sea was dark, crashing savagely against the rocks that formed breakers along the deserted Israeli coast. Grey clouds scudded across the sky, ripped by the fierce winds that crested the murky waves with white horses. Christie closed her eyes and bent her head. She burned to feel David's arms around her, for him to be there to help her through all of this.

She had never felt so alone in her life.

A sharp knock on the door drew her back to the present. She turned round and stepped through the French window, shutting out the sound of the angry sea behind her, and closing the manila folder, whose contents were spread out on her bed. She must shake off the despair that threatened to engulf her. She had a job to do – one upon which many lives could depend. Only when that was completed could she crawl home and let the pain within her take over.

She opened the door to a dark-haired Arab, his slender frame clad in a well-cut khaki suit, a heavy and expensive Breitling watch at his wrist and a worn leather briefcase under one arm. His expression was one of polite curiosity.

'Mrs Bradley?'

Christie smiled at her new matrimonial status, but did not attempt to disabuse her visitor of the notion, or to open the door further. 'How can I help you?'

'My name is Mohammed Ashref, of the World Relief Agency for Palestinian Refugees. We spoke on the telephone.'

443

'Mohammed, of course.' Christie extended her hand warmly, and her visitor shook it carefully. 'Please forgive me, do come in.'

Christie stood aside and the diminutive relief worker walked through into the room adjoining Christie's bedroom, which she had turned into a makeshift office.

'Coffee?'

'*Shukran*, that would be very pleasant.'

Christie dialled room service and requested two cups of fresh ground coffee. She replaced the receiver and sat down in an armchair opposite Mohammed, clearing a space for his briefcase on the crowded table between them.

'Mohammed, I am so sorry about Marina,' Christie said earnestly, leaning forward, her sea-green eyes bright with tears. 'She was a good friend of mine, although we haven't seen each other much recently, since she came back to Israel. We were at Oxford together. She was a wonderful person, very independent, but always there if you needed her. I shall miss her.'

Christie could see the emotion in the young Arab's eyes. 'I, too, will miss her, very much. She meant a great deal to me.'

A knock at the door signalled the arrival of their coffee, and Christie opened it to admit an Israeli waiter bearing a large silver tray. He glared contemptuously at the Arab seated near the window, but remained silent as he placed the tray on the table. Christie said nothing until he had gone, then handed one steaming cup to Mohammed and added an extra spoonful of sugar to her own.

'Mohammed, you said on the telephone yesterday that you had something important to tell me, but that you had to see me in person.'

The relief worker tasted his coffee and nodded. 'I could not tell you over the telephone. I did not even realise that

444

it was significant until you called me. I am still not sure . . . perhaps I am jumping to conclusions . . . but I will leave you to be the judge of that.' He paused, gazing at her intensely. 'Marina was very anxious that I did not tell anyone, but I think I have to trust you.' He was silent for a long moment. 'She said you were her friend. Anything I can do to catch Marina's killers, I will do.'

Christie frowned. 'You don't believe the official theory? That Palestinian terrorists murdered her for being a collaborator with the Israelis?'

Mohammed leaped from his seat, his dark eyes blazing fire. 'That is what they are saying? The Israelis! How dare they utter such things! After all she had done to help her people! She gave her life for them!'

Christie clasped the young Arab's shoulder with compassion. 'I don't believe it, either,' she said softly, as he sank back into his chair. 'I think Marina unknowingly became involved in something far more serious than she realised. I am beginning to understand what that was, but I need to know everything. And then to stop it.'

Mohammed's shoulders shook as he bent his head, dashing his hand across his eyes to hide his tears. 'I am sorry. I cannot bear to think of what they did to her.'

'I know.' She touched his arm gently. 'Mohammed, what was it that Marina told you?'

Mohammed shook his head dully. 'She did not say much. She just gave me this.' He held out a small bulky envelope, which Christie could see he had not opened. 'She said something about vitamins. A new drug, which Doctor Joseph was giving all the young girls at Dar el-Baran, a village in Gaza. Vitamins that also provide immunisation. And she told me to keep this envelope safe.'

'That's all?'

'She said nothing else.' He gazed up at her, his dark eyes

445

clouded with pain. 'Mrs Bradley, why did they kill her?'

Christie sighed deeply, and reached out to grasp the unhappy young Arab's hand. 'Mohammed, my friend, I don't know. I hope that this will tell me.'

After the relief worker had left, Christie opened the envelope and stared quietly at the small clear plastic packets of white powder. She knew instinctively that it was the piece of the jigsaw she had been looking for.

'I think it's time to bring in the experts,' she murmured to herself.

■ INN, LONDON
30 September, 7.20 p.m.

Sir Edward Penhaligon gazed for a long moment at the confidential memo that was lying on his desk. He steepled his fingers beneath his chin and leant back in his leather chair, his slim ankles encased in their supple handmade shoes crossed beneath his desk. This was a problem he would have to deal with immediately.

A shaft of mellow light glinted through the window, and reflectively Sir Edward studied the London skyline silhouetted against the deep red cast of the sunset. He had no idea how this girl had managed to find out as much as she had, but his most pressing concern now was damage limitation. Fortunately he was ideally placed to achieve it.

Sir Edward ran one slim finger down the close lines of type, searching for the relevant paragraph. Ben Wordsworth's memos, confidential or otherwise, had a habit of burying the important information in the midst of a great deal of chaff, a deliberate device calculated to pass the maximum number of motions through the Board meeting with the minimum amount of objection, predicated on the

446

accurate notion that most of the members would not possess sufficient interest – or wit – to persevere through the maze of utterly irrelevant detail. In this instance, however, this foible had served Sir Edward well, since what Ben considered mere camouflage provided Sir Edward – for once – with the one item of information he required.

Included on the grey memo, which bore the legend 'Printed on recycled paper, please recycle', were the detailed budgets of the several restaurants and shops in the News Mall, the schedule for the next series of Management Orientation Seminars (providing 'an overview of Company policies and procedures' which Sir Edward felt would be a revelation in itself), various proposals for amendments to Operation OpenEnder including the relegation of the President of the United States to Category Two and the Duchess of York to Obits.Gen., details of planned coverage of next week's Conservative Party Conference in Blackpool which Ben planned to oversee in person, draft copies of the new Fire Drill, and announcements of births (Stork Report), engagements (Getting Hitched) and marriages (Wedding Bells) – deaths and retirements having being thoughtfully omitted from the agenda so as not to lower morale or raise interesting questions concerning the operation of the Pension Fund, a subject on which Ben had been particularly sensitive since the Maxwell exposé. But what interested and perturbed Sir Edward was the Futures list of the reporters and crews who had been assigned to cover the various breaking of potential stories across the world.

'Peter Princer (corr), Steven Bower (ed), Andy Fairburn (cam/sound). Venezuela, follow-up to last week's attempted coup. Interview with Pres, army officials etc. Contact difficult, though they have the Inmarsat with them, 00837 1504726. Return tba, prob Monday.

447

David Cameron. On leave at home in Rome. Back on shift Tuesday 20 October.

Christie Bradley (no crew). Recce in Israel re follow-up to People Bomb series. Why is refugee population declining? Contact Sheraton Hotel Tel Aviv, 010 9723 5286222, room 313. Returns Heathrow, Friday 17.40, El Al 102.'

Sir Edward had been unhappy about authorising the death of the WRAPR girl in the first place. The confident reports of their agents in the field that the Operation had not raised any suspicions amongst the refugee community had not allayed Sir Edward's private fears that something was wrong. It had been too smooth, too easy, and his journalistic hackles had risen with the instinct that had guided him to the top of his profession. He had been as concerned as the others when the girl started asking questions about Dar el–Baran, but not particularly surprised. At least then he had known from whence the danger threatened, and at that stage, the situation had been manageable. But the others had panicked, and opted for a more permanent solution, one to which he was reluctantly forced to accede in the face of their determined pressure. He had still maintained that some subtle disinformation would have been far more effective, and a great deal less public. But had he known then that the girl was a friend of one of INN's most persistent and astute reporters, he would never have countenanced their solution.

The intercom on his desk buzzed.

'Sir Edward?'

Sir Edward pressed the talkback impatiently, tossing the memo on to the desk as he straightened up and drew his gaze back from the Hockney print on the wall. 'Yes?'

'Mrs Kelly is here to see you, sir.'

Sir Edward muttered under his breath. 'Indeed? Prescient woman.' He thought for a moment, then pressed the intercom. 'Five minutes.'

He stood up and moved to the window, staring expressionlessly down at the rain-slicked street below. Neon lights glowed hazily in the smeared darkness, and he could hear the swish of the traffic cutting through puddles at the side of the uneven road. The windows of Aristotle's wine bar on the opposite side of the street were already steamed up by the press of people inside. In the distance, the silhouette of London was now studded with white, yellow, orange lights, streaked like meteors through the blurred, rain-lashed window. The Bradley girl problem made it imperative that his more far-reaching plans be executed without delay. He turned his back on the window, his mind slicing through the facts and sifting his options. He had to be in an invulnerable position, able to move quickly, efficiently and – most importantly – undetected. Control of INN had always been desirable. Now it was essential.

Sir Edward had not wanted to tighten the noose about Dalmeny de Burgh's neck. The Minister for Energy was a useful friend to have, and Sir Edward had hoped that their sympathetic views would ultimately lead to a quiet exchange profitable to them both. Indeed, given sufficient time and patience, Sir Edward had no doubt that Dalmeny would have eventually succumbed to the substantial financial lure he was offering, and a gentlemen's handshake would have been all that was necessary to render Sir Edward's position a good deal more secure. Now, however, he could no longer afford to be lenient. The Bradley girl was denying him that valuable commodity, time. And Dalmeny was proving somewhat reluctant to sell his INN stock. Sir Edward was thrust into the distasteful position of persuading Dalmeny somewhat more forcefully than hitherto that he needed Sir Edward's friendship rather more than he needed the ten percent in question.

Christie Bradley he would deal with later. It would

require nothing as dramatic as the unhappy solution to the problem posed by the WRAPR girl. But it would be necessary to end her career. *Irrevocably*. A shame, but these things happened. She would be a casualty of war. Not that she would ever know it.

The door opened, and he looked up as Caryn entered hesitantly, her Versace silk shirt glowing, her make-up just a touch too obvious. Sir Edward smiled. Her unexpected arrival was fortuitous, given the circumstances. She would be perfect. And he had no doubt that she would enjoy carrying out her instructions to the letter.

'Caryn, darling,' he said smoothly, as she wafted over to him on a cloud of Shalimar and kissed him on the cheek. He took her hands in his, kissing the top of her head with gallant courtesy. 'I wasn't expecting you until next weekend.'

'Edward, I *have* missed you,' Caryn cooed, withdrawing from his cool embrace and perching herself on the edge of his desk provocatively. 'Darling, there's something I have to tell you, and it simply couldn't wait. I hope you're not going to be angry.'

'My dear. With you?' Sir Edward said, with a dismissive wave of his hand. He moved towards her, gazing into her eyes with an intensity that she found faintly disturbing. 'But I have something to tell you which I think will prove to be a little more important.'

Sir Edward watched as Caryn tried unsuccessfully to fathom the unreadable expression in his eyes. He knew her intimately, understood her every emotion, every thought that passed through her head. She played her games, and he played them with her, always waiting for her just a few steps ahead. He knew what she wanted, and he would give it to her. But the price would be high. He knew that she suspected what he was, that she sensed he would be a difficult man to outmanoeuvre, and a lethal

450

man to cross. But he was also aware that she found the danger of it exciting; even now, her pupils were dilated with desire as she tried to decide which strategy she would use to persuade him that she had left David's protection for him, even whilst she dreaded telling him for fear of what he would do. Sir Edward knew that Caryn was in love with David Cameron. But that didn't worry him. She needed him. He required her. They were perfectly matched.

Sir Edward smiled with the confidence of a man who knows he is going to win once more, and took her hands in his.

'Caryn darling, I want you to marry me,' Sir Edward said. 'No, don't say anything just yet. I'm afraid there *are* one or two conditions.'

Chapter Sixteen

■ LANGAN'S BRASSERIE, LONDON
7 OCTOBER, 1.20 p.m.

Morgan de Burgh leaned across the starched white linen tablecloth and reached for another breadstick from the basket in the centre of the table.

'I can't help it, I find these irresistible,' she said, snapping the thin stick between her fingers. A solitary ring with an emerald the size of her thumbnail glittered on her left hand.

Victoria smiled in return. 'It's the little things in life that are so addictive,' she said sympathetically, sipping her Perrier slowly.

'Like men,' Morgan replied acidly.

Victoria laughed nervously, uncertain how to respond to Morgan's directness and the feral light burning in her strange silver eyes. She already found Morgan de Burgh fascinating, exciting, and amusing, but she was distinctly unsure of her ground. She was terrified of appearing provincial or Non-U or – worse still – *dull* to this unpredictable and unconventional woman.

Lunches in Victoria's diary were neatly bracketed according to type: power lunches, invariably with men, at which you flirted and teased and played games and signed contracts; girlie lunches, full of gossip and confidences and envious glances at each other's latest designer outfits; and, very occasionally, intense Affair-by-Lunches, conducted with plenty of smouldering eye-contact and carefully accidental brushing of hands across the tablecloth. Lunch with Morgan de Burgh looked like it was going to be all three. Victoria sighed enviously. It was easy to flout the rules when you were rich, well-born and married to power. When you were part of the world that made those rules.

'Would madam care to order?' the waiter said, addressing himself to Morgan.

'I'll have the spinach soufflé, then the chef's salad, but no dressing, with extra radicchio and capers,' Morgan ordered crisply.

Victoria hesitated, her eyes flickering distractedly across the menu, longing for just a little of the other woman's self-assurance and poise as she tried to make a decision. If she followed suit she might look unimaginative and – *horrors* – naive, but if she opted to follow her own initiative, she might select the 'wrong' choice. She was acutely conscious of the myriad intricate rules governing what one might order for any given social situation, although she had a strong idea that Morgan would ignore them all. Victoria did not dare. Was this a light luncheon between acquaintances, or a lengthier business lunch? Had Morgan ordered a salad because she was dieting, or because she had another engagement to which she was hastening? If she chose Perrier again she might appear naive and too conscious of appearances, but dare she order wine alone if Morgan wasn't drinking?

The waiter glanced across at her, masking his impatience when he recognised her face. He groped for a name whilst his face remained expressionless and his attitude politely attentive. Television, not film, obviously, or he'd have no trouble identifying her. Not enough glamour for an actress, and her couture outfit, whilst expensive, was

453

not sufficiently haute to bracket her within the exclusive circle of the Women Who Lunch. After a moment he gave a mental shrug, unable to place her, and quickly relegated her to the restaurant's unofficial 'C' list. Famous enough to get a table at Langan's on a weekday, possibly even downstairs. Friday and Saturday evening? Forget it. Exile to the upper floor where the soufflé was never served. But she was with Lady de Burgh, so she obviously had a few of the right connections. His smile became a touch more deferential. Lady de Burgh was 'A' list, along with the likes of Soraya Khashoggi, the Duchess of Westminster and Elizabeth Taylor. The rules were simple: you had to have money or breeding, and preferably both.

Morgan sensed Victoria's indecision, and lifted one elegant eyebrow. 'I do recommend the chef's salad,' she said casually, picking a piece of lint off the shoulder of her Jasper Conran jacket with a flick of her burgundy nails. 'It's always excellent, although they do tend to suffocate it rather with dressing. And a Puligny Montrachet, I think. Victoria?'

Victoria smiled thankfully, closing the menu and returning it to the waiter. 'I'll be guided by you,' she said, smoothing her hair carefully against the nape of her neck. She was glad she had selected the Armani. Its understated elegance and sophistication always made her feel chic and well-dressed, particularly when she was insecure and on her guard. Restaurants like Langan's instantly chipped her painfully-acquired veneer of confidence and reduced her to the ingenuous schoolgirl she had once been; the child who had spent so many unhappy hours agonizing over why, despite her parents' vast newly-minted fortune, she remained outside the exclusive social circles that formed at her costly private school. But patiently she had watched and listened and learned, and now she wore their clothes, she had adopted their accent, she possessed the status

454

symbols that were a shorthand in their world – the original black Chanel handbag, the Vuitton luggage, the Hermès scarf. She skied at Klosters and lazed on the beaches of Eleuthera, she was invited to Henley and Ascot, Cannes and Cowes. She had become obsessed with such hallmarks of wealth and power. But underneath, she knew that no matter what she did, this world would never be truly hers.

Victoria glanced across at Morgan, who was raking the crowded restaurant with her arresting tip-tilted pale-grey eyes, searching for acquaintances, her shingled white-blonde head tilted confidently towards the room. Victoria sighed again. Morgan epitomised all that she longed for and wanted to be. When Morgan ordered a meal, there was none of the apology and petition for approval in her voice that Victoria could not exclude from her own. How ever much she wanted to deny it, the truth was inescapable. Breeding. Class. Like style, it could never be acquired by those who were born without it; that innate arrogance and sense of belonging, automatically sensed by those who catered to the every whim of those with good blood and old money and endless power.

Victoria bit her lip in frustration. It was the same when she visited Michaeljohn, the exclusive West End hairdressing salon patronised by members of the Royal family and the more chic celebrities. However much she was paying for a service, she always felt that whilst they accepted her money graciously, as those bestowing a favour upon which a price could never be set, they would never seek her patronage as they did that of their more distinguished and well-connected customers, however hard she tried to lure them. Victoria dressed more carefully for a session of lowlights with Joanne and a cut with Kevin than she did to meet Audrey Hepburn and Anthony Hopkins at the BAFTA awards.

Morgan turned to face her, and met Victoria's cool blue eyes with her own startling silver ones, her long lashes and dark eyebrows a striking contrast to the platinum whiteness of her cropped hair. 'Nobody here I know, so we won't be disturbed, which is just as well. I want to talk to you.'

Victoria laughed self-deprecatingly, fiddling nervously with the clasp of her discreet Cartier bracelet. 'Sweet of you, Morgan, although I'm sure it's not true.'

'Why?'

Victoria looked startled. 'Why what?'

'Why should I not want to talk to you?'

Victoria was unnerved by the way Morgan had sliced through the polite conventions that habitually governed such social lunches, gazing into her face with an intensity that seemed . . . almost . . . well, *interested*.

'I think there's more to you than hairspray and designer clothes. I want to know what it is,' Morgan said.

'I'm not sure what to say . . .'

'Yes you are. You're just too afraid to say it.'

Victoria sat stunned into silence, not knowing whether to be insulted, flattered or amused. She toyed with her silver cutlery, relieved for the distraction that the waiter provided as he placed their soufflé on the table. He poured a little of the Puligny Montrachet into a thin-stemmed glass on Morgan's left, and waited for her to try it. She waved her hand at him dismissively, and he quietly filled her glass and that of Victoria, before melting into the shadows.

Victoria regarded the other woman thoughtfully as she spooned the soufflé, slotting the few facts she already knew about this unusual and magnetic woman into place with what she was experiencing now. Thirty-something, undoubtedly striking but not classically beautiful, Morgan de Burgh was married to one of the most attractive – and

456

certainly one of the most wealthy – Conservative Ministers in Major's Cabinet, although coming from one of England's most distinguished old families, she was extremely rich in her own right. Along with *Tatler*'s other readers, Victoria knew that Morgan gave parties that Dempster would kill to be admitted to, moved freely in European Royal circles, dismissed the most established Hollywood celebrities as tacky non-entities, and had never watched a television programme in her life, even though her husband owned a tenth of INN. She was renowned for her idiosyncrasies, particularly in the eccentric way in which she dressed; her boyish figure suited the nineteen-twenties mens' suits she favoured, and her trademark long, slim amber cigarette-holder drew the eye to her elegant, tapering hands.

But what *Tatler* had not revealed to Victoria was this woman's hypnotic, mesmerising qualities. At this moment, she resembled a shadowy, silver-grey cat, waiting to pounce, and Victoria decided that she did not intend to play the mouse. Hairspray and designer clothes indeed.

'Morgan, it's sweet of you to invite me to lunch like this, but I can't help wondering . . .'

'Why?'

Annoyed at being once again anticipated so accurately, Victoria shrugged. 'If you like, yes.'

Morgan laughed, tilting her head backwards to expose her blue-veined milky-white throat, and Victoria felt a rush of nameless excitement. Morgan was completely female yet curiously sexless, a dangerous, exhilarating, terrifying creature, outside the bounds of everything that Victoria had ever known. She felt an urge to flee the table before she was drawn into that translucent grey gaze, but at the same time she could not move away.

Victoria watched with fascination as Morgan bit into a piece of crisp celery with sharp white teeth and slipped it

457

between her lips, tapping the remainder absently against her pale cheek. Unexpectedly, Victoria felt a sudden flood of arousal between her legs and her nipples hardened automatically against the soft silk of her blouse in response to the latent sensuality of Morgan's gesture. Utterly horrified, she lowered her gaze as she blushed with shame. She had never felt such a magnetic pull of intimacy towards anyone, much less another woman – and one she had barely met – and the arousal appalled and shocked her. Victoria crossed her ankles firmly beneath the heavy linen cloth and thrust unbidden images from her mind. Perhaps she was being over-sensitive, letting her middle-class prurient imagination run away with her, reading a hidden message where none had been intended. Then she eyed the secretive smile around the other woman's wide mouth, and did not know what to think.

Morgan's direct gaze did not leave Victoria's face as she picked up her glass and sipped the pale wine appreciatively; her manner slid effortlessly from the sensual, pagan creature of a moment ago to polite social hostess, so that Victoria wondered again if she had imagined everything.

'I should warn you. Macbeth is in your midst,' Morgan said cryptically, watching for Victoria's response over the rim of the glass.

Victoria did not give her the satisfaction of a reaction and silently Morgan awarded her the point. 'Penhaligon. He is plotting,' Morgan added, smiling dryly. 'With or without a cauldron.'

This time Victoria responded, cutting through the myriad layers of subterfuge and discretion that Morgan was weaving before she became entangled. 'Plotting *what*, exactly?'

'Ah, I was rather hoping you could tell me that.'

'What makes you think he is plotting anything?' Victoria asked curiously.

'He wants Dalmeny to sell his shares in INN to him,' Morgan said succinctly. 'I suspect Dalmeny isn't the only person he has asked, since he needs more shares than that to take control.'

'You think that's what he wants to do?'

'Don't you?' Morgan countered. 'I am quite certain he means to wrest control of INN from that charming man, Ben Wordsworth, but the question is: Why? What is he going to do with the company? Frankly, my dearest Victoria, the answer to that question fascinates me.'

And you're not the only one, Victoria thought cynically. I'm the one whose job is on the line. 'Will Dalmeny sell?' she asked.

'Not until I know why Penhaligon is aiming to take control, and who else has agreed to sell to him. It might be more interesting to see who else enters the market, don't you think?'

'And Dalmeny agrees?'

'But of course. I've let him think it's his own strategy. I always finds that works best.' She licked her scarlet lips. 'Although if I can do it, so can another woman. Luckily, so far I've been better at it than any of those who've tried.'

'Don't you mind?' Victoria said, astonished at her frankness.

'Not while he's so easy to lead, darling, why should I mind? He's a sweet boy, but frankly I don't care two figs where he chooses to spend his nights of passion. Or afternoons, for that matter.'

Victoria barely noticed the waiter as he whipped away their dishes and replaced them with the salad. 'But why do you tolerate it?' she asked, shocked by Morgan's acceptance of the situation. Fidelity was unimportant to her – after all, she did not practice it herself – but discretion was surely vital. Wasn't that what being Upper Class was all about?

'Why not?' Morgan answered, picking up her fork. 'Darling, you really should try the radicchio, it's delicious. Dalmeny doesn't bother me, and I don't bother him.'

'You mean he lets you . . .?'

Morgan's voice pealed with laughter at Victoria's obvious discomfort. 'He lets me have affairs? But of course. Why do you think I asked you to lunch?'

Victoria laughed uncertainly, and drained her wineglass without even noticing. She knew what was happening, although she could not quite confront it directly, not yet. But she wanted to be with this woman more urgently than she had ever wanted anything in her life, to inhale her, absorb her, *become* her. With Morgan, suddenly she felt real. Morgan challenged her, forcing her to question every aspect of her life; Morgan wanted substance not illusion, and she was unrelenting in her refusal to accept anything less. She was a siren lure that drew Victoria to her, fascinating her because in her Victoria was discovering her own self reflected, and it was a self that – for the first time – she was beginning to respect.

She was unaware of the small smile of satisfaction on Morgan's lips, or the intensity of the other woman's gaze as they completed their meal, lightly discussing the latest collections from Milan and Paris, and deploring the weather.

Morgan's driver was waiting at the door of her Bentley as they emerged into the watery October sunshine.

'You will join me for coffee?' Morgan said, the question robbed of any query by the cool authority in her voice. 'I do *so* want you to see my home.'

Victoria glanced down at her, realising for the first time how tiny Morgan was. 'I have to get to INN soon; I'll be anchoring the studio end of the Conference this evening,' she said reluctantly, torn. Few people were actually permitted into the de Burgh's inner sanctum

Morgan smiled knowingly. The first step was always the hardest, but that was why she was here: to make it easy. Theatrically she rolled her eyes. 'That dratted Party Conference! Dalmeny talks of nothing else. I do get so frightfully bored with them. Do you have to go right now?'

'Not quite immediately . . . I could telephone Ben . . .'

'That's settled then,' Morgan said, ushering Victoria into the car before she could object further, and sliding in after her. 'Cuthie will take you to the very door and no one will know what you've been up to.'

Victoria sank into the soft leather upholstery with a delicious sense of playing hookey, and being old enough to get away with it. She used the car cellphone to tell Ben's secretary that she would be late, and as she replaced the telephone, vaguely she wondered what exactly it was she would be getting up to. Determinedly she dismissed all thought from her mind and closed her eyes, relishing the sense of anticipation that coursed through her veins. Her body was relaxed, fluid against the seat; the tension and apprehension that usually filled her every waking moment was absent for the first time since she was a tiny child. She knew Morgan saw the fine lines around her eyes, the silver threads mingling with the darkness of her hair, the tiny scars from the Brazilian cosmetic surgeon; that Morgan saw past the aristocratic pretensions Victoria cultivated, beyond the Armani suit, the Cartier bracelet, to the terrified bourgeois middle-class woman beyond; my God, Morgan probably even knew she was over forty. There was no point pretending otherwise or attempting to conceal those hated signs of her age, because Morgan knew it all – knew it, and did not care.

As the Bentley snarled to a halt in the traffic, Morgan winked at her, and Victoria stifled the urge to giggle.

461

Morgan drew her tongue lasciviously along her lips, straightening her face abruptly as Cuthie glanced in the rearview mirror, pouting wickedly when his eyes returned to the road. Victoria laughed aloud unselfconsciously, and Morgan clapped in approval.

'She's got it! By George, I think she's got it!'

Victoria blushed, but laughed again. She felt delicious and free, as if she had been released from the murderous grip of an eighteenth-century corset. Suddenly she realised that she had been fighting all her life to be something that, ultimately, she did not really want, and suppressing a vital part of herself in the process. Why *shouldn't* she be attractive and intelligent and – she screwed up her courage – over forty? Why on earth should she pander to Ben Wordsworth's perception of women as pretty faces, empty heads and open legs? She was a professional journalist, not a movie starlet, wasn't she? Instinctively she knew that this fascinating, dangerous woman would find Paragon's bee-stung pouting lips and voluptuous youthful body profoundly uninteresting, and she hugged the thought to herself with secret glee.

Beside her, Morgan permitted herself a small self-congratulatory smile as she regarded the newsanchor, whose exultation was a tangible presence in the luxurious car. Deliberately she allowed herself to become caught up in Victoria's childlike anticipation of nameless adult wickednesses, neither of them uttering a word as the Bentley eased its way through the London traffic towards her home. Even Morgan – experienced as she was in matters such as these – had had no idea that this electricity would spark between them, drawing them irresistibly together, or that Victoria would possess such spirit. She had given the newsanchor a glimpse of a world in which all the Rules were made to be broken, and the intelligent, freethinking, independent woman that Victoria had so long stifled beneath her designer clothes was suddenly making her presence felt. Morgan had no wish to break the spell.

Unexpectedly, she realised that her own mask of eccentricity was in reality highly conventional, that – unlike Victoria – she was risking nothing. Her power and money and status protected her against the dangers of the games she played. Suddenly she wanted to take the risk, embrace the danger.

Neither of them spoke as Cuthie drove the Bentley into the underground parking area of the Belgravia apartment block and left them at the concertina black-and-gilt wrought-iron door of the ancient lift, which creaked as it took them slowly upwards towards the fourth floor. Victoria barely noticed the exquisitely decorated apartment as Morgan drew her through the many rooms towards the bedroom. There would be plenty of time later to admire the wall lined with cream and blue striped silk, the sapphire-brocaded sofas, the rich Aubusson rugs carelessly thrown across the deep ivory carpet, the twisted wrought-iron art-deco lampstand, the Picasso sketches discreetly framed against the walls.

Morgan paused as they wordlessly crossed the threshold of the elegantly appointed master bedroom, her arm casually around the waist of the older woman. Victoria's eyes were drawn towards the vast four-poster double bed, its heavy crimson counterpane drawn back to expose rich cream Pratesi sheets. Scattered across them were a dozen long-stemmed magnolia roses, their heady perfume filling the room. Heavy floor-length wine-red velvet curtains concealed the window seats set into the wall opposite the door; facing the end of the carved wooden bed was a deep, recessed fireplace, a glowing smokeless coal fire burning in the grate. On either side of it were winged armchairs upholstered in crimson brocade to match the hangings of the four-poster bed, and on a tiny seventeenth-century carved table between them a bottle of champagne was cooling in a burnished silver ice-bucket. Next to it, a matching candelabra held six brightly burning candles, which, together with the fire, provided the only illumination. It was a room of seduction, and Victoria smiled.

'I'm not sure if I should be flattered that you went to so much trouble, or insulted that you were so sure of success,' she said ruefully.

Morgan closed the door and crossed the room swiftly, kicking off her exotic handmade Jimmy Choos and carelessly shrugging her fifteen-thousand-dollar gold-embroidered smoking jacket on to the floor. 'I will treat you better than you treat yourself,' Morgan replied, smiling enigmatically. 'And certainly better than any man has ever treated you. And in return – you will probably break my heart.'

Victoria watched without fear as Morgan undressed unhurriedly in front of the fire, shedding her black twill trousers and winged shirt on to the floor, until she stood clad only in scarlet La Perla lace panties. Slowly she removed them, so that she stood naked. Her small tip-tilted breasts needed no support, and Victoria drew in her breath at the sight of the slim figure in front of her. She was so tiny that her head barely reached Victoria's shoulder, the shadowy outline of her ribs just visible beneath her thrustingly confident breasts, above a waist so narrow a man could have held it in his grasp. Morgan's alabaster skin was gilded gold with the light of the fire and to Victoria she seemed suddenly classically flawless, like an ancient statue. Suddenly she realised why. Morgan's satiny mound was completely hairless, giving her an ethereal, unhuman appearance, as if she were carved from the whitest marble. Victoria's cunt spasmed in response, and she let out a small moan.

464

Slowly Morgan raised her arms in a wide embrace, and dreamily Victoria moved towards them, feeling as if she was suspended in a tank of warm water in which every movement was unhurried and delicious. Morgan's soft fingers undid the tiny silk buttons of her shirt, sliding down her chest to unfasten the waist of her Armani trousers. As she moved her deft hands down Victoria's slim legs, she rolled back her stockings, stroking the downy hairs of her thighs, and hooked her little fingers into the narrow satin band of Victoria's panties, drawing them downwards to join the pile of unconscionably expensive clothes scattered on the floor. Morgan buried her face in Victoria's bush, inhaling the sweet scent, her warm breath sending a pang of longing through the other woman. Victoria reached her own hands around her back and unhooked her bra, so that her soft breasts tumbled free. It was Morgan's turn to gasp as she saw the full ripeness of the figure before her, its tensile lines honed to perfection by hours of obsessive aerobics and the skill of the surgeon's knife.

'Never change,' she murmured as she rose, kissing Victoria's cheek with controlled passion. Mentally Victoria tore the surgeon's card into tiny pieces and consigned the loathed leotard to the incinerator.

They moved towards the bed, not touching, revelling in the complete sameness yet utter difference of their bodies. Morgan's skin was milky white against the sheets, Victoria's the peachy bronze of summer beaches and exclusive London beauty salons. The younger woman's body was boyish and slim-hipped, her pert breasts tipped with small, chocolate nipples that tilted upwards. Next to her Victoria felt indescribably sexy and curvaceous, her lush figure ripe and inviting, her pink cinnamon nipples erect with desire. The two heads – cropped platinum blonde and groomed dusky nutbrown – bent towards

465

each other, and their lips met. Their tongues touched and for a moment they did nothing but explore each other's taste and sense and feel.

Victoria felt desire flood through her as it had never done, a tingling that began between her legs and stirred an answering response in her breasts, developing into a burning need to possess and be possessed by the woman whose skin was fire against hers. Morgan's hands moved across the satiny surface of her body, stroking her thighs, her breasts, her stomach, brushing almost imperceptibly across her bush so that Victoria's engorged clitoris strained in response, craving for that fiery touch to return. She lay on her back as Morgan knelt astride her, and gasped as the other woman teased her taut nipples against Victoria's own. Morgan smiled, holding herself above Victoria on her forearms, tensing and relaxing her body so that her breasts ebbed and flowed against the other woman's nipples, the soft flesh pillowing together.

Slowly, tantalisingly, she bent and took Victoria's left breast in her mouth, her tongue teasing the stiffened pink tip as her hand worked expertly against Victoria's right breast. Arrows of fire sparked from her nipples at Morgan's touch, and she felt silver hooks of pleasure trailing outwards across the surface of her body as Morgan drew her nipples in and out, in and out of her moist, sweet mouth. Her cropped hair was soft and silky against Victoria's throat, and she bent to kiss it, twining her arms around the other woman's slim back, stroking her hands along the firm globes of Morgan's buttocks. The longing inside her to feel Morgan's touch . . . to have Morgan's smooth mound pressing hard against her own . . . to feel Morgan's erotic lips against her bush rose to an almost unbearable pitch, and instinctively Victoria's fingers reached past the cleft of Morgan's buttocks to find the other woman's hungry clitoris.

466

Morgan arched her back as Victoria's touch sent flames of desire flickering through her, her skin so sensitised that the least whisper was magnified a hundredfold and rippled outwards to encompass her whole body. Morgan had slept with so many men – and women – but had never experienced this intensity of feeling which went beyond passion, beyond lust, to pierce her protective barriers and reach the real woman beneath. Her right breast nudged questingly against Victoria's mouth, her hardened nipple darkly erect, and the other woman opened her lips unconsciously, drawing the taut, firm flesh between her lips, sucking hungrily, the palm of her hand rolling against the surface of Morgan's left breast. Morgan shuddered uncontrollably as Victoria's sharp white teeth bit down against her flesh, her tongue teasing the bud of her nipple with taunting strokes, flicking back and forth across the surface.

Victoria moaned with escalating passion as Morgan's smooth mound rubbed deliciously against the softness of her own, their juices flowing and mingling, their breasts grazing against each other, their kisses feverish. With an effort, Morgan summoned her mind back into control and curved away from Victoria, bending her head to whisper into the hollow of the other woman's neck.

'This is for you, remember,' she murmured softly, biting and kissing Victoria's skin with quick movements. 'Otherwise, you might not come back for more.'

'I'm addicted already,' Victoria panted, gasping and writhing under Morgan's expert hands and mouth, unaware that she, in her turn, was driving the other woman to distraction with wanting. 'What have I been missing?'

'Oh, you are about to discover *exactly* what you've been missing,' Morgan whispered softly, her hand moving slowly down Victoria's silken skin to part her thighs

467

with an imperceptibly soft caress. 'And so am I.'

Victoria's legs opened under Morgan's hand, and suddenly she felt the soft touch of Morgan's darting tongue against the lips of her cunt, creating tiny whorls of pleasure around her clitoris and causing Victoria to cry aloud and clutch the creamy sheets with her fists. As gently as if she were separating two sheets of gold leaf, Morgan parted Victoria and drove her tongue into the musky moistness. Her other hand ran brands of fire across Victoria's breasts as she teased them, and Victoria spasmed against Morgan's mouth as the other woman drank her greedily. The pulsing between her legs intensified to an almost unbearable peak of pleasure, the craving for satisfaction arching her body on the bed. Her two hands sought and found Morgan's springy breasts, and she rolled the hard mocha nipples almost roughly between her fingers, winding her tanned legs around the whiteness of Morgan's lower back. She felt the other woman quivering against her as her mouth teased and worried and sucked at Victoria, the two of them surging together towards climax.

Suddenly Victoria's eyes opened wide as she felt Morgan's cool fingers sink deep inside her, the tips pulsing urgently against the soft damp walls within her. Morgan slithered upwards along Victoria's shuddering body, her fingers still probing inside the other woman, her thumb rubbing rhythmically against Victoria's clitoris, as she kissed her full breasts with unrestrained passion. She lifted her head to Victoria's mouth, and as Morgan's lips met hers, Victoria tasted her own muskiness, her arms reaching to embrace Morgan's body as their legs tangled together. Victoria's thighs spread wide to embrace the other woman, and she rocked her hips hungrily, drawing Morgan into her, holding her as Morgan picked up her rhythm and adapted it to her own.

468

Morgan broke away, her silvery eyes fixed on Victoria's cool blue ones, a wicked smile curving lips swollen with desire. 'I think this is what they call the anchor position,' she breathed.

Any response Victoria might have made was sublimated as Morgan's quick fingers found the tiny place inside her that they had been seeking, that Victoria had never known was hidden within her. She screamed as the pleasure overwhelmed her, driving every thought from her head as the pulse between her legs and her taut nipples became the only focus of her existence. Her skin burned. She was no longer sure where Morgan began and she ended; she felt breasts and she was breasts; she felt Morgan's satiny mound against her own lush chestnut hairs and could no longer tell the difference. The fiery trail of pleasure emanated out from their centre and consumed them, silky skin against silky skin, soft willowy limbs entwined together, a tangle of lust and softness and sensation and sex.

They screamed and shuddered and moaned as they came, their bodies pressed tightly together as again and again they arched away and back towards each other with quivering, rippling movements. Afterwards, for a long moment, they could not move, gazing wordlessly into each other's eyes.

And then it was Morgan's turn.

■ INN, LONDON
   12 OCTOBER, 9.52 p.m.

'I promise you, it's true,' Rich whispered.

Dom slithered along the back of the gallery with an updated list of the running order for the Party Conference coverage. 'Can't be.'

469

'On my honour . . . well, what's left of it . . . they do.'

'Do what?' Jerry demanded, taking his place at the back of the control room and surveying the production team with the disconsolate air of Wellington in charge of Greenham Common.

'We were just admiring the enterprise of a few young men who seem determined to defy the censors and view INN as it is meant to be,' Rich explained.

'I wouldn't mind seeing that for myself,' Jerry muttered darkly.

Dom grinned. 'Apparently, in certain Moslem countries, several religious young ladies are employed to spend their days inserting electronic blocks on the screen to obscure portions of the female anatomy offensive to Moslem sensibilities.'

'Half their luck,' Ollie said, flinging on to Jerry's desk a copy of the scripts the Conference newscasters would be reading down the line from Blackpool, and beating a hasty retreat before the Producer asked any awkward questions.

'Ah, but that's not all,' Dom laughed. 'They're persistent chaps. Where there's a willy, there's a way.'

Rich attempted to keep a straight face, and failed. 'What the charming young ladies don't realise is that it's common knowledge throughout the Moslem world that a black handkerchief, held over the television screen, neutralises the electronic effect and reveals all.'

'You're kidding?' Jerry said disbelievingly. 'Where's the key to the Obit Box? I intend to be the first to hold a black handkerchief over Paragon Fairfax to see if it works with her.'

'On-Air in three minutes,' Annie, the PA, chanted.

'We're going to frighten the shit out of people with this programme,' Jerry said. 'A solid half-an-hour of Tory

470

politics, and we're not even giving them a health warning.'

'Two minutes forty-five to go.'

Muriel, the Director, crossed her fingers. Party Conference coverage was always a nightmare; it required precision co-ordination from the anchor in the London Studio, the presenter based in the Conference Hall, and another correspondent picking up live comment from party delegates in their hotel lobby, as all three threw the bulletin back and forth to each other. Into this explosive mix, she had to add reports of the day's events, which were invariably sent late and longer than expected, requiring last minute cuts, plus unpredictable interviews with whichever politicians the fixers at Blackpool had managed to haul out of the hospitality bar. It was like juggling half-a-dozen greased balls from a high-wire trapeze – and that was when the satellites, microphones, earpieces and newscasters all worked.

'Are you happy, Blackpool?' Muriel asked into the intercom in front of her.

On the screen in the corner of the gallery, Sir Edward Penhaligon could be seen standing on the red plush balcony of the Conference Hall, untidy rows of empty seats visible in the background below. A brief wide-shot revealed Jeremy Paxman in the box next to the INN position, making a few late adjustments before Newsnight went on air; further along the hall, an ITN crew was belatedly setting up arc-lights for News at Ten.

The camera jiggled to signify that the cameraman was satisfied with the picture. Sir Edward smoothly shot the cuffs of his shirt, revealing a glimpse of discreet smoky topaz cufflinks that precisely matched his silk tie. Livvy, his field producer, straightened the impeccable lines of his grey Savile Row suit, concealing the earpiece cord behind his head, and whisked a sheaf of conference notes from the balcony shelf out of the way. Sir Edward smoothed his silvery hair back from his forehead, and slipped his reading glasses into his breast pocket. He gave a swift thumbs-up in response to Muriel's question, carefully readjusting the earpiece in his ear.

'A little tighter on the shot, Dave,' Muriel said down the line to the Blackpool cameraman. 'We don't want to see all their empty lunch wrappers on the seats behind him.'

'Is Christie with you?' Jerry interrupted. 'Her story still isn't in yet, and we'll need her to give us a live update at the end of the programme from Sir Edward's OB position.'

On the screen, Sir Edward raised one eyebrow in polite disinterest, glancing through the notes on his clipboard before handing it back to Livvy. 'Ms Bradley? I am afraid I cannot see her at the moment.'

'She'll be there,' Ollie said, handing the graphics girl a list of the names of the Blackpool interviewees so that she could programme the computer which would generate the subtitles. 'Never missed a feed yet.'

'On-Air in one minute.'

Muriel's glance moved across to the next screen. 'Everything OK, Imperial?'

Charles Silversmith was already sitting in place in the lobby of Blackpool's Imperial Hotel, where most of the Conservative Members of Parliament were staying. Half-a-dozen junior MPs and Conference delegates were perched nervously on a circle of gilt chairs beside him, matriarchal bosoms and kipper ties to the fore. A crowd of substitutes and hangers-on were standing in the background, ready to seize their moment of fame should the opportunity arise. Others circulated mindlessly about the lobby, sidestepping the cables which snaked around the camera position to the OB van parked outside the hotel, and artfully sneaking glances at the camera as if they had only just noticed it was there. Sweat gleamed on the foreheads of the delegates trapped under the glare of the arc-lights, and several had the desperate air of children forced to take part in the annual Nativity play, longing to flee if they could only figure a way out through the rows of parents.

Muriel suddenly saw Charles pick up a crystal glass of amber liquid and take a deep gulp, replacing it surreptitiously on the floor beneath his chair. From the look of him, she strongly suspected that it wasn't his first. He jumped as she addressed him again, and innocently tapped the tiny microphone clipped to his paisley tie as if he had been having problems with his reception.

'Loud and clear,' he said, his enunciation revealingly precise.

'Dammit, Ginny, get that bloody glass away from him,' Muriel ordered into the microphone. Her gaze returned to Victoria in the Studio.

'Thirty seconds,' Annie said.

'For God's sake,' Muriel heard Charles complain. 'Bloody miserable Whitehouse brigade. There may be teetotallers who are fun, but I've never bloody met one, that's for sure.'

'Edward, as soon as Victoria has read the general intro from the studio here, we'll come to you for the round-up on the day,' Jerry said crisply. 'If you throw back to Victoria after your interview with Heseltine, she'll then come to you, Charles. At the end of the Conference wrap, Victoria will anchor the rest of the day's news from the Studio, then come to Christie for a final update.'

'On-Air in fifteen.'

'Don't forget, Victoria, plenty of sexual chemistry in the handover,' Jerry said, throwing his arms up into the air with the enthusiasm he usually reserved for conducting

473

Last Night of the Proms from his armchair at home.

'Why's Jerry so excited?' Rich asked.

'It's the first day of the relaunch, or hadn't you noticed?' Rochelle replied, tapping the keys on her computer to check the latest wire-stories.

'Five . . . four . . . three . . .'

Rich looked surprised. 'What, again? This programme's had more relaunches than the bloody Shuttle.'

'On-Air!'

Victoria started reading the introduction, her voice cool and professional, a window depicting the Conservative torch over her right shoulder. Jerry paced up and down the gallery as she spoke, seizing the late scripts from the GAs, who raced from the newsroom down to the control room with each story as soon as it had been completed and printed out. 'Rich! There's a sentence here without a verb in it!' Jerry yelled as he scanned the latest to appear.

'Yes, rather stylish I thought,' Rich said absently, concentrating on Victoria as she wrapped the topics discussed during the day's conference, and making sure her words matched the graphics appearing on the screen.

'Something strange about her,' he whispered to Dom. 'She looks so bloody cheerful.'

'Perhaps she's on a biorhythmic up,' Dom suggested.

'Whatever that is, I want one,' Ollie grumbled, appearing at the door of the gallery and beckoning to Jerry. 'The only person who writes to me these days is the subscription girl at *Time* magazine.'

Jerry turned round and frowned at Ollie. 'Bugger off, Ollie. Can't you see I'm doing a sodding programme?'

'I've got the bloody Fraud Squad upstairs,' Ollie retorted indignantly. 'What the fuck do you want me to do?'

Jerry buried his head in his hands. 'Why me, God?' He

looked up just as Muriel prepared to switch to Charles at the Imperial Hotel, and recoiled in horror as he saw the newscaster lurch against a young, attractive female delegate, attempting to fasten a microphone to her fluffy pink jumper. 'For Christ's sake, where's he trying to put it? On her bloody nipple? Edward, we'll have to come back to you!'

Dom threw his clipboard on the floor and darted over to Ollie, who was now hopping from one foot to the other. He pushed the News Editor out of the Gallery, and the two leaned against the door, blocking out Jerry's howls of misery.

'What's going on?'

'It's that bloody accountant, Daniel. It seems he's been playing away with his company credit card, and that's just the beginning.'

'So what's the big deal?' Dom asked, puzzled. After all, it wasn't exactly the first time. Ben Wordsworth had put half a dozen prostitutes on his card when he was in South America, and calmly pointed out that it was all tax deductible when the statements arrived.

'Well, it wouldn't be so bad, if they hadn't also picked up two dozen amateur video tapes of him and his rent boys . . . shot on INN cameras.'

'Just in time for INN's Christmas video releases,' Dom said dryly. 'Bet it does better than *The Royal Year*.'

'I just hope he authorises my expenses before he gets marched out,' Ollie said mournfully.

'You'd better make sure you get an interview with him first,' Dom said. 'Ben wouldn't be too pleased if you got scooped on this one.'

'Funny you should say that,' Ollie groaned. 'He asked if he could make his one phone call when they arrived. Unfortunately, it was to the *Daily Ethic*.'

Dom grinned. No one could accuse INN of being dull.

Before he could reply, Jerry's shrieks of despair reached a crescendo and hastily Dom ducked back into the gallery to rejoin the fray.

'Dom! Get me a line to Imperial! That drunken bugger's taken his earpiece out!' Jerry screamed.

In the lobby of the Imperial Hotel, Ginny closed her eyes in despair and buried her head in Sam's shoulder. 'I daren't drag Charles out of shot in case Jerry cuts to him,' she groaned. 'But he can't carry this one off, he's too far gone. Jerry will be going crazy.'

'Never mind Jerry, Ben will personally crucify Charles if we don't sort him out,' Sam said, trying not to notice how good Ginny's body felt against his. 'Jerry can't use him like this anyway. How the hell did he get so drunk without anybody noticing?'

Ginny shrugged hopelessly, and glanced at INN's current output in the monitor propped up on two empty Edit Pack cases in the corner of the room. Victoria was conducting a lengthy interview down the line with Sir Edward on the outcome of the Government's new proposals to kick-start the economy, but despite the unusually intelligent edge to her questions, it was clear she could not fill for much longer.

Sam ducked down to put himself below the level of the camera and hurtled towards the cluster of delegates around Charles. Ginny turned to the telephone balanced precariously on top of the monitor, its red light flashing violently to make up for its enforced On-Air silence. She took a deep breath and picked up the receiver.

'Can you sober him up or not?' Jerry howled down the line.

Ginny winced. 'Not, I think,' she said, watching as Sam attempted to intervene between the newscaster and the attractive female delegate who was fighting off Charles' assaults on her clinging Angora jumper with visible reluctance. After all, pixillated or not, he *was* Charles Silversmith . . .

Back in London, Jerry threw his scripts on to the floor of the control room, and hurled the telephone receiver towards the bank of television screens, cursing colourfully when its lead brought it up short and the telephone tumbled heavily on his ankle.

'Rochelle!' he shouted at his Chief Sub. 'We'll have to go with the Thatcher Comeback story!'

'There's no information on that, it's all invention!' Rochelle shouted back, scanning the wires in desperation.

'Well, go away and invent some more!' Jerry screamed, hauling the telephone receiver back up to his ear by the spiral wire. 'Rich! Give me a fifteen second intro and take it to Victoria in the Studio!'

'This story doesn't need a lead-in, it needs an apology,' Victoria snapped tartly from the studio, as Muriel rolled a pre-recorded piece on the Chancellor's speech.

'Who switched *her* on?' Jerry asked in disbelief.

'One forty-five on this piece,' Annie intoned.

'Ginny! Get Charles right out of the bloody shot before we get taken off the air!' Jerry yelled down the telephone line.

He watched as Ginny drew her finger across her throat to signify that the shot should be cut, and Sam forcibly dragged Charles away from the scrum of MPs and delegates towards the back of the lobby. He did not move quickly enough. A barrage of paparazzi flash bulbs illuminated the hall, and the startled newscaster pitched forward on to the floor as he tripped over the OB cables.

'Coming to you, Edward,' Muriel said, as the package drew to a close.

Sir Edward neatly fielded Victoria's question about the rumours of a return to the benches by Lady Thatcher, smoothly picking up the bulletin as she handed to him.

477

With no trace of the chaos in the gallery that he could hear in his earpiece, the veteran newscaster calmly assessed the latest opinions from the conference delegates, filling the time informatively and efficiently. Having dealt thoroughly with the issue, he returned to the planned running-order and began to read the pre-written introduction to Christie's package on the PR campaign behind this year's conference.

'You'll have to roll Christie's package into the bulletin live from there, Blackpool,' Muriel said. 'We still don't have it here in London.'

'What the hell are you talking about?' Livvy shouted down the line from the Conference Hall. 'We haven't got it here!'

'Fifteen seconds left on this lead-in,' Annie said, referring to the script in front of her from which Sir Edward was reading.

'What's going on?' Jerry shouted. 'Are you telling me that not only have I lost one newscaster, now I have no story?'

'Edward, can you fill for a moment?' Muriel said calmly. 'We have a slight problem this end.'

Jerry picked up the receiver linking him to Ginny at the Imperial Hotel. 'Ginny, sweetheart, this is it,' he said briskly. 'I want you on air in thirty seconds. Pick up Charles's script and give me everything you've got.'

At the Imperial, Ginny dropped the telephone and sank on to the Edit Box. Sam reappeared as she dazedly scrabbled among the wires on the floor for Charles's discarded microphone. 'He wants me to take over,' she murmured, stunned. 'I can't do it, Sam.'

'Baby, of course you can,' Sam said, raising Ginny gently and leading her over to Charles's vacated seat. The delegates smiled encouragingly at her as she sat down, and Sam worked the microphone cable around the bump of her stomach. 'You'll be a hit. It's easy, just ask them the most obvious questions you can think of, and everyone will love you.'

Ginny glanced into the camera lens, wondering how on earth Christie could make it look so easy when she went live. It was a different ballgame, being this side of the lens. Thank God she didn't have time to think.

'Imperial, coming to you in fifteen,' Muriel said down the line.

Ginny gave a nervous thumbs–up and wondered whether the fluffy angora or the lurid paisley tie would be able to answer her first question better. God, what was her first question?

'Our correspondent, Ginny Templeton, is at the Imperial Hotel now. Ginny, what has been the response to the day's events among the delegates?' Victoria asked.

Ginny turned towards the lens. 'With me to answer that question first is . . .' she glanced at her script, 'Philippa Beeton. Mrs Beeton, what did you make of the Chancellor's speech?'

'Wonderful! Bloody wonderful!' Jerry enthused from the gallery, as the fluffy angora began to speak.

'You're doing fine,' Muriel said in her earpiece, while the gallery breathed a collective sigh of relief.

Ginny moved calmly from one delegate to another, cutting short their ramblings without seeming to interrupt, making sure everyone had the chance to voice their opinions. She did not have time to wonder if she was asking the right questions, or to feel self-conscious about her appearance. Her voice seemed to be coming from a distance far outside her as she rode on automatic pilot, her journalistic training coming to the fore and unerringly guiding her through the debate.

As she handed back to the Studio after five minutes, the entire gallery cheered, and Sam dashed from the shadows

to seize her in a hug that had more passion than congratu-
lation in it. 'You were fantastic!' he shouted, whirling
Ginny around the makeshift studio in the Hotel lobby.
'They loved you! Damn it all, Ginny, *I* love you!'

Ginny smiled dizzily as Sam came to rest, and laughed
with shy pleasure as the delegates applauded. Suddenly
she realised how terrified she had been, and hugged Sam
in mingled relief and delight.

'I couldn't have done it without you,' she said warmly.
'You were wonderful, Sam.'

'Baby, you did it,' Sam enthused, his strong arms
tightening around the gentle swell of her waist. Suddenly
the look in his bright blue eyes grew serious. 'Ginny, I
meant what I said. I love you. I have done for . . . oh, as
long as I can remember.'

Carefully he put her down on top of the empty Edit
Box, and fixed his eyes on hers. 'My darling, will you
marry me?'

Ginny's hands reached out automatically for the sides of
the silver box as she sought to steady herself. Wordlessly
she gazed at him, too stunned by the love she saw
reflected in the clear depths of his eyes to answer.

'Please say yes,' Sam pleaded, kneeling on the floor and
clasping her hands in his as he looked up at her. 'I love you
and . . . whoever else comes along,' he added, stroking
her stomach. 'I know you don't love me, not yet, but I
promise you, I'll make you happy. Please, just say yes.'

'I don't know what to say . . .' Ginny murmured,
feeling the reassuring pressure of his hands around her
own. She thought of the strength of the man in front of
her, the warm support he had given her which, until this
moment, she had not really appreciated. Suddenly she
imagined it gone, and the emptiness that flooded through
her shocked her. She realised that she had come to rely on
Sam, his silent, undemanding loyalty and friendship.

Every day he greeted her with a smile, encouraging her, supporting her, enfolding her in his easy companionship, expecting and asking for nothing in return. In a thousand ways he had been there for her, in a way that no one ever had before; not Nick, and certainly not Charles.

With Sam she did not feel the searing, white-hot flare of infatuation that had consumed her relationship with either of those two; Sam did not fire her senses, or set her heart pounding with anticipation. But as she thought of him, she felt a reassuring inner warmth spread deep within her; a steady glow that instinctively she knew would never burn out. Sam would never wittingly bring her the pain that Nick and Charles had delivered; he would never betray or desert her. She did not doubt that Sam loved her, and would turn the soft radiance of his affection on her child.

A tiny spark of hope flared within her, and, startled, she recognised it as the start of love. It would take time and energy and effort to nurture it into the full and generous relationship of giving and loving that Sam deserved, but it was there.

'Oh, for God's sake, say yes!' Jerry shouted down the line. 'I've still got a show to finish!'

'In that case . . . yes, Sam, I would love to marry you!' Ginny smiled, blushing deeply.

Sam shouted in triumph, and gathered her in his arms. 'You'll never regret it, I promise, my darling,' he said, smothering her in kisses as the delegates cheered.

'Coming to you, Blackpool, at the end of Victoria's wrap,' Muriel shouted above the calls of congratulation that were echoing along the length of the gallery.

'Two minutes,' Annie said from the London control gallery as she checked her stopwatch.

'Where the hell is Christie?' Jerry asked, glancing across at the empty camera position in horror.

481

'Livvy!' Muriel said urgently down the line. 'Can you get Christie down here *now*?'

'I haven't seen her for hours,' Livvy replied tearfully. 'I've no idea where she is. I've been trying to tell you.'

'For Christ's sake!' Jerry shouted. 'Go and find Edward and get him here to fill for her!'

'I'll try,' Livvy said, flinging down the telephone and pushing unceremoniously past the Newsnight team to try to catch up with Sir Edward, who was making his way back down to the body of the Conference Hall where Dalmeny de Burgh was waiting to greet him.

Sir Edward turned as the young field producer dashed up to him, clutching the edge of his sleeve in her desperation to propel the newscaster back to the camera position in time to close the bulletin. Smoothly he extracted himself from her grasp, his face betraying none of his satisfaction that Christie's absence had been so severely exacerbated by Charles's unforgivable condition. He called to Dalmeny that he would meet him at his hotel in one hour, and calmly walked back towards the camera position, his stride brisk but not urgent. Deftly he clipped on his microphone and took his place once more before the camera, listening for Muriel's instructions through his earpiece as he waited for his cue. As Victoria handed to him from the Studio for the last time, he summarised the day's news succinctly, glossing the facts with his habitual acute analysis, and closed the programme with an urbane smile that revealed nothing of the mayhem that had ruled behind the scenes.

Sir Edward left the camera position without waiting to take Jerry's call of thanks and congratulations, smiling briefly at the field crew as he removed his earpiece and effectively silenced the exuberant exultation of the gallery.

Swiftly he left the Conference Hall and waved away the

cab that was waiting for him outside. Tonight he preferred to walk.

He drew a deep breath of the crisp night air, his leather soles making no noise as he walked briskly towards his hotel. His face bore an expression of quiet reflection. It had been absurdly easy. In one stroke he had made the Bradley girl appear both incompetent and unprofessional. Her defence – that Sir Edward himself had told her that her segment of the programme was to be replaced so that she could interview the Minister of Defence for the Late News Show – would be regarded with, at best, scepticism and dismay, and at worst, outright disbelief. After all, with Sir Edward himself emphatically denying any such conversation, what other conclusion could be drawn than that the girl was frantically looking for an excuse for her mistake? And soon, very soon, it would be known what was behind her desperation. Jeopardising the programme would be the least of the accusations levelled against her, when he'd finished with her.

The Bradley girl herself, of course, would eventually work out who lay behind what had happened, if not why. But too late – her credibility, and her career, would be destroyed forever. He had already all but made sure of that. Just one more move was required.

Sir Edward reached the public telephone booth at the edge of the promenade outside his hotel. He paused for a moment and rested his hands on the rail that bordered the wall in front of the beach. He gazed impassively at the inky blackness of the sea as it crashed against the shore. Its power was wild and untamed. Sir Edward smiled fleetingly into the darkness, then straightened up without haste and moved towards the telephone kiosk. Calmly he lifted the receiver and inserted several coins. He did not intend there to be any record in the hotel of the numbers he was dialling now.

Twice his slim fingers moved to punch the digits he required. Both conversations were brief and one-sided. When he replaced the receiver, there was a grim smile on his face.

Her credibility would be lost forever.

Sir Edward breathed in the salt from the sea as the wind whipped around him, and crossed the road to make his way up the small incline towards the Imperial Hotel. He had considered every angle carefully and made every suitable provision. He would arouse no suspicions. There would be nothing to connect him with the scandal about to engulf Christie Bradley and drag her down to a depth of disgrace from which she would never recover. The one dangerous action his strategy demanded had been success-fully completed without witnesses.

Or so he thought.

One person *had* seen him.

Chapter Seventeen

■ BLACKPOOL CENTRAL POLICE
STATION, LANCASHIRE
13 OCTOBER, 04.00 a.m.

Christie sank back against the cold stone wall of her prison
cell, her legs curled against her chest on the grimy plastic
mattress. Slowly she laid her head on her knees and
wrapped her arms around her ankles. She closed her eyes,
despair filling her mind. Suddenly she doubted her ability
to fight the unknown but powerful and implacable enemy
who seemed so clearly bent upon destroying her, as she
fought to stem a rising tide of fear, desperately trying to
organise the few facts she knew in her mind. She would
need every ounce of her intelligence if she were to make
sense of this chaos.

Slowly she raised one hand and touched the bruise
spreading across her cheekbone, wincing as her fingertips
found the swelling. Resisting arrest. It would be laugh-
able, were it not so dangerous.

Christie stood up, moving towards the end of the cell.
She gazed up at the barred window, the moonlight gilding
her face with a strange translucence. Her bare feet were
cold on the stone floor. They had confiscated her stockings, along with her belt, shoes and scarf, when they had
strip-searched her. She had been told it was to stop her
from harming herself.

She turned around and paced back towards the door of her narrow cell, wondering if even now someone was watching her through the spyhole set into it. She felt violated and humiliated by the invasion into her privacy. Until now, she had never understood what it meant to have the weight of the Establishment set against her. Always, in the past, when she had confronted authority, it had been as a journalist with the power of INN on her side. Now, she was utterly alone.

Again she suppressed the flicker of panic that ran through her. Firmly she forced herself to concentrate on finding a way out of this situation. From the moment the Drugs Squad had swooped on her hotel room in Blackpool, she had had nothing to help her but her own wits. She had to use them well.

She sat down on the hard wooden bench, and slowly replayed the events of the last few hours, trying to put herself in the mind of the unknown enemy who had laid this trap. Only by doing that could she hope to discover his – or her – identity. The four grams of cocaine that had been discovered in her briefcase had been deliberately planted there. But why? And by whom?

Four hours ago she had accompanied the Drugs Squad officers to the local police station, and had listened dazedly as the Custody Officer there had read her rights to her. Shaking with shock and disbelief, she had contacted her family's solicitor in Sussex, James Delahay, who, until now, had never had to do anything more than draw up a will for her. She had listened as his calm voice told her to co-operate but admit to nothing.

'But I haven't *done* anything!' Christie had protested.

'Of course you haven't,' James had reassured her. 'Just wait until I get there. It'll take me a few hours to drive up to Blackpool, but the roads won't be too bad at this time of night. I'll be as quick as I can.'

Christie glanced at the lightening sky beyond the barred window. It must be almost dawn. She wished she had been permitted to keep her watch so that she could tell what time it was. God, she hoped James would arrive soon.

She turned towards the door as she heard footsteps echo in the hall outside. The bolts scraped against the metal door as they were pulled back, and the door swung wide to admit the portly frame of her solicitor.

'James! Oh, thank God!'

James Delahay nodded to the police officer behind him to indicate that he could leave them alone. As soon as he had gone, James wrapped his arms around Christie in a hug of reassurance. 'Don't worry, sweetheart, we'll soon have you out of this.'

Suddenly the shock hit her afresh, and she started to sob into his shoulder. Quietly he guided her over towards the bench and sat her down. After a few moments she turned to face him. 'Oh James. I just can't believe this is happening.'

'I know, Christie, I know. Don't worry, we'll sort it out. Why don't you tell me about it, from the beginning?'

Calmly she told him everything she could remember, from the moment she had been awakened in her hotel room by the slam of her bedroom door as it had been forced open by the Drugs Squad. As James listened and nodded, coolly professional, Christie felt for the first time since this nightmare had begun that there was some solidity to the shifting grounds beneath her feet.

James thought for a moment after Christie had finished speaking. 'It's obvious that whoever put the cocaine in your briefcase must have tipped off the Drugs Squad. But that still doesn't answer the question why. Someone must want you out of the way pretty badly. Any idea who?'

Christie shook her head. James stood up. 'OK, let's go and face the music.'

She was immeasurably grateful for James' reassuring presence as the police officer conducted a fifteen-minute taped interview with her. She denied having any knowledge of the cocaine with a quiet vehemence, part of her mind still whirling with questions as she wondered who could want her out of the way enough to destroy her life. James squeezed her hand as she was formally charged with unlawful possession of a controlled drug. He ascertained that the drugs had already been sent for forensic tests, and that her hotel room and her flat in Islington had both been searched, and nothing else had been found.

'OK, sweetheart, this is where I have to leave you,' James said, as she was returned to her cell. 'They'll let you out on bail as soon as they've finished fingerprinting you and taking your photograph. Then it's all up to me.'

Christie sat and watched as the small square of dark sky that she could see gave way to pale grey and then to pink and orange. Whoever had planted the drugs in her room must have done it the previous evening. It was the only time she had left her briefcase unattended. She had been away chasing an interview with the Minister of Defence for the Late News Show at Sir Edward's request. Someone must have been monitoring her every move very carefully.

Suddenly Christie understood. Only one person could have known that she was going to be away from her room that night. She had no facts to back up what she suspected, no proof. But it was the only answer that made sense.

But would anyone believe her?

The door clanged open and Christie jumped as the Custody Officer entered her cell. 'OK, you can go now.'

She stared at him in confusion. 'I can go? What about bail?'

'You have bail on your own recognisance – that is, if

488

you promise not to skip the country. You're free to do as you wish pending a hearing at the Magistrate's Court in four weeks' time.' He threw the clothes which had been confiscated earlier on to the bench. 'Look sharp, darling.'

Christie dressed and made a futile attempt to eradicate the signs of her sleepless night. Her hair was dishevelled, her face tearstained. She hoped she could reach the sanctuary of her hotel room before she saw anyone she knew. She fled from her cell without glancing backwards, and stood in the entrance hall of the police station, willing herself to walk into the watery October sunshine with her head held high. She had done nothing wrong, she reminded herself. She had no reason to be ashamed.

'Quite a star, I see.'

Christie turned to the police officer on the front desk. 'I'm sorry?'

The policeman held up his copy of the *Daily Ethic*. 'Front page, no less. Didn't realise we had a celebrity in our midst.'

Christie stared at the grainy picture of herself. The officer tossed the paper across the counter. 'Here, you can keep it if you like. Souvenir of your stay here. I've got work to do.'

She took it dazedly and walked out into the early morning, neither knowing nor caring where she was going. She looked at the paper. The *Daily Ethic* had done its worst. The tabloid journalists, always out to take a swipe at what they saw as the unfair glamour of television news, were having a field day with INN. Splashed across the front page was a picture of Charles Silversmith sprawled on the floor of the lobby of the Imperial Hotel, the caption 'Tired and emotional?' beneath it. The second leader carried a blurred photograph of herself and told readers to see pages four, five and six for 'the full story.' And the *Ethic* had scored a hat-trick with a picture of

489

Daniel, the accountant, next to a detailed and salacious account of his activities as a paedophile and fraudster.

But the newspaper reserved the greatest number of column inches and its most severe disapproval for herself. Two full pages covered in equal measure her unprofessional absence from a vital live broadcast, the lightning raid on her hotel room, and her subsequent arrest for possession of cocaine. The inference was that she had been unable to go on air because she was high on drugs, and it was implied that it was not the first time her colleagues had been forced to cover for her. Christie's past reportage had been dragged out and re-examined in the light of the 'recent discovery.' Much had been made of her frequent trips to South America, her legendary calmness on camera, her ability to function in the field on two or three hours' sleep a night for weeks on end.

Christie stared at the newspaper in disbelief. Was there any part of her life that they had left untouched?

And then she turned the page and saw the photograph of David.

Every aspect of her relationship with him had been cruelly exposed and distorted. Unnamed sources attested to their joint reporting from Kosovo, their mutual absence at the time Nick Makepiece had been kidnapped, David's inexplicable infatuation for the 'Siren of the Newsroom'. Her reputation had been expertly and thoroughly destroyed. She had been presented as a ruthless, ambitious young woman prepared to sleep her way to the top, who had distributed her favours willingly amongst her colleagues.

The assassination of her character was both clever and effective. Even if she could have afforded the outrageous expense of litigation, the damage had been done. Someone had planned to destroy her career utterly and irrevocably. And it seemed they had succeeded.

But the most agonising part of it all was the pain she imagined would be in David's eyes as he read the piece. Her heart clenched in anguish. She knew how ridiculous the suggestions were, how distorted the facts had been; yet, in black and white, they seemed convincing. Much as the tabloids were ostensibly despised, the most outrageous fantasies were given credibility simply by appearing in print. She knew love made David vulnerable. Every inner doubt which he could possibly have harboured in the depths of his soul would be dragged out and ruthlessly exposed when he saw this, giving substance to his deepest unnamed fears. How could his love for her possibly survive such a ruthless onslaught?

Suddenly Christie found she was facing the truth she had evaded for so long. She forgot her ruined career, the threat of imprisonment, her total humiliation by the tabloids. All that mattered was David. All she wanted was to feel the reassuring warmth of his arms around her, to draw on his strength and love. She could not imagine how she had withheld herself from him for so long. *Amoud fiki*. She would die for him. If he loved her, if he could forgive her the confused impulses which had made her run from him, she could survive even this.

Without him, she had no life left.

■ REGENT'S PARK, LONDON
   12.10 p.m.

Caryn Kelly knew exactly what she was doing.

Awkwardly she extracted two of her Louis Vuitton suitcases from the storeroom in the entrance hall of Sir Edward's apartment, careful to ensure that they left no mark on the black and white marble tiles as she dragged them free. With a brisk kick of her heel she shut the storeroom door and carried the empty cases upstairs, glancing cursorily at her fingernails to make sure that she had not chipped them by her efforts. Her suede-clad feet made no sound on the soft Savonnerie carpet that graced the hall, and swiftly she manoeuvred the two cases past the elegant walnut occasional table and the priceless collection of Oriental porcelains discreetly displayed in a fourteenth century carved cabinet; it had been in Sir Edward's family for generations. She did not pause now to savour the tastefully appointed apartment; if her labours bore their expected fruit, all this would be hers in a matter of weeks. The Matisse painting and the da Vinci drawing would greet her every time she passed through the length of this hallway; the recessed alcoves which sheltered two fluted cloisonné vases, the exquisite Degas dancer, the collection of antique inlaid Syrian jewellery boxes; all would soon be a familiar part of her surroundings forever. Sheraton and Aubusson, Cartier and Chagall. She had a price, and it had been paid.

Caryn slid the larger of the two suitcases on to the burgundy damask coverlet which sheathed the vast double bed, and unclasped its leather straps, glancing at her watch as she opened the case out. Twelve fifteen. She had barely enough time, if she was to make the train by ten past one.

'Madam, the taxi is here.'

Caryn spun round and saw Isabella, the nanny, hovering nervously in the doorway. Sandy was cradled in her arms, his plump legs wrapped around her hips and his chubby arms wreathed about her neck. He reached out his hands to his mother with a tentative smile which did not quite banish the wariness in his dark eyes. Caryn's glance travelled dispassionately over his small form. Sandy dropped his arms. He buried his head in the softness of Isabella's shoulder.

492

'Tell the driver to wait,' Caryn said tersely. She crossed the room and opened the door to the dressing room which contained seven rails of her clothes. 'And take that child out of here.'

Isabella flinched at the animosity in her voice, wishing desperately that she could protect the child from its mother's rejection. Young as he was, he understood that somehow he had incurred his mother's bitter displeasure, and that the tall, loving father figure who had protected him for so long had suddenly vanished from his life. Only Isabella was left to stand between him and the source of that relentless dislike. The little boy began to cry softly as Isabella fled from the room, hugging the child and murmuring soothingly to him. His mother shut the door behind them with a decisive slam.

Caryn frowned briefly as she sifted swiftly through the tissue-wrapped clothes hanging in the wardrobe. She had dismissed Sandy from her mind as soon as he left the room. After all, she had to. That had been one of the conditions.

So many delicious decisions. Her hands slid through shimmering silks and soft wools, creamy lace and translucent chiffons. The litany of exclusive and unconscionably expensive couture designers was her personal mantra, and she recited it reverently as she selected each outfit. Donna Karan's white chiffon shirt, teamed with the Dolce & Gabbana choker-necklace. The grey pinstriped Jean Paul Gaultier catsuit and matching lace-up waistcoat, the Emma Hope shoes, the Nicole Farhi suede jacket with its wool wrap skirt, and the Krizia wool jacket edged with velvet trim. The fake white leopard Joseph coat, of course. The MaxMara wool suit, but with the Georges Rech sweater. And the lethal Martine Sitbon black dress, with its wicked satin and laces and rows of ruched and pleated chiffon, that had proved to be

Dalmeny de Burgh's undoing.

Caryn smiled in satisfaction. Seducing Dalmeny had been extremely simple. And it had also been a pleasure.

A flicker of desire ran through her at the memory. Unconsciously her left hand reached to cup her breast and caress its nipple. She closed her eyes as she felt again the sinuous rustle of the black satin as it slid from her body, the fire in Dalmeny's hands as they roamed freely over her skin, the heady taste of his tongue on hers, the intoxicating sensation of his mouth savouring the hollows of her neck, the softness of her breast, the musky sweetness at the tops of her thighs. Dalmeny had been an expert and accomplished lover, his hands practised as he caressed her, his thrusts sure and certain as he plunged into her. Her recollection was tinged with a regret that the experience would never be repeated. Dalmeny had also been charming and full of good humour, his self-deprecating comments endearing, his manner boyish. Unbidden the thought flashed through her mind: *as David had been when she met him* . . .

With a start her eyes flashed open, and resolutely she clamped down on the memories his name evoked; it was the bittersweet taste that tainted every waking thought and every sleeping dream. David would never be hers; the game was over.

But for one last throw of the dice.

Swiftly Caryn folded the outfits she had selected and placed them in the open suitcase, adding silken layers of camisoles, panties, suspender belts and stockings, expertly separating them with pink wafers of tissue paper. Seducing Dalmeny might have been enjoyable, but it was part of a wider vision than hers. Charming and accomplished though he had been, he had been no match for her. She had lured him to her bed for one purpose alone. Sir

494

Edward had required that the Minister for Energy be placed in a position of supplication, for reasons which he did not explain and which she had no desire to pursue.

The photographs had been delivered to Dalmeny's home forty-eight hours after their passionate and compromising embraces had taken place, in an envelope empty except for a single newspaper cutting, the masthead of the *Daily Ethic*. Despite the evident distance from which they had been taken, the pictures were both graphic and self-explanatory, depicting the clearly identifiable Conservative MP in an imaginative variety of positions which he knew would end his brilliant career at a single stroke should they be made public. It was only natural that Dalmeny should turn in desperation to his loyal and trustworthy friend, Sir Edward Penhaligon, and beseech him to use his considerable influence to persuade the Editor of the scurrilous tabloid, Denzil Calhoun, not to publish. Dalmeny knew that there was an unspoken code that such a favour would have to be returned.

But this move was hers alone.

Edward knew nothing of what she planned to do. Before she sold herself to him completely, she intended to take her own, very personal, revenge on the man who had rejected her. David Cameron might not want her, but he would never forget her.

Caryn placed an exquisite black silk teddy edged with antique coffee lace into the suitcase, separating it from a matching peignoir with a final layer of tissue paper. She smiled as she closed the lid and fastened the leather straps, lifting the suitcase on to the floor and replacing it with the smaller Vuitton grip. With quick steps she crossed the room to her elegant dressing table and gathered her Chanel make-up bag in her hands, rapidly adding to its contents a variety of powders, shadows, blushers and lipsticks. She drew her jewellery box from its place at the bottom of her lingerie drawer, unlocking it with the tiny silver key to reveal an array of necklaces, bracelets and earrings which she had garnered from her many lovers during the course of her marriage to Sebastian. In their midst was now added a glittering marquise emerald ring, which Edward had given her exactly twenty minutes after he received the telephone call from Dalmeny saying the INN shares were now his. He had then thrown her on to the bed and taken her with such force that she had felt the painful imprint of his possession for several days.

It was the sinister danger that she sensed lurking at the bottom of Sir Edward's soul that so inflamed her desire and drew her inexorably to him. No matter the cost.

Caryn returned to the bed and slipped the Chanel bag and the relocked jewellery case into the Vuitton grip, which she closed firmly and placed by the side of the suitcase already on the floor. 12.40.

With a sigh of impatience, she opened the door and walked down the upper hallway towards the makeshift nursery. Sandy's brightly coloured toys and child's clothes looked out of place in the restrained elegance of Sir Edward's guest bedroom, his small form adrift in the expanse of the double bed. Isabella was stroking his forehead, love and affection visible in the soft depths of her eyes.

'When is Sandy coming back, madam?' she asked hesitantly, turning to face Caryn as she strode into the room.

Caryn smiled grimly as she gathered Sandy's tiny sweaters and trousers in her arms, flinging them with swift disregard into the multi-coloured hold-all that was open on the floor beside the bed. 'Soon. This is just for a while . . . so that Edward and I can get to know each other. He'll be back soon.'

'I don't understand . . .' Isabella said in confusion.

'Oh, don't worry, he'll be well taken care of,' Caryn said dismissively, regarding the child in the bed without emotion. In the end it had not been a difficult decision, particularly when she thought of all that Edward would bring her.

'He's going back to Mr Cameron then?'

'Mr Cameron?' Caryn laughed shortly. 'Good heavens, no. He will never see this child again.'

'Then where is he going?' Isabella asked. She stood up and gripped the edge of Caryn's cream and navy Ralph Lauren suit. 'Where is he going, Mrs Kelly?'

Caryn shook the girl off, glancing distastefully down at her sleeve. 'You forget yourself,' she said curtly. 'Kindly get the child ready to leave.'

She spun on her heel as Isabella wordlessly gathered Sandy in her arms, hugging his warm little body close to her, burying her face in the downy softness of his hair. She felt his arms wrap themselves about her neck, his sleepy wriggle clutching at her heart and twisting it in his tiny fingers. She had cared for him for all the fifteen months of his young life; it had been her arms that held him, her hand that tended his cuts and wiped his tears, her heart that showered him with the love his mother denied him and his father had never been able to give him. She was all he had ever known, and he was more precious to her than anything else in her own life. Resolutely she suppressed the tears that threatened to fall, afraid she would upset him, and dressed him in his favourite Mickey Mouse outfit. She kissed his upturned face and summoned a smile.

'You look wonderful, little fellow,' she murmured, tickling his stomach so that he laughed gleefully. 'Do you have a smile for me?'

'Have you finished?' Caryn said, appearing at the

497

doorway. She crossed the room and picked Sandy up before Isabella could reply.

'Bring his clothes downstairs. The driver's waiting.'

Sandy sensed his mother's anger, and his lower lip trembled. He twisted in her grasp, his hands reaching out towards Isabella for her reassuring warmth. Caryn pinioned him firmly in her arms so that he could not struggle, and left the room. His unhappy cries echoed down the hallway as he realised that he was being separated from Isabella.

Caryn frowned in annoyance. She had no compunction in fulfilling the second of the conditions which Edward had demanded in return for the lifestyle she coveted. Sandy was an encumbrance she could well do without. She had never wanted any child but David's. Her heart twisted fleetingly as unwanted memories flooded through her, and a bitter anger replaced the pain.

She frowned as Sandy's wails grew louder. For heaven's sake. He would only be gone a couple of months at the most. Just until Edward got used to the idea.

If only he would stop crying.

'Madam, his bicycle,' Isabella said, hastening after her with the toy clutched in her hands. 'Please . . . he loves it . . .'

'For God's sake!' Caryn said, exasperated. 'Leave it! He has more than enough toys already. Go and open the door.'

Isabella left the brightly coloured tricycle at the top of the stairs and hurried down them to open the front door of the apartment, trying to block out the screams of the child as tears flowed unchecked down her cheeks. With some sixth sense the little boy understood that he was being taken from everything he knew, from the only person who loved him, and his shrieks redoubled as Caryn marched swiftly through the doorway to the woman

498

waiting in the taxi. His tiny hands clutched the elegant lapels of her jacket, and she fought to disentangle herself as the woman reached out to take the hysterical child.

'Mrs Kelly . . . are you sure?' the woman asked, enfolding the screaming boy in her arms with concern.

'Yes, I'm sure,' Caryn said coolly. 'Didn't you have something for me to sign?'

The woman regarded Caryn with a mixture of dismay and surprise. She had seen mothers hand over their children to her for temporary fostering with anguished misery, with misgivings, even with relief. But she had never witnessed such an utter lack of care, tinged with a bitter emotion that seemed to be almost pleasure.

Caryn tapped her foot on the ground impatiently, and the woman recalled herself. Still holding the sobbing boy, she scrabbled in her bag with one hand and extracted a sheaf of papers. 'If you would just sign these,' she said anxiously, kissing the little boy's head in an attempt to soothe him.

Caryn scrawled her name without a second thought, turning and walking back up the steps. She did not look back.

Her mind was already on her next move.

■ IMPERIAL HOTEL, BLACKPOOL
  6.00 p.m.

Admission to the hotel was simple.

Caryn walked confidently towards the lift, an expression of cool assurance that brooked no discussion on her face. She had already obtained the room number she required. With a brief, dispassionate glance around the lobby, she entered the lift alone and selected the floor number she wanted. Moments later she emerged into the deserted corridor, a Vuitton suitcase in either hand, and scanned the oak-panelled doors in both directions before turning to her left. As Caryn had expected, a maid was still making her way down the series of rooms, a cart laden with miniature bottles of shampoo and bath foam parked outside the room she was currently cleaning, an untidy heap of sheets piled on the floor against it. Caryn put the two suitcases down and waited expectantly for the maid to emerge.

The girl looked up as she came out of the room, her arms filled with damp towels and crumpled pillowcases. She glanced at the elegantly dressed woman standing in the corridor, noticing immediately the glittering emerald ring on the woman's left hand, the exquisitely cut cream and navy suit that she recognised as outrageously expensive, the Vuitton luggage at her feet.

'Can I help you, Madam?'

Caryn smiled charmingly, an expression of slight embarrassment and tentative excitement on her face. 'I *do* hope you can, although I know I shouldn't ask you,' she said. 'I would be *so* grateful if you could do me a wonderful favour, although I quite understand if you can't.'

The girl smiled encouragingly. 'I'll do my best, madam,' she said, putting the soiled linen on top of the pile already next to her cart.

'That's so sweet of you,' Caryn smiled, opening her Vuitton grip and extracting a card. 'My husband's staying here, I think. I'm sure you've seen him before . . . David Cameron, the INN correspondent?'

The girl's eyes widened as she read the name on the card. 'Oh yes, Mrs Cameron, I saw him on the TV last night. He's really your husband? Ooh, you are lucky.'

If only you knew, Caryn thought bitterly. 'I've been travelling for absolutely ages,' she said instead, with a rueful smile. 'We haven't seen each other for weeks. I can't tell you how much I miss him when he's away. I think you probably see him as much as I do!'

'Do you know all the other people on the TV?' the girl asked, deeply impressed. David Cameron was famous. I mean, he was a real star. Wait till she told Hilary. 'Have you really met Paragon Fairfax and Trevor McDonald and Anne Diamond and people?'

Caryn concealed her impatience. 'Oh yes, some-times . . .'

'Ooh! What're they like, then?'

Caryn shrugged her shoulders with a charming smile. 'Oh, they're terribly nice, you know. Almost ordinary. Just like you and me, really.'

For God's sake, this was getting nowhere. And she wished the wretched girl would stop calling her Mrs Cameron. She clamped down on the desire to scream and resisted the powerful urge to glance at her watch. She smiled again and smoothed her hair so that the auburn curls just whispered against the cream collar of her suit. 'I don't want to be a bother, but my husband will be back soon . . .'

The girl straightened up, completely charmed by the warmth and friendliness which Caryn emanated, keen to reciprocate. 'How can I help you then?'

'Well, I don't want to get you into trouble or any-thing . . .' Caryn demurred. 'It's just that my husband isn't expecting me back until tomorrow, and I'd so like to surprise him . . .'

The girl nodded sympathetically. 'Ooh, that's so *romantic*,' she enthused, gazing at Caryn with frank admiration. 'You must be so in love, then.'

Something like that. 'I knew you'd understand,' Caryn gushed. She tilted her head to one side and smiled winningly. 'I just need you to do a little thing for me . . .'

501

'Ooh, anything, Mrs Cameron, you only have to ask.'

'Well . . . you see . . . I wanted to be right there waiting for him when he comes home,' Caryn said, with a tiny smile of embarrassment. 'Only I don't have a key to his room, and I didn't want to ask reception downstairs in case they told him and spoiled the surprise . . .'

The girl pulled a large bunch of keys from her apron pocket with an air of efficient complicity. 'Don't worry, Mrs Cameron, you leave that to me. He'll be thrilled, I'm sure.'

Caryn sighed with relief as the girl darted down the corridor and stopped outside the room she had indicated. 'This it, then?'

'I think so, yes,' Caryn replied, as the girl slid the requisite pass key easily into the lock and opened the door. 'Yes, this is David's room, I'd recognise his things anywhere. All those electricity cables . . .' She gave a little laugh. 'I'm surprised he doesn't fuse the whole hotel sometimes, the tricks he gets up to with those.'

'Is there anything else I can do, Mrs Cameron?'

Caryn smiled at the girl as she carried the two Vuitton cases across the threshold. Discreetly she extracted a twenty-pound note from her bag. 'You've been absolutely wonderful, I don't know what I would have done without you,' she said, crossing the room swiftly.

The girl glanced at the money and held up her hands in protest. 'No, Mrs Cameron, I couldn't take that,' she said, stepping back a pace. 'It was so sweet of you to talk to me, you don't have to give me anything. Honest. It was a pleasure.' She smiled. 'And if there's anything else . . . anything at all . . .'

'No, no, you've done more than enough, thank you so much,' Caryn said.

She waited until the maid had gone, and shut the door firmly behind her. Swiftly she lifted the larger of the two suitcases on to the bed, smiling bitterly as she unfastened the leather straps and extracted the black silk teddy and peignoir. With practised movements she secured the case shut again and concealed it in an alcove set to the left of the door for just that purpose. Coolly she withdrew her Chanel make-up bag from the Vuitton grip, then glanced at her watch. Perfect timing.

Caryn undid the gold buttons of her Lauren jacket and shrugged it off, carelessly casting it onto the bed. Calmly she kicked off her suede pumps and removed her trousers and the pale cream silk blouse that she had been wearing. She scanned the room and located the wardrobe, moving towards it on stockinged feet. An unexpected dagger of pain shot through her as she opened it and saw David's familiar shirts and suits already hanging on the rails. She closed her eyes and gripped the door, inhaling the warm, fresh scent of him that still clung to his clothes. For a moment she felt dizzy with loss and misery, a deep and hopeless longing swamping her with startling strength. Abruptly anger replaced the pain and she hung her clothes amongst his in the grip of an emotion she did not care to recognise.

She did not pause to reconsider. Her anguish fed the malevolent fury that consumed her and strengthened her determination. Calmly she removed the remainder of her clothes, sliding them into the drawers set at the back of the wardrobe. She sprayed a fine mist of Shalimar across the smooth contours of her naked body before slipping into the exquisite black silk teddy. Then she crossed the room and sat down in front of the mirror, resolutely closing her mind to the memories that David's things evoked as she pushed them to one side of the dressing table. Loose change, taxi receipts, the cufflinks that had belonged to his father.

Caryn tilted back her head and opened her eyes wide to

503

receive the drops of belladonna from a bottle in her Chanel make-up bag. She straightened her head and glanced critically at her reflection. Nothing else gave her eyes that sleepy liquid lustre that suggested complete sexual fulfilment and sated passion. She took a sable brush from the Chanel bag and passed a translucent shimmer of powder across her face, before stroking her cheeks with blusher and dusting the lids of her unnaturally bright eyes with subtle shades of ochre and russet. Expertly she sheened her lips with a trace of Vaseline and disarrayed the controlled curls of her auburn hair with her fingers. Slowly she assessed her image in the glass, running her hands thoughtfully across her creamy freckled shoulders, smoothing the black silk and coffee lace over her breasts. She looked as if she had spent most of the day in bed with a man who knew precisely how to please a woman.

She looked exactly as she intended to look.

Caryn rose and moved towards the Vuitton grip which she had left beside the door, extracting two Baccarat champagne flutes and a vintage bottle of Dom Perignon. David's last Christmas present to Sebastian and herself. The cork popped softly as she pushed it expertly with her thumbs. Smoothly she filled the two glasses, standing the bottle on the dressing-table and taking a deep draught from each glass before placing one on either side of the bed. She stepped back and scanned the room rapidly. From the doorway, only the bathroom and a tiny sliver of the bedroom were visible. The bed itself was impossible to see unless one walked directly towards it. Caryn smiled. This was the one part of her strategy which she had been forced to leave to chance, but the room could not have been more perfectly arranged if she had designed it herself. Deliberately she left her peignoir in a silken heap on the floor beside the bed, and slid beneath the coverlet.

Her assessment had been extremely accurate.

When David entered the room a few minutes later, he dumped his bag unceremoniously by the door and walked straight towards the bathroom without glancing towards the bed, as she had known he would. Moments later she listened with painful pleasure to the sounds of the water sluicing over David's body as he stepped under the shower.

She had already left a message, apparently from David, for Christie at her hotel.

Now all she had to do was wait.

■ BLACKPOOL, LANCASHIRE
  7.05 p.m.

'This the place, Miss?'

Christie opened her eyes abruptly and glanced at the imposing facade of the Imperial Hotel. In her hands she clutched a message that David had left at her hotel, asking her to come to him as soon as she could. She did not know what he was doing in England. She was just grateful that he was here. He was her lifeline.

'Yes, thank you.' Christie climbed out of the taxi and fumbled in her jacket pocket for some change. Distractedly she paid the driver and took a deep breath.

She turned and walked into the hotel, acutely conscious of her dishevelled appearance and the lurid bruise on her cheek. She had sunk into an exhausted sleep the moment she reached her own hotel after leaving the police station, and had only been awakened when the concierge telephoned David's urgent message through to her. She had not even stopped to shower before dashing from her room to go to him. She crossed the carpeted lobby swiftly without approaching the reception desk, and entered the lift alone. Thankfully she leaned her back against the panelled wall and regarded her reflection in the mirror with detachment. She had never imagined coming to David like this, in these terrible circumstances. Her jeans were grimy, her coffee-coloured tweed jacket creased and torn where one of the police officers had thrown her roughly into the cell, her leather ankle boots scuffed and muddy. The face that looked steadily back at her was ashen with fatigue and stress; the purpling bruise on her cheekbone stood out in stark relief against the whiteness of her skin, her eyes were shadowed and hollow. She looked and felt as if she had just fought her way single-handedly across a warzone. Tiredly she passed a hand across her forehead as she pushed her hair out of her eyes.

It was only the thought of being with David that gave her the strength to keep going.

She had not seen him since that terrible day after Nick's capture, when she had retreated into a world of guilt and grief, unable to let David in. Now, at the lowest point of her life, she acknowledged how much she loved and wanted him, and suddenly he was here, in Blackpool, to be with her. When she most needed him, he was here.

The lift stopped and its doors hissed open quietly. Christie closed her eyes for a brief second and stepped out. A few more moments and she would be in David's arms, his lips would be against hers as he kissed her fears away, his strength giving her life as he told her she was no longer alone. She would never leave him again. With a sudden renewal of hope and excitement, she reached his door and tapped on it hesitantly. Her hand moved against the polished wood and she realised that the door was already ajar. David was waiting for her. *Oh, God, she loved him so much.*

Christie crossed the threshold and a part of her died as she took in the scene before her. David was standing in the doorway to the bathroom, his hair damp from the shower, droplets of water still gleaming on his tanned chest, a white towel wrapped around his waist. For a fleeting moment she thought she saw her own shock and horror reflected in his eyes. Dazedly her gaze moved towards Caryn, who was sitting up in the bed against a heap of pillows, a glass of champagne in her hand. A remote part of Christie registered the expensive silk peignoir trailing on the floor, the half-empty glass on David's side of the unmade bed, the dishevelled aura surrounding the other woman, her auburn hair disarrayed, her cheeks flushed, her pale eyes bright and satisfied. Those eyes told Christie everything. Slowly she backed away, unable to turn and break her gaze, fumbling for the door handle behind her.

David stood frozen in disbelief. He stared at Caryn for one long, endless moment, the hatred and contempt on his face so powerful that she shrank back against the pillows despite herself. She felt the depth of his anger as if it was a tangible presence in the room, and fear entered her heart.

David swung round towards Christie, and his hands reached towards her. 'Christie . . .'

His movement broke the spell which had rendered her immobile, and with a low moan she stumbled through the door, tears blinding her as she ran the length of the corridor and pummelled the lift button with the palm of her hand. She clutched the wall with both hands, her head lowered, drawing deep breaths. A distant part of her heard David calling her name as the lift arrived and she fell into it, not knowing and not caring what she did or where she went. All she wanted to do was to put as much distance as possible between herself and the man she had loved, the man she had lost forever.

In the hall, David beat on the lift doors as they shut behind her, shouting her name over and over again. At length he stopped and turned away, despair swamping him. He had come all this way to Blackpool the moment he had learned that Christie was there, determined to win her back to him, no matter what it took. At last he had broken free of the past, and had been able to offer himself to her, fully and unconditionally.

Now he knew it was hopeless. She would never trust him after this. He had lost her.

He looked up and saw Caryn standing, dressed, in the doorway of his room, a defiant expression on her face. He grasped her shoulders, forcing her back against the wall.

'What the hell are you playing at, Caryn? What are you trying to do to me?' he shouted, his face white with fury. 'What have I ever done to you to deserve this?'

Caryn's eyes blazed as she looked into his. 'I loved you, but you didn't care, did you?' she cried. 'You never cared about me. Only about Sebastian, and Sandy. Never me. *Why*? What's so wrong with me that you couldn't love *me*? No one could love you as much as I do. We could have had so much. Why did you have to throw it all away?'

David stared at her in disbelief. 'There was never anything between us!' he shouted, shaking her. 'There never would have been. You're crazy, Caryn. Crazy!'

'Crazy for loving you?'

He threw her away from him so that she stumbled and almost fell. 'Love? Your kind of love is destructive, corrosive. You want to possess me, to own me. You never loved me. You're not capable of love.'

'I was! I was!' she screamed, tears pouring down her cheeks as she grasped his arm, forcing him to face her. 'I was, until I met you! Whatever I am, you made me this way!'

He shook his head. 'No. There comes a time when we all have to make our choices, to decide how to be. You

508

made your choice.' His voice was cold and filled with contempt. 'You have no one but yourself to blame.'

Caryn recoiled against the corridor wall as his words hit her. 'She'll never come back!' she shouted desperately. 'You'll never have her, just as I have never had you. You'll be alone, forever!'

'Perhaps I will. Right now, I can't imagine wanting anyone else ever again. And whatever mistakes I've made in the past, I have to live with them. But at least I will never have to live with you.'

She looked at him hopelessly as he turned and threw her bags into the hall. 'David, please . . .'

'Go. Just *go*. I never want to see you again. I daren't. Next time, I might kill you.'

He slammed the door of his bedroom shut and leant against it. He thought of the pain he had seen in Christie's eyes as she ran from him, and his heart turned over in misery. There was nothing he could do to help her. Anything he said to her now would be futile. How could she possibly believe him?

Suddenly he longed to obliterate everything from his mind, to exist without thinking or feeling, to lose himself completely. He had had enough.

He crossed the room and picked up the telephone. He dialled the number of the Foreign Desk at INN and waited impatiently for it to answer.

'Sam? David here.'

'David! Good to hear from you. I thought you weren't back from your leave until next week?'

'I wasn't. I'm in Blackpool,' David said. 'Don't ask why. Just get me out of here. Fast.'

'I thought you'd never ask,' Sam said, relief in his voice. 'We've missed you. It's been pretty busy lately, and we could use another pair of hands. Want to travel?'

'As far away as possible. Preferably to where the action

509

is. I don't want time to think.'

Sam laughed. 'Kosovo suit you? Pretty active there.'

He thought again of the pain in Christie's face. He closed his eyes. 'Kosovo would be perfect.'

■ IMPERIAL HOTEL BAR, BLACKPOOL
7.20 p.m.

'You're a miserable bastard, Dave,' Andy grinned.

The cameraman shrugged, a wicked gleam in his eye. 'No one's forcing you to listen,' he answered.

'For God's sake, are you going to shut up or what?' Steve said indignantly, leaning forward and turning up the volume.

From the speaker on the bar came the unmistakable sounds of a woman's sighs as she was thoroughly and enthusiastically screwed. The three men could hear the deep pants of the man labouring on top of her and the rhythmic rattle of the bed as the couple's excitement began to mount and their bodies came together with slick passion. The woman's moans became sharper and more prolonged, shrill cries of appreciation and excitement, her partner responding with renewed application to the task in hand. As the pace grew faster the woman's shrieks intensified, her breathing coming in rapid, shuddering gasps, her groans overlaid with the stronger, deeper sounds of her partner's pleasure. They panted with a perfect synchronisation they could never have achieved at any other pursuit. It was clear from their obvious enjoyment and skill that they could not possibly be married; at least, not to each other. The headboard beat a thunderous tattoo against the wall, the overworked springs resounding with the echoes of the writhing bodies on the bed. Suddenly the woman screamed as she reached her climax.

510

'Oh, fuck me Jimmy, you legend, fuck me!'

As one, the three men gathered around the speaker fell against the bar, helpless with laughter and clutching each other for support, their mirth drowning out the equally over-excited drama to which they had been party.

'Legend?' Steve gasped as he fought for breath.

Andy and Dave shrugged as they looked at each other. 'Legend,' they confirmed rapturously, gazing in delight at the blushing speaker from which more muted gasps were now emanating.

An amused voice spoke from behind them. 'OK, you miserable sods, what have you been up to?'

'Nothing the *Daily Ethic* needs to know,' Andy said amiably, moving to allow the tabloid reporter to reach the bar and taking a deep gulp of beer from his glass.

'Let me be the judge of that,' Damon replied with a grin, signalling to the barman to approach. 'OK, what'll it be, lads? Same again?'

'I'm not sure he's got it in him, after that,' Dave said.

The long-suffering barman approached the cluster of journalists with a resigned expression on his face. After six years of Party Conferences he knew better than to interfere with the respected Members of the Press in the determined and enthusiastic pursuit of their duty. At least this lot still had their clothes on and weren't eating the glasses yet. Give it another few rounds.

Damon eyed the speaker on the bar with suspicion. 'OK, spill.'

Steve swirled the beer in his glass, glancing over his shoulder with exaggerated care to check who else was in the bar before speaking. 'We just decided to have a harmless little wager,' he said innocently. 'Passing the time, that's all.'

Damon lifted one eyebrow sardonically. 'You lot are about as harmless as an exocet missile in a kindergarten.

511

Tell Uncle Damon everything or I might have to let that nice Mr Wordsworth know where you're all hiding. He's been out looking for you.'

Andy held up his hands in surrender. 'We'll talk! We'll talk!'

'Or rather, we'll let you listen,' Steve grinned. He reached forward and turned up the volume again.

'Jimmy, baby, that was out of this world,' a breathy feminine voice gasped. 'You can adjust my focus any-time.'

'Want to play with my tripod?' a male voice said suggestively.

'Mmmm, baby, I can feel something developing right now . . .'

'You bastards,' Damon said, shaking his head appreciatively. 'How'd you do it?'

'Simple. We wired him up,' Andy said.

'She's his sixth this week,' Dave added. 'I don't know how he does it. He's not exactly Chippendale mate-rial . . . more like MFI. At this rate he'll have a bloody telegram from the Queen by Christmas.'

'It's his technique. He's not afraid to beg,' Andy commented.

Steve turned as he saw Damon looking over his shoul-der with an expression of unconcealed admiration on his face. ''Fraid not, old son,' he said, clapping Damon on the back. 'That's our Christie, and the last thing she needs right now is you.'

'Jesus, I don't know if what they're saying is true, but I'd give half my damn salary to find out,' Damon said, his eyes following the beautiful but distraught girl as she fled past the open door of the bar to the main door of the hotel. 'Sod it, I'd give the bloody lot for just half a chance.'

'Leave it out,' Andy said, his laughter fading. He grimaced at Damon's suggestive grin. 'Forget it, mate, she doesn't play away, least of all with us. But she's a great correspondent, and I hate to see what your paper's doing to her.'

Damon shrugged defensively. 'Hey, guys, nothing to do with me,' he said. 'I'm just as surprised as you are. Our revered leader Denzil Calhoun doesn't share his thoughts with lowly hacks such as me.'

Andy took another swallow of his beer and frowned. 'Somebody's playing games, and I'd like to know who.' He moved aside as two men in immaculate Savile Row suits approached the bar. 'That whole scene was a little too smooth for my liking. They were just a bit too ready for her. What the fuck were they doing searching her room in the first place?'

'Yeah, well, that's the way it goes,' Damon said, draining his glass. 'Wordsworth's been playing with fire for a bloody long time. INN's fair game these days. Something like this was bound to happen.'

'Why her? She's the straightest bloody reporter we've got,' Steve said bitterly. 'When you think what some of them get up . . . Christ, half the bastards we get as correspondents spend most of their time chucking caviar down the toilet to up their hotel bills, and then make a mint when they claim their expenses at the official exchange rate whilst at the same time they're dealing privately on the black market. Christie doesn't even fiddle her taxi receipts.'

'That's not what the papers are saying,' Damon shrugged. 'Doesn't gel, if you ask me.'

'Exactly,' Steve said angrily. 'For God's sake, she saved my life in Kosovo. I *owe* her. I just wish I could figure a way to help.'

'Should get your boss to have a word with Calhoun,' Damon said, indicating to the barman to refill his glass. 'They're supposed to be good friends, or so I've heard.'

'Wordsworth and Calhoun?' Dave asked in surprise.

'Hardly,' Damon answered sceptically. 'No, Penhaligon. Seen him a few times with Denzil. Annabel's, Langan's. Strange, really. They don't seem the type who'd have much in common.'

'You're not kidding,' Steve said thoughtfully.

Andy grinned as sounds of life came from the speaker, and pulled the stereo nearer towards him across the counter. 'Sounds like Our Jimmy's giving her one for the road.'

'Oh, baby, fuck me hard, give it to me good,' the woman screamed.

An appreciative audience gathered around the speaker. Several other men leaning against the bar moved closer to the journalists as the barman admitted defeat and joined them with another round of beer. The woman moaned softly, her voice muffled by an unknown portion of her partner's anatomy.

'Jesus fucking Christ!' the man next to Andy yelled suddenly, slamming his glass of whisky down on the top of the bar. 'That's my fucking *wife*!'

Steve dived for the telephone and punched Jimmy's number as the man fled the bar, his face working with demented fury. 'That bugger Jimmy needs a wife to keep him under control,' Steve grumbled as he waited for the cameraman to pick up the receiver. 'This kind of excitement I can live without. For God's sake Jimmy, answer the bloody phone.'

'He's got a wife,' Andy observed. 'Quite a few of them, in fact. Trouble is, none of them are his.'

The group around the speaker settled down expectantly to wait for the next act in the drama, draining their glasses and passing a glass dish of peanuts along the bar as they chatted in the muted tones of a West End theatre audience waiting for the curtain to rise. Idly Steve thought he

514

might issue programmes next time.

None of them even noticed the woman who entered the bar alone and sat down at a table on the opposite side of the room, her pale eyes bright with satisfaction, as she smoothed her hair into place over the collar of her cream and navy jacket. Her fingers touched the cut on the side of her cheek where she had fallen against the door when David threw her away from him. It had been worth it, just to see him lose control. To make him feel a little of the pain, the anguish, the humiliation that she had experienced at his hands. And this was just the beginning. She would make sure of that.

Caryn smiled. She was sure Edward would not object to her little jaunt to Blackpool when she told him that Ben Wordsworth and Paragon Fairfax were having an affair.

■ PEMBROKE HOTEL, BLACKPOOL
   11.10 p.m.

Christie lay curled up on her bed in the foetal position. A distant part of her tried to believe that she would survive this, that the agony would pass. But memory was treacherous, cruelly replaying the treasured moments of her time with David and then cutting to that last, final scene with terrible precision. She was dying inside from a thousand cuts inflicted by a thousand shattered images. Had it all been an illusion, a lie, a pretence? Could she have been *so* wrong?

The telephone rang beside her, and automatically she reached for it, her instinct as a journalist switching into gear. She held the receiver against her chest as she sat up, fighting to clear her head, and drew a deep breath.

'Yes?'

'Christie? Is that you?'

515

'Jack?' Relief flooded her voice. 'Oh Jack, thank God. I thought it was . . . never mind. It's just good to hear your voice.'

'Christie, are you OK?' Ginny's brother asked with very real concern. He had known that she would be at her most vulnerable after the tabloid's vitriolic assault, but until now he had never doubted her ability to fight it and survive. Christie had never been afraid to battle for justice. But the defeated sound of her voice appalled him, and suddenly he was not so sure.

'I can't deal with this,' she sobbed, her voice raw with grief. 'I just can't take any more. It's too much.'

Jack sighed softly. 'Oh, baby, it's not going to last. I promise you that,' he said quietly. 'Just hold on a little longer. You're not alone. We're here for you.'

Christie smiled fleetingly through her tears. Jack was one of her closest friends. Her affection for him was deep and honest, despite the scene she had witnessed between him and Nick on the tennis court at Ben Wordsworth's party. He had always been loyal and true to her, and she responded now to the care in his words. 'It's more than the newspapers, Jack,' she whispered.

'David?'

Christie gasped at the pain the mere mention of his name sent streaking through her. 'I saw him, Jack. With Caryn. He was in bed with her. Oh God, why did he lie to me, Jack? I don't understand it, I don't understand any of this.'

'I think I do,' Jack said grimly, more to himself than to her. He paused thoughtfully. 'Christie, I can't believe he's having an affair with her. David told you it was over between you two?'

'He didn't need to,' Christie answered, flinching again at the memory. 'I had a message from him, asking me to come to his room. He told me he loved me, Jack. I

516

couldn't hold out against him any longer, I needed him so much. But when I walked in, she was there in bed with him.'

'Christie, has it occurred to you that David would hardly have set himself up to be caught like that?' Jack said disbelievingly. 'He's crazy about you, you know that. Think about it. Just think about it. Promise me, Christie?'

'OK, Jack, I promise.'

Jack sighed grimly. He knew there was only one thing that could help Christie survive this. Her journalistic instinct was stronger than anything else, and right now he thought it was the only chance she had of holding herself together. He prayed it was enough.

'Baby, hang on in there,' Jack urged. 'I need you to be strong. You have to help me now.'

Something in his voice caught Christie's attention, and she forced her mind to concentrate, to reach outside her own torment. 'I'm here, Jack,' she said.

'Christie, we've got a hell of a fight on our hands,' Jack said wearily. 'I've just had the results back from the package you sent me. It's not good.'

Christie straightened up, a sudden rush of adrenalin filling her with a pulse of excitement that she had not expected to feel. 'Tell me, Jack.'

'You were right. Jesus, Christie, I can hardly believe it.'

Christie reached for her notebook. 'I'm ready.'

'Those tablets are *not* a vitamin, that much was easy to find out. I gave it to a friend of mine here, who analyzed it as a favour,' Jack said, running his hand through his hair distractedly. 'He was horrified when he ran it through a few tests. It's one of ours.'

Christie sat back on her heels, stunned. This was hardly the latest lipstick. Her mind raced furiously.

'One of yours?'

'It's not something we've done a great deal of research

on, it's far too experimental at the moment,' Jack explained. 'But I know what it is. It's called Loc33. It's a sterilising drug.'

'A contraceptive?' Christie asked incredulously.

'It's more than that. It's cheap and very simple, since it can be administered by injection or in tablet form. It's also extremely effective: just one dose is enough. And it's irreversible.'

'Enough for what?'

'Enough to sterilise a woman forever.'

Christie was stunned. 'Who developed it? Why?'

'I can't tell you why. You've probably got a better idea than I have, to be honest. But it's certainly not legal. Our Research Department have been looking into several alternatives to the current Pill, but this Loc33 is nowhere near ready to be released on to the market. I can't understand how you got hold of it.'

'It's on the market all right,' Christie said grimly. 'And it's certainly being used. Who runs the Department, Jack?'

'The Research Department is very tightly controlled,' Jack answered slowly. 'No one working there is given any more information than they absolutely *have* to have, to prevent industrial espionage. You wouldn't believe how much money is involved in this kind of contraceptive work. Almost more than there is in AIDS research.'

Christie scribbled furiously on her notepad as Jack spoke. She was on the edge of a story that could split the world apart, and her every sense was alert.

'Go on,' she said.

'Well, each researcher answers only to one person, the Managing Director of ChemCo,' Jack said. 'His control is absolute. It's the only way the company can guarantee to keep the kind of work we do secret. He's the one person who holds all the pieces of the jigsaw puzzle. It's all down to him.'

Christie knew what his answer would be, but she asked him anyway. 'Who is he, Jack?'

Jack's voice sounded grim on the end of the telephone. 'Who else? Sir Edward Penhaligon.'

Chapter Eighteen

■ KENT, ENGLAND
   15 October, 2.30 p.m.

'So it's over.'

   'I'm so sorry I had to be the one to tell you.'

   Odile Wordsworth looked across at the courtly old
gentleman seated on the sofa in front of the window. 'Oh,
no, Mr Foley, I'm so glad you did. It would have been
terrible to find out some other way . . . from the newspapers, or on the television.'

   Harry Foley inclined his head in acknowledgement. He
had dreaded this conversation, but his own innate sense of
duty forced him to complete the task with as much
compassion as possible. There had been more than
enough pain already.

   He was quite well aware of Sir Edward Penhaligon's
motives in letting him know that his wife Paragon was
sleeping with the Editor of INN. Nevertheless, he would
do as Sir Edward wanted. He would sell. He had already
instructed his stockbroker to draw up the necessary papers
that would enable him to divest himself of his shares in
INN, and had informed Sir Edward of his decision. He
had no wish to have anything more to do with INN, a
company headed by a man who had so ruthlessly deceived
him.

   Or with the wife who had so ruthlessly betrayed him.

'I always knew that Ben had never been faithful to me,' Odile said quietly. Her gaze flickered across the silent television screen in the corner of the room, which showed David Cameron reporting from a bombed-out village somewhere in Kosovo, before returning to Harry. 'I just never dared to admit it, not even to myself. I didn't want proof, because then I knew I would have to do something about it. And, despite everything, I didn't want to lose him.'

Harry sighed. Her feelings echoed his own with an ironic accuracy. He had lived with the painful reminder of his mistake every single day of his two-year marriage to Paragon Fairfax. The easy companionship which she had initially provided had faded almost as soon as they had completed their wedding vows. Bitterly he realised that he had been fooled into a desperately unsuitable marriage by Paragon's skilled display of sympathy and understanding, her promises of friendship and her readiness to listen. He had been so terribly lonely since the death of his beloved first wife, Philippa. The inevitable whisperings of amusement that had accompanied his re-marriage with a girl almost forty years his junior had been difficult to withstand, but he persevered. He had been determined to stand by his choice, however misguided it might have been. Unquestioningly he had sanctioned her demands for designer watches, couture clothes, expensive cars; he knew her for what she was, and he accepted it as part of the price he had to pay for his error.

Having made Paragon his wife, Harry had resolved to fulfil his obligations, whatever his personal misgivings. He had contributed financially to the formation of INN in order to provide Paragon with the showcase she desired, and had watched with quiet acceptance as she rose to the intoxicating heights of one of the most envied jobs in television journalism. Later he had denied his own

521

instincts of business and principle to protect her, refusing Sir Edward Penhaligon's generous and reasonable offer to buy his shares in INN. Much as Harry had sympathised with Sir Edward's desire to restore the qualities of hard news, expert analysis and editorial responsibility to the news network, he had put Paragon's interests first. He had never expected her love; all he had ever wanted was her loyalty.

But now he understood she had denied him even that.

Harry turned to Odile, infinite sorrow for her and regret for his own foolishness in his expressive grey eyes. 'What will you do now?'

Odile shrugged her shoulders eloquently. 'I will survive,' she said simply.

Harry regarded her with renewed respect. The upright woman on the elegant Chesterfield gave little indication of the unhappiness she must currently be experiencing. Odile displayed instead the resolute courage that he recognised as an integral part of her aristocratic French upbringing, her backbone firm and straight, the dark eyes meeting his filled with resignation and unselfish sympathy. Odile reminded him in so many ways of Philippa; they shared the same finely-drawn cheekbones, the same mobile, expressive mouth, the same shapely head and slender neck. Harry saw in her the courage and spirit his first wife had possessed, the strength of character that enabled both women to withstand the most cruel onslaughts of fate and chance, the inner composure that leant a depth and timelessness to the classic beauty they both shared. He could not comprehend how such a faithless, uncivilised man as Benjamin Wordsworth had ever captured the elegant, intelligent woman before him.

Harry smiled to himself. Who was he to pronounce upon the strange twists human relationships gave to one's life? No doubt Odile entertained similarly incredulous thoughts about his own marriage.

Odile sighed and rose, crossing the elegant drawing-room to stand beside the tall French windows that looked out upon the lawn. She rested for a moment with her forehead pressed against the glass, her left hand holding back the heavy Regency striped curtains. 'It must be hard for you,' she said compassionately, her eyes following a fox as it darted across the grass, disappearing into the damp mists that wrapped the lower half of the garden. 'Betrayal is such a complex feeling. It hurts in ways that are so unexpected.'

Harry thought again how much courage this woman possessed, and how much understanding. He had faced and survived horrors that he prayed she would never know, her life had been sheltered and protected in ways his had never been. Yet now she comprehended his confused feelings with an instinctive wisdom that he, for all he had endured, had never learned.

Harry had believed he had experienced the full range of human emotions in his lifetime. Those who had lived through the nightmare of the Holocaust were seared irrevocably by its horror. He had tasted grief, terror, anger at the death of his father, and the murder and rape of his mother; he had come to terms with fear and his own desperate fight for survival that overrode all other instincts of selflessness, heroism, loyalty. That bitter realisation that at the bottom of his soul lurked a desire for life that outweighed all nobler emotions was the most harsh lesson he had ever had to learn. That and the terrible guilt that he alone of his family had survived.

He had fought hard to overcome the terrible legacy of the Nazis, to keep his spirit and his faith in humanity untainted by the cynical despair that destroyed so many of his people. And he had succeeded. From the ruin of war-torn Europe he had escaped to achieve personal happiness and professional success. He had created an empire of exclusive hotels that spanned the world and catered to the elite of society, savouring his triumph all the more because he had known poverty and despair. He had survived his overwhelming grief for his beloved Philippa when she died, battling his anger and loneliness to finally achieve a measure of quiet acceptance. With Paragon he had sought not love but friendship and companionship, the chance to share a little of his hard-earned wisdom with someone for whom he cared. It had pleased him to be her mentor, and he had enjoyed teaching her a little about his world. He had believed there was nothing left for him to learn.

But Paragon had taught him something of her own.

Betrayal.

Would he ever be sure of himself again?

'You must not doubt yourself,' Odile murmured, as if she had known what he was thinking. 'If you trust someone you can never really be betrayed, only mistaken. You must forgive yourself. Trust is part of being human. It is not a weakness, but a strength. You would be a lesser person without it.'

'You are a remarkable woman,' Harry said quietly.

Odile shook her head gently. 'In a strange way, for me it is almost a relief that it's over.'

'You sound so final. Are you sure?'

'Aren't you?' Odile countered softly.

'Yes.'

Odile crossed the room, her soft cream wool skirt swishing as she moved, and knelt on the floor at his feet. She took his old hands in his, her face upturned towards him, her amber eyes soft with compassion. 'Mr Foley, do not let this destroy your faith, your hope,' she said quietly. 'If you do, then it has all been for nothing.'

Her hands encircled his in an unselfconscious gesture of

affection, and suddenly Harry felt a comfort and reassurance he had not experienced since he lost Philippa. 'My faith has survived far more than this,' he said softly, smiling down at her, his grey eyes filled with the unutterable ancient weariness of his race. 'My dearest Odile, you have given me so much. I came to comfort you and instead . . . my dear, I cannot begin to thank you.'

Odile smiled and rose gracefully, her hands still clasping his.

'If you need a friend, I am always here.'

'I know. And thank you.'

The warmth of her words stayed with him as he drove his Silver Cloud along the winding autumn roads towards London, a bridge of friendship across the ravine of mistrust that Paragon had forged. He slowed the Rolls to a gentle meander, pausing every few miles to allow the more impatient drivers on the road to pass him. The rich russet and ochre of the turning leaves on the trees that arced across the road made a pathway of riotous colours, softened in the distance by the haze that hung over the valley as he passed through it. A fragment of a long forgotten poem came to his mind, and he murmured it softly. *Season of mists and mellow fruitfulness, Close bosom friend of the maturing sun* . . .

Harry smiled in fond recollection at Keats' poised words. Autumn was the boundary between summer and winter, between growth and decay, and the poem expressed a mood of calm acceptance mingled with a sense of the movement and processes of time at work that Harry suddenly understood. *Where are the songs of spring? Aye, where are they? Think not of them, thou hast thy music too.*

Yes. He had his music too. Paragon had not destroyed that.

The mood stayed with him as the fields gave way to

villages and later towns, and he entered London with mixed feelings of resignation and an inner peace that had eluded him until now. May and December were never meant to be together; he had paid the price of an old man's foolish dreams. Already Paragon seemed a distant part of his past. He would survive. The wounds would be painful, but they would heal. He thought Odile too would emerge from her personal ordeal with her integrity and faith intact; she had grown beyond Ben Wordsworth long ago. Finally she would be free to be herself.

Idly Harry wondered how Paragon and Ben would fare now that they were forced into each other's company by default. He grinned with satisfaction at the thought. They would drive each other crazy.

He walked into his penthouse office at the Mayfair Foley Hotel with a step far lighter than the one with which he had left it. He paused in surprise as he crossed the threshold, when he saw a slim, pale young woman already sitting on the wine-red leather sofa in his outer office. He had no appointments for that afternoon. His secretary shrugged as he raised a questioning eyebrow at her.

The girl stood up and extended her hand. 'Mr Foley, I'm so sorry to interrupt you like this, but it is terribly important that we talk. There is something you must know.'

Harry Foley pressed his fingers together and regarded Christie for a long moment. His grey eyes were clouded by doubt and foreboding at what she had told him, and for several minutes after she had ceased speaking he sat immobile, his brain rapidly assessing the information she had given him.

He tapped his fingers against his lips and leaned back, watching her steadily. She was even more beautiful than he remembered at their last meeting six months ago, and his brow furrowed as he attempted to define the change. His eyes ran over her rich gold hair, the make-up that was deftly but discreetly applied, but failed to hide her paleness. Her deep-grey Louis Feraud jacket and trousers were expensive but understated, the outline of her soft breasts just visible beneath her cream silk camisole. About her throat she wore a strand of unusual black pearls that he recognised instantly as expensively real, and a slim Guy Laroche watch was fastened about her wrist. She exuded class and style.

Suddenly he realised the difference in her. The expression in her green eyes was that of pain and hard-won understanding. It gave her a new depth which went beyond the undeniable attractiveness of her features and hinted at the character beneath, adding a new aura of compassion and simple strength to her startling beauty.

Yet this was the woman whom the papers were branding a cocaine addict.

Harry found the integrity he sensed in her character impossible to reconcile with what he had read about her. He frowned. Could she be believed? Could he trust her?

'Miss Bradley, the implications of what you are saying are more perhaps than either of us can comprehend,' he said at length.

Her expression did not waver. 'I know,' Christie said quietly. 'But I thought you, above all others, would want to prevent it.'

'You have incontrovertible proof of what is happening? You know, you really *know*, it is true?'

Christie sighed wearily. 'Mr Foley, I would give a great deal not to have to face this too,' she said. 'It is more horror than I ever imagined. But yes, I know it is true. I have been to the Palestinian camps. I have asked questions that can't be answered. It's happening. It's real.'

'A moment, please,' he murmured, closing his eyes and leaning back.

Was what she was saying really so unbelievable? There had been rumours of similar happenings in the Balkans, of Serbs forcibly sterilising Muslim women, or impregnating them with their own seed. And Israel? Were some of those in Israel above such acts?

Harry leant forward, his arms resting on his desk, his grey eyes meeting Christie's. 'And you are sure of the source?'

'Loc33 is a unique drug,' Christie said, choosing her words with care, aware that she had only one chance to convince him. 'It possesses a chemical fingerprint that has not been found elsewhere on the market. Only one company manufactures it, and they have not officially released it as yet; it is very much in the experimental stages.'

'ChemCo?'

'ChemCo,' Christie confirmed. 'A friend of mine who works in the Research Department recognised it as being Loc33; he says the chances of another company having developed and refined it to this stage of development are negligible.'

'But there *is* a chance?'

'Mr Foley, life is not composed of absolutes,' Christie said, pushing her hair back from her forehead. 'There is always a chance that one is mistaken, that there is an alternative. But one weighs the possibilities, and one makes a decision that tallies with the facts as closely as possible. One can do no more.'

Harry leaned back again and listened to the echo of her voice in his head. *It's happening. It's real.* His instinct told him to trust Christie, he sensed the stamp of truth in her story. Yet the man she accused was one of the most respected broadcasters in the world, renowned for his

528

rectitude and probity, the one voice of reason in the tabloid mire into which INN was fast descending. The man to whom he had just agreed to sell his shares in a company he no longer trusted. Was there no end to human treachery?

And against that he had the word of a woman who had been utterly discredited, branded as unreliable, untrustworthy, immoral. Was what she said the truth, or vengeance against the company who had instantly dismissed her the moment her career erupted in a blaze of scandal? Was the horror real, or the result of a personal vendetta against the most prominent man in that company?

'Miss Bradley, what is it you want me to do?'

'Help me fight,' Christie said simply.

Harry ran his left hand through his silvery hair, his right beating a tattoo on his desk. He felt every one of his sixty-three years as he thought of what that battle would involve. He would have to commit his considerable resources and put his own personal integrity on the line in order to fight, and once started there would be no turning back. He wanted to flee, to hide from this world of cheating wives, treacherous colleagues, unscrupulous friends, where nothing was as it seemed, where everyone wanted something from him and would do anything – say anything – to get it. Who was lying? Who was telling the truth? He had every reason to believe Sir Edward, every reason to doubt Christie Bradley. And yet his instinct told him otherwise.

Could he believe her? Dare he trust his judgement?

'I will think about what you have told me,' he said at last. 'I can say no more.'

Christie closed her eyes in defeat. He did not believe her. It was too late. Penhaligon's smears had discredited her so thoroughly that even this man would not accept the truth when she placed it before him. She had come to him because she knew what he had endured at the hands of the Nazis. He of all men knew the depths to which human beings could sink, the instinctive desire of a race to survive, the blindness of a world to see what was happening until it was too late. But she sensed his withdrawal, the prevarication in his promise to think about it further. She had gambled and lost. She could do no more.

Slowly Christie stood, and held out her hand, a final plea on her lips. 'Please. Before it is too late. Help me stop it happening again.'

Harry shook her hand, knowing that she understood the evasion in his words, trying to still the doubt about the rightness of his decision in his mind. He felt a flicker of shame.

She deserved his trust.

■ THE BOWER CLUB, LONDON
18 OCTOBER, 7.30 p.m.

Sir Edward Penhaligon glanced up as the club steward approached and gave his customary discreet cough into his hand.

'Sir Edward? Your visitor has arrived.'

'Have him shown over to me.' Sir Edward indicated his glass. 'And another of these.'

'Very good, Sir Edward.'

Sir Edward watched, a smile of satisfaction on his face, as the club steward walked away. The final piece of the puzzle was about to be slotted into place.

Caryn's information on Paragon and Ben could not have been timed more fortuitously. Even with the shares he had acquired from Dalmeny de Burgh, and his old friend Patrick Courtenay's promised support of the World News Service, he could still command control of only

530

thirty-eight per cent of the INN Board: more than Ben Wordsworth's thirty-two per cent, but not enough to force a vote of no confidence and oust the Editor altogether. Until Caryn had seen Ben Wordsworth and Harry Foley's attractive young wife entwined about each other as they disappeared into a bedroom at the Imperial Hotel. Caryn had done well.

He was glad he had married her.

She had willingly complied with all his suggestions, understanding the tenets of their partnership without needing to be told. He would never trust her, of course, but that was an irrelevancy. She had given him INN, and he had been happy to provide her with the name and status she craved. He glanced at his watch. As of three-and-a-half hours ago, she was Lady Caryn Penhaligon. Idly he wondered if she realised exactly what kind of deal she had struck, the extent of the payment he would demand from her. Dalmeny had been just the beginning.

He looked up as Harry Foley approached his chair, guided by the club steward.

'Sir Edward.'

'Harry, good to see you. I'm glad you could make it. Drink?'

'No thank you. This won't take long.'

Sir Edward glanced at the other man in surprise. Foley's face remained expressionless, but Sir Edward could see that he was carefully controlling himself. His grey eyes were unreadable, his movements formal and precise as he seated himself in the leather armchair next to that of the broadcaster. Sir Edward frowned. His instinct as a journalist told him that there was something seriously wrong, and his senses were immediately alert. He doubted that Foley had agreed to forgive his errant wife and changed his mind about selling; Paragon had responded to the revelation of her affair by moving straight in with a somewhat startled Ben Wordsworth, no doubt believing it to be an adroit career move. Sir Edward had a feeling this was far more serious.

'You'll forgive me . . .?' Sir Edward asked, indicating his Scotch.

'Please, go ahead. I suspect you will need it.'

Sir Edward slowly placed his glass on the table between them, and leaned back in his armchair. His lips tightened as he took in the naked hostility on Foley's face which the other man attempted but failed to conceal.

'May I ask what this is all about?'

'You may ask, but I'm sure you already know.'

Sir Edward laughed amiably. 'I'm afraid we seem to be talking at cross-purposes. I thought we were finalising the transfer of your stock to me . . .'

'Things have changed a little. I am perfectly prepared to explain it in great detail to you. Via the kind offices of the *Daily Ethic*, or perhaps a broadcast on the Early Evening News. The choice is yours, but I suspected you would prefer a private conversation.'

Sir Edward felt a terrible foreboding as he regarded the implacable expression on Foley's face. This was far more than the mere question of adultery, or even the acquisition of an international news network. Somehow, *somehow*, Foley knew.

'I think you had better tell me exactly what you mean,' Sir Edward said coolly, all traces of good humour now vanished.

'Tell me, how long did it take you to plan and execute your programme of elimination? How many years did it take to develop your solution?' Harry leaned forward in his chair and hissed each word with barely controlled anger. 'How long before you came up with your answer to an insoluble problem?'

Sir Edward thought rapidly. What Foley actually *knew*

532

was irrelevant. What he could *prove* was what mattered. He had to know how much that was. Denial was pointless: he had to draw Foley out.

'I could tell you the whole story, of course,' he said calmly, picking up his glass and sipping the Scotch. 'The years of trial and error after I inherited ChemCo. The pain of watching my mother's people, my own people, driven back against the wall by the Palestinians, a demographic gun held to their heads. The desperate search for a way out, a way that only I could provide. But I suspect that you already know it.'

'But why? Tell me, *why*?'

'Why me?' Sir Edward said consideringly. 'Because I am now part of the British way of life does not mean I forget my blood, my inheritance. I am half Jewish. English society may choose to forget that my mother was a Jew, but I haven't. I am in a position to be of real help to my people. Why not me?'

'You have denied the chance of life to hundreds – thousands – of human souls! You have destroyed the future of thousands of women! How can you justify what you've done?'

A fire burned in Sir Edward's eyes, and he leaned across to the other man; their eyes locked across an unbridgeable gulf of understanding. 'You are Jewish. You should understand how I feel.'

'Do two wrongs ever really make a right?' Harry asked despairingly. 'We have been wronged, yes, we have been wronged. We have been hounded, tormented, ignored, murdered, yes. I was there. And yes, I know the battle did not end with the Holocaust, nor with the war of 1967, nor with the PLO. It is still going on. But you have made yourself no better than they are.'

Sir Edward sat back in his chair. 'We have tried understanding, tolerance, patience, and where has it got us? How many times have we sat back and waited for the world to come to our aid, waited in vain? Who was it the Iraqis bombed when the Allies came to the rescue of Kuwait? Whose soldiers are shot every day as they protect their own land? Who are always the first to die?'

'Do you really believe this is the only way to fight?'

'What choice do we have?' Sir Edward asked. 'There is no other solution to the problem. We cannot live together. There has been too much death, too much pain, for there ever to be forgiveness. There can be no peace in Israel until one side defeats and destroys the other.'

'It is their land as much as ours,' Harry said wearily.

'It is our home! It is the only home we have! Do you think they will show any mercy if they manage to take control? No. This way there will be no war, no needless dying. No blood has been shed. No lives have been lost.'

'You are destroying the future of a whole people,' Harry said softly. 'I can't let you carry on doing it.'

Sir Edward smiled grimly. 'I don't think you can stop it.'

Harry shook his head. 'No. But you can. And you will.'

The two men gazed at each other for a long moment. Harry felt infinitely weary. He understood the forces that had driven Sir Edward to take the path he had chosen, he sympathised with his motivation. He knew that Sir Edward believed absolutely that there was no other way. But Harry could not condone what he had done.

'Would you like to tell me why you think I might do that?' Sir Edward said at length.

'I know you developed Loc33. I know it was administered as a vitamin in Dar el-Baran, and later in other Palestinian villages,' Harry said. 'I know that the Israeli Government is not a party to what is happening, although a few of their officials are involved. I know who, I know how, I know when, I know where.'

Sir Edward laughed. 'Proving it might be a little difficult.'

Harry acted as if he had not spoken. 'I know that you tipped off the Drug Squad, I know that you planted cocaine in Christie Bradley's hotel room. You one mistake. You were seen. I also know that you orchestrated the Press campaign to discredit Christie, and I can prove it. So her integrity will not be questioned, as yours will. Christie will be able to testify to what she has discovered without fear.'

Harry caught a flicker of unwilling respect and a faint acknowledgement of defeat in the other man's eyes, and for the first time he dared to permit himself to hope. Penhaligon's cooperation was vital; if Harry were forced to make Sir Edward's activities public in order to halt them, the ensuing retaliatory bloodshed in Israel and across the world would be unthinkable. It could be the trigger which detonated the powder keg that was the Middle East. Harry was treading a fine line. He had to force Penhaligon into a corner by convincing him that the proof against him was overwhelming and undeniable. He also had to offer Penhaligon an escape route, an alternative that was sufficiently attractive to prevent him from forcing Harry's hand.

'Why are you telling me all this?'

'I am going to give you a choice. You can either do exactly what I suggest, or I will reveal your activities. Not to the police, that would be too simple. To the Palestinians.'

'They would eliminate me,' Sir Edward said without emotion. 'That I can accept. But they would hold my people responsible. My people would bear the brunt of retaliation. It would all have been for nothing.'

'Yes.'

'You would do that, knowing what it might mean?'

535

'If necessary, yes. If there was no other way to stop you.'

Sir Edward had often wondered what he would do if he was discovered, accepting the risks he took as an inevitable part of the war he waged. It seemed now that he was about to find out. He found the taste of defeat unpalatable but not unbearable.

'Continue,' he said to Harry.

'You will ensure that the distribution of Loc33 ceases immediately. You will hand over control and ownership of ChemCo to your nephew, who is not a party to any of this. You will agree to sell me all the shares in INN currently in your possession at the market price, and your connection with either company will be completely severed. You may plead reasons of ill-health, if you wish, which I shall not contradict. And you will leave this country within twenty-four hours. The final choice of destination is yours, but you must never return here.'

It was better than he had dared hope. 'Anything else?' he said dryly.

'I have already had this conversation with two people. My lawyer, who has instructions to reveal everything should anything untoward befall either myself or Christie Bradley. And Denzil Calhoun, who will publish a complete vindication of Christie's character and reputation.'

'Indeed?'

Harry smiled for the first time since he had walked into the Club. 'Mr Calhoun was more than anxious to extricate himself from any link with you, once I made the situation clear. Most helpful, in fact. Particularly when I pointed out that I shall be the new majority shareholder in INN.'

'That *would* help your position with Denzil, yes,' Sir Edward murmured.

'Fortunately the memories of those who read the tabloids are notoriously short; today's news is tomorrow's fish-and-chip wrappings, as they say. I suspect the great British public will take the beleaguered Christie to their hearts when they understand the cocaine was an unfortunate error on behalf of the police. Mistaken identity, perhaps.'

'And how will you persuade the Drugs Squad to take that generous view as well?' Sir Edward asked coolly.

'I assume you have a good contact with the Squad, otherwise you would not have been able to frame Christie in the first place. You will telephone your loyal friend and explain the change in the situation to him. How you do that is your concern, but you will ensure all charges are dropped and a full, public apology is made.'

'You seem to have thought of everything, but do you really think it will make any difference in the end? You must know that Arab and Jew will go on fighting each other, until one day, one side wins. At least my way, the cost in lives would not have been so high.'

'Your price was still too high for me to sanction its payment.'

Sir Edward drained his glass and replaced it on the table. 'I take it I am at least permitted to return to my home?'

'No. Anything you want, you may send for.'

Sir Edward met Foley's eyes for one last, long minute. They shared the same heritage, the same background, the same ancient blood. But in beliefs they could not have been further apart. He understood his defeat and accepted it. In a war, battles were won and lost. His one regret was that he had failed to wrest INN from Ben Wordsworth's hands. Sir Edward's commitment to maintaining the integrity of television journalism was as deep as his loyalty to his own people, however unscrupulous his methods of achieving his aims. But, as majority shareholder, perhaps

Foley would now be able to temper Wordsworth's influence. Whilst they differed on so many things, Sir Edward had no doubt that Foley agreed with his view of Ben's Editorship.

And twenty-four hours would be more than enough to transfer the remainder of his funds out of the country.

'In that case, I think I had better telephone my wife.'

■ REGENT'S PARK, LONDON
8.10 p.m.

Caryn listened to the telephone ring and ignored it. If it was important, they would call back. Smoothly she soaped her shoulders, relaxing as the warm water lapped against her body, soothing away the world. She lifted her left hand from beneath the bubbles and regarded it with satisfaction. The simple gold wedding band was more valuable to her than the glittering emerald ring. Lady Caryn Penhaligon. It had been worth the price of losing her child, seducing Dalmeny, that Edward had demanded. It was worth any price.

With a sigh of contentment Caryn stood up and stepped out of the bath, her polished toes sinking deeply into the soft pile carpet. She reached for her white bathrobe and slipped her arms into it, deftly twisting the belt around her waist. She glanced at her watch on the dressing-table as she emerged into the bedroom. 8.15. That gave her less than an hour before she had to meet Edward at Annabel's. Thank God she had already packed for their honeymoon.

With a swiftness born of long practice Caryn applied her make-up; her hand paused over her array of eyeshadows as she debated which colour to choose. With a smile she rejected the soft fawns and russets which Edward

538

favoured, selecting instead a vibrant plum and deep rose which made her cerulean eyes even more startlingly pale. After all, she did not have to cater to his every whim any more. She was married now.

The game had only just begun.

And the challenge of it appealed to her. To control a man such as Edward would be an achievement indeed; the promise of the contest filled her with mingled fear and exultation. She would do it.

Or be destroyed in the attempt.

Caryn peeled off her bathrobe and tapped a heap of perfumed talcum powder into her hand, dusting it across the smooth contours of her body, leaving a faint imprint of her feet in the powder she had spilled onto the white carpet. She wriggled her shoulders in delicious anticipation. Three weeks in Nassau. Every door would be opened to her now that she was Edward's wife; they would mingle with the elite of society, attend the most exalted society occasions. Perhaps even join the ranks of those aristocratic celebrities who graced Dempster's gossip column, an accolade of social chic that had so far eluded her.

Resolutely she suppressed the mingled longing and anger that twisted her heart inside her when she thought of David, trying to dispel the bitter taste of the realisation that she had not known what it was to love until she had already thrown it away. She would not make the mistake of caring twice. With Edward she would enter a battle of wills: from him she would have the challenge, the recognition, of an equal adversary. And if she failed – it could not be more painful than the defeat she had suffered in love, at the hands of David.

Maybe one day this terrible loneliness would disappear. *Forget him. Forget him. He is nothing to you now.* She unlocked her jewellery case and drew a rope of antique baroque pearls from it, teasing through the jumble of bracelets, necklaces and rings to find the matching earrings that Dalmeny had bought her after he received the photographs, the gesture of a gallant loser. She laughed softly. A gentleman to the last. She glanced at her watch. 8.50. Damn.

Rapidly Caryn crossed the room and opened the door, fiddling with the clasp of one of her earrings. She heard the insistent shrill of the telephone once more, and hastened her steps.

She did not notice the brightly coloured tricycle until it was too late.

Desperately she tried to regain her balance as she stumbled against the toy, her ankles twisting in her high shoes. She felt a searing pain in her shoulder as she fell against the wall, and reached out frantically for something to halt her descent. Her hands found only empty air. With a terrible scream she plunged headlong down the stairs, tumbling and twisting and turning as she fell and the steps reached up to meet her. Her forehead caught the marble edge of the lowest stair as her back slammed into the floor at the bottom, her body twisted at an unnatural angle. The tricycle tumbled slowly after her, and came to rest just inside the door. It lay on its side, the upper wheel turning slowly and silently in the air, until it finally stopped moving altogether.

Slowly Caryn opened her eyes. She saw the tricycle with perfect clarity, and breathed a sigh of relief. No double vision, so she had probably escaped concussion. She gasped at the white-hot pain that speared her injured shoulder as she moved her arm to touch her face. Her fingertips came away redly wet from her forehead. Damn. Fervently she prayed it would not scar. Carefully she felt her cheekbones and nose. Nothing was broken, thank God. Apart from the gash in her temple, her face was undamaged. Bruises and cuts would heal. She had been extremely lucky.

Damn that child. She would kill him if she ever saw him again. She lifted her head cautiously. The pain knifed through her shoulder as she moved her arms to take her weight, and she bit her lip as carefully she tried to sit up.

It was then she realised she could not feel her legs.

She could feel nothing at all below her waist.

Slowly, terribly, she began to scream.

And scream.

Chapter Nineteen

■ ATHENS AIRPORT, GREECE
1 NOVEMBER 2.00 p.m.

Christie sat down on a pile of silver camera boxes that belonged to the World News Service and watched as INN's camera equipment was loaded into the back of a Hercules C-130 transport plane. God, six tonnes was a hell of a lot of gear, but then these sturdy military aircraft were built to take that kind of weight. She sighed. It would be good to be working on a real story again, far out of the reach of Fleet Street's finest. She wanted to cover the news, not be part of it.

The tabloid interest in her had been fuelled to fever pitch by the *Daily Ethic*'s article which had followed Harry Foley's meeting with Sir Edward Penhaligon. Two days later, the paper had proclaimed that there had been an 'outrageous' miscarriage of justice, and had hinted mysteriously at a devious dirty tricks campaign against her. Christie had smiled when she had seen it. She should have known that Denzil Calhoun would find a way to transform his abrupt volte-face into newspaper sales. Thanks to him, she had become hot property. Her story had elements of everything guaranteed to improve newspaper circulation: television glamour, intrigue, sex and drugs. Journalists had besieged her flat, shouting questions and taking photographs of her every time she had stepped outside. She had developed a lasting sympathy with the Royal Family.

But what they all really wanted to know was whether she and David planned a future together.

She cupped her chin in her hands, sadness clouding her eyes. Somehow, somewhere, David and she had lost whatever future they might have shared in a maze of guilt and misunderstanding. How had it been possible for two people who had loved each other so much to utterly destroy their relationship?

Christie knew now that David had not been having an affair with Caryn Kelly. Jack's shrewd comments had provoked her into finding out what had really happened that terrible night at the Imperial Hotel, no matter how much the truth might hurt. Slowly she had pieced the story together, using all her skills as an investigative reporter. Finally she had managed to track down the chambermaid who had let David's 'wife' into his hotel bedroom, and Christie had learned firsthand the power and hatred of a woman scorned.

Yet her anger was directed not at Caryn, despite the damage she had done, but towards herself. *She* was the one who had failed to trust David; not once, but twice. She had run from him in her anguish over Nick's abduction; and then she had run again from the scene in the Imperial, without even giving David the chance to explain.

Now, it was too late.

However much she told herself that any woman would have misread the scene as she had done, she could not forgive herself for doubting him. She should have known that David would not lie to her. She should have known that he would never have broken his promises to love her. And now the damage had been done. Their trust in each other had been broken.

She had spent the last two weeks desperately trying to come to terms with the fact that she had lost David forever. It had taken all her strength to keep going, and she welcomed this chance to escape into her work.

The irony was that she was going to Kosovo to join the INN team who were already there. And amongst them was David.

'This water all yours?'

Christie glanced at the cardboard boxes of bottled water which were piled haphazardly on the tarmac, and turned to the World News Service producer. 'Think so. All the ones marked with the INN logo are ours, anyway.'

The WNS girl frowned. 'We didn't think to bring any bottles to take with us. Can we have some of yours?'

'You didn't order some yourselves?' Christie said in surprise. 'Surely your Foreign Desk knows that there's no longer any running water in Kosovo?'

'They do, yes, but I forgot to do anything about it.'

Christie looked up as Steve joined them on the airstrip. He thumbed towards the airport handlers who were still loading the heavy editing boxes into the gaping maw of the Hercules. A fine mist of rain started to fall. 'Those guys are doing well, so far. About two-thirds of our stuff is already on board. Another half-hour should do it.'

'I hope you're putting all the INN gear on first,' the WNS girl said tightly. She pulled her anorak hood over her head as the rain fell more heavily. 'I want our equipment put on last, so that we're first to unload off the plane once we land in Kosovo. WNS chartered the Hercules, remember.'

Steve held his hands up in surrender. 'Sure, sure, no worries. Whatever you say.'

'So it's OK if we have some of your water then?' the WNS girl said, turning back to Christie.

'Bit of a problem there, darling,' Jimmy said, appearing

behind her. He winked at Steve. 'It's already been loaded on the plane, along with the rest of the INN gear. We put it on board first, as you requested. It'll take ages to unload, and I'm sure you won't want to wait around.'

'Yeah. We'd hate to slow you down,' Steve added.

The WNS girl glared at them. Before she had a chance to frame a suitably cutting reply, she noticed two baggage-handlers trundling a canary-yellow flatbed trolley laden with equipment away from the Hercules. She darted after them, waving frantically. 'Hey! Stop! That's my trolley! You can't take that! Where are you going?'

'I think I'm in love,' Steve said, his hand over his heart.

Christie dug her hand into the pocket of her jeans, hooking the heel of one boot over the lip of the silver editing box. The rain had given her skin a damp sheen. 'Beggars can't be choosers. We were lucky to find a plane willing to fly into Kosovo at all.'

'Yeah. But we pay half the flight charter and she gets to make all the rules.'

'That's partly our fault,' Jimmy said fairly. 'Philip Cunningham wouldn't commit INN to chartering the Hercules in case none of the other networks joined us, and we couldn't split the cost. Instead, he waited for WNS to take the risk and charter, and now we have to pay the penalty for piggy-backing on their ride.'

Christie stood up, straightening her khaki jacket and picking up the Billingham bag that contained the essential items with which she always travelled. 'I'm going to check that our equipment is all safely on board,' she said to the camera crew as she ducked under the propeller of the plane. 'Keep an eye on the WNS gear as it's loaded, and let me know how full the plane is. CNN want us to bring in a few pieces for them if we have room.'

'Will do.'

Christie darted up the three steps into the Hercules and

paused a moment, pushing her damp hair out of her eyes as she scanned the interior. Nearly a hundred pieces of equipment had already been stowed in the centre of the vast plane; webbing straps held them loosely in place. Folded against the sides of the aircraft were simple red canvas seats which, once in place, would leave little space between the occupants and the equipment on board. The Hercules had been designed for efficiency rather than comfort; the tiny circular windows let in little light, and the metal floor was a maze of bolts and rings to which the cargo could be secured into place with the heavy-duty webbing in almost any combination of positions.

She knew from experience that the flight would be uncomfortable, cold and extremely noisy, akin to travelling in the hold of a commercial airliner. They had little choice. There was no other way to transport both themselves and the INN equipment into Kosovo at such short notice. They were fortunate that the UN had at least managed to secure the airport and the surrounding hills there. Until now, the only way into the war-torn country had been the hazardous overland journey through Albania which Christie and David had undertaken on their previous visit to Kosovo.

She wondered fleetingly how long the air route would stay open. With Turkey, Bulgaria and now Greece on the threshold of war, they had no guarantees that the air corridor would hold up long enough to provide the journalists with a safe way back out of Kosovo. The terrible and bloody sundering of Yugoslavia was as nothing compared to the conflict which now threatened to engulf the Balkan states, and perhaps spread into the heart of Europe itself. And Kosovo was the flashpoint.

The West was still desperately trying to prevent the bloodshed from escalating yet further. They had deployed UN forces with a new directive to actively peace*make*, as well as peace*keep*. Now, the approach of winter heralded problems in supplies of both food and ammunition, and each of the numerous warring factions was desperate to gain as much of both as they could before the snows arrived and made transport impossible.

David had predicted exactly this situation when they had left the country four months before. Christie's heart turned over as she thought of him. If only things could have been different between them.

'Hi, gorgeous. Ready to roll?'

Christie turned as Steve dumped a large box on the floor of the aircraft. He glanced around for something to secure it.

'What the hell have you got in there?' Jimmy asked as he came on board. 'He peered suspiciously into the box, which clinked as Steve wedged it between two struts of the aircraft.

'Six bottles of gin, and half a dozen of Scotch. But for Christ's sake, don't tell WNS. If we're too heavy and something has to get left behind, I don't want it to be this. I have a feeling it wouldn't be regarded as essential supplies.'

'That's a matter of opinion,' Jimmy said.

Christie smothered a laugh as the WNS girl pushed past them, her cropped hair bristling aggressively in all directions. 'We'll be taking off in five minutes,' she said curtly. 'What's so funny?'

Christie shook her head wordlessly, and the girl stalked into the cockpit, pushing past the vast lacing of webbing that protected the electronic heart of the aircraft from being damaged by loose equipment during landing and take-off.

The twenty or so journalists, cameramen and technicians, who formed the remainder of the INN and WNS teams, made their way into the belly of the Hercules, dumping their personal bags into the few spaces that were left around the camera gear. The baggage-handlers gave a few straps a final desultory tug before disappearing down the ramp of the Hercules. It closed slowly behind them.

'No complementary champagne? No ditsy stewardess telling me how to inflate my lifejacket and which emergency exit to use?'

Christie smiled as Jimmy fastened the seat-belt across his lap. 'Don't worry. I'll tell you when to jump.'

Steve slid into the canvas seat next to her, and nodded towards her Billingham bag, which she had left on the floor. 'I'd hold this next to you, if I were you,' he shouted over the noise of the engines as they started up. 'The way that gear's piled up, the chances are that half-a-dozen boxes will fall our way when the plane takes off.'

Christie reached for the bag and wedged it between her feet. Abruptly she caught hold of Steve's arm as the Hercules took-off and she was thrown sideways against him. 'Hey, I'm sorry.'

Steve grinned. 'No need to apologise. I love it when a beautiful woman can't put me down.'

The aircraft stabilised into its flight, and most of the other journalists unbuckled their seatbelts and stood up, replacing one or two boxes that had slipped free of their fastenings, and chatting as they passed around cans of coca cola and bottles of water.

Steve waited until the others had moved away towards the rear of the plane and turned towards Christie. 'I haven't had a chance to say this before, but I'm so sorry about everything you've had to go through,' he said quietly. 'You didn't deserve that kind of treatment from the Press, or from anyone else for that matter.'

Christie smiled tiredly and leaned back. 'Thanks, Steve. It makes all the difference, knowing that your friends still

548

care about you.' She paused, reaching for a bottle of water on the floor. 'As a journalist, I'm used to being on the other side of a camera and asking the questions. It was quite a shock to be on the receiving end.'

'Some of the things they said were pretty cruel.'

She sipped the water. 'The worst part was knowing that thousands of people would be reading these terrible lies, and believing I was really like that.'

'Well, you're the darling of the nation now,' Steve laughed.

'Something like that.'

Suddenly Steve's face grew serious, and he clasped her hands in his. 'You deserve a break, Christie. It's been a rough year for you, with Nick's kidnapping and everything. We all miss him, of course, but I know he was a very close friend of yours.'

'If only I knew he was even still alive,' Christie said sadly. 'But we've heard nothing. It's so hard to keep on hoping.'

'I know.'

Both of them were silent for a moment, thinking of their colleague still languishing somewhere in the shadowy depths of Beirut. If he wasn't already dead.

Jimmy wandered back towards them and sat down on one of the edit boxes. 'Talking of Beirut, is Bob Carpenter still there?' Steve asked.

'Far as I know,' Jimmy shrugged. 'Why?'

Christie frowned. 'I can't think why Ben is letting him stay there,' she said. 'It's so dangerous, and INN is pretty high profile at the moment. Sam was saying that Bob's working on some secret deal Ben's cooked up between the Arabs and the Israelis. Anyone would think Ben's *trying* to get Bob kidnapped.'

'Couldn't happen to a nicer man,' Steve said dryly. 'But Bob won't leave. He's still chasing an RTS. He's been

549

after one ever since ITN's Jonathan Munro snaffled it from him last year.'

'Not a chance,' Jimmy said dismissively. 'David Cameron will win every award going for the Dakovica story he did in the summer.'

Christie looked away. No matter how much she told herself she would get over David, the pain still remained locked inside her, as raw as ever. She wondered if it would ever really disappear.

Suddenly the plane banked to the right, and Christie fell forward onto the boxes in front of her. She gasped as the sharp metal bruised her ribs.

'What the hell was that?' Jimmy exclaimed.

Steve leaned forward to help Christie up, his hands grasping her wrists firmly. An unreadable emotion filled his eyes as he looked at her. 'You OK?'

Christie sat back into her seat. 'I'll be fine.'

His hand did not leave hers. 'Are you sure?'

'Really, just a few bruises.'

She smiled at him warmly. They had become very close since she had saved his life in Dakovica, and his support had meant a great deal to her in the past few difficult weeks. Their friendship was strong. When you were on the road together, you came to know almost everything about your colleagues: their strengths, their weaknesses, their dreams and their fears. You shared experiences that formed an unbreakable bond between you.

'Christie . . . I've been meaning to ask you . . .'

The plane banked sharply again, and the WNS girl appeared in the doorway to the cockpit. Steve sighed.

'We can't land at the main airport in Kosovo,' the WNS girl said. 'There's a gunfight going on, and we've already been shot at. We'll have to land at an airstrip outside the main town.'

Jimmy groaned. 'Bloody place. Trouble with Kosovo is

550

that everyone's got a gun and an attitude.'

'Is there any way of letting our guys on the ground know?' Christie asked.

'We've radioed to the Tower at the main airport and asked them to let everybody know what's going on,' the WNS girl said diffidently. 'Down to them now.'

'Let's hope our trucks get the message and go out to the airstrip. It'll be hell to move our gear if they don't show,' Jimmy said. 'And without transport, we're sitting targets.'

'Can't help that,' the WNS girl said, turning and disappearing back into the cockpit.

'Great,' Jimmy said. He winked at Christie. 'I suppose a quick bonk is out of the question while we're waiting?'

She laughed and shook her head. Jimmy was not to be deflected. 'How about a massage then?'

'I pay thirty pounds for a massage from this girl in Soho,' Steve said indignantly. 'Why should you get it for free?'

'Thirty pounds?' Jimmy said disbelievingly. 'I don't pay thirty pounds for sex.'

'Ah, you would if it was with Paragon Fairfax,' Steve said.

'That's a different matter altogether,' Jimmy grinned. 'Now she's *worth* paying for.'

'I doubt Ben Wordsworth feels the same way,' Christie said. 'I can't help feeling sorry for him. Not only has Odile thrown him out, but Paragon turned up on the doorstep of his London *pied à terre* last week and moved in, lock, stock and overdraft.'

'Careless talk costs wives,' Jimmy said laconically.

Christie laughed. 'And meanwhile Harry Foley is revolutionising INN by introducing alien concepts such as ethics and integrity. And now he's got Victoria . . .'

'What about Victoria?' Steve asked.

'You don't know?' Jimmy said. 'She only turned up for the Early Evening News last week dressed in a tie-dyed kaftan, complete with beads, open-toed sandals and an holistic aura. She keeps eating lentils and pulses and has decided the only way to achieve true spiritual healing is to forsake material possessions and donate her entire wardrobe to Oxfam.'

'We'll have the best-dressed down-and-outs this side of *The Clothes Show*,' Christie observed.

'We *are* talking about Victoria?' Steve said incredulously.

'It's amazing what love can do,' Jimmy added. 'She's run away with Morgan De Burgh, no less. They're living in a lovenest in Hampshire, getting in touch with their psyches.'

'How's Dalmeny taking it?' Christie asked. She glanced across at Steve, and smiled affectionately at him as he ran his hand through his crisp, dark curls. He was a good friend, and an attractive man.

But he wasn't David.

'Dalmeny's the hero of the hour,' Jimmy said. 'Everybody's terribly sorry for him, and the PM has apparently decided to give him the FO as a consolation prize.'

'I can't quite see Ben embracing the idea of Victoria's new image wholeheartedly,' Steve said. 'In his view, women aren't even supposed to think they *might*, much less decide they *can*, get better sex without him. Hasn't he dived through some loophole in her contract by now? He always puts at least three in.'

'Can't afford to,' Christie said. 'Now that Sir Edward Penhaligon's retired, and Charles has been demoted to Religious Affairs Correspondent, Ben daren't risk losing any more newscasters. And Victoria's ratings have gone through the roof since she came out of her Designer closet.'

They felt the change in pressure as the Hercules began to descend, and the journalists around the aircraft moved back to their seats. With a jolt the plane landed, sending half a dozen pieces of equipment tumbling against the webbing which protected the front of the aircraft.

Slowly the Hercules came to a halt, and Christie climbed down the steps on to the sandy runway that was being used as a makeshift airstrip in order to avoid the conflict raging around the main airport. In the distance a number of trucks were speeding towards the aircraft. 'Looks like someone at INN got the message,' she said over her shoulder. 'The trucks are here for the gear, anyway.'

Some of the journalists climbed out after her and wandered away from the Hercules, welcoming the chance to stretch their legs after being cramped in the hold of the aircraft. Christie, Steve and Jimmy stood chatting at the side of the airstrip as they waited for the trucks to reach them, shivering in the cold November air.

The co-pilot stuck his head through the open door and called towards them. 'We're going to taxi to the end of the airstrip before we unload, in case anyone else needs to land here in a hurry. We don't want to be in the way,' he said. 'Want to come back on board for the ride, or will you meet us at the end of the runway?'

The three of them looked at each other. 'Might as well go with them,' Christie said. 'At least it'll be warmer.'

She waved at a couple of WNS journalists who were further away, pointing towards the opposite end of the airstrip to indicate to them to meet the Hercules there. The trucks which had been heading in their direction stopped, and waited at the side of the airstrip as the WNS journalists walked towards them. Christie climbed back into the plane.

Steve turned towards her. 'Christie . . . there's

something I wanted to tell you . . .'

Suddenly the pilot threw the engines into full throttle and the Hercules jerked forward, throwing those on board against the sides of the aircraft. Christie clutched some webbing securing the equipment nearest to her and struggled to regain her balance. Steve threw his arm around her as there was a sickening thud and the entire aircraft shuddered with impact.

'I give up,' he murmured.

'What the hell was that?' she gasped. 'Why have we taken off? I thought we were just taxiing to the end of the airstrip?'

'I'd very much like to know,' Steve said. 'That sounded like our landing gear to me.'

Jimmy made his way towards them through the maze of equipment boxes that had fallen loose as the Hercules had lifted sharply into the air. 'Bloody typical!' he stormed. 'There I was, having a quiet pee behind the plane. I stand deliberately downwind, and what does the sodding pilot do? He turns the engines on and suddenly I'm peeing into a gale. I only just got back on board in time.'

'Half the WNS team are still on the ground,' Steve said angrily. 'I'm going to find out what's going on.'

He climbed over the tangled equipment and disappeared into the cockpit as the aircraft banked and the pilot attempted to stabilise the flight. Steve's face was grim when he returned a few minutes later. The other journalists gathered around him.

'I'm afraid it's serious,' he said, cupping his hands around his mouth so that he could be heard above the noise of the aircraft. 'The jolt you felt as we took off was the landing gear hitting a sandbank at the end of the runway. This plane is too heavily loaded to take off on such a short airstrip, particularly when its surface is not tarmac but sand damp from too much rain. We only just managed to avoid crashing on take-off as it was. And without landing gear, we have a major problem.'

'Why did we take off at all?' a WNS cameraman asked shakily.

'I haven't a clue, and neither has anyone else, as far as I can see,' Steve said, frowning. 'That WNS girl of yours ordered the pilot to take the Hercules up for some reason, and as she is the one who chartered the aircraft, he agreed. His conduct was irresponsible, not to say downright bloody dangerous.'

'So how serious is serious?' Jimmy asked.

'We didn't actually lose the wheel, but part of the landing gear is out of action, which means we can't get the righthand wheel down. We're going to try to winch it down by hand, but even if we do, there's no guarantee it'll hold up when we land.'

'Where are we going to now?'

'We're heading back towards the main Kosovo airport,' Steve said. 'Apparently the fighting there was just a skirmish, and the UN are back in control. Let's hope so. There's nowhere else we can land.'

'What if the landing gear doesn't hold up?' Christie asked.

'If it doesn't, the chances are the wing will hit the ground. That could cause the plane to cartwheel, or it may send sparks flying and that could ignite the fuel. Either way, we're in trouble.'

'Oh Christ, the gasoline,' Joe, the WNS cameraman, groaned. 'We've got twelve drums of bloody fuel on board.'

'You've got what?' Christie said incredulously.

'Maddy – our producer – insisted that we fill the fuel drums with petrol and bring them with us, since it's so difficult to get fuel in Kosovo. I told her it was against

555

regulations to fly with it, but she's not the kind of person who takes no for an answer.'

'We have to get that to the back of the plane,' Steve said urgently. 'We've got to lash everything down securely; if we have to crash land, we don't want six tonnes of editing equipment tumbling down on top of us.' He eyed the many boxes which had broken loose during their unexpected take-off. 'These will have to be fastened down a lot better than they were last time round, or we will have no hope of surviving this. Joe, if you and Jimmy take the far end, I'll start this end with the others. Any questions?'

The journalists shook their heads and fanned out along the length of the plane, transferring as much of the heavy equipment as possible to the left-hand side of the aircraft, which still had a functioning wheel. Two of the flight crew came through into the hold, and began to try to winch the landing gear down by hand. Christie joined Steve in drawing the webbing around the metal boxes, crossing and re-crossing over the equipment to make sure it was as securely lashed as possible. As soon as they had finished one set, they moved along the aircraft to the next.

'What are our chances?' Christie said quietly.

Steve paused. 'About thirty per cent,' he said at last. 'And even if we don't explode on impact, there'll still be some casualties.'

A cold knot of fear gathered within Christie. She had faced danger many times, but it had always been fast in, fast out. If she were ever shot, it would be quick and over before she knew what had happened. But this was different.

She knew that it would take at least two hours to get to the main airport, since they would have to fly without pressurising the aircraft whilst the flight crew were working on the landing gear. That would mean flying low, which would slow them down. Two hours to lash the

556

equipment and prepare themselves for an emergency landing which they had a thirty per cent chance of surviving.

Some of them.

■ KOSOVO
5.30 p.m.

David pressed his foot to the floor on the accelerator and slammed the gears into third as the jeep slewed around the bend. He felt the rear wheels slide on the icy surface of the road, and ruthlessly changed into fourth gear as he came out of the turn. The engine screamed in protest.

'David! For Christ's sake, slow down!' Andy shouted, bracing himself against the dashboard. 'It won't help Christie if you're killed on the way to the airport!'

'I have to be there,' David said mechanically, his eyes on the road. 'I have to be there.'

'Yes, but it would be nice if you're in one piece,' Andy retorted.

David shrugged and did not let up. 'You don't have to come with me.'

Andy gripped his shoulder. 'Where else would I be, David? I may not be able to help the guys on the plane, but I think you could use the company.'

David drew a deep breath and slowed the jeep a fraction. 'You're right. I'm sorry. It's just . . .' His voice cracked.

'You don't have to tell me, David. I know.'

David stared into the darkness ahead of him, seeing only Christie's face as he swung the jeep around the sharp bends. He had fled to Kosovo in an attempt to bury himself in his work, to obliterate the pain of losing her. And, for a time, it had worked. He had been so preoccupied with surviving that he had not had time to think. He had buried his feelings deep within him, and had managed to convince himself that he would be able to treat her as just another colleague when she arrived.

And then he had heard over the radio that her life was in danger, and suddenly nothing else had mattered.

He slammed his fist on the steering wheel in frustration. He should never have let her just walk out of his life without making some attempt to keep her. He should have gone to her, explained what Caryn had done, *forced* Christie to listen to him. *He should not have let her go.*

If only he was given a second chance, he would not make the same mistake again.

'We're nearly there,' Andy said quietly. 'The UN checkpoint is just ahead of us.'

David slowed the jeep as they neared the makeshift barrier and wound down his window. He handed his INN Press pass out to a UN soldier for inspection, and after a cursory glance, the soldier waved him through. David abandoned the jeep near the airstrip and ran towards a group of UN officials who were clustered on the tarmac, Andy following him.

'What's happening?' David asked urgently. 'Where are they?'

'They're still on their way. Don't worry, we're doing everything we can,' one of the soldiers replied reassuringly. 'We're in constant contact with the pilot, and we've got all the emergency services standing by.'

'What emergency services?' David shouted angrily. 'We're in the middle of a bloody warzone! What can you possibly do?'

'Hey, calm down,' Andy said. 'They're doing their best.'

'Let's hope it's good enough,' David retorted, his face grim. He spun on his heel and walked towards his jeep.

558

Andy shrugged apologetically at the UN official. 'I'm sorry about that. He's pretty hyped up at the moment. His ex-girlfriend is one of the people on board.' His gaze did not waver as he met the other man's eyes. 'How bad is it?'

'They've been lucky so far,' the soldier replied evasively. 'If they'd been in any other type of aircraft other than a Hercules, they would have been wiped out on take-off. But those planes are pretty sturdy. They were very fortunate . . .'

'I said, how bad it it?' Andy gripped his arm. 'I want to know the truth.'

The UN soldier sighed. 'If we had a full fire service standing by, cutting equipment, foam . . . I'd say not good. Without any of that, I have to say their chances of making it are pretty small.'

Andy glanced over at David, who stood staring up into the darkness. Damn it. David was so much in love with her.

A young UN soldier came up to them, holding a radio to his ear, and saluted smartly. 'Excuse me, sir. The plane's coming in.'

■ C-130 HERCULES, KOSOVO
  6.15 p.m.

'OK, everyone. I want you to sit down, listen, and do everything I tell you. No questions. Your lives may depend on remembering this.'

The flight engineer looked around the aircraft to check that he had everyone's attention. 'We have managed to winch the landing gear down, and we've chained it into place. That means we will try to land on two wheels. However, we have no guarantee that the damaged landing gear will hold up. We just have to hope.'

He began to hand out the pillows and sleeping bags which the journalists had brought with them in anticipation of rough conditions in Kosovo. 'Wrap the sleeping bags around you, and put the pillows on your knees,' he said. 'When we land, you must brace yourselves, putting your heads forward and your hands around your head. If you have any spare blankets, wrap them about your heads too for added protection. The pillows should prevent your faces from being hit by flying debris.'

Along the length of the plane, the tense journalists worked the sleeping bags around their legs and bodies, trying to control their fear. 'As soon as we have come to a complete rest, leave the aircraft as quickly as possible, putting as much distance between it and yourselves as you can. Don't stop to go back for anyone; as soon as we land, the emergency crews will commence rescue procedure.'

'Nice to know they care,' Jimmy muttered, as the flight engineer returned to the cockpit. 'Can't I just go back for that bloody girl who got us into this in the first place?'

'Wish I could find the gin,' Steve said, glancing around the heavily fastened equipment. 'Damned if I can see it under that bloody lot.'

'If we go up in smoke, I'll know where you are,' Jimmy said. 'I'll just look for the blue flames.'

The flight engineer re-appeared in the aircraft hold. 'We'll be landing in approximately five minutes,' he said. 'When I give the order to brace, do it immediately.'

Suddenly Christie longed to feel David's arms around her, just once more, and the chance to tell him how much she loved him, would always love him. Their misunderstanding seemed so irrelevant now. They had both been so afraid of making themselves vulnerable, so aware of the risks. But wasn't that what love was all about?

'About two minutes,' the engineer called, settling himself in a canvas seat near the access to the damaged landing gear. He eyed the undercarriage with concern, checking for signs of stress on the chain holding it in place.

Quietly the journalists wished each other luck, aware that some of them, if not all, would probably die. They fell silent, each preparing for the final few moments which might be their last. Death was a risk they all ran so often during the course of their work, and all accepted it; but facing the reality was a test none could be sure of passing.

'Brace! Brace!'

Christie threw her head against the pillow on her knees, holding a blanket tightly around her face and tucking her legs beneath the seat. She inhaled the mingled scent of damp wool, machine grease and fear, waiting for the thump which would signal that they had landed, dreading what might come after.

'David, I love you,' she whispered.

Suddenly the Hercules jolted as it hit the ground. Christie felt the aircraft lurch as it bounced into the air and hit the tarmac again. Her head pressed against her knees, she heard the roar of the engines in reverse thrust as they tried to slow the aircraft down, the thunder of the equipment as the boxes slammed against the walls and the floor and each other, the screams as some of the boxes broke free and collapsed on to those nearest to them.

The aircraft lurched towards the right, and Christie heard the engineer cry out in fear. 'Jesus! We've lost her! We've lost the landing gear!'

The right wing tip of the Hercules grazed the tarmac as the starboard wheel collapsed. A shower of sparks flew into the air as the wing shattered and the plane cart-wheeled slowly across the tarmac, flames billowing out from the tail as the drums of fuel exploded.

Christie could see nothing as she buried her head deeper into the pillow on her lap. She felt the world spin crazily around her as the aircraft collapsed on to its side. The

561

stench of burning filled the air, and she was aware of screams and a sudden, unbearable heat.

Distantly she heard Steve's voice calling her name, and struggled dizzily to unfasten the unfamiliar seatbelt. It opened and she struggled to her feet not even sure which way up she was. The list of the Hercules made it impossible to keep her balance, and she fell awkwardly back into her seat, choking as thick, oily smoke filled the aircraft. Through the gloom she saw Steve standing half-upright, clutching the side of the plane a few feet from her. He worked his way backwards along the fuselage towards her, hand over hand, trying to shield his eyes from the glare of the fire in the tail of the plane. 'We have to get out of here!' he shouted. 'Now!'

The aircraft shuddered beneath them as it broke apart. Suddenly one of the editing boxes came free from its fastenings.

Christie did not even feel the blow that sent her tumbling, unconscious, across the floor.

Two hundred yards away from the burning aircraft, David broke free from Andy's restraining grip and raced across the tarmac towards the Hercules as it lay, broken in two, in the fields to the left of the airstrip. Andy ran after him and caught his shoulder, whirling him around.

'There's nothing you can do!' he shouted. 'You'll get yourself killed!'

'She'll die in there!' David shouted back. 'I can't just sit here and watch her die!'

'You can't help her! For Christ's sake, David, listen to me! You won't be able to reach her! No one can!'

'I can *try*, for God's sake! *I can try*!'

He wrenched himself free from the cameraman and ran towards the Hercules. UN soldiers were already pumping water on the burning plane from two fire trucks, but their efforts were futile against the strength of the fire raging out of control. Without foam or cutting equipment, there was little they could do. Those who tried to reach the aircraft door were beaten back by the flames, and stood helplessly listening to the agonised screams of the people trapped inside.

Suddenly the emergency door opened, and David saw Steve stumble out, his face blackened by smoke, his hands bleeding and blistered where he had fought his way across the hot metal of the camera boxes. David pushed two UN soldiers out of the way and raced towards the injured man, his muscles aching with effort. He hauled Steve away from the intolerable heat of the aircraft, and frantically shook him by the shoulders.

'Where is she, Steve? For Christ's sake, where is she?'

Steve stared numbly into his face, the flames reflected in his eyes. Slowly he shook his head, tears rolling down his cheeks. 'I tried to save her, believe me, David, I tried. But I couldn't reach her.' His voice broke. 'I couldn't reach her.'

'No! Dear God, *no*!'

David staggered backwards, his mind refusing to accept what Steve was saying. Andy reached towards him, but David pulled away, his face working with rage and pain.

'No! I won't let her die! I'm not losing her now!'

Before either of them could stop him, David ducked past them and reached the emergency door, gasping as the heat hit him. He took a deep breath and dived inside the aircraft.

He could see nothing but the swirl of smoke and the red glow of fire as flames licked through the plane. Choking, he squatted down, trying to fill his lungs with the purer air near the ground. The floor listed crazily beneath his feet, and he clung to the webbing straps as he worked his way into the aircraft, shouting Christie's name over and

563

over again. He stumbled, then shuddered as he saw the broken, lifeless body of the flight engineer. *Dear God, where was she?*

The heat grew stronger as he battled past the red-hot casings of the editing boxes towards the rear of the plane. His head swam with lack of oxygen, his hands were raw and blistered. Sheer strength of will drove him to keep struggling foward when every instinct shouted at him to get out.

Suddenly he saw her.

She lay limply at the side of the aircraft, a heavy camera box across her legs. Her eyes were closed, her body motionless. David did not even have time to see if she was still breathing. With a strength born of desperation he hauled the box away from her and caught her up in his arms, then plunged blindly back towards the emergency door. He could see nothing in the smoke-filled aircraft, but he felt the faint coolness of the air blowing in through the opened door. With one last supreme effort of will, he threw himself through it.

Coughing painfully, he drew fresh air into his lungs, and raced back across the tarmac towards the airport terminal, dimly aware of other fleeing figures as he ran. Suddenly a tremendous force hit him from behind, and he threw himself on the ground, protecting Christie with his own body. He glanced behind him as the Hercules exploded into a brilliant ball of fire.

He felt Christie's neck with one hand, searching for her pulse. For a moment he could not feel it, and panic swept through him. He moved his hand, and suddenly it was there. Faint, but it was there. She was alive.

Warm arms reached around him and helped him stand upright.

'She's going to be OK,' Andy said, clasping his arm. 'You saved her life. She's going to be fine.'

564

'I won't leave her . . .'

Andy pulled him to one side as the International Red Cross team lifted Christie's unconscious form carefully on to a stretcher. 'No one's making you,' he said. 'But you have to let them look after her now.'

David walked slowly beside the stretcher, gazing at her pale face, his heart pounding inside him. He could not lose her now. He turned to Andy.

'Steve? Jimmy?'

'They're alive. Jimmy's got some bad burns, but he'll make it. Steve will be fine in a few days.'

'And the others?'

Andy gripped his hand. 'No.'

'*No one?*' David gasped incredulously. 'There were over twenty people on that plane!'

'They couldn't reach them. Steve and Jimmy were lucky. They were thrown near the emergency exit when the plane broke in two. The others had no chance.'

David stared at Christie. 'She nearly died. Andy, I nearly lost her.'

'Yes, but you didn't. You saved her life.'

They reached the truck that was serving as an ambulance, and the Red Cross team lifted Christie into it. David climbed in after them and crouched on the floor next to her, holding her hand in his. A thousand thoughts filled his mind, every one of them directed towards the beautiful woman beside him. The truck jolted as the ambulance workers drove towards the airport terminal, and suddenly Christie stirred. She opened her eyes as David took her in his arms.

'You really meant it, didn't you?' she whispered as he clung to her. '*Amoud fiki.* You would have died for me.'

'I had to find some way of stopping you running away from me again,' David murmured.

'You know what they say if you save somebody's life.

You're responsible for them forever.'

'Forever. That sounds good to me,' David smiled.

And then he kissed her.